A POLITICAL AFFAIR

A POLITICAL AFFAIR

a novel by

Mickey Ziffren

DELACORTE PRESS/NEW YORK

Published by
Delacorte Press
1 Dag Hammarskjold Plaza
New York, N.Y. 10017

First printing

Designed by Laura Bernay

Library of Congress Cataloging in Publication Data
Ziffren, Mickey.
A political affair.

I. Title.
PZ4.Z674Po [PS3576.I35]   813'.5'4   79-12598
ISBN: 0-440-07227-1

To my beloved sleep-in editor
without whose discouragement
this book would never have been written.

A POLITICAL AFFAIR

CHAPTER
One

"What did you say the President said?"

Norah Jones Ashley looked up at her husband. The Academy Award–winning actress's famous green eyes, their extraordinary color intensified by the dark velvet of her robe, were wide with disbelief.

"I said, the President wants you to run against Richard Hardwick for Hardwick's seat in the Senate," Tom Ashley repeated.

Norah felt her hand tremble, clattering the thin china cup on the mahogany table between them. "What did *you* say?" she asked.

Tom Ashley stretched his long legs out in front of him, reached for the humidor, and chose a cigar. He sniffed the cigar appreciatively, looked at her with amusement, and answered. "That I thought you'd be a marvelous candidate. The best."

"You've gone mad, Tom. You and the President are insane." Raising her voice, Norah said emphatically, "I won't do it!"

The President of the United States and his old college roommate, her husband, had reached a summit decision without the slightest understanding of what they were asking of her. How could Tom do this to her, even if he couldn't possibly know the origin or the depth of the revulsion she felt at the mere mention of Richard Hardwick's name? She and Tom had never indulged themselves in that titillating idiot game of revealing to each other their personal past histories. They both had too great a sense of privacy for that sort of thing. Perhaps they should have played true confessions after all, Norah thought ruefully. Then she wouldn't be sitting here in a state of shock, riddled with guilts, feeling deceitful and terrified.

She felt a wave of nausea at the memory of the dingy row house in north Philadelphia and the waiting on tables for the meager scholarship; the very smell and feel of the long forgotten poverty washed over her. Her past was a closed book. She had long since slammed the covers shut. And she damn well intended to keep them shut. It had nothing to do with her relationship with her husband. But now, an unaware Tom and the President were unleashing the painful memories she had willfully blocked all these years. Damn them! Richard Hardwick. A skeleton-rattling campaign against Richard Hardwick. It was unthinkable.

The Ashleys had been served their coffee in the library. It was to this room they gravitated when the two of them were alone. Large windows at each end opened on the formal front garden and the sloping green expanse of well-tended lawn that stretched out toward the pool. The floor-to-ceiling bookshelves and the light brown leather chairs exuded an air of warmth and intimacy. But the usually soothing effect was lost on Norah.

Tom pulled a silver cutter from his pocket and neatly snipped off the end of his cigar. He was puzzled by her vehement reaction. Even after all these years he had difficulty discerning the "real" Norah from the "actress" Norah. But his gut feeling was that her response this time was a genuine one, and it puzzled him. The President was giving her the chance of a lifetime. Surely she must be aware of that. He lit the cigar and exhaled the fragrant smoke, studying her carefully.

"Andy Watkins, Sam Bradshaw, John Mellon, and Dan Brookings are flying out tomorrow to discuss it with us," he said matter-of-factly. He paused, and added, "At the President's request, of course. I've told Mrs. Manley they'd be here for dinner."

"Terrific," Norah snapped, glaring at him. "*You're* arranging dinner parties and volunteering *me* for a race I have no intention of making. I mean it, Tom."

Tom leaned forward. "Knock it off, Norah. You *know* as well as I do, getting rid of Hardwick in California is crucial to the President's reelection. What's all this silliness about? You *know* you'd love to make a run for it.''

She'd love to run for the hills, that's what she'd love to do. She stared at Tom in angry disbelief and shook her head.

But she knew him well enough to know that he was in dead earnest and was not about to be put off easily. Tom wasn't a man given to embarking on loosely conceived, harebrained schemes. Other than the romantic gesture he'd made twenty years ago, when he'd bought a huge block of Paragon Pictures stock in order to meet her, Paragon's number-one star, she couldn't recall his ever having acted on a mad impulse. And he had even managed to turn that romantic, spontaneous indulgence into a sound business investment. He'd met and married her, and then the stock he'd bought in order to do so had quadrupled in value. No, this was no whimsical bright idea. He and the President had thought it through carefully. They had decided on their own, without consulting her, that she would run for the Senate. Damn them! Even if she wanted to explain why she couldn't, which she didn't, what could she say? Richard Hardwick belonged to the edge of another time, bound in with the most painful memories of her life, and she wanted him, and them, to stay erased.

There was no way Tom, the secure upper-middle-class banker's son, could possibly understand the vehemence of her reaction, even if she could find a way to tell him what it had cost her to get where she had been in life when they'd met. True, he'd made his vast fortune on his own. Nobody handed it to him on a silver platter. Tom had brilliance and ingenuity and grit. He had parlayed a small family inheritance with his wizard talent in electronics and created Ashley Dynamics at a time when most people had never even heard the word *computer*. But he hadn't had to invent himself out of nothing.

He'd always *known* what to wear and what to say and what to eat when and what utensil to eat it with. She'd known none of that. She too had raw intelligence and grit, period. But she had to learn who she was and how to move and speak and what colors emphasized the color of her eyes, what fabrics moved with her body. She had manners and style because she'd sweat blood to learn them.

There were still some people who remembered the young Norah, that ambitious girl full of bright potential. Not all of them had been her friends, and that was another reason she wasn't about to risk having her past dredged up and scrutinized in a vicious political campaign.

Tom poured himself some coffee, his temper mounting. "Stop acting as if I've betrayed you. The party's without any strong candidates at this particular time. You know it as well as I do. And Hardwick will capitalize on that. The President is asking *you* to help him. With good reason. Every son of a bitch in the Senate gets up in the morning, looks in the mirror, and with very little effort convinces himself he'd make a better President than the guy sitting in the Oval Office. Do you think Hardwick's any exception? The President's been biting hard on the bullet since the day after his inauguration. Taxes, price controls, federal spending, conservation—all the stuff people hate facing up to hit him at once. You know it. Christ! The press didn't even allow him the three-month honeymoon. They dug right in and started blasting." He looked at her intensely. "How can he possibly push through positive programs with the dissidents in his own party joining the opposition and the press and ganging up on him? He's vulnerable as hell. On one hand, he's being shafted by his former colleagues, and on the other, there's Hardwick salivating in the wings, egging them on, and building his own prestige. The President's in real trouble, Norah."

"Baloney!" Norah snapped angrily. "The President doesn't come up for reelection for another two years! Anyway"—she waved her hands as if to brush the discussion away—"it's smart politics to get the nasties over with early in the first term." She grimaced. "This hysteria is ridiculous. At best, Hardwick represents a small, conservative—"

Interrupting her, Tom leaned forward, his dark, intelligent eyes riveted into hers. "You're wrong; dead wrong, my dear. Hardwick is big trouble. The President's private polls show a widespread base of national support for him—not just some small cadre of hard-core disappointed Reagan lovers. Hardwick's got unlimited resources. He's the darling of the real-estate lobby, the munitions industry, and the right-wing labor bosses. As minority leader he can carp about the insolubles like taxation, inflation, and unemployment without having to deliver a single solution. Every time there's a fuckup in foreign affairs, the President carries the blame and Hardwick crows, criticizes, and waves the flag. His backers are straining at the bit to get their man into the White House and put themselves in the power position. He's on the

Senate Appropriations Committee. What's more, his wife's got a fortune ready to spend to make herself First Lady. Hardwick can cut the President off at the knees, Norah." Tom brought his clenched fist down on the coffee table, rattling the china. "He's got to be stopped *now!* Two years more of that bastard Hardwick's machinations and they won't even need an election! He'll walk into the White House over the President's dead body."

"If *you* feel so concerned and so obligated, *you* run, Tom. The President was *your* college roommate, not mine!" Norah flashed.

"If I thought I could, I sure as hell would," he said ruefully. "I don't have charisma on the soapbox. You do and you know it! And you owe it to him to use it."

Norah faced him and shouted, "I don't owe the President a goddamn thing. He owes *me* for all the campaigning I've done for him every time he's run, from his first congressional campaign on up! And most of all" —she bit her lip to hold back the angry tears—"I don't owe him the horror of exposing myself in a dog fight with that—that reactionary bastard, Richard Hardwick! I won't do it!" She turned her back to him and stared out of the window.

Tom shook his head. Not only had his beloved wife run for intraparty office with relish, she'd served as state chairwoman and national committeewoman with extraordinary skill. She had raised enormous sums of money by virtue of her own connections and her willingness to stump the state attending dinners and meetings in the cow counties, where titled party officials—much less one who in her own right was a worldwide celebrity—had never been seen before. It was as if the political arena had replaced the stage for Norah, and she knew how to use it with the same professionalism and the same success.

If the President had chosen someone else to run against Hardwick, she'd have unquestioningly devoted herself to the candidate's cause with whatever expertise and energy she could muster. Why did running against him herself terrify her?

Could it simply be the fear of losing? Had fear triggered her outburst? Had he totally misjudged her?

Puzzled, he walked to the window where she stood, silent and withdrawn, and put his arm around her shoulder. "My darling, this reluctance isn't at all like you," he said reassuringly. "All you're being asked to do is what you do well—seduce the audience. The floor of the Senate's a pretty good stage."

"I know that, but—" She looked at him gravely and said, "I won't have our lives disrupted. I won't do it. Forget it, Tom!"

As if dealing with a recalcitrant child, Tom took her hand and said gently, "Come, sit down with me and let's talk this over calmly."

Norah settled herself silently in the deep armchair. Tom pulled up a hassock for himself and sat at her feet. "I spend as much time on company business in the East as I do in the West. You know that. So whether our base is in Washington or California, it will make little difference. Our lives won't be disrupted. I'll take a leave of absence and manage the campaign for you. We'll go into this together. What do you say?"

"Listen to me, Tom," Norah said. "There must be a dozen members of the congressional delegation who'd jump at the chance to run—not to mention several other actors." She paused and smiled. "Try Jane Fonda. Chuck Heston, maybe?"

Tom winced. He knew he was manipulating her for the President's sake, and he felt guilty about it. But she was the best shot the President had. Hardwick must be eliminated as a contender for the Oval Office. The President had confided in Tom, and Tom couldn't bring himself to break the President's trust. He had told Norah the overt reasons for running against Hardwick. They were clear enough for anyone to understand. He would not tell her the President's private desperate reason. At most, he rationalized, he was guilty of omission. She must be persuaded to run.

"Don't get smart, darling. It's not only your movie star charisma the President needs, but your astonishing political skill, and you know that!" Tom said quietly. "If you don't grab the brass ring now, love—when it's offered—you'll become the kind of woman you hold in contempt. You'll have a life of boring luncheons, do-good committee meetings, long fittings in the dressing room, visits with masseuses and hairdressers." He touched her cheek. "Finally, a nip here and a tuck there. Or"—he paused—"is it possible you're afraid of campaigning—of losing?" He looked at her probingly.

Afraid? Norah thought. She'd *never* been afraid. She had the constitution of an ox for all her fragile looks. The appalling food, the discomfort, and the bone-aching fatigue of a campaign held no special terrors for her. As for losing, it wasn't losing the campaign that terrified her; it was the prospect of destroying the life she'd carefully nurtured with her husband, this man who was backing her against the wall. Campaigns were brutal and dirty, under the best of circumstances. This one Tom proposed would be unthinkably so.

"I'm not afraid of losing, Tom," Norah said. "Truly I'm not! We've supported plenty of hopeless causes and I've made my share of bad films. I know how to lose. But I'm not an office seeker. The thought of it appalls me. Actors and politicians have a terrible disease in common—narcissism. So—" She repeated, raising her voice, "So! After twenty years I've finally learned how to deal with individual human beings instead of mobs, and to commit myself to meaningful causes instead of applause. Now you and the President, in your infinite wisdom, decide for me that I should once again involve myself in the business of whoring after audiences. Replace my box office appeal with voting-booth appeal."

Tom looked at her searchingly. "Are you saying running has *no* appeal for you? That using your talents to get yourself elected to the Senate is *abhorrent?*"

"Exactly!" she said emphatically. "Politics is an avocation for me, just as it is for you."

But she knew she was lying. Suddenly she felt a wild longing for the spotlight. How many centuries had it been since she'd warmed herself in its brilliance? And what a stage! The United States Senate. A whole new life. Tom had struck home when he talked about the aging-actress syndrome. She would be an ingenue again on the floor of the Senate, with a whole new worldwide audience to play to. And somehow, somewhere in the back of her head, the thought of revenge was tempting. She could play dirty, too. Richard Hardwick might take a fall, and he had it coming.

Tom stood up, exasperated. "An avocation? Bullshit! What the hell is this all about, Norah? Peter's at Harvard and as good as gone from our lives. You've held every possible intraparty office from national committeewoman to state chairwoman and done an astonishingly good job at it. You're as close a friend of the President's as I am."

He laid down his cigar and walked toward her. He bent his long agile frame and put his fist under her chin. He raised her face to his and kissed her gently. "This scene is totally out of character. You *know* you'd love to head the ticket. The President's choice; center stage, star position." Tom lowered his voice and said, "He needs you desperately, Norah. We owe him all the help we can give him. Come on. Cut the Miss Movie Star number and admit it."

Norah pushed his hand away angrily. "Don't cue me."

He was hounding her, she thought. He had his teeth tightly clamped on her jugular. She knew her husband was using her for the President's sake, and she was bitter with resentment and frustration. She would not allow herself to be used, and she could not tell him why.

"If you're so anxious to please the President that you don't care about me, Tom, then our marriage is in as much trouble as you claim *he* is."

Tom turned ashen. He moved toward her, eyes flashing. "I don't 'claim,' I *know!* You'll have to take my word for it. In *trust!*"—he spat the word—"whether you like it or not. But I can tell you this for sure," he admonished. "Hardwick represents the worst elements in the country. He's a dedicated hawk. He holds détente in contempt, and what's worse, he's dangerously close to the lunatic nuclear-trigger-happy fringe in the Pentagon. The Strangeloves! He's their mouthpiece and patsy for Christ's sake! You know that!"

Norah threw her head back and laughed. "You mean I'm the McGuffin in the script?" she mocked.

Tom drew his brows together and scowled. "McGuffin?"

"Actor talk," she said sarcastically. "Hitchcock's term for the diversionary subplot to keep the audience away from the real thing. In this case, it seems that the President's scared shitless of having to face Richard Hardwick. We wouldn't want the folks to know about that, would we?" she said with a sneer.

"That's unfair, Norah. It's more than that. You'd really make a damn good senator. True, we've got Sam Bradshaw in the Senate. He's all right, if he can stay awake long enough to vote. But he's hardly the one to rally the kind of support for the administration that you could. The President needs a strong senator from California as desperately as he needs to get rid of Hardwick," he insisted, trying not to think how close she was to the truth. "It's his home state."

Norah drew in her breath, the mocking expression gone. "Are you saying I must run for the Senate to save my son and the nation and the state of California from Richard Hardwick? There's no one else around in this huge state to make the race?"

Tom nodded, his eyes fixed on hers. "Yes, goddamn it, I am!" He came closer to her.

"I have no choice then, do I?" she said. "You're not asking me, you're *telling* me!"

Tom exploded. "Jesus Christ, Norah. I tried every way I knew not to put it to you like that, but your goddamned prima donna ego forced—"

In speechless anger, before he could finish, she raised her hand to strike him. He caught it in midair, and she started to cry. My God, he thought, I've pushed her too far. Suddenly she seemed frail and intensely desirable. He pulled her toward him roughly and kissed her with ferocity. He wanted her. She was his, every inch of her was his. Nobody else's. He lifted Norah in his arms and carried her to the couch, pulling at the dark velvet negligee. They made love in absolute silence with a violence they had never known before.

As they lay exhausted, he whispered, "You have to trust me." And Norah knew that was the end of her protests.

CHAPTER

Two

R ichard Hardwick of California, Senate minority leader, member of the powerful Appropriations Committee, and front-runner for his party's presidential nomination, drove his car through the imposing wrought-iron gates which protected his Foxhall Road estate in Washington, D.C. The gates had swung open at his approach. Winding past the carefully tended sloping lawns, savoring the subdued elegance of his private fiefdom, he brought the car to a halt under the huge portico and left the keys hanging in the ignition.

Someone else would put it in the garage for the night. The front door opened at the sound of his footsteps. He enjoyed that: the silent service, the rewards of success.

"Good evening, Theodore."

The butler, his face expressionless, held the door ajar. "Good evening, sir."

"Is Mrs. Hardwick at home?"

"Yes, sir. Madame is in the library."

Christ, he thought, and sighed, she's had a headstart on the martinis. That was the other side of the coin. The "price."

He followed Theodore across the polished parquet of the entrance hall to the library. The butler held open the paneled door for him to enter. The moment he saw her, he knew his suspicions were accurate. His wife's posture was too erect, her movements too careful as she rose to greet him, drink in hand. There would be rough seas ahead tonight. Yet even on the verge of drunkenness Virginia reeked elegance, her auburn hair pulled back into a knot at the nape of the flawless neck, the long robe flowing gracefully.

His lips brushed her pale cheek dutifully. "What will our very next President have to drink this evening?" she asked, her voice overly polite.

"Scotch, and easy on the water." He settled into the deep leather chair and held up the evening paper for a shield.

She brought him his drink. "I saw those polls, they're very encouraging. You should be pleased."

Taking the drink and settling into the business section, he grunted an "Um-hum."

Refilling her own glass, Virginia Thayer Hardwick thought bitterly of her father. Even in death the Colonel was finally getting his way. Richard, his surrogate son, was firmly on the road to the White House. But then, the Colonel always did get his way, didn't he? Only he hadn't lived to see this. Too bad. At least he'd seen her marry the man he thought might well be elected President. That was the best she could do for him. Compensation enough for his disappointment in having a daughter, not a son.

She settled herself in a corner of the brown velvet settee and studied her husband. Richard had aged well. The lines at the corners of his mouth and across the brow added character to his overly handsome face. The graying, sandy hair and lines appeared deliberately drawn as if by a skillful makeup artist. The long-muscled athlete's body still showed no signs of flab. Perfect presidential casting! Why the hell should the cold son of a bitch show his years? His goal was the presidency. No personal drama had been permitted to interfere with that. His monomania protected him from the wear and tear of love. And hurt.

Her face hardened. "Who do you think they'll run against you for the Senate?" That should get a small rise out of him, she thought.

He glanced up from the paper, rattling the ice cubes in his drink. "They don't have anyone, really. When's dinner?"

"I asked Theodore to serve us here. It's cook's night out. He should be along any minute. Goddamn it, Richard, put that paper down and *talk* to me!" she ordered shrilly.

With a shrug of resignation, he lay the paper aside. "Okay, what *shall* we talk about?"

Theodore's knock saved him, but he knew that the reprieve was only temporary. Once Virginia was on track, there was no diverting her.

"Shall I set the table in front of the fireplace, madame?"

"Please, Theodore."

Under Richard's appreciative eye, the butler swiftly spread the white linen and placed the gleaming silver and crystal and iced salad plates on the table. Fine china platters held thinly sliced pink beef, and cold, pale asparagus, each stalk carefully peeled. Holding the wine out for inspection, Theodore asked, "Shall I pour, sir?"

Virginia took over. "Thank you, no, we'll serve ourselves. I'll ring when we're through." She drained the last of her cocktail as Theodore left the room.

Holding her chair for her, determined not to be forced into a scene, Richard asked pleasantly, "What, my dear, would you suggest we talk about, since we must talk."

"You, of course, and the upcoming election you seem so cavalier about."

He felt the bite of her tone. Antennae up, and firmly resolved to keep his temper, he said quietly, "I am following your dear father's sound advice. I do my job in the Senate well and visibly. There's no one of any consequence looming on the horizon to challenge my reelection to the Senate. There's no reason to get excited."

Virginia sipped her wine, raised the thinly arched eyebrows, and fixed him with her agate-colored eyes. She leaned across the table and said softly, "Ah, but there is!"

"Is what?" Hardwick asked, spearing himself a piece of roast beef.

"Someone of considerable consequence to run against you, someone quite formidable, in fact, with higher public visibility than you have," she said with relish.

"Who?" He looked up. Well, at least she had his attention. She put down her glass with care, eager to savor his reaction to the fullest.

"Mrs. Ashley."

Looking genuinely puzzled, he asked, "Mrs. Ashley? Now who the hell is Mrs. Ashley?" He couldn't place the name.

A shocked expression crossed her face, and she said in a dismayed tone, "Heavens, Richard, I don't believe it! *Everybody* knows Mrs. Ashley. If you don't know her, she must be the only actress you haven't known—and fucked—since you turned twenty-one. She's the former Norah Jones. Remember her?" She could see him flinch.

Did he think she didn't know about his women? Did he think she didn't know about that slut Dorothy Johnson, little Miss Wonderful and her "Have a Good Day, U.S.A." blah-blah show? There wasn't one of the hundred members of the Senate who wouldn't drop everything for a chance to get the exposure Johnson's show gave. But it was Richard who was on her program every five minutes. Clearly he was sleeping with her. Not that Virginia gave a damn.

Having made her husband noticeably uncomfortable, she went on relishing her success. "Don't you remember? She married Thomas Ashley, the computer millionaire. She was the national committeewoman for California—remember we saw her at that premiere?"

He flinched again, and she paused to drink in and savor his discomfort.

"Oh my yes," she gushed, "she's the darling of all those bleeding-heart liberals and the Jews, wetbacks, and niggers—"

"For God's sake, Virginia—"

She knew he loathed her using those words. Not that he wasn't a bigot himself. He was just too bloody hypocritical to say so out loud. He was terrified she'd slip and use those pejoratives in public.

"Oh dear, I mean 'blacks,' " she corrected herself in mock dismay and shrugged. "They never vote for you anyway. Norah Ashley's husband is buddy-buddy with the President. They were college roommates or something. Since you're beginning to look like a threat to the great man, Ashley won't hesitate to pour a fortune into her campaign, for the President's sake as well as his wife's."

She reached for a stalk of asparagus, held it in her hand, and bit into it, studying him as he mulled over what she'd told him.

He put down his utensils and glared at her. "What kind of nonsense are you talking? They'd be crazy to run an actress against *me!*" His voice went up. "Anyway, why would she do it? She just plays with politics. Who fed you this crap?" he snapped.

"I have *my* sources. I happen to know that the President really is going to lay the pressure on her, and I think it's a brilliant idea. They haven't got anyone else and that's the truth," she said emphatically. She reached

for the wine bottle, refilled her glass, and held the bottle out toward him.
He shook his head.

"She'll give you a tough race," Virginia continued. She let it sink in.
His face began to redden, and Virginia observed with pleasure the bulge
of a small vein at his temple. It was a certain sign of his anger.

"Oh, my"—she frowned—"I've offended the distinguished senator,
the great cunt collector." Enunciating each syllable with exaggerated care,
she continued, "Norah Jones Ashley is going to oppose you for the
Senate, my darling. And in my very *humble* opinion, she's got a good shot
at winning."

"You don't know what the hell you're talking about, Virginia, and, as
usual, you're drunk." He reached angrily across the table and took her
wine glass. "You'd better ring for Theodore to bring some coffee. You
need it," he said contemptuously.

She tried to retrieve her glass, but he grabbed her wrist roughly and
held it.

"Let go, you're hurting me!"

The bitch, the consummate bitch! She'd invented this garbage story in
order to bait him. He hoped. Or did she really have a source? Norah
Jones! Releasing the narrow wrist, reddened by his grip, he shouted,
"Where did you hear this, goddamn it? You are going to tell me what
you're talking about, and without the charming asides."

Virginia rubbed her wrist, her eyes narrowed to slits. "Tell you what?"
she slurred. "That you're a cunt collector, or that Mrs. Ashley is going to
screw you out of the Senate?"

He gripped the table and pushed his chair back, overturning his half-
filled wine glass. A dark red stain spread over the white linen cloth.

Virginia stood up and reached for her napkin to dab the spilled liquid.
She made a little clicking noise. "Oh dear, dear," she said mockingly, "I
have upset you, repeating all that silly gossip about your sexual prowess.
Shame on me!" She shook her head and looked at him, wide-eyed. "But
Mrs. Ashley is not gossip! Andrew Watkins, old Sam Bradshaw, John
Mellon, and the President's nig—uh—I mean, that overbred black
houseboy of his, Brookings, are on their way to California right now, this
very minute, in the President's very own Air Force One. And what's
more, they're going to have a nice little din-din with Mr. and Mrs. Ashley
to discuss you know what."

"Who told you that?" he demanded angrily.

Ignoring his question, she put down the napkin and grimaced. "Oh my, what a mess."

"Who told you?" he repeated, glaring at her.

Rubbing her wrist conspicuously, she looked up at him, wide-eyed. "John Mellon. He'll be the one to scrutinize all your senatorial records for bits and scraps of corruption and to decide what issues Mrs. Ashley should bear down on. He's so clever at that."

She could see the anger boiling, his face turning bright scarlet. Any minute now he'd explode. Her spirits soared with self-satisfaction.

"And why would Mellon confide this in *you*?" he asked contemptuously.

Looking directly at him, she picked up her wine glass and refilled it. Taking a small sip, she moved toward him.

The scents of perfume and liquor enveloped him as she brought her face close to his. The usually tranquil mask was twisted with hatred.

"Because we're lovers," she hissed triumphantly, and she delighted in his look of shock. She'd hit on target. He hadn't expected that.

"He told me about the President's plan to screw you, while we were screwing each other." She threw her head back and drained her glass.

Hardwick stood silent.

"And for your information, my *dear* husband, John Mellon is a lot more competent at screwing than you are—as I recall." She broke into a scream of high-pitched laughter.

Richard Hardwick could taste the rage welling up in him, his breath came in gasps. As if it had a life of its own, he felt his arm reach out and strike her face. The laughter stopped. The glass fell from her hand. She rushed at him, clawing him with her nails. Blind with fury, he struck her again. She reeled back against a small table alongside the velvet settee, crashing it over, screaming, "You bastard, you dirty, rotten bastard!"

Horrified by his own violence, he moved toward her. "My God, Virginia, I didn't—" he gasped.

Her hair fell away from the carefully coiled knot, the agate eyes looked at him in terror. "Don't touch me!" she shrieked, and she fled the room.

He stood frozen, listening to the clacking of her heels on the foyer floor and the repeated screams of "The bastard—bastard!"

He heard Theodore's astonished shout of "Madame—" then silence, followed by the sudden roar of a motor turning over, tires screeching, shaking him out of his torpor.

Hardwick bolted to the front door, past the startled butler, and rushed down the stairs to see the car swerving erratically across the lawn at breakneck speed. Christ! She was at the wheel, blind, crazy drunk! The stark headlines flashed before his eyes, "Wife of Senate Minority Leader Arrested for Drunk Driving!" The minute she hit the street, the cops would pick her up. He started to run down the long, green slope, his heart pounding in his ears, screaming, "Virginia! STOP! STOP!"

Oh God, why didn't she just go over a cliff and disappear? How could she do this to him? Suddenly the car changed course and headed directly toward the high stone wall encircling their property. He ran, screaming her name, his lungs bursting in his chest. She was going to kill herself! Within seconds the car crashed full force into the wall. Metal struck and crumbled against the rock, thundered into the evening quiet. The car door flew open, hurtling Virginia's limp body out onto the lawn. Richard Hardwick gasped for breath and doubled over in a paroxysm of uncontrollable retching.

CHAPTER
Three

Norah stepped out of the shower, all her anger and fears replaced by a wild sense of elation. Of course Tom was right. What did it matter that something had happened so long ago to a Norah she could barely remember? She'd overreacted, perhaps because Tom had put the President's request to her so unexpectedly and caught her off guard, making Richard Hardwick, whom she'd long since put out of her mind, loom up again to scratch at the past. The hell with that. This was *now.* Now she really wanted to run for the Senate. In her own way, she was as committed to the President's cause as Tom was. Years of campaigning in his behalf were an integral part of her marriage.

She wrapped herself in a large Turkish towel and walked toward the French doors leading to the small walled garden directly off her dressing room. Pushing the doors open, she breathed in the warm, fragrant scents. Thin-stemmed translucent poppies, deep orange, contrasted with the pale yellow of early jonquils. All the colors in her garden were intensified by a background of textured greenery growing against the encircling brick wall. Norah felt a never-ending sense of pleasure at the sight of this small private place.

Abruptly a vision of north Philadelphia came into her head. The cramped interior of her father's house, the musty odors of cooking carried by the steam heat to every corner, those inescapable smells, that relentless misery.

And Papa, the trolley car conductor, she thought bitterly. The Saturday night bully, reeking beer and staggering into the house full of bravado, stumbling up the stairs, only to collapse on the bed in a drunken stupor before Mama and she could pull off his shoes. All she'd ever dreamed of then was "out!" Well, she'd made it out. Not that Papa hadn't fought her like a steer every inch of the way. When she'd gotten the scholarship to Temple University, he'd sneered. "College! For what? So you can marry some jerk who's too good for you?" Well, she'd earned her parole, waiting on tables, typing papers, doing *any* crummy job that came her way, paying rent to Papa too, putting the butter on *his* table. Papa. Killing the joy when Guido'd offered her the small ingenue role in his Broadway production after he'd seen her perform in the college repertory company. "Big producer, my ass!" Papa had screamed. "He's a filthy wop who wants to get into your bloomers. You little whore! And you'll let him, won't you?" She could still see him, red-faced and leering, poised to strike her.

But Mama had grabbed his hand. For once Mama had gathered the strength to fight him. Norah's eyes filled. God knows how she must have paid for that defiance. At least Norah had been able to thank Mama with money for that act of courage. But she'd never been able to get her to leave him. That still hurt. Norah sighed. Her parents were dead now. Still she'd not forgiven him, the bastard, not even in death.

Calling his own daughter a whore. What the hell was a whore anyway? She'd loved Richard and Guido, each differently perhaps, but nevertheless, loved them. And there hadn't been any others, only Tom. She'd made her commitment to Tom and kept it gladly. Whores didn't do that. Norah mulled. A whore is a creature to be used by men. Wasn't that what the word meant? She was closer to fitting the description now. She was being used all right and with her own consent.

The gloomy recollections were abruptly interrupted by the ring of the house phone. Norah came in from the garden and reached for it, relieved to return to the present.

"Good morning, madame. Mrs. Manley wants to know, does the guest count still stand at four? And what time will dinner be, please?" The butler's voice was anxious.

"Good morning, McPherson. Tell her I'll be there as soon as I check with Mr. Ashley."

Manley was sticky about time. The tensions would be mounting early, as they always did when there were to be dinner guests on short notice. Mrs. Manley was endowed with a great cooking gift; God had shown less generosity to her nervous system.

Norah sighed and dried herself hurriedly, reached for her robe, and kicked her feet into her slippers. Opening the door, she collided with Tom, sleepily groping his way to his own dressing room. For all his drive and energy, he was, in contrast to Norah, a slow starter in the morning. He claimed they had compatible neuroses and incompatible metabolic systems. He insisted that early morning studio calls had permanently damaged Norah's habits.

"Smoke signals are emanating from the kitchen," she told him hurriedly. "What time will they be here?"

Tom yawned and ran his fingers through the thatch of short-cropped gray hair. He leaned toward her and kissed the hollow at the base of her throat.

"None of *that,*" she said firmly.

"I told them seven thirty," he answered, his eyes fully open now. He put both his hands on her shoulders, looked into her eyes. "We're going to win this, you know," he said.

"I hope you're right! Still—nobody ever started out to make a bad film, Tom." Norah's face clouded.

He held her close to him. "We'll get you a good script, darling."

Disengaging herself, Norah said impatiently, "The script in the kitchen is going to be a bummer unless I get there on the double."

"That woman's got more clout with you than the President or I do," Tom said ruefully.

"Damn right," she flung at him on the way out. "Neither of you jokers can cook."

Norah was certain Tom would keep his word, allow his subordinates to manage Ashley Dynamics, and make the campaign with her. She felt an urgent sense of excitement, a lifting of her spirits, as she headed toward the kitchen. She found herself looking forward to the political talk, the strategy, the tensions, and the relentless march to the first Tuesday after the first Monday in November. If she was to be the candidate, she would run her own campaign; there would be no manipulation by Tom or the President. On that she was absolutely determined.

* * *

Dinner was flawless, from the clear soup to the tangy lemon mousse. It reenforced Norah's conviction that Mrs. Manley was worth the occasional kitchen drama.

Sam Bradshaw, the senior senator from California, was seated to Norah's right in deference to his rank as majority leader. A small dapper man with an Adolphe Menjou mustache, Bradshaw was given to dozing off on the floor of the Senate even during a heated debate. He'd been dubbed "Sleepy Sam" by an impudent broadcaster.

The nickname had stuck. Rather than resenting what was intended as a slur, he made good use of it and played to the gallery with gusto. Sam had a way of closing his eyes and nodding off, head bent forward, chin tucked into his chest, and, when it was least expected, he'd throw back his head, open wide the baggy owl's eyes, and deliver a salient verbal thrust. Although he was rumored to be something of a ladies' man himself, he had a huge appetite for gossip concerning the extracurricular activities of his peers. Disarmed by his narcoleptic symptoms and his somewhat dotty air, the unsuspecting would blurt out confidences to him. These indiscretions were promptly banked in his encyclopedic memory and drawn upon when he deemed it necessary. Secure in his power, ranking member of the President's own party, Sam Bradshaw was a man to be reckoned with. He had free access to the Oval Office, and if the President, his fellow Californian, wanted Norah Ashley to run for the Senate, Bradshaw could be relied upon to do his utmost in her behalf. Norah did not underestimate him.

She had placed Andrew Watkins, the chairman of the National Committee, to her left. His Santa Claus exterior was a disarming camouflage that served the shrewd and ruthless political strategist well. His bright blue eyes twinkled behind rimless glasses, and a nimbus of gray hair fringed his balding pate. Other than Tom, Andrew Watkins was the President's most trusted friend and longtime ally. Since the President's earliest days in Washington as the freshman congressman from the Eighteenth Congressional District of California, the chairman had been his strong supporter.

Watkins and Tom had drifted into the garden during the cocktail hour, and Norah suspected Tom had informed him of her capitulation. It amused her that, as if by tacit agreement, the subject of the Senate race had thus far been carefully avoided. The conversation at table was general, gossipy, and interesting. She was curious as to who would bring up the race and when. She was certain it would not be Mellon or Brookings, who were seated on either side of Tom at his end of the table.

The White House congressional liaison, John Mellon, was rumored to be brilliant and both sexually and ethically amoral. He firmly attached himself to the center of power no matter who wielded it. For all his addiction to fine tailoring and made-to-order shirts, his ever-present cigarette and his unfortunate tendency to weight gave him a dusty, rumpled look.

In contrast, Daniel Brookings, the President's press secretary, a former Rhodes scholar and a highly articulate political barracuda, bore himself with an innate elegance. Tall and lean of frame, with his black skin drawn tight over his high cheekbones and strong features, he wore his black hair cropped close to his skull. Daniel Brookings was respected for his skillful duels with the White House Press Corps. He used his quick wit and personal charm to protect the President with flair and firmness.

Sam Bradshaw made the first move. Finishing the last of his wine, he dabbed his lips with the white linen napkin, placed it on the table, and cleared his throat. "You set a very good table, my dear Norah," he said appreciatively. "I should like to pay my compliments to the cook."

No director could have made a better choice than the voters did in casting Sam for the role of senator, Norah thought, as she said to him, "Mrs. Manley would be thrilled, Sam. Come, I'll introduce you."

He rose to pull back Norah's chair and lowered his voice. "And then, my dear, we must get to the business at hand."

Norah stood up, signaling Tom.

Hands wrapped in her apron, face flushed, and beaming with pride, Mrs. Manley accepted the senator's excessively gallant compliments. The tigress had been turned by Sam's charm into a cream-filled pussycat. The embattled kitchen would, to Norah's relief, become a haven of tranquillity. For a while, at least.

Putting her arm through his as they walked through the living room, she said with a laugh, "You ought to negotiate with the Russians, Sam.

You're a marvelous diplomat. You've saved my home—at least my kitchen."

"Enlightened self-interest!" He patted her hand and said, "I want to be invited back. And I want you to save the administration." He looked at her probingly. The laughter evaporated.

When they reached the library, they found Tom and the others settled in the deep couches flanking the bright-burning fireplace. McPherson had already served them the chilled stingers for which he was justifiably famous.

The butler immediately offered one to the senator, who readily accepted it with a lame protest: "I have absolutely no character vis-à-vis this poison." He took a small sip and raised his eyes to the ceiling. "Perfection! Where shall I sit?" he asked.

Norah directed him to the large leather armchair backed against the bookshelves, and she pulled up a small chair for herself. She felt like Joan of Arc facing the tribunal. I must stop dramatizing myself, she thought, refusing McPherson's offer of a drink. She wanted a clear head.

"I take it you've all been informed of the President's decision that I should run for the Senate, and Tom has told you I've agreed to do it. Right?" She didn't wait for their answer. "But there are some questions I'd like to ask. If that's okay?"

Bradshaw nodded. "Of course, my dear!" He smiled at her benevolently.

"Have any of you geniuses considered the negative factors? I'm a woman and an actress."

Mellon put his cigarette down and reached in his pocket for a slip of paper and looked up at her appreciatively. "Being a woman used to be considered a fifteen-percent handicap for a candidate. Today, it puts the odds to even." He studied the paper. "No, it's a slight advantage. One percent, two, maybe, not enough to matter."

"And being an actress?" Norah asked.

Watkins was quick to answer. "It certainly didn't hurt Reagan or George Murphy. Even Helen Douglas made it to Congress, and if it hadn't been for the McCarthy horrors, she'd have beaten Richard Milhous what's-his-name for the Senate."

"What about my positions on the issues, Andy? Have you thought about that?" she questioned the chairman, aware of his hostility to what he called the "goddamned dame problem." "I've been pretty vocal for abortion, the ERA, busing, and a few others that might cause some trouble for the President." She looked directly at him. "And I have no intention of changing my opinions."

Tom interrupted. "We've been through enough negatives. Let's talk about the plus factors first." Andrew Watkins sat back and accepted the cigar Tom offered him. "The congressional delegation should be unanimously in favor of Norah's candidacy. She helped on all of their campaigns when she was national committeewoman." He grimaced. "Or is it person? —whatever. Anyway, they're all of them obligated to the President."

Watkins interrupted. "And to you, as I recall. You helped finance most of 'em."

Tom nodded. "And of course she has a strong base in the Hollywood community by virtue of her career."

"What about Lowman at Paragon Pictures?" Brookings asked. "Isn't he the emperor of Hollywood? Will he be with us?"

Norah laughed. "The empress is my closest friend, and they go back with the President almost as far as I do. What about labor?" she asked. "Will they go along?"

Tom raised his eyebrows. "Karl Auerbach is head of the labor council, and he's already told the President he'd be for you, Norah. I'm sure the Boss talked to him before he called me," he said. "You should be in good shape with the liberals and the minorities; you supported Martin Luther King and Cesar Chavez earlier than anybody. And you're publicly committed to Israel. You can count on the Jews."

He turned to Watkins. "She's weak with the oil people, the conservative farm bloc, and the nonliberal business establishment. That's Hardwick country."

Andrew Watkins puffed his cigar. "Well, we've got a pretty broad base for starters." He turned to Mellon and asked, "Have you found out who the hard-noses have in mind to run for our party's nomination? I've heard some rumblings about a character by the name of Chisholm. Is he for real?"

"You bet he is," Mellon replied, the plump face showing concern. "He's attractive, articulate, and smart as hell. He may be the chancellor of that dumb-dumb Pacific College in Santa Barbara, but he's also on the boards of some pretty smart corporations and foundations. What's more, he's been vice-chairman for the State Committee in his own district. He has a public image as an educator, not that of some polarized right-wing nut, although that's what I think he is." He scowled. "He'd be a very effective candidate for the anti-President, anti-Norah bunch to rally around. I wouldn't be at all surprised if some Hardwick money found its way into his coffers. Oh, no"—he shook his head and made a sucking noise —"he's for real!"

He was interrupted by McPherson, who addressed himself to Daniel Brookings. "Excuse me, sir, the White House is calling you. You can take it at the desk, if you wish."

"Thank you, McPherson." He picked up the receiver. "Brookings here. . . . *She what?*" he gasped. The intensity of his tone riveted all attention in the room. "In her own driveway? Jesus God! Has anyone talked to Hardwick? . . . I'll bet! What about the servants? . . . Un-hum, yup, fine. Make the usual condolence statement, Mabel, about the President and the First Lady's shock over the tragic loss, and that the senator and his family are in their prayers, or whatever."

He hung up the phone and shouted, "Quick, the television! Virginia Hardwick drove her car into the garden wall at their Foxhall Road place. She was pronounced dead on arrival at Georgetown Hospital." He told them, "An excessive amount of alcohol showed up in her bloodstream. That won't be made public, at least not yet. The senator's spokesman claims Hardwick's in a state of shock and unable to answer any questions."

John Mellon turned pale. He reached for a cigarette and sank back into the couch, incredulous. He felt numb, thinking of Virginia on the coroner's table. She'd had the body of a girl. He closed his eyes and tried not to envision the scene. When he looked up, Andrew Watkins was staring at him. He knew! Mellon felt it at once. There were no secrets in Washington.

CHAPTER
Four

A solemn-faced commentator, microphone in hand, overcoat collar raised against the chill of the wet night, stood surrounded by a silent, grim-faced crowd of onlookers. "Ladies and gentlemen," he reported, "the hospital has just confirmed the death of Virginia Thayer Hardwick, wife of Senator Richard Hardwick of California. Mrs. Hardwick apparently lost control of the family car this evening and crashed into the stone wall surrounding the luxurious Hardwick estate. She was pronounced dead on arrival at the hospital."

There was a visible stirring in the crowd, and the commentator explained, "There's Senator Hardwick now."

Richard Hardwick, bareheaded, his face shielded from the camera by his aides and uniformed police, was seen entering a black limousine, which sped away immediately, led by a motorcycle escort, sirens screeching. The reporter moved to the left of the screen and shoved his microphone toward a distracted looking aide, who pleaded, "Please! Please! Ladies and gentlemen! There will be no statement at this time. The senator is obviously in no condition to speak for himself. He will meet with you in the Senate Briefing Room tomorrow morning at ten o'clock and answer any questions you might have to ask him at that time. No cameras will be allowed." The men and women of the press kept crowding around him. He shook his head and pressed himself into a waiting car.

The commentator faced the cameras again. "The late Virginia Thayer Hardwick, wife of the senator from California, was a well-known Washington hostess and the only child of the late, legendary Colonel Elwood Thayer, whose empire included the Thayer newspaper chain, numerous television stations, and vast oil, real-estate, lumber, and agricultural holdings. He served as chairman of the Board of Trustees of Whitmore College until his retirement in 1972. The Colonel was credited with having been instrumental in the elections of former President Nixon and former Governor Ronald Reagan. Colonel Thayer died earlier this year. It was rumored that he was actively engaged in promoting his son-in-law's expected bid for the presidency.

"Reliable sources indicate that the late Mrs. Hardwick had been deeply depressed by her father's death this year.

"She is survived by her husband and a daughter, Mrs. Marianne Redfern.

"We now return you to your regular program but will keep you informed of any further developments concerning this tragic affair as we receive them."

Tom switched off the television.

"He killed her, the son of a bitch killed her," Mellon hissed, draining his glass, unmindful of the cigarette ashes dropping on his trousers.

Andrew Watkins studied him through hooded eyes. A chill of apprehension ran through the chairman of the National Committee. The congressional liaison's visible agitation confirmed the validity of the FBI report on Virginia Hardwick the President had asked for. There had been an affair between the Colonel's daughter and Mellon. True, Mellon was only one of many. The list of her conquests looked like a congressional directory. She'd been flagrantly unfaithful to Hardwick for years, not that *he* was any rose. Still, the chairman had felt uneasy about having Mellon close to the Oval Office after he'd read the report. But the President had pooh-poohed the idea of booting him. He needed him. Besides which, the whole mess was like walking through molasses. There was no way of knowing whether or not Virginia had any knowledge of the President's encounter with her father, much less if she confided in Mellon or if her father had confided in her. Neither seemed likely. Still, there was no point in taking any chances now. Norah's campaign was supremely important to the President. Maybe California would be the best place to put Mellon on ice for a while, as far away from the White House as possible. Just in case.

"Now, now, John," Senator Bradshaw said sympathetically, "whatever else he is, Hardwick's no murderer. I know the man. Cold, yes! Killer, no! Apparently Virginia was loaded. What was that you said about the alcoholic content, Dan?" he asked.

"There's a report, but it's not checked out yet. It appears to have been pretty high," Brookings answered.

Norah sat silent. Virginia Hardwick was dead, the circumstances of her death clouded. Poor thing, life hadn't been all that wonderful for her. Norah went to the bar, poured herself a glass of Scotch, and filled it with ice from the silver bucket.

Tom watched her, thinking, she's shaken by this. It makes Hardwick a human being, not just an abstract thing, "the opposition." Was she feeling pity for him? Would it inhibit her willingness to take him on? Would he play the grieving husband? Would that soften her? He looked across the room and saw Mellon slumped in his seat, stunned and pale. Jesus! He'd forgotten about Mellon's involvement. The FBI report! No wonder he looked stricken. Poor devil. Andy had wanted him sacked the minute they found out he was messing around with Virginia Hardwick. Now, with the real—What was it Norah had called it? The real "McGuffin"—hanging in Damoclean fashion over the President's head, maybe it'd be best to keep Mellon in California.

Tom glanced at the chairman, who was studying Mellon, his expression troubled. He caught his eye and cocked his head questioningly. Watkins nodded almost imperceptibly. They were of the same mind. Turning to Brookings, he asked:

"What effect do you think this'll have on our campaign?"

Brookings looked thoughtful. "Depends on how he uses it. I think it's a shrewd ploy, having a press conference tomorrow. Damn clever of them. He's got to be in a state of shock and look dreadful. The press are human, after all, they'll treat him sympathetically."

Mellon sat up straight. "They must have had some kind of donnybrook. Saying she was distraught over her father's death is pure crap. *Depressed* is going to be the—the key word." He knew damn well she wasn't that!

God Almighty, they'd been together—when was it—yesterday? Light-years away. Not that Virginia ever pretended the affair was more than it was. Nor had he! But one thing was certain, she sure as hell hadn't been depressed. Obviously there'd been a domestic fracas and she'd gotten smashed. Well, he'd better snap back into the present. "He'll get the sympathy vote for the moment, but it's a long time till November."

"What do you think about it, Norah?" Sam Bradshaw asked. "This could make it somewhat more difficult for you to go after him."

She looked at him, rattling the ice in her glass. "What do I think?" She wasn't likely to tell him what she was thinking. There but for the grace of God— The man she'd seen on the screen being hustled into the limousine was surely not the Richard Hardwick she remembered. Well, she wasn't exactly the starry-eyed ingenue she'd been either. Norah felt Tom studying her. He was wondering how this would affect her willingness to run. He needn't worry. She found herself anxious to get the machinery cranked and moving.

She raised her brows and took a sip of Scotch. "It would have been better to run against Hardwick right from the start and ignore Chisholm or whomever they put up against me in the primary, the way the President used to do it—but now? We'll have to see how he handles it. What's the daughter like?"

"I met her at the Hardwicks'," Bradshaw answered. "They entertained frequently in that fancy place of theirs on Foxhall Road. Poor Virginia did a lot of that. The daughter's name is Marianne. She's married to Bailey Redfern, a pretty boy who's big on tennis and horses and doesn't give a damn for politics. She looks just like her mother. There was some talk they didn't get along too well."

"Will she stand by her father?" Norah asked.

"Probably," John Mellon said as he joined Norah at the bar. He held the inevitable cigarette while he refilled his glass from the chilled pitcher of brandy and mint.

"Why should she?" Norah questioned. "If her mother's death was the result of some terrible quarrel with her father, wouldn't she be hostile to him?"

Sam Bradshaw shook his head. "It was the old Colonel who reared the girl, not Hardwick and Virginia." The shrewd eyes narrowed. "That old bastard had his heart set on Marianne's daddy going to the White House,

and, like her mother, what the Colonel wanted, she wants. Hell, why else
would Virginia have stayed married to that bastard other than for her
father's sake? No sir!" he said emphatically. "Marianne'll hang in. You
can—"

He was interrupted by the ring of the telephone. Brookings reached for
it instantly.

"Brookings here," he said, his face turning grim as he listened. "Yessir,
I'll tell them." His mouth went slack and his expression changed to one
of surprise. "I beg your pardon, Mr. President." His face broke into a
broad smile. "Why, of course I would, sir. That is, if she'd like me to. Yes,
Mr. President, she's right here. I'll put her on." He motioned excitedly
to Norah and stood up to give her his chair as he handed her the receiver.

"Hi, darling—" Norah quickly corrected herself. "I mean, Mr. President."

He chuckled and the famed voice said, "Call me what you like. I'm
going to call you Senator, my girl."

All her resentment against him dissipated. She could envision the strong
mobile face and the steel blue eyes that darkened ominously when he was
angered. They had been bright with the look of victory the first time she'd
met him, when Tom took her to those dingy congressional headquarters
nearly a quarter of a century ago. His first election night, his first win. Tom
predicting he'd be President. He'd been right about that.

She herself had been totally apolitical then, totally wrapped up in her
career at Paragon Pictures. Norah the superstar had thought the word
incumbent meant a supine position. But, through Tom, politics became her
territory, too. It had provided her with a new kind of audience, a live one,
through three congressional, one gubernatorial, and finally a presidential
campaign. All of which she had enjoyed in behalf of the man on the other
end of the phone.

Tom, the born pragmatist, saw politics as a vehicle for good, despite its
flaws. He loved the role of mastermind and used it as a diversion the way
other men did golf or tennis. But for Norah, it developed into a passion.
Certainly her beauty and acting ability helped, but it was her ability to
project the depth of her concern which evoked the strong response from
her followers. She sometimes wondered whether it was a real passion on
her part or just her deep-seated actress's need to arouse the emotions of
her audience. Whatever the reasons, she had learned how to exploit it.

And the President never showed any compunctions about exploiting it in his own behalf.

He was right. She was his best available shot.

"Look here, Norah, we're going to send Hardwick back to Orange County. But I think this mess makes it a different ball game. He's not going to have any real opposition in his own primary and he's going to milk his bereavement for all it's worth. He's going to use it like he used her fortune, to further his career. He's not above that, you know."

"I know," she answered. Ah yes, she knew.

"Well, Norah, don't you worry about it; I'm going to loan Dan to you so we can use your talents to the maximum. That is, if you'd like having him handle the news media in your campaign. If Hardwick wants to sit back on his ass and act like there's no campaign going on, we'll see to it that you'll be on the front page of every paper and the cover of every goddamn magazine sitting on the racks."

"I'd love it, Mr. President. I need him." As soon as she'd finished the conversation and hung up the phone, she rushed over to Brookings and threw her arms around him and shouted, "You're mine, mine, mine. Tom, he's going to come to California!"

Brookings hugged her and shouted, "Ole Massa say I'm to help this honky actress beat back the noble representative of 'all white America.' Ah'm gonna get out of that backbiting cesspool, the District of Columbia."

Tom said, "That's marvelous, Dan. God knows, we need you. The primary is the most lethal of all political encounters. If it's handled with the maximum exposure for Norah and the minimum amount of venom to foul up the finals, by God, we'll take the son of a bitch in November."

Dan Brookings' face turned serious. "By the way, this is the latest. The butler claims Mrs. Hardwick had been doing some pretty heavy drinking before the great man arrived home. It seems that after he'd served them their dinner, he heard the sound of raised voices. Next thing he knew Mrs. Hardwick came running out of the house with the senator in pursuit. He made a special point about 'the madame's' having been extremely upset by the death of her father. The butler's been with the family a long time and isn't about to admit to what everybody in Washington suspects, that she's been into the drinking thing for years."

Watkins noted, "Mellon's right, the 'deeply depressed' phrase about the death of that miserable old bastard, her father, is the alibi. Can Hardwick sustain a sympathy vote for eighteen months?"

"No," interrupted Brookings, "but it sure as hell will give him the excuse to sit on his hands during the primary. If I were advising him, I'd suggest he lay back and let the opposition beat its brains out while he collects condolences, attacks the administration, and makes like a statesman in the Senate, revving up for the finals."

Andrew Watkins nodded. "He can keep right on doing his bit in Washington. He's on the air every five minutes anyway, carping at the President. Between 'Meet the Press' and 'Face the Nation' and morning and nighttime 'yak' shows, the bastard's getting to be as visible as Coca-Cola. This new development should make him even more desirable to those media vultures." The eyes grew hard behind the bright lenses as he glared at Senator Bradshaw. "I hear he's going to appear on your friend Dorothy Johnson's morning show again."

"I didn't know about that!" Bradshaw answered, genuinely surprised. "I'll have a talk with the little lady when we get back," he said, scowling.

Was it possible Dorothy was messing around with Hardwick? he thought angrily. She hadn't returned his last few phone calls. Her crotch was some sort of political weather vane. She must think Hardwick's a shoo-in. Well, all the more reason to go after him.

"Do that!" Watkins said, directing his attention to John Mellon. "Have you found anything on Hardwick that looks suspicious?"

"Nothing tangible yet," Mellon answered. "There hasn't really been time. But on the surface some of his votes seem peculiar to me. Why?"

"Well," the chairman said, running his fingers across his pate, brushing back the nonexistent hair, "if we could get something on the son of a bitch, he'd have to get off his duff to defend himself, wouldn't he?"

Mellon nodded agreement. "We haven't researched him in depth, but his labor votes have a pattern. He's a big anti-labor guy except if it's a close one and—"

Watkins picked up his cigar, looked his most avuncular, and said thoughtfully, "Maybe we ought to ask the President to loan you to Norah along with Brookings here. If she could get a handle on any funny business, his current grief situation would have to be put aside—now wouldn't it?"

Tom was quick to back up the chairman. "It would be a great help to Norah, John, if the President let you stay here for the campaign."

Mellon frowned. "Here?" Then he questioned, "It'd be much easier to check him out in Washington, wouldn't it?"

Watkins, his voice firm, replied, "No, John, I think you'd be more help to the campaign if you stayed in California for a while. I'll talk to the President about it."

Mellon studied the miniature snaffle on his Gucci shoe. He wasn't being asked. He was being told. Christ, obviously they knew about him and Virginia Hardwick. They probably had a file on him just like they did on everyone else, these self-righteous hypocrites. Washington was one big monkey cage; everyone watched everyone else's indiscretions. The chairman wanted him out of the White House. Norah's campaign was to be his Siberia. Ever since Carter, they'd gotten holy. He looked up and smiled as best he could. "Of course, I'd love it, if it's all right with the President. And if Norah wants me, that is. I'd, ah—be delighted," he said.

The President wouldn't gainsay Watkins and Tom if they insisted that necessity demanded his exile. There was no use in protesting. John Mellon thought of Virginia and wondered why he felt so stricken by her death. It wasn't love. Well, if they were going to put an apple in his mouth and serve him up on a platter to Norah's campaign, maybe, just maybe, he could have a hand in sinking the bastard who drove her to kill herself.

CHAPTER
Five

R ichard Hardwick flung himself into the one deep armchair in his living room and pressed his hands over his eyes. It was the only chair in the formal room in which he felt comfortable. Virginia had permitted its presence under heavy protest. He had insisted on having at least one piece of furniture of his own to sit on among the delicate fruitwood Louis XIV chairs and pale green silk settees. He had always felt the trespasser here. It was very much Virginia's domain. The portrait of her, white shouldered in a white damask ball gown, hung above the scrolled marble fireplace. Even in death her presence dominated the room.

He couldn't rid himself of the horrible specter of her bloodied face even as they lowered the flower-banked coffin into its resting place in the freshly turned earth. The nightmare vision would remain with him for the rest of his life.

He shuddered, put down his hands, and looked up at his daughter, Marianne. She silently handed him a drink. Bailey, her husband, leaned against the fireplace, the even-featured handsome face despoiled by the surly mouth. Virginia, who had loathed him, claimed he was born with a birth defect: a permanent sneer.

"How'd it go, Senator?" he asked, studying his father-in-law's appearance. Even Bailey found himself shocked by the puffy bloodshot eyes and the yellow cast of Hardwick's tanned skin. The press must have really shafted him at that conference. He looked ravaged.

Hardwick shook his head. "I don't know, I just don't know." He bent over and gulped his drink, the usually erect posture collapsed into an exhausted slouch.

Marianne, drained of color, her pallor exaggerated by the unrelieved black of her dress, pulled up a small stool at the foot of his chair. The white skin and copper-flecked auburn hair emphasized her Thayer inheritance. Although taller and more robust than Virginia, she moved with the same effortless grace. The resemblance was eerie, as if the dead woman's ghost had entered her daughter's body.

But the agate eyes, so much like her mother's, looking into his were as sad as Virginia's had been cold. "They went after you?"

He shrugged. "No, not really. If you take the press's hostility toward me into account, I'd say, by their standards they were being considerate. It was just tough. That's all."

Marianne stood up and walked over to the fireplace, ignoring Bailey. She studied her mother's portrait and asked hesitantly, "Did they bring up the drinking thing?"

"No, they didn't—I did," he stated quietly.

She spun around, horrified. "How could you? What a rotten thing to do." Her voice grew loud. "Did you have to muddy her up now? What concern is it of anyone's? She's dead!" The eyes narrowed, and she looked at him with distaste. "Or were you playing for sympathy? A cheap shot to pick up a few votes?" The eyes flashed, the sadness gone.

He sat up straight and glared at her. "I really don't need this now, Marianne. I'm not going through any more goddamn inquisitions and certainly not from you." His face reddened. "Christ," he shouted angrily, "are you so naive as to believe that the coroner's report won't *show* the alcoholic content, or that Theodore won't be put under oath at the inquest and asked to tell what the hell went on here?"

He stood up and faced her. "Your mother was drunk when she killed herself. Besides, everybody in town knows she was a full-blown alcoholic. I was trying to save her reputation, if not for her sake then for ours, by saying she was in a depression brought on by your grandfather's death. The press had the decency to make mention of it, even though they knew goddamn well that it was a crock of shit. The Colonel was hardly cut off in his prime," he snapped.

Bailey broke the silence and said sarcastically, "My, my, 'of the dead say nothing but good.' Please, Senator, you're shocking my poor, bereaved wife. You know how close she was to her mommy." He made an attempt to put his arm around Marianne's shoulder. She recoiled from his touch.

Hardwick lurched toward him. "Shut up, you bastard. Do you hear me?"

Bailey sighed. "Temper, temper, and at such a time! I can see when I'm not wanted. I'll just leave you two to your terrible grief." He brushed his lips across Marianne's cheek, walked to the door, and held it open. Looking at Hardwick, he said in an exaggeratedly solicitous tone, "Maybe with your tragic loss and all that, they won't bother looking into the Beau Soleil deal. If the environmentalists ever join up with the Justice Department and figure out how you and these distinguished partners of yours managed to screw 'the peepul' out of their parkland, you may need all the sympathy you can get, Senator. Good night, sir." He bowed with exaggerated servility and slammed the door shut.

"What Beau Soleil deal? What park? What does he mean?" Marianne asked, rubbing her cheek with the back of her hand.

"He doesn't know what the hell he's talking about." Richard picked up his drink and sat down again in the chair, putting his feet up on the stool. He really needed Bailey to give him that shit. "How the hell did you ever marry that creep?"

Bitterly, she answered, "I suppose I had nothing better to do after lunch." She settled herself on the settee alongside the fireplace and folded her hands in her lap. "I want to know what *really* happened," she said, quietly looking directly at him, waiting.

He returned her gaze, too exhausted to dissemble.

"She *was* drunk and hysterical and especially hostile when I got home. We quarreled bitterly—more so than usual—I lost control of my temper —inexcusably, and then— What more can I tell you? I don't think you want the details of the quarrel, do you?"

"No!" She shook her head. "Considering your relationship, it's a wonder you even bothered to fight."

His voice lowered to a whisper. "Listen to me, Marianne, I had no hand in her death, and depression is as accurate a description for alcoholism as any other. You *know* what she was."

Marianne stared at him, incredulous. "I *don't* know what she was. How could I? All I know is that she was a cold, indifferent mother who wanted me as far away as possible. Concha and my grandfather raised me. *She* didn't want to be bothered. For that matter, neither did you." Her eyes began to fill with self-pity. "Did she *ever* love me, or you? Did you love her, or was it the Thayer money? The power? Did you kill her soul long ago, or what? Why did she marry you? What kept you together? Where did it all begin?" The questions poured out accusingly.

Had Richard Hardwick ever loved his wife? The Colonel himself had chosen Hardwick to be his daughter's consort. He had acquiesced willingly. Had Richard Hardwick and Virginia Thayer been put through a computer, the results would have read, "flawless match." He'd married her for what her father offered him. She, him, because there was only one place the Snow Princess of the Casa Thayer could go—to the Casa Blanca. He would be the vehicle to get her there. That was what he offered her.

Well, the Colonel had gotten his money's worth—a male to manage his empire and bed his insatiable daughter. Although Richard hadn't provided Colonel Thayer with a grandson, he'd sired a daughter whom the old pirate unabashedly adored. More important, Richard was the Colonel's passport to the Taj Mahal of power—the White House. The old robber baron, unable to attain it on his own, wanted his son-in-law to fulfill his unrequited political dreams. He himself was too remote, too powerful and distant, with no talent for the glad hand, the pressing of the flesh. He was unelectable and he knew it.

Returning to Marianne, Richard said, "It was all so long ago, I can't remember who did what to whom or where or why. My relationship with your grandfather began when I was a bottom-of-the-ladder junior partner at Baxter and Wall. I'd developed considerable expertise on the subject of oil and gas leases. So when your grandfather, who was a very important client of the firm, acquired some oil properties, they assigned me to him. It was heady stuff for a young lawyer, scratching his way to the top. The Colonel was pleased with the work I did for him, and we actually developed a genuine fondness for each other during that time. I guess I had a fierce need for a father figure and he for a son. A psychiatrist might have diagnosed it that way." He shrugged. "After he returned to California, he invited me to visit at Casa Thayer. I guess I'd been anointed before I got there.

"The first time I laid eyes on your mother, she was dismounting her horse. She seemed to be totally weightless. I thought her the most graceful woman I had ever seen. Your grandfather was waiting for me at the great oak door to the Casa, very much the grandee. Little Manuel was at his side. I guess Concha's son-of-a-bitch nephew must have been three or four at the time and the Colonel doted on him. It was such a magic world, Marianne, for an ambitious young lawyer. You were born into it and take it for granted. I was reared in a tract house in Riverside. It was overwhelming." He found himself pleading for her to understand.

"No, I don't. I don't take it for granted," she answered. "It's just the only world I feel safe in."

He was startled. "Safe? Safe from what?"

"I don't know." Her face clouded. "The Thayer demons, perhaps. They're less apparent to me at the Casa."

He drew in his breath. What tormented her? Did she carry her mother's seed of self-destruction? If so, she needed a better man than Bailey to save her.

He pulled himself up out of his chair, crossed the room, and poured himself another Scotch.

"Did you ever love anyone?" she asked.

How could he tell this distraught woman, his daughter, that he had never been in love in his life with anything except power. The multiple octopus tentacles of Thayer wealth and power were the potent moving forces of his life. They had become a part of him. Richard was not a man to indulge himself in backward glances. His choice had been inevitable. The sweetness of the summer with Norah dimmed with the passage of time. Perhaps he couldn't love. Ginny had thought so; well, she couldn't either. At best, she had assuaged her momentary appetites with alcohol or men or whatever came her way. Beneath her apparent fragility had been an animal's strength, and an animal's appetites. These she inherited from the Colonel. But not his self-discipline. No, unfortunately, she hadn't been heir to that.

Marianne had been a tiny infant when the doctors told him and Virginia that there could be no more children. Virginia was not meant to multiply; Marianne's birth had brought her close to death. Perhaps that was why she cared so little for the child and willingly allowed Concha to rear her at Casa Thayer. There was no way to know now.

When Marianne was a small child, he was the newly elected senator from California. His political star was on the rise. Arriving home unexpectedly, in a banal, cheap scene of discovery, he found Virginia naked on the couch in this same room, his executive assistant sprawled across her. She mocked his outrage, and as the horrified, spluttering lover reached for his clothes, she made no attempt to cover herself. Her pale, patrician face calm, eyebrows raised, she said, mockingly, "Come now, Senator, don't bother playing the aggrieved husband, your passion is vote counting, not fucking. Since there will be no grandsons for Papa and no sons for you, why bother to pretend? I shall do as I want and screw whom I want where I want. Tonight was stupid and indiscreet." She made a chagrined face. "How careless of me to embarrass the future President! I'll be more careful next time."

They never slept together again. But she kept her word; he never knew where, when, or with whom she indulged her appetites until that terrible last night.

The actual truth was that once his ego recovered, it hadn't mattered to him. She was a brilliant hostess, adroit at handling the social needs of his political life. This was all he required from her and she enjoyed the role.

For now, at least, Dorothy Johnson fulfilled whatever libidinous needs he did have. TV superstar and interrogator, she was as deeply involved in her own career as he was in his. She made no clinging noises, no excessive demands on his time. His aura of power and her total lack of sexual inhibition worked well for the both of them. Sure, she thought she'd use him for her own purpose. No chance. No one was going to use *him*.

Only once could he remember having been deeply aroused. That had been during his bittersweet love affair with Norah Jones. A few years back, he and Ginny were the guests of a movie mogul (he couldn't even remember the man's name, now) at a Hollywood film premiere. There had been the typical Barnum and Bailey atmosphere. Long lines of hearse-like limousines glutted the boulevard, klieg lights pierced the dark sky, grandstands overflowed with screaming fans. Ginny detested the entire scene. The limousines disgorged their passengers to loudspeakered introductions and screams of approval from the bleachers. In the distance he'd seen Norah step from one of those cars, Thomas Ashley at her side, tall, elegant, and aquiline. She smiled to the cheering mob with a grace and vitality that separated her from the others; she was a presence, a new Norah. The young actress had turned into a distinguished, handsome woman. Age had refined her features, and she exuded a shimmering quality, a sense of stardom and beauty honed by time. He had felt a sudden pang of longing. Ginny stiffened. "Who's that?" she had asked their host.

The mogul had answered, "That's Norah Jones, honey—*some* gorgeous lady. Much more beautiful now." Sighing, he added, "Too bad Ashley's so loaded she doesn't need to act. Politicks a lot these days, plenty smart, too!"

After a complex search for her number, he made up his mind to call her on the pretext of "lunch for old time's sake." But the telephone froze in his hand. Of course, she'd refuse him. God knows he had it coming. There was no point in making an ass of himself.

That had been almost three, or was it four, years ago? It didn't matter. But that she should be planning to run against him was unbelievable. That son of a bitch in the White House must have put her up to it.

Suppose she made it through the primary? He, the reliable, distinguished, incumbent senator, would paint her as a dumb movie actress, a rich dilettante, a do-gooder, a nigger lover, a sloppy bleeding heart. He'd call her the President's puppet. He'd wrap her in that package and send her home to her millionaire husband, special delivery.

The President was his true target; he'd treat Norah for what she was, a diversionary tactic on the road to the real battle. Norah would provide nothing more than the framework for his attack on the President. Whatever temporary emotion he had felt back then was long since gone.

Returning to Marianne, he said, "There's no point in rehashing my life with your mother. It's *you* I'm concerned about. Darling, we haven't bared souls to each other, ever. But will you answer a question I've had about you for years? You're a brilliant, beautiful, adorable young woman. Why did you marry that sneering, unsubstantial jackass, Bailey Redfern?"

He moved toward her. They stood and faced each other in silence while he waited for her answer.

"Do you really want to know the truth?"

"Yes!"

She swallowed hard, closed her eyes for a moment. Then she looked up at him and said softly, "Because I loved Manuel"—she paused and her voice went flat—"and he wouldn't have me!"

Hardwick was horrified. "Manuel? Concha's nephew? And *he* wouldn't have *you?*"

"Yes, Manuel, the housekeeper's nephew," she said dryly. "Or as he calls himself, 'the Colonel's pickaninny.' The house nigger's nephew. He seems to feel that one member of his family warming a Thayer bed is enough. He was too proud to have me and suggested I marry one of my own kind. So, my dear father, since you're suddenly interested in my case, that's precisely what I married," she said with a sneer. "Tom, Dick, Harry, Bailey; one of my own kind. What difference?"

Hardwick sat down, muttering in disbelief. "Jesus Christ! *A Chicano!*"

"I had to marry somebody, didn't I?" she said defensively. "What else was I trained for? Expected to do? God knows, Bailey had all the proper credentials. Well-bred, good family, lovely public manners. How was I supposed to know he was a twisted, useless rotten monster with nothing but the Thayer money in mind?" she asked plaintively. "He courted me with damn near medieval gallantry. At least you gave my mother a child, which is more than Bailey can do for me." She paused, her eyes filled. "Suppose Concha *was* Papa Colonel's mistress. I don't give a damn. She was the only mother I ever had!" she shrieked at him. Then, lowering her voice, she asked, "She was his mistress, wasn't she?"

"So what? I don't know, Marianne. How the hell should I know? It doesn't matter, does it?" He threw up his hands. "She's a very rich woman now. The Colonel left her a great deal of property and stocks. For my part, I'm glad he did; she earned it for rearing you, whatever his other reasons. That little bastard Manuel has some nerve criticizing the Colonel, much less Concha. Who the hell does he think paid for his education at Harvard? His mother? The house she lived in with him? The Colonel gave it to Concha. His mother never had ten cents to her name that she didn't get from Concha." Richard's face grew red with anger. "After all Concha and this family did for that self-righteous card-carrying hostile shit! He's a goddamn ingrate! A rabble-rouser! That's what he is!"

Marianne looked at him coldly. "You can call him what you like. I call him a proud man."

Hardwick felt his gorge rise. "Have you been seeing him? Tell me the truth, Marianne. I want to know."

Her eyes flashed with sudden hostility, and she said ruefully, "Not that it's any of your business, but no. *He* won't see me!"

"Marianne," he said hesitantly, "I know I haven't the right to collect any chits from you but—I have a favor to ask."

She shot up her eyebrows in the same way as Virginia; the resemblance chilled him.

"A favor of me? What could you want from me?"

"To help me in this campaign. I need you badly."

She broke into shrill laughter. "Me—the political illiterate?"

"I'm not joking. I'm begging. With your mother's death, especially under the circumstances"—he paused, his face grim—"your presence at my side would go a long way to—"

"To remind the great unwashed of your sincere bereavement," she mocked. "Your devoted daughter, the image of your poor dead wife, her beloved mommy, standing by your side? Is that what you want?"

He nodded. He wasn't going to play the hypocrite with her. She felt an overwhelming wave of desolation. At least if she agreed, it would give her an excuse to be away from Bailey. That much it would do. The tears began to flow unchecked. "We're both so alone, so terribly alone," she sobbed and flung herself weeping into his arms. That was something Virginia Thayer Hardwick had never done.

CHAPTER
Six

Within a few weeks the framework for Norah's campaign machinery began to creak into position.

The mechanics for mounting it were classic. Before Norah would make a public declaration, the search for appropriate headquarters was launched statewide. Personnel to staff them were hired. Stationery, posters, car stickers, were ordered. Committees were formed, volunteers sought out and organized. Politicians have subzero credit ratings and with good reason. History has repeatedly proven them to be poor economic risks. Losers spend as much money as winners, sometimes more. Both leave a holocaust of financial disaster in a wake of unpaid bills. The old saw "You can't raise money on a dead horse" is a proven truism in politics. Telephone companies and printers, radio stations and the television networks demand not only prepayment but early reservations as well.

From the opening gun until the moment the polls close, *money* is the top priority concern. Since the dismay born of Watergate, even where the regulations do not limit the size of an individual contribution, public opinion does. This enlarges the number of contributors needed to underwrite the cost of campaigning. Money remains the mother's milk of politics. In any campaign, a finance chairman by necessity must be named at the earliest possible moment. For Norah's campaign the obvious choice was Walter Lowman.

Not only was Walt Lowman the chairman of the board of Paragon Studios, the undisputed Supreme Chieftain of the movie community, but he was the richest and most powerful of all the studio heads. Like the Ashleys, he and his ebullient, outspoken wife, Tillie, were devoted to the President's cause.

Walter Lowman's business dealings spread across every facet of the community. No call from him would go unanswered. No request would be ignored. The favors he had performed for others were legion; the sums of money he donated to various causes beyond counting. And he himself was the most skillful money raiser in the community. In a company town Walt Lowman was the company. And a social invitation from the Lowmans was not a request but a mandate.

Walt had brought Norah to Hollywood from Broadway. He was the first to sense her "screen" potential. Paragon was her alma mater, the mother convent.

Tillie Lowman had befriended Norah from her starlet days on. When Norah catapulted into stardom, it was Tillie who guided her through the social maze. Although men dominate the workings of the film industry, their consorts control the Rubicon of social acceptance. Some have themselves been the beauties who filled the fantasy lives of millions of Americans, others made their mark privately in the bedroom. They are, for the most part, intelligent, stylish, and tough and are frozen in time at the approximate age of thirty-five. A hard-core cabal of these women could and often did doom a chosen victim to social Siberia by virtue of exclusion. It was especially dangerous for a young and talented actress whose beauty might threaten them. Tillie's approval and friendship were equivalent to a papal blessing and provided Norah with an open passport at the beginning of her career. Their friendship grew and deepened with the years. It was the Lowmans who first introduced Norah to Tom when he became a major stockholder of Paragon Pictures. The Lowmans were the people to whom the Ashleys, still, felt the closest.

It was imperative to have them involved in the campaign. Norah, herself, as a matter of courtesy, went to see Walt in the white marble "tower of terror," from which he ruled his domain and where she herself had begun her own film career.

The office was just as Norah remembered it, unchanged by time. Although the Lowmans' private life-style was baronial, Walt's office was sparsely furnished in sterile glass, stainless steel, and soft black leather. The dark mahogany desk was immaculate with the minimum of necessities visible. Walt Lowman never put off anything. There were no piles of unfinished business in sight. Only the material on which he was working lay on the polished surface. Small-boned and slim, of medium height, he had an innate elegance that belied his impoverished beginnings.

Since he and Tillie often dined with the Ashleys, he'd been surprised when Norah called and asked for an appointment to see him. The intelligent, perpetually tanned face broke into a smile at the sight of her, his star, back in his office at her old studio. Walt had no doubts as to the purpose of the visit; still it pleased him that she'd come. He kissed her and asked jokingly in his soft voice, which in temper lowered to a whisper, "Did you come to tell me you're ready to go back to work, darling?"

Norah leveled her gaze at him fondly. "Quite the opposite. I have a job in mind for *you*!" She laughed. "Guess what?"

He drew his brows together and looked at her in mock seriousness. "My God, McPherson's quitting and you want me to mix the stingers. Right?"

Norah shook her head. "Wrong," she said, knowing full well that Tom and possibly the President had already approached him in her behalf.

He pulled up a chair for her in front of the desk, but he remained standing, leaning against it, while she settled herself.

"Would you believe I want you to serve as my finance chairman—?" She looked up, eyes large. She lowered her voice. "What's more, I want Tillie's lily-white body too. I need her to tackle the fat-cat consorts."

Walt snorted, "Sweetie, me you've got. You didn't even have to ask—but Tillie—" His mouth pulled into a lopsided grin. "That's a whole other story—you know how she hates committees." He bent down and kissed her again. "I'll make a deal with you. I'll tackle your campaign finances —you tackle my wife." He straightened up and leaned toward the intercom.

"Now I have a favor I want from you," he said to Norah. He pushed the intercom button and called into the machine. "See if you can get Lisa up here. I'll wait."

A disembodied secretary's voice replied, "Yessir," and then came back a few minutes later: "I'm sorry, sir, she's in the middle of a scene. Do you want to—?"

"Never mind," he answered disappointedly and switched off the box. He pulled up a chair alongside Norah. "You know this new young actress we have on the lot, Lisa Ryder?"

Norah tried to place her but couldn't and said apologetically, "I'm embarrassed to say I don't, but you know Tom and I don't—"

"I know," he sighed. "The only time you see a film these days is when you come to dinner. Thank God Paragon doesn't have to depend on the two of you to go to the movies, or our stock would be worthless. Anyway," he continued, "Lisa's got the makings of a real star. She can romance a camera like . . ."—his look softened—"just like you could. But she's one of these modern young women who're given to that 'I want to know who I really am' crap."

"Walter Lowman!" Norah exclaimed. "With Tillie for a wife and me for your next senator, are you making male chauvinist noises? I don't believe it!"

He grimaced and made sucking noises through his teeth. "This new breed is a whole other story. So you and Tillie are tigers." He shrugged. "But you sure as hell know who you are, and you don't have to run around in circles finding yourselves."

"Maybe we just hide the search better," she commented dryly.

"Anyway," he continued, "Lisa is convinced that you're not only the greatest thing that ever hit the screen but a totally fulfilled human being —whatever the hell that is! I thought it would be nice to have her meet you. Maybe you can find a place for her in the campaign." He drew a deep breath. "She's a hot property, and we don't need another meshuginah Marilyn Monroe, God forbid! So if she's happy and busy in between pictures, she might find herself a lot faster—"

"I'd be thrilled to have her," Norah assured him. "A 'hot property' could add a lot of zing to the campaign."

* * *

"I'll give you the money! I'll sell the jewelry! Anything! But if you think I'm going to muck around with a lot of dull broads—even for you—" Tillie Lowman shrieked at Norah, "never!"

But for all the kicking and screaming, it was Tillie who gave Norah her first major fund-raising event. She took the upstairs room at the Bistro, the favorite watering hole of the Hollywood establishment, and threw a splendid luncheon, collecting a fortune in Norah's behalf.

There was no need to pressure Karl Auerbach, head of the labor council, into action. He was panting at the starting line, wildly anxious to get into Norah's campaign. Auerbach was totally committed to the defeat of Richard Hardwick, whose political posture he detested. He admired and respected Norah and considered whomever the right wing of the party chose to oppose her no more than a fly on the lion's paw.

His wife, Evelyn Curtis Auerbach, successor to Norah as national committeewoman, was a brilliant organizer in her own right. Over the vehement objections of her rich, conservative family, the former Philadelphia Main Line debutante had not only fallen in love with the gruff labor leader but insisted on marrying him. And then to their absolute horror, she espoused his political philosophy as well.

It was she who conceived a plan to utilize the vast untapped volunteer power lying dormant throughout the state and dubbed it "Bag It for Ashley."

Her plan was to hold a "Bag-It Day" each week in as many communities as possible across the state, encouraging the volunteers to bring their own lunches (*sic* the "Bag-It") and address and stuff envelopes to raise large sums of money by means of small donations. This would galvanize a committed corps of volunteer workers for Norah who would be useful now and invaluable in the finals, which concerned her most, as they did Karl.

It was an easy way to assemble the woman power which, by necessity, formed the basis of all grass roots movements, despite the advances made by the feminists. And it would create sufficient support and spirit to augment the impersonal but necessary media campaign.

Tom, who took no campaign title, headed the loosely knit brain trust consisting of the Lowmans and Auerbachs, Brookings and Mellon. The President had readily agreed to loan John Mellon to the campaign. Norah was deeply grateful, believing that the President was depriving himself of Mellon's services for her sake.

As the early activities began to take form, Norah felt like a boxer. Managers and trainers prepared her and propped her up. Yet when the bell sounded and center ring time came, she'd be alone in the ring facing the opposition, chin out. The time of sparring ends at the mystical moment the battle is joined. Whoever her opposition might be, she herself would be obliged to plead her own case.

The chaotic tempo of these early weeks, which Tom called her "slugger-in-waiting" period, helped divert her anxieties. Her spirits vacillated from exhilaration to apprehension. The self-doubts peaked at night. Tom would wake to an empty bed and find Norah in the library reading the stack of position papers supplied by Mellon.

Norah embarked on her first statewide swing in behalf of the "Bag-It" operation directly after the press conference Brookings called for her to announce her candidacy.

Evelyn hosted the opening event. The rambling Auerbach house was crowded with photographers, press people, and distinguished women addressing envelopes, munching sandwiches, and sipping white wine. Norah went from group to group, thanking them for their help. Tillie, all pink silk and pale linen, was at her side, whispering names Norah might have forgotten. Living with Walt had developed Tillie's facility to remember names. Walt could recall the title of every film he'd made, its gross intake, each scene in it, in sequence, and the role each employee had played in the making of it. But put him in a receiving line, and the name of the familiar person whose hand he was about to shake was erased from his memory. Tillie would skillfully fill in the gap for him. Now she was doing the same chore for Norah. Forgetting a name might bruise an ego in Walt's case. In Norah's it could cost a vote.

Norah noticed an extraordinarily good-looking young woman dressed in a turtleneck and blue jeans, head wrapped in a brightly colored scarf, sandwich in hand, pen in the other. She was working feverishly, oblivious to the photographers swarming around her.

"Who's that?" Norah whispered anxiously.

Tillie looked at her in disgust and hissed, "Don't you know?"

Norah shook her head, unable to place her.

"You're as bad as Walt! Come with me, dummy, that's Lisa Ryder, the hottest thing at Paragon since you deserted. Didn't Walt tell you about her?"

Norah's face lit up. "Of course. She's going to find herself or something."

Tillie took Norah's hand and led her toward the young actress and chuckled. "Walt could afford to be magnanimous and release her to work for you. Her next picture doesn't start for a few months. She thinks she won one."

Seeing their approach, Lisa jumped to her feet and came to them. The photographers' flashbulbs exploded as Tillie introduced them, and Norah knew at once that Lisa Ryder's presence would be invaluable to the campaign.

Intelligent blue eyes, large with excitement, Lisa Ryder spoke in a husky voice soft with the traces of a southern accent not yet conquered. "I feel just terrible that I didn't get to see you at the studio, Mrs. Ashley. The bahstards wouldn't let me off the set." The words poured out in a breathless rush. "I told Mr. Lowman I wanted to meet you and that I was determined to work on your campaign, on *my* time for *my* own sake, instead of being nothing more than a slave on his Paragon Plantation. I carried on so he had nothing to do but agree to let me have a leave of absence to work for you. The very idea of a woman, and an actress at that, going to the Senate of the United States absolutely blows my mind. I *gotta* have a hand in it." She paused for breath and looked at Norah searchingly. "That is, if you'd like me to."

Norah took the younger woman's hand in both of hers. "Like you to—?" She laughed. "I'd be thrilled and grateful."

The beautiful young face turned earnest. "I don't mean just to be a decoration. I mean to really help, to do something meaningful. Something from *here*!" She tapped her forehead. "Something that's my own. Do you know what I mean, Mrs. Ashley?"

Did she ever? Norah felt her years as the young woman spoke. She had become a symbol to this beautiful young woman who was just about where she herself had been twenty years earlier. Lisa was struggling to find out "who she really was" and believed the campaign would serve as the illuminating vehicle. Norah hoped that if she found the "real Lisa Ryder," she'd like her. There was a calculated risk to the quest. She studied the younger woman's face, her green eyes looking searchingly into the young actress's deep blue ones.

"Of course I know what you mean. The loss of identity is one of our occupational hazards." She paused. "Look here, political seas can get rough and dirty and mean, you have to expect that. But you'd add a lot of dazzle to this trip." She leaned toward the young woman and kissed the smooth cheek and wondered. Had she herself ever been that young, that breathless?

"Bag-It" took off like a rocket, and for ten successive days, Norah flew up and down the state with a merciless Evelyn Auerbach and a starry-eyed Lisa Ryder, who loved every minute of the exhausting pilgrimage. Tillie refused to join them, explaining it was not her style of travel.

"Evelyn," Norah whined, "do I have to keep eating those dreadful egg sandwiches and addressing all those damned envelopes? I'm on the road to a heart attack and bursitis."

The hazel-eyed patrician yawned. "Oh dear, the candidate is bored." Then, giving Norah her coolest gaze, the well-bred voice contemptuous, she said, "You hang in there, or I'll deck you with a swift kick in your well-photographed ass! We have the makings of a fine volunteer organization—which you, by the way, taught me was the key to a successful campaign. And I really don't give a damn about your cholesterol count. Or your ouches."

"Evelyn, your Main Line graciousness is slipping!" Norah smiled. "I don't see how Karl's held up all these years."

Evelyn threw her head back and laughed. "Simple! He is convinced he married beneath himself!"

By the time the exhausted women returned to Los Angeles, they had established a statewide network of volunteers and the beginnings of a huge mailing operation. And Lisa Ryder had become an integral part of the campaign.

The President's endorsement brought offers of support from every segment of the community. Norah and Tom gave endless dinner parties, the guest lists laden with tycoons, politicians, lawyers, educators, intelligentsia, and labor leaders. Walt Lowman arranged a series of crash sessions with directors and writers to brainstorm a maximum-effective media image for Norah. The bulk of the voters would be swayed by what they saw on her television spots. They had to be created by the best pros in the business.

Planning, preparing, and organizing the campaign during the early weeks gave Norah a sense of energy she had long since forgotten she possessed. There was a renewed closeness to Tom. They were in it together, locked at the hip. It was rehearsal time.

The curtain went up the day Dr. Norton Chisholm, chancellor of Pacific College in Santa Barbara, called a press conference to announce his candidacy for his party's nomination in opposition to that of Norah Jones Ashley.

"How can he do that?" Lisa questioned Dan Brookings as they settled themselves to watch the broadcast in the main room of Norah's headquarters.

"Do what?" he asked with a scowl.

"Why, declare himself against Norah! They're both in the same party and *she's* the President's choice!" Lisa's tone was indignant. "That's just like he's defying the President."

Brookings looked at her with astonishment. What the hell was this little Miss Southern Beauty doing in a political campaign? Sarcastically, he drawled, "Missy Lisa, ma'am, I jes' keeps forgettin' you all's so young and innocent." Ignoring her angry look, he continued, "Since time immemorial, spitting in the President's eye has been an intramural party sport. In recent years—" He paused. "You're too young to remember, of course, but Eugene McCarthy, George McGovern—not to mention that home-grown California hero, Ronald Reagan—took on—" Before he could finish the sentence, the television screen reflected Chisholm's image and the room grew silent.

Square-jawed, clear-eyed, the sandy hair cut short, an enameled American flag pinned prominently to his lapel, he faced the cameras seated in his book-lined office overlooking the Pacific. "As a patriot and an active member of my party, I feel duty-bound to challenge Norah Jones Ashley's bid to depose the incumbent senator from California in the November election. The people and the party must have a choice. I admire her as an actress but deplore her ties with the leftist elements in our social and political spectrum. But most of all, as a third-generation Californian, I resent her being a handpicked candidate and the President's puppet. The primary is historically a matter to be settled by the *people* themselves." His face grew stern. "No one, not even the President of the United States, has the right to tell the people of the sovereign state of California whom they should nominate to represent them. I deplore his misguided highhandedness," he said sternly.

"The American people are desperately seeking moral leadership. With the help of God I believe I can provide that leadership. I am beholden to no man. I pledge to serve all the men and women of California and not just the privileged, the underprivileged, the blacks, the whites, the young, or the old, to the best of my abilities. I welcome this opportunity to be of service to my party, my state, and my nation"—his voice grew louder —"and to the Christian principles which have made us great!"

Norah's supporters watched the broadcast at the newly opened Ashley headquarters with amusement. There were shouts of ridicule. "Do you believe that mother?" "Jesus and the American flag."

John Mellon, cigarette clenched in his teeth, face glum, protested, "I sure as hell do believe him. Remember Reagan? He was plenty effective with all that crap about the American flag and the Panama Canal." He shook his head, spilling ashes. "And broadcasting his love of Jesus sure as hell didn't hurt Carter. Norah may need him herself."

Brookings scowled silently. Lisa Ryder stood up from her desk and said with concern, "Why is everyone laughing? I think Chisholm's scary."

Brookings looked at her, surprised. "Do you now, Miss Ryder? May I ask why?" There was a touch of amusement in his voice.

She angrily leveled her gaze at him. He was so goddamn patronizing with his Washington savvy, his Oxford education, and that black chip on his shoulder.

"Because he looks and sounds like educated Klan. That's why, Mr. Brookings." She reached across for one of Mellon's cigarettes.

Brookings pushed aside a pile of papers and found a package of matches and held out a light for her. She inhaled the smoke and studied him, her voice quiet, the anger muffled. "Why don't you cut out the crap and stop patronizing me? And you can call me Lisa, Dan," she snapped.

"Okay, Lisa," he said, ashamed of his hostility. Southern accents could still hackle him. At first, when Norah suggested using the young actress as a substitute for herself when overscheduling demanded an alternate speaker, he thought it an insanity. But despite his doubts he had to admit she'd proven a quick study. She grasped the issues easily and charmed the audience. Now in a headquarters filled with people who were supposedly politically experienced, she was among the few who sensed the real threat in Chisholm's candidacy.

Mellon sat lost in his own thoughts, ignoring the others, and mused out loud, "That pious prick's no joke. Where's he coming from? Who's backing him? He's not just some kook from left field. He's a college president.

even if it's a lousy college. And academicians are hardly rich. You can't run without money. He's got the smell of the states' righter on him with that 'sovereign state' crap. Is that shorthand for antibusing, antigovernment controls? *Oil* maybe? Gun control lobby maybe? Translated, he is saying that a man's home is his castle, down with the environmentalists, the feminists, forced integration, the President's tariff program, and anything else that's to the left of McKinley, *sic* anti-Christian principles, whatever they are." He stubbed out his cigarette and pulled a fresh one from his breast pocket. "What are his party credentials?" He looked up at Brookings. The press secretary shrugged. "He was state committee chairman in a district that's so heavily weighted against us you can put our entire party registration in your eye without blinking. And that business about Norah being the birdbrain actress who's the handpicked stooge of the President," Mellon said. "That's sure to be the line Hardwick's going to lay on her in the finals—if she wins. If there's any funny money floating around, it could be Hardwick's, and we better find it and fast." His face was grim.

CHAPTER
Seven

Within days of Chisholm's declaration, it was apparent that his campaign was professionally organized. Wherever Norah appeared, an army of placard carriers was there too, carrying signs warning of subversion and implying that she had communist ties. A cadre of neatly dressed middle-aged men and women, they marched silently, in front of churches, synagogues, hotels, and union halls.

"Don't Bus Our Babies." "American Food for American Children." "Keep the Kremlin out of California." "Babies Have the Right to Life."

Just as Richard Nixon had painted Helen Douglas into the left-hand corner during the McCarthy madness that ravaged the country in the fifties, by cliché and innuendo Chisholm was locking Norah into every possible controversial issue. The laughter and the confidence in Norah's headquarters died abruptly. They hadn't anticipated Chisholm's malevolence nor his strength.

John Mellon, the sleeves of his rumpled blue shirt rolled above his elbows, sat in his cluttered cubbyhole of an office opening the mail. Reaching across his desk for the box of kitchen matches, his arm knocked over a half-filled paper cup of cold coffee.

"Christ," he bellowed, "somebody get in here and clean up this fucking mess."

A young, black woman ran in with a rag and a stack of Chisholm's latest campaign literature. Mopping up the spilled liquid, she pushed aside a pile of papers and deposited the new material in its place.

Mellon studied it in silence, ignoring her hostile mumblings. His anger mounted as he read the pamphlets, oblivious to the young woman's presence. All his worst apprehensions were being realized.

The latest Chisholm brochure was clearly meant for mailing to lily-white neighborhoods. It carried a photograph of Brookings, holding a drink in his hand, standing next to Lisa Ryder in a low-cut dress. It was taken at one of the cocktail parties in Norah's behalf. Brookings' blackness was exaggerated by Lisa's fair-skinned blond beauty. The picture had been cropped and reworked so that it appeared as if the two of them were alone. It was captioned: "This is the man the White House sent to California to aid Norah Jones Ashley. Do you want *him* masterminding your senator?"

The next mailer Mellon opened portrayed a shirt-sleeved Chisholm, smiling broadly, sandy hair ruffled, standing alongside the Reverend Isaiah Smith, pastor of the Olive Street Baptist Church. The two men were surrounded by a cluster of small black children.

On the flip side of this one, which was obviously targeted to black neighborhoods, was a picture of Norah taken at some goddamn Hollywood premiere; diamonds sparkled in her ears, a soft fur was thrown over her bare shoulders. "Which candidate do *you* think cares?" the caption read. The caption was effective.

Mellon looked up at the young woman, who, rag in hand, was mopping up the last of the coffee.

"You," he barked. "What's your name?"

"Barbara."

"Can you type?"

She nodded.

"Then type a memo, and I want copies to Tom, Norah, and Brookings. No more diamonds or fucking minks for Norah until this thing is over!"

She nodded and left the room. Mellon heard her typewriter clacking. He turned his attention to the morning's mail. Half the envelopes were soggy with the spilled coffee. Mellon hoped no checks had been destroyed. Interspersed with the usual congratulations, offers of help, and checks, which he carefully put aside, were a number of hate letters. They were more vicious than any he'd ever seen. Hate letters were a phenomenon endemic to all campaigns, but these amounted to an onslaught. The vituperative quality of the unsigned ones, which were always the most hostile in character, was too great to be ignored. The insidious and frightening quality and quantity of the mail alarmed him.

He called for a meeting in Norah's office and arrived with his hands full of pamphlets and letters. Throwing the first pamphlet on Norah's desk, he snarled, "Look at this crap."

Norah paled and held the Dan-Lisa pamphlet out to Tom. He studied it and shook his head.

"Do you think maybe we ought to keep Lisa away from Dan?" Mellon asked.

Tom looked up at Mellon, the hawklike features stern. "Nobody bothers with that kind of garbage these days. Ignore it," he ordered and threw it in the wastebasket.

Mellon shrugged, reached in his shirt pocket for a cigarette, and coughed. "You're the boss. Take a look at these." He handed him a stack of the hate mail. Tom began to flick through the letters.

"What about protection for Norah?" Mellon asked.

"Protection for me. Are you crazy?"

"Shut up, Norah, and listen to this," Tom said and went on to quote from some of the letters.

" 'God punish you, you atheist bitch. How dare you face decent people? We know how you got where you are. We know all about how you got your money. You sleep with dirty jews and nigger lovers. Watch out! You not get away with it.' "

He threw it on the floor and picked up another without looking up and read.

" 'You try to kill the little good babies. You a disgrace. A bad woman. You need a big beating and a fucking. You Commie whore-woman.' "

Before he could reach for another, Norah protested, "Stop, Tom." She looked at him with dismay. "It's just the same old hate-crazy nonsense. You're both turning paranoid." The very idea of protection was offensive to her. "Do you mean to tell me I can't run for senator from the state of California without being surrounded by bodyguards? You're as gaga as the letter-writing loonies. I won't have it," she said angrily. "That's just giving the kooks credence, letting them think we take them seriously."

"Bullshit," Tom interrupted. "John's right. This is not the *usual* hate mail. Now you just listen to me, Norah. The characters who're writing this filth"—he grimaced at the pile of mail—"are the nuts in the lonely rented rooms. And they're dangerous. They can't be discounted anymore. Lee Harvey Oswald, Sirhan Sirhan, James Earl Ray, and John Wilkes Booth were kooks. It only takes one kook with one gun to change the course of history. Chisholm is deliberately picking the scabs off of the bigotry endemic to all kooks—psychos—loners. We're ripe for an assassination. John's right," he repeated. The set of his jaw made clear to Norah that arguing was useless. She would have bodyguards. Security personnel were promptly added to the campaign entourage and posted at the Ashley home in Bel Air as well.

* * *

By the time Chisholm's campaign against Norah reached its crescendo, one month before the primary, its monied extravagance was not only visible but baffling. Even oil interests and real-estate lobbies did not commonly invest unlimited sums of money in challengers with no credentials who opposed established candidates endorsed by the President of the United States. The usual ploy for the big businesses was to give each candidate some token funding—just in case. Mellon was certain of two things. One, that Chisholm's real money source was as limitless as it was covert, and it had to be uncovered if Norah was to survive the primary.

The second was that Chisholm had established himself as the rallying force for a genuine groundswell of deep-seated dissatisfaction. The well-dressed people who were responding to his thrusts were bitter about taxes; threatened by blacks, young people, and big government; anxious about the dwindling power of their dollars; puzzled at the feminist movement; and appalled by the breakdown of what they considered the American way. Chisholm was their man. Norah's campaign was painfully aware that no amount of party organization could fend off a genuine, emotionally triggered movement. Only disillusionment with Chisholm himself could break his momentum.

When the educator appeared on a well-financed, skillfully produced statewide television broadcast, billed as a "Chat with the People of California," it was publicized in advance by full-page advertisements in the press and minute spots on the air. Chisholm blatantly exploited the Reverend

Isaiah Smith's support. The pastor boasted a huge following in the black community, and his picture with Chisholm effectively contrasted with that of Dan Brookings and Lisa.

Reverend Smith joined Chisholm in his televised "chat" and eloquently discussed the need to elect a man who understood the "true problems" of the disadvantaged, one who didn't mouth a lot of double-talk about so-called "equal opportunities." What his people needed, Smith pontificated, were jobs and food. He accused the "former Miss Jones" of being a tool for special interests and no friend of his black brethren. Then he introduced a *real* friend, Norton Chisholm.

The California press carried excerpts from the broadcast. But it was the Thayer chain's coverage, in bold print on the front pages of all its newspapers, which triggered Mellon's increasing suspicions that Chisholm was Hardwick's creature. The chain made blatant use of Chisholm's attack on Norah as the basis of its lead editorials. What had been a gnawing doubt became a full-fledged conviction.

"It's obvious," Mellon screamed at Karl Auerbach, waving the newspaper at him. "The *Thayerville Press* is a house organ for Hardwick. They're not going this far out on the limb for some schmuck nonentity. Hardwick is involved in Chisholm's campaign. Christ, it makes sense, doesn't it? If the bastard loses, he's had enough exposure beating on Norah to make her a pushover for Hardwick in the finals. The only thing they didn't count on is that he would develop a following." He threw the paper on Karl's desk. "But they'll pay him off, and he'll make a few token noises in the finals, and Hardwick will be home free."

"We've got to find out how the Hardwick people are funneling that money to Chisholm," Karl Auerbach said disconsolately. And, silently, everyone in the room agreed.

The erosion was visible. Norah's appearances drew smaller audiences. The monies for her campaign trickled in slowly. Tom and Walt Lowman, and even the President himself, were constantly on the telephone, pressing for contributions.

If Chisholm was taking money from Hardwick and they could prove it, maybe then, just maybe Norah would have a chance. Mellon was spurred by the hope that if he uncovered the evidence, his exile would be over.

Brookings was more concerned about the black vote, which rightfully should have been Norah's, than the question of money. "Brother Isaiah

Smith carries heavy clout in the ghetto and he doesn't come cheap. He's a boughten black bastard and Chisholm's bought him," he snarled. No one in the campaign had even considered the possibility of black defection to a conservative such as Chisholm. The President's popularity and credentials were thought to be foolproof. And Norah was respected and loved in the ghetto.

"What makes you so sure that Chisholm bought Reverend Smith, Dan?" Karl Auerbach asked cautiously. "You people are really getting paranoid."

"Because *I* bought the son of a bitch for the President in the *last* election. I carried the cash myself. That's how I know!"

Mellon mumbled, "It's the money, always the money."

They were riding back from a labor rally. Norah's reception had been lukewarm. "Hardwick's financing Chisholm in order to shoot down the President. But maybe the real problem is that some of what Chisholm says hits home," Brookings said. "Norah is rich, she is famous, and what's more, she's too goddamn grand. Chisholm is presenting her as an actress and a wealthy leftist dilettante who's patronizing the blacks and the middle and lower classes. And he's doing a damn good job of it. You yourself went after her on that, John."

"Why the hell don't you curtail those goddamn high-minded briefings? She already knows too much for her own good. My people don't like their politicians or their women too smart!" Karl snarled.

"All she's got to do is stand up and say, 'I know what your problems are. When I'm elected, I'm going to see that they're taken care of' and get the hell off the stage and start shaking hands. Keep her away from *Women's Wear Daily* and the Bistro and all that crap." He shook his finger at Mellon. "And get her away from those smart-assed young lawyers and their fucking position papers! Lock them up in that squirrel cage of yours and let 'em work on the financial scandal you're so fanatic about."

The briefings stopped and Mellon enlarged his research operation. Other than an occasional visit with Tom and a series of low-keyed meetings with earnest-looking young men and women carrying bulging briefcases and portfolios, he began to work unnoticed and separate from the day-to-day campaign.

CHAPTER

Eight

"**I**nternecine cannibalism and chaos are endemic to primary fights," Andrew Watkins pontificated, helping himself to a second serving of crème brûlée.

"I *know* all that," the President said irritably, "but I'm going out to California anyway. I euchred Norah into this, and I've got a responsibility to continue to help her. Anyway, Liz is after me to get out there," he sighed. "She's frightened for Norah. And the truth is, I'm worried too."

The two men were having dinner alone at the priceless eighteenth-century dining table in the family quarters of the White House. The First Lady had excused herself directly after cocktails on the pretext that she was certain they wished to talk privately.

The chairman knew the Chief had no secrets from his wife. Obviously, the First Couple had caucused in bed. He'd learned from bitter experience there was no way to beat it. She'd lobbied the President into this kamikaze trip. No need for her to loiter. Her mission was accomplished.

He took another spoonful of the rich dessert. It was marvelous—probably a splash of rum was what gave it the indefinable kick. Damn it! Why didn't she stick to running the White House, which she did so brilliantly, instead of screwing around with politics?

The cuisine was the finest it had been since Jacqueline Kennedy shook up the White House kitchen.

The black butler silently served them their coffee.

"Thank you, Foster, I'll ring if we need you," the President said, dismissing the man with a nod.

As soon as they were alone, Watkins continued, "You can't get away with it, sir. The shit will hit the fan. An incumbent President is bound by tradition not to get himself caught up in a primary hassle. Do you remember what happened to FDR when he went out to California for McAdoo?" The blue eyes lost their twinkle. "Californians are as bad as the Texans. They hate carpetbaggers. You're a native Californian, but you've transcended the native-son bit. You're the President. Native sons with that kind of muscle are resented. And what's more, Chisholm has already tried to smear Norah as a puppet, the President's choice. Now you want to go out there and fuel that mess? It's crazy!" he insisted. "Your hold on the electorate at this moment is at best tenuous. Breaking the rules won't help things."

I don't need him to give me a lecture on political tradition, the President thought angrily. I wrote my goddamn doctoral thesis on it. Screw the incumbent neutrality taboo! So Roosevelt got his tail kicked in for campaigning in McAdoo's behalf when Downey challenged his bid for re-election in the late thirties. He'd survived the thorny business of carpetbagging quite well indeed. What's more, FDR got himself firmly reelected, carpetbagging and all.

Big deal! Every taboo in politics had been flaunted one time or another. And successfully, as often as not. He had to take the risk. Not for Norah, but for himself. There was no choice. Liz was right, he sighed, grateful for her loyalty.

He frowned at the chairman, took a sip of his coffee, and pushed away the dessert. "Goddamn it, Andy. I'm not going to play the hypocrite. I have a personal preference. It's Norah! It's hardly a secret. I'm going out there and say so. I can't let Chisholm win the primary. Hardwick'd destroy him in the finals with one hand tied behind his back. If Norah makes it, she can win in November. At least she'll have a chance."

He stood up, walked over to the sideboard, and poured two snifters of brandy from the crystal decanter. He handed one to Watkins. The chairman accepted it, knowing that further argument was futile. The ball game was over.

The President reiterated, "I've got to take the risk." He looked at his watch and reached for the telephone placed at the far end of the table. "Let's see. It's about five thirty out there." He picked up the phone and said, "Get me the Ashleys, Mabel."

* * *

After the President's phone call, Tom replaced the receiver at a loss for words, his face grave with concern.

"How do you say, 'No thanks, don't help me' to a President?" Norah agonized.

Tom's eyebrows shot up. "Goddamn it, you *don't!*"

* * *

Lisa Ryder, her breasts straining the tight T-shirt showing under her safari jacket, handed a cup of coffee to Dan Brookings and kept one for herself.

"Calm down a minute, Dan, and explain this to me. I can't figure why the fact that the President is coming here to campaign for Norah is so awful," she complained. "People are running around going bananas and looking morose. Even Norah's acting as if she's about to be put against the wall. The Auerbachs are frenetic. Walt Lowman has actually descended from the tower and is locked in with Tom. And he *never* comes to the headquarters. Mellon's off someplace, and I can't find anyone who'll tell me what's so terrible. I would've thought everyone would be thrilled!" she said emphatically and seated herself opposite him.

God Almighty, Dan Brookings thought, why didn't this crazy bird leave him alone? He wasn't running a political science seminar. He had enough problems scheduling the President's visit and finding housing space for the media people who would come along with the presidential party. The press and TV and wire service pack had to be taken care of properly. They were a gaggle of prima donnas and, God knows, Norah had enough difficulties without antagonizing *that* bunch. Naturally Mellon was off someplace as usual, playing sleuth, being no help to anyone.

Despite his annoyance, he was grateful for the coffee. He put down the phone and looked at her appreciatively. She really was a number-ten fox.

The sun-streaked hair hung loose, framing her face. The large, intelligent eyes fringed with heavy lashes looked at him questioningly.

"Missy Lisa," he said mockingly. "Y'all know what a carpetbagger is, don' ya, honey?"

She put her cup down. The fine-boned face, treasured by cameramen, was distorted in an angry grimace. "Damn you, Dan," she said indignantly, "cut that out. All I did was ask a perfectly sensible question and you start giving me the little miss baby-doll southern crap again." She stood up to leave, glaring at him.

He reached for her wrist to detain her, making the peace sign with his free hand. "Pax, fair lady, I'm just an harassed, smart-assed nigger going berserk. Sit down and I'll try to explain why the Commander-in-Chief is giving everybody a pain."

She sat down, unsmiling. "Some nigger! You're a snob, a fucking snob in any color!"

The press secretary burst into laughter. "All right, it goes like this. The President's arrival is going to bring the Chisholm forces out en masse, screaming 'carpetbagger' from one end of this state to another, and it's going to rub off on Norah. And right now, that's not the kind of help she needs."

"So why's he coming, if it creates problems? Norah told him not to."

"Because in his mind he thinks he can beat the odds and help himself by helping Norah. She can't very well say, 'You're not welcome here, Mr. President.' No way! He's the President! If she wins, he's a hero. If she loses, he's a martyr. Martyrs are sacred cows. Right?"

"Maybe he's right and you all are wrong." She sipped her coffee and said thoughtfully, "He seems to think he can help. Maybe he knows something you don't."

Eyebrows raised, Brookings asked quietly, "Wanna bet?"

Lisa nodded. "Yes, I do! I'll bet you a dinner in the restaurant of the winner's choice."

Brookings was taken aback. She was suggesting they have dinner together, publicly. Was it possible she hadn't seen Chisholm's flyer? He looked at her tentatively.

"Bet?" she repeated, holding out her hand.

He took it and said, "Sure, sure. Thanks for the coffee. I'd better get back to scheduling." He picked up the phone and said, "Get me the

Fairmont in San Francisco and then ask Karl if I can see him about getting his people out on the streets for a well-organized, impromptu spontaneous welcome for the President."

Mellon stood at the door, nodded to Lisa, and waited for her to leave. "You'd better scratch that bet and forget the payoff, no matter who wins or loses," he said quietly and turned around and walked down the hall.

CHAPTER

Nine

The news of the impending visit by the President, and the unusualness and irregularity of his intervention in a state primary in Norah's behalf, received wide media coverage and publicity. Large, enthusiastic crowds greeted him as he rode through the streets of San Francisco, Los Angeles, and San Diego, Norah at his side. The money-raising dinners given to fill the campaign coffers were sellouts. Even the governor, who had been careful to avoid involving himself in the intraparty primary battle, was forced to appear with the President. The banners and placards held aloft by supporters along his travel routes read *"Viva el presidente y Señora Norah,"* "We want Norah for Senatorah," and the like. But interspersed among them were the ones saying, "Yes on President, No on Ashley," and "Don't Carpetbag for the Ashley Hag." "Mr. President, Go Home."

Chisholm was on the air constantly milking the carpetbagging issue. In Washington Richard Hardwick made use of the California visit to intensify his attack on the administration and accuse the President of playing cheap politics while the nation went leaderless.

In the campaign itself things got uglier. Lisa Ryder, agitated and stricken, rushed into Norah's office. She reached across the desk and flung a letter in front of Norah. Written across the smudged notebook paper in childlike handwriting were the words *nigger fucker.* "It came addressed to *me!*" she gasped, looking stricken.

Norah crumpled it angrily in her fist and shot it into the wastebasket. "Damn them! Where did you get this? Did it come to your house?" she asked anxiously, fearing for Lisa's safety.

Lisa shook her head. "John Mellon gave it to me."

"Mellon!" Norah exclaimed. "Why would he show that garbage to you? I'm going to have a talk with him."

"Oh no! It was my fault," Lisa said quickly. "I guess I asked for it!" She was close to tears. "You see in the last weeks, Dan's deliberately avoided me and every time I got near him—somehow Mellon managed to come between us so Dan could drift away. I had enough. It was so obvious that I decided to put it to Mellon—" She paused and nodded toward the wastebasket. "That's when he handed me the vile thing!"

Norah sighed. "I'm sorry, Lisa, but can you imagine what poison comes in the daily mail that John secs?"

"So Dan avoids me," Lisa said angrily. "You mean the no-good trash —the pigs who write that sort of venom—control *us?* Dan can't speak to me because of *them?*"

"I'm afraid he thinks so," Norah said resignedly. This was really what she needed with things as they were, she thought bitterly. She felt an overwhelming sense of fatigue and leaned back in her chair.

Lisa observed her guiltily. "God Almighty, with all you've got to worry you. I come in and lay my dumb problems on you." How many of the sordid letters had Norah herself received? she wondered. "I'm sorry, Norah, really I am! You've just got to win. You've got to beat that terrible man. I'm going to ignore the letter and Brookings and Mellon, too. You've got to win!" she repeated.

"I'm trying, Lisa, I'm trying," Norah said wearily. "Now don't worry about those two snubbing you. They'll be okay as soon as this bloody primary is over," she reassured the young actress. "Don't worry, it'll all be fine."

But she didn't believe it herself. Her worst fears were being realized. The President was damaging his own case as well as hers. In his desperation to beat back Hardwick, he seemed to have lost his political judgment altogether. The violent reaction to his visit was too well orchestrated to be the product of Chisholm's organization alone. It was damnably sophisticated and professional, out of Chisholm's league. Hardwick's people had to have a hand in it. She no longer envisioned Hardwick as a man on any personal level. He was an abstract, invisible creature—"the enemy." She clung to the hope that Mellon's singlemindedness, which all of them had mocked in the beginning, might bring in some pay dirt. It was now that Norah's early years of show business discipline stood her in good stead. The actress Norah managed to project a calm, cheerful public face while the acid dripped slowly on her nerves.

Tom watched her anxiously as she maintained her poise, concealing the fatigue, smiling, handshaking, exuding confidence.

Tillie, too, worried over her, and said bitterly to Walt, "She deserves another Oscar for her brilliant performance in 'losing.' "

Norah's facade finally shattered on the last night of the President's visit. It wasn't Chisholm but Brookings who cracked the calm outer shell and broke through to the harassed candidate.

They were having sandwiches and coffee in the presidential suite at the Fairmont after a huge, garish, "money" dinner, when Dan arrived, looking grim. The President had made an eloquent speech in Norah's behalf, and she, in turn, had delivered the best and most moving address of her campaign.

Lisa Ryder, leading the Pledge of Allegiance, brought cheers and whistles of approval. The atmosphere was warm and high-spirited. The crowd was as enthusiastic as the dinner was inedible.

Tillie rose quickly to greet Brookings, noted his appearance, and thought, He's not buying this death rattle euphoria, poor bastard. "Have something to eat," she urged, solicitously. "You look exhausted."

Norah waved to a place to her left.

The President admonished, "Don't look so dour, Dan. Things went very well tonight. I think we've turned the corner."

Brookings remained standing, his face grave.

John Mellon pushed away the remains of his sandwich, lit a cigarette, oblivious to the press secretary, and said to Norah, "Look here, I'm going to Thayerville in the morning to do some research. I've got a hot lead that Hardwick—"

Brookings interrupted him. "Mr. President, I would like to resign from Norah's campaign."

Startled, the President put down his fork and asked the earnest-faced black man, "What the hell are you talking about? Why?"

"Because I'm a handicap to the campaign, sir. I'm the vehicle for bigotry. A black albatross. Norah's in enough trouble without my adding to it."

"Sit down," the President ordered, pointing to the vacant chair. Silently Lisa poured a drink from the bar and handed it to the press secretary, who accepted it without taking his eyes from the President's face.

"What the hell makes you think you're so important?" the President snarled. "You're the press secretary, not the central figure. Norah is!" He waved his hands toward her. "Because you're black?" he asked, angrily. "Didn't she march with King and walk through Watts during the riots? They're throwing it at her anyway. It's got nothing to do with you. How arrogant can you get!"

Brookings glared at him, trying to control his temper. "I don't think I'm arrogant, sir, and I don't think I'm a central figure. I'm a problem in this campaign. I'm being pictured as being involved with Lisa here"—he nodded in her direction—"in order to emphasize the racial issue. I'm an issue just like you're an issue, Mr. President," he shot at him. "I'm being forced front and center in order to sidetrack the focus of the campaign. My own people consider me an Uncle Tom, and to Whitey I'm a smart-assed nigger . . . an agent of the White House; which in their book has no place in this campaign. Right now, it's the fellow out there in the tract house, the mobile home, the small apartment, whose vote counts. That guy will go into that booth and pull the lever for Chisholm unless something changes fast."

Norah sat silent, eyes wide with disbelief; the dark velvet of her dress emphasized her pallor. Tom sensed the depth of her dismay and struggled with his own doubts as he watched her. Lisa leaned against the bar, looking from one to the other. Even Tillie was speechless.

The silence was broken by Karl Auerbach, who pushed back his chair at the far end of the table, lumbered over to Brookings, and said, contemptuously, "It's apparent they don't hand out Rhodes scholarships for judgment." He addressed himself to the President. "Take him back to Washington, sir. Stupidity is valuable there. They buggered the manhood out of him at Oxford. He'd be just great in the State Department with the striped-pants nances."

Brookings jumped up and flew at the unruffled labor leader. Lisa screamed. Tom and Mellon rushed toward the enraged press secretary and pulled him away from Karl.

Norah brought both her fists down on the table full force and shouted in a voice which had been heard in the back row of many a theatre, "Stop it! Goddamn it, stop it."

Tom was startled by his beautiful, disciplined wife, distorted with rage, yelling like a fishwife. He rested his hand on her shoulder and said, "All right, Norah. Now calm down, all of you." He turned to Dan. "I hate saying it, but I think you're right. The truth is that you're not just a decoy but an issue, and that you're being used to fuel the hate." He paused and drew in his breath. "I don't like to buckle to the bastards, but I have to agree, it would be best for you as well as Norah if you resigned. I think he should, sir," he said to the President, and turned to Karl Auerbach. "And you, my friend, owe Dan an apology. It takes a great deal of courage for him to resign."

Karl grimaced. "I'm sorry, Dan, I really am. I guess we're all unraveling." He put out his hand. "But I still think you should stay."

The press secretary took the proffered hand and accepted the apology in silence.

The President felt his insides turn over. Unable to look Brookings in the eye, he stared at the tablecloth and drew on it distractedly with his fork. Then he said brusquely, "Dan's right. So's Tom!"

Lisa's eyes filled, and she bit her lip to hold back the tears. She'd been certain the President would side with Karl and insist Dan stay on. "My God, and they say Hollywood's corrupt!" she said.

Ignoring Lisa's outburst, Norah said firmly, "I disagree, Mr. President."

"It's not easy for any of us," Tom intruded. His tone was conciliatory. "We all feel terrible that it's come to this. It's not a personal matter. Dan knows that, Norah. It's a *political* decision, and the President and I think it's a wise one."

Fuck them. They weren't going to cost her the Senate, nor the race against Hardwick. "Don't be so goddamn patronizing!" Norah's eyes flashed. "It's my neck that's on the block. I'm the one taking the flack. *I* am the candidate, and *you* volunteered me. Remember? Don't you think I see those dingy placard carriers or know that I have guards surrounding my house and me? I know goddamn well the trouble I'm in."

Tom was shocked by her vehemence. Before he could answer, Andrew Watkins, silent until now, said soothingly, "Now, my dear girl, we all know how upsetting this is for everybody, especially you. But you must understand that the President's future and that of his entire administration is in jeopardy. There's more involved than your campaign for the Senate. Of course we have your interests at heart as well as his. I tell you, Dan is doing what's best for both of you."

"Is he now?" she asked dryly. "That is in your judgment, of course?"

"In my judgment, yes!" the chairman answered firmly.

"Well, I don't accept your judgment." Norah stood up and faced the President, color mounting, her voice growing loud. "You drafted me, Mr. President," she said bitterly, "and I suspect it was for reasons of your own to which I'm not privy. But if I'm to stay in this race, you geniuses aren't going to sit back and tell me how to run it. It's going to be *my* way or *no* way." She moved toward Brookings, her finger pointed at him. "And you're not going to quit on me, do you understand? I'm not going to let those bastards say I dumped my black press secretary while Chisholm's running arm in arm with that cheap crook, the so-called Reverend Smith. That's what they want me to do, and I won't, I won't do it!" she repeated.

Dan looked at her in astonishment and then burst into a laugh. "You mean, I'm your token black."

"Damn right you are!" she shouted.

My God, thought Tom, she means it. He was stunned by her performance. She had never before gainsaid his political judgment, much less the President's. In politics, she'd always been his disciple. Now she was demanding to be the leader. Suppose she pulled out if this demand wasn't respected? He believed she might. His darling Norah had taken the bit firmly in her own teeth.

The President got up and put his arm around Norah's bare shoulders and hugged her to him. But her expression didn't change. It had a hardness Tom had never seen before.

In an effort to calm her, the President said, "Okay, boss, you're in charge. If you insist—" This was all he needed, to have his appointed candidate bolt.

"I insist," she snapped.

The President looked at Tom and raised his brow questioningly.

Tom answered coldly, he had no choice. "Brookings stays, the candidate has spoken!" Things were suddenly different. Some changes come unnoticed in small ways. A look here, a word there. Not this one. This one hit like a sledgehammer. Suddenly he wished he'd never gotten his wife into this campaign.

Lisa, unable to contain herself, blurted out, "How can you all be so cynical?"

Norah smiled mockingly, "It's not beer and skittles, little one! And I'm not playing Rebecca of Sunnybrook Farm. You think *this* is rotten?" Her eyes narrowed. "If I make it to the finals, which I have in mind to do— my way—" she added emphatically, "Hardwick may have us thinking fondly of Chisholm."

CHAPTER
Ten

Johan Mellon squeezed himself dejectedly into a vacant booth in the only bar in Thayerville and adjusted his eyes to the dim light. The day had been a frustrating and futile bust. He looked at his watch. The only flight out of Thayerville wouldn't leave for another two hours, and he might as well have a drink. Nothing of any consequence had turned up for all his trouble, not from the cab driver, the liquor store, the real-estate office, or any of the other standard sources. Sure, everybody knew the Thayers. That is, they knew *who* they were. Wasn't the town named after them? Oh yeah, of course they'd vote for Hardwick. He was the Colonel's son-in-law. Shame about poor Virginia Thayer—the Colonel's daughter. Sad business. They damn near bowed from the waist when they said "the Colonel," not "Colonel Thayer," just plain "the Colonel." He was the *padrón,* all right, the father of this particular county. Oh God, how Mellon longed to be back in Washington and out of this boring lotus land. I'd kill for a lunch at the Sans Souci, he thought wryly.

He opened a fresh package of cigarettes, the second, or was it the third? Christ, the day wasn't even half done. If this misbegotten campaign ever ended, he'd go to one of those clinics and kick smoking cold turkey. Hypnosis, maybe. He inhaled the smoke deep into his lungs. The blond, middle-aged waitress, hair piled into a lacquered pagoda, took his order for a Scotch and water. She wiped the Formica table with a used paper napkin, then dumped the full ashtray into the soggy napkin. She brought him his drink and smiled, revealing a disconcerting gold-framed front tooth. Bitterly, Mellon thought it wasn't likely that anybody from the Casa ever stopped off in this dump. The Rancho Café looked no more promising inside than it did from the street. His vision cleared and he noted the few figures standing or sitting at the bar with the neon Schlitz sign across the mirror. Small ranchers, maybe a truck driver. Still, it seemed to be the only place around. Maybe the waitress was talkative. It was worth a try.

"Guess you get a lot of important people with Senator Hardwick coming from here?"

She shrugged. "Nah—he's not here all that much, stays in Washington mostly." Her face lightened. "When the Colonel was alive, things was different. He always come in; if'n he had business to do, he'd bring whoever he ran into with 'im and buy drinks for the house. Always asked a person how things was. Real friendly." Her face saddened. "It ain't the same since he passed. Course, Bailey comes in a lot when he's around. Hardwick's son-in-law, you know. He don't talk to nobody. Real stuck-up." Her face took on a conspiratorial look. She leaned forward, engulfing him in a cloying wave of cheap perfume, and whispered, "That's the ranch foreman over there." She indicated a jeans-clad figure sitting at the bar.

Sensing he was being discussed, the man slid off the chair, turned around, and looked directly at them. He moved slowly toward Mellon's booth with an air of feline grace, carrying his drink. His face was extraordinarily handsome, the eyes very dark below the thick, well-arched brows. He pressed close to the waitress and grabbed her large buttocks with his free hand.

She slapped his hand away. "Cut it out!"

"Aw, Helen baby, you know you love it." He smiled provocatively, revealing even white teeth, and slid effortlessly into the cracked vinyl seat alongside Mellon. "You're crazy about me, aren't you, sweetheart? Bring another round."

She looked at him with distaste. "You're a goddamn smart-ass freeloader. Watch out for him, mister, he's no damn good. Just because he works at the Casa—" She went to place the order.

"I'm Lon McFarland, ranch foreman at Casa Thayer," he volunteered. "You here on business?"

"Not exactly," Mellon answered.

The dark brows drew together, giving him a look of malevolence. "What kind of crappy answer is that, stranger?" He mimicked Mellon's voice, " 'Not exactly.' "

He had the look of the quick-to-anger drinker.

Anxious not to rouse him, Mellon lied, "I'm doing a study of leading California families for the university, and of course, the Thayers—!" It was as good an explanation as any.

"A professor, huh!" McFarland took a match from the striker and chewed on it, studying him. "You mean you're gonna write a book about the Thayers."

"Well, I guess you'd have to call them one of the 'leading families.' They'd just be a part of it, of course. The waitress tells me you're their ranch foreman. Imagine you get to see a lot of celebrities," he ventured.

"Nope. Hardly nobody much visits the Casa now, specially since the Colonel passed. Bailey and Marianne—that's the Colonel's granddaughter, Marianne Redfern, and her husband—they live there. They don't entertain at all. There's a lot more action when the senator's around."

The waitress brought their drinks and scowled at the foreman. Mellon reached for the check. McFarland made no effort to stop him.

"No kidding." Mellon held out his cigarettes and struck a match for the both of them.

The foreman blew the smoke through his nostrils and gave him a knowledgeable look.

"One time he even flew out with that broad who's on TV all the time. Dorothy Johnson, you know who I mean. She may be a big cheese to some people, but she looked like a piece-a-tail to me."

"Doesn't he have a lot of big shot politicians around?" Mellon asked.

"Who knows?" McFarland said with a shrug, waxing loquacious. "How the hell can you tell what they are?" He paused and frowned. "Christ, he even had that little professor who's running against the actress at the Casa with a big black nigger. The Colonel must of turned over in his grave. You can bet they didn't have no niggers up here when the old man was alive. This one was a preacher with the collar backwards, but he still was black as coal."

He leaned forward. "If you really want to know what goes on at the Casa, you ought to try to talk to that Mexican housekeeper who runs the place. There's a lotta yak in these parts that she was plenty close to the

Colonel." He winked. "I mean close! But she's a snotty old bitch. Don't know if she'll tell you anything much. What the hell! You can give it a try."

He lifted his drink. "Well, here's to you! Whadja say your name was?"

* * *

John Mellon returned from his trip to Thayerville looking even more remote and distracted than he'd been before he left. The activities in his cubicle grew in intensity as he continued to keep them separate from the rest of the headquarters. The campaign itself became increasingly frenetic. Mellon's isolation was barely noticed.

Barbara Potter had all but forgotten about him and the noncommunicative young men and women who rushed in and out of the smoke-filled cubbyhole. She was in the midst of an assignment for Karl Auerbach when she heard John Mellon shout, "Hey you, Palmer, Porter!"

Resentfully she went to the door of his office.

Rolling down his shirtsleeves, snuffing out a cigarette in the overflowing ashtray, he reached for his jacket and said, "Come on. We're going out to lunch. I want to talk to you."

"I can't!" she protested, "I'm in the middle of something for Karl. It's urgent."

"Forget it," he ordered and grabbed her wrist, pulling her down the hall.

She walked rapidly alongside him, avoiding collision with the oncoming pedestrians on the crowded noonday street. He held the door for her as they entered the Italian restaurant at the corner. The short plump proprietress lit up in a smile at the sight of Mellon and signaled him past the waiting customers to a corner table. He must eat here regularly, Barbara thought. It was probably as far away as he ever got from the office.

"Ah, Signor Mellon," the woman said, "the veal is beautiful today!"

He grunted consent. "Fine. Two antipastos and some chianti." He looked questioningly at Barbara.

"Oh sure, fine!" She placed her elbows on the checkered tablecloth, rested her face in her hands, and stared at him, wondering why he'd brought her here.

"How'd you get into this campaign, Betty?"

"Barbara," she corrected. "I got into it because I think Ashley's better than Hardwick and Chisholm's no good at all. And mostly because I want a woman to win it."

"Oh." He looked at her with interest as if he were seeing her for the first time. "Suppose she loses? What will you do when it's over?"

"Win or lose, I'll go back to law school." Barbara observed his astonishment with satisfaction. "I'm taking the semester off."

His eyebrows shot up. "Why didn't you tell me?"

"You didn't ask me." She looked at him with amusement. "And I don't do windows!"

Mellon threw his head back and laughed. "I guess I deserve that."

"You sure as hell do." She leaned toward him. "So you don't have to waste any more time trying to be polite, I'll give you the whole story. My old man helped start the Janitors Union and I walked the picket lines when I was fourteen. I'm the first person who ever received a scholarship funded by the Janitors Union. I'm in my second year of law school and I'm going to specialize in business law. None of the public defender crap for me. That's okay for rich kids. But I want to know all about money. That's where the power begins. And before this campaign is over, I'm going to find out about politics because that's where the power ends up." Without waiting for him to comment, she announced, "And for your information, John Mellon, I intend to be the first black woman elected as attorney general of the state of California and maybe of the United States."

Mellon was speechless.

"Now," she said matter-of-factly, "suppose you tell me why the hell you're taking me to lunch."

"Okay," he answered, looking at her in astonishment. "I need your help. You're born here, aren't you?"

Barbara nodded.

"I want a rundown on that phony bastard, the so-called Reverend Smith. Do you know anyone who belongs to his congregation?"

The waiter brought them their first course, poured them each a glass of the sharp red wine, and left the wicker-covered bottle on the table.

John held up his glass and nodded. "Cheers."

"Cheers," she answered. Who'd she know who was mixed up with that old fraud? Mellon drained his glass, refilled it, and attacked the antipasto.

Barbara watched him, wide-eyed. No wonder he looked like a sack of potatoes.

"Listen, man," she admonished. "If you want to make it to the finals, you better slow down."

"Never mind that." He paused and broke into a smile. "Barbara—can you think of any way to infiltrate that church?"

"Well, there's my Aunt Ethel," she said thoughtfully. "She's big on God. I think she's a church hopper. Would you like me to talk to her?"

* * *

On a fine spring morning, two weeks before the primary election was to take place, Barbara Potter marched into Mellon's cubicle, carrying a Xeroxed sheet of paper in her hand, and waved it triumphantly under his nose.

"Hey you, *watch* it!" He grabbed the Styrofoam cup of steaming coffee and snarled, "You damn near spilled—"

Holding up the cup to keep it from tipping, he looked at the paper she held in front of him and whistled. Running his fingers through his hair, he stared up at her incredulously and asked, "Is this for real?"

She pushed a pile of printed material off the folding chair next to his desk and settled her lean, jeans-clad body into it.

Reaching for a cigarette from the open package on his desk, she commanded, "Light, please." Drawing in the smoke, she said evenly, "My name is not 'you' or 'hey you.' I would remind you it's Barbara, Barbara Potter. And from now on, you arrogant bastard, *you* can mop up *my* coffee, dump *my* ashtrays, and address *me* with some respect."

Oblivious to the tirade, Mellon studied the paper, shaking his head with amazement. "That's it. My God, you've got it." He took the surprised young woman's face in his hands and kissed her, shouting, "I love you, love you, Barbara Porter. How did you get this?"

Freeing herself, she screamed, "Potter! It's Potter, not Porter, you birdbrain!"

"How did you do it, Barbara P-O-T-T-E-R?" He rocked back in his chair, shaking his head.

"No problem," she answered. "I told my aunt I wanted to find God!" She rolled her eyes heavenward. "Father forgive me! Damned, if she didn't take me to meet the Reverend Isaiah himself. He felt me up and down but good"—she snickered—"as he was leading me to the Lord. Christ! I even got baptized for this campaign."

John Mellon rocked forward and broke into loud laughter. "How was the water?"

"Lukewarm," she said, giggling. "I hung around the church a lot, to Aunt Ethel's joy. I guess bringing in a fallen-away Christian is some kind of special passport to heaven," she mused. "I made a point of getting chummy with some of the Reverend Smith's older parishioners. I figured they might know something about him I wanted to hear. Boy oh boy, did they ever! The older women are pissed with that black Rabbi Korff. It seems his holiness has been neglecting Mrs. Smith in favor of some young chick. There were rumblings that he'd even gone as far as purchasing a house in Malibu for himself and his little friend. That's all I needed."

She stood up and blew smoke toward Mellon. "I planted myself in the Hall of Records until I found this title deed. Smith's funhouse in Malibu seems to have cost just about the same amount of money those Elwick Foundation people donated to his so-called youth project. And here, look at this—! These show that something called the Elwick Fund for Political Education made a grant to the 'Olive Street Youth Council' for a hundred thousand dollars."

"What's the Olive Street Youth Council?" Mellon asked.

"There is none," she said quietly, and asked, "What's the Elwick Fund anyway?"

John Mellon scowled. "Obviously a contraction of the sainted Colonel Elwood Thayer's first name and the noble senator's last name. Hardwick appears to be crazy for the name Elwick. His Elwick Foundation Management Corporation is negotiating a Mickey Mouse real-estate deal in northern California. It's called Beau Soleil. We're scrutinizing that one with a beady eye and now this one." He whistled softly. "Hardwick's branched out into tax-exempt foundations. How did you get this stuff?"

She pursed her lips and blew a thin ribbon of smoke toward him. "After all, I'm into business law and trusts are in my line of trade. Let's just say I borrowed it."

*   *   *

"Where'd you get this?" Tom asked Mellon, an expression of dismay on his face.

Papers were strewn over the refectory table in the Ashley library. Norah sat rifling through them, ignoring the men. Mellon had come up with proof positive of a Hardwick-Chisholm involvement. She was stunned and exhilarated. This stuff might put her over the top. Make the difference!

Mellon was about to answer Tom's anguished question when he noticed the library door was open. He turned to close it. He wasn't about to take any chances. He had insisted on seeing them alone and away from the headquarters. Leaning against the door, he faced Tom and waved the hand holding his cigarette, nonchalantly, his expression impassive.

"Oh, we—uh—just kind of *borrowed* the stuff."

Tom leaned his elbow on the table and rubbed the inner corner of his eyes with his thumb and forefinger. God Almighty, this driven son of a bitch was plummeting them into a disastrous scandal. He felt sick. Did Mellon really believe they could get away with this? He must be mad.

Oblivious to Tom's distress, Mellon went on excitedly. "Remember when the President was here, the night Brookings threw his fit? I told you then I was going to Thayerville to have a look around."

Tom shook his head. No, he didn't remember. He preferred to forget the entire disastrous presidential visit.

"Well," Mellon continued, "I inadvertently ran into this fellow in a bar who turned out to be the ranch foreman for the Thayers at that Casa what's-its-name. He was only too happy to talk about some of the comings and goings of the last few months up there. With a little research on the passenger lists at the local airport I was able to verify what he'd said and put a few things together. Of course"—he winked conspiratorially—"I felt we ought to reward him for his troubles."

"You bought him!" Tom gasped. Didn't this fool understand about corrupt campaign practices? Had he been on the Potomac so long that he'd lost his judgment?

Mellon shrugged. "Nothing like that. He came cheap, a few drinks and a hundred bucks for his troubles." Seeing the shocked expression on Tom's face, he said quickly, trying to reassure him, "We only 'borrowed' this stuff to Xerox it." He waved his hands at the papers in front of Norah. "We didn't keep the originals, only the copies." He smiled knowingly. "I can always say the tooth fairy left the material under my pillow." He moved toward Norah and said happily, "Hell, they'll be so busy explaining themselves, they won't have time to question us."

Tom's usually impassive patrician visage was distorted with rage.

"Goddamn you, John," he shouted, "you've created a Watergate West. We can't possibly use this stuff! Bribery and stealing!"

Mellon looked as if he'd been struck. He had finally managed to find the means to salvage Norah's faltering campaign and this holier-than-thou asshole was berating him! Before he could speak, Norah interrupted, her gaze fixed on Tom, her voice soft.

"My darling. You're dead wrong. You simply can't equate this to Watergate. The crux of that scandal was the abuse of presidential and governmental power. God knows this has nothing to do with that kind of thing. As for corrupt practices"—she threw up her hands—"what could be worse than an attempt to sabotage the two-party system, which is exactly what Hardwick's trying to do." Her eyes grew wide. "Tom, you're the one," she continued, "who taught *me* that the two-party system is crucial for a healthy democracy! Here we have that man, Hardwick, running on the opposition ticket and making a blatant attempt to handpick ours. Financing my opponent! Choosing his own challenger! Why it's a disgrace!" She looked shocked. "It's absolutely scandalous. We *owe* it to the public to air this filthy plot to abrogate their right to participate in an open primary!"

She faced Mellon, pointing her finger at him in angry jabs. "I did *not* order this caper, John. I wouldn't have even considered such a thing had you consulted me." Her expression was stern. "Which you did not! And I can assure you if any such shenanigans take place again, I'll fire the bastard who initiates them and dares to risk my good name. I'll have his head!" she said emphatically. She turned to Tom. "I never wanted to be a candidate because it's a dirty rotten business. You insisted on my making the race. You assured me it was the right thing to do," she reminded him and sighed. "But as long as we have all this material, wouldn't it be silly not to use it? Isn't it our duty to expose them for the monsters they are?"

She believes her own rationale, Tom thought. Her performance was stunning and she'd managed to convince herself. Perhaps she had a point. It was too late in the game to be squeamish and pull back. Not if she was to win. He looked searchingly from her face to Mellon's. How in God's name could they have thought that the congressional liaison would have used any knowledge he might have picked up from Virginia Hardwick to hurt the President? He was fanatically loyal. Tom wished to God they'd left Mellon in Washington.

"We'll go ahead with this at once," Norah said.

Tom closed his eyes and nodded. There was no use arguing further.

He ordered Brookings to call a press conference for Norah to disclose the "Plumbers West" findings the following day. The salient points were carefully leaked to the news media early in the day. The conference had been deliberately scheduled for the afternoon in order to milk the maximum coverage on the evening news broadcasts on both coasts. The hope was to force Hardwick to enter the campaign to answer the charges.

Mellon and his troops had spent the day briefing Norah, carefully rehearsing her for the announcement, anticipating the questions she'd be asked, shooting them at her one after another. They were satisfied she was ready.

The AP man shot the first question. "Are you accusing Senator Hardwick of handpicking your opponent?"

"No," she answered. "I'm not accusing him of handpicking *my* opponent. I'm simply providing the evidence that proves Hardwick financed Chisholm in Chisholm's quest for our party's nomination. Hardwick is trying to handpick his *own* opponent."

"Mrs. Ashley, are you charging the Reverend Isaiah Smith took money under false pretenses?"

Here Norah's actress quality served her well. Large-eyed and serious, she shook her head and said in mock dismay, "Heavens, no! Of course not! There's nothing false about it. It's an obvious fact that Reverend Smith received payment for services rendered—to Dr. Chisholm."

* * *

Satisfied with Norah's performance, Karl Auerbach didn't wait for the conference to end. Shoving his way through the mass of waving, shouting reporters and excited campaign workers, he returned to his own office and immediately placed a call to the central labor council.

"I want a hundred thousand copies of Norah's statement sent out to every union local and shop steward and especially the goddamn Teamsters!" he screamed. "No, I don't know who the hell's going to pay for it! I'll worry about that later. You just get someone over here to pick up a copy of her statement! On the double!" He slammed down the phone and lumbered into John Mellon's office. Mellon looked up from the pile of papers stacked in front of him. He had no need to waste time watching the press conference circus. "She doing okay?" he asked.

"She's doing great!" the labor leader snarled. "But I want you to get those smart-assed lawyers of yours in here. They already know what she's going to say. Christ, they wrote it! I want every one of those geniuses on the streets taking a demographic poll all through the night, in the saloons if necessary, so I can have it in my hands by morning. Do you understand, John? I want to give the momentum as much thrust as I can while it's rolling with us!"

Mellon raised an eyebrow and looked at him questioningly. "Suppose you don't get what you're looking for from your poll?"

Karl snorted. "I'm the one who's going to analyze it. It'll say anything I want it to say. By the time Fields and Gallup get theirs out, mine'll be all over the place. And it will announce a massive swing back to Norah."

*   *   *

Dr. Chisholm refused to be interviewed or to answer any questions concerning Norah's press conference. The attorney for the college president made a brief statement on the steps to the school library, saying that since his client was planning to sue Mrs. Ashley for libel, it was on his advice as counsel that Dr. Chisholm would make no statement. He concluded by saying, "The whole disgraceful affair is a matter to be settled in the courts and not the press."

The Reverend Smith made a one-word comment, "Racism," but Richard Hardwick met with the press in his office in the Senate Building.

When he was questioned, Senator Richard Hardwick said he was profoundly shocked and aghast that the family funds had allegedly been so ill used, explaining that due to his recent bereavement, his senatorial duties, and whatever little campaigning he was doing in California, he had not paid as much attention to the family holdings as he should have. He added that any persons found to have engaged in this seemingly shameful affair would be discharged at once, if the charges were true. Some persons had acted without his knowledge; probably out of misguided, good intentions, which, nevertheless, in no way excused them.

Even Mellon had to admit as he and Karl watched him that Hardwick handled it skillfully. He'd removed himself from direct involvement and milked more sympathy at the same time. Well, Mellon was working on a few more surprises for the grieving widower.

Karl's polls didn't need much distortion; they were substantiated by the professionals. Chisholm's credibility had taken a mortal blow. His most vehement supporters, the ones who had seen in his self-righteous evangelistic posture an example of old-fashioned virtue, were bitterly disenchanted by the disclosures, and their anger at their champion was as intense as their support of him had been earlier.

As Chisholm's money sources dried up, his media blitz dwindled to an occasional radio advertisement, disappearing along with his chances for victory.

The former omnipresent placard carriers all but vanished.

Norah's rallies drew large and enthusiastic audiences in places where earlier her advance people had had difficulties filling a room, much less a large hall. Black ministers flooded the campaign with invitations for Norah to address their congregations. They made a point of deploring Chisholm's and Smith's collusion and vigorously expressed their support of her candidacy.

Karl Auerbach was no longer obliged to beg, wheedle, and cajole organized labor for endorsements. They volunteered them.

For Norah it was the beginning of the home stretch. She forgot the inhibitions Tom had felt about the source for the attack. She had Hardwick on the defensive and Chisholm on the ropes. That was what mattered.

CHAPTER
Eleven

The Ashleys were among the first to cast their votes at the local schoolhouse early election morning. The media people and reporters were waiting for them in the school gymnasium, converted for the day into a polling place. As soon as they arrived, Norah was surrounded by exploding flashbulbs and TV reporters holding out their long-stemmed microphones, shouting "Hold it." "Let's have one coming out of the booth." "Do you think you'll win?" "How does it look?" Norah posed and smiled and nodded, and held her arm high, fingers crossed. The intensity of the campaign, the disclosures, made the famous Norah Ashley especially newsworthy. The other voters and poll watchers crowded around her. It was her home precinct; neighbors greeted her warmly, and to the delight of the photographers a stout, elderly woman, an "Ashley" button pinned prominently on her large bosom, kissed Norah on both cheeks and assured her she'd win. Finally her bodyguards were forced to make a path for her and Tom and firmly pressed them into the waiting car.

They were driven directly to the main headquarters. There the atmosphere was one of frenzied optimism. Karl Auerbach's booming voice carried across the large room. This was what he'd planned for during the long days of the primary. For him it was the test of his power and expertise, the moment of truth.

"I want every one of your goddamn votes out in the Hawthorne area," he roared. "She's strong there! You bet she's going to win— big! . . . We'll send that sniveling little crook back to Santa Barbara, maybe with a detour in the cooler for corrupt campaign practices. . . . Forget San Marino, Sam! It's the pits. . . . We'll sweep it without those bastards!" Catching sight of Norah, he put down the phone and moved toward her, pushing aside the people crowding her. Putting his hands firmly around her waist, he lifted Norah off the ground and whirled her around triumphantly.

"Put me down, you nut! You're going to break me," Norah protested breathlessly.

He lowered her gently and chuckled. "You're a tough little cookie, Ms. Ashley. You won't break. You're going to win this pissing match, lovie, and I mean in November too. The primary's *over!*"

"Not the way you're carrying on," Norah said, laughing.

His face grew serious. "What are you doing here anyway at this hour?" he asked, cocking his head questioningly. "Candidates are supposed to rest on election day!"

"This one's campaigning." She lowered the pitch of her voice, imitating him. "I want every one of your goddamn votes out in the Hawthorne area!" Suddenly she felt her mouth go dry and a hard knot in her stomach. Her high spirits dissipated into a rush of anxiety. Suppose she lost? Were they deluding themselves? she wondered. The confidence, the bravado wavered.

Karl, sensing her anxiousness, put his large square fist under her chin and lifted up her face. He looked into the green eyes and said reassuringly, "It's just plain stage fright, babe. I'm queasy before every negotiation." The craggy face broke into a smile. "You're going to win! The folks are going to put the boot to that holier-than-thou faker, I promise."

Norah whispered, "Promise?"

Karl nodded. "Go on, Norah, hit the streets and cover the neighborhood headquarters; that'll give you back your confidence. My nostrils are quivering with the sweet smell of victory. And for God's sake, take Tom with you. I don't need him here bugging me."

"And take Auerbach too!" Tillie called out. "He thinks he's playing General Rommel deploying his troops across the Sahara. He's driving everyone, including his wife, crazy. Isn't he, Evelyn?"

Evelyn nodded agreement from the far end of the room, where she was supervising the phone bank operation.

"No way," Karl shouted. "I'm going to yell my people into the voting booths!"

Tom had disappeared. Norah worked her way through the milling crowd toward the offices in the rear of the building. She found him in John Mellon's cubicle, surrounded by people, seated on the edge of the cluttered desk, phone held to his ear. Barbara Potter was grimacing and shushing so he could hear. He looked up and saw Norah and held the instrument toward her. "It's the chairman." She took the phone from him. "Hi, Andy!"

Watkins, his voice excited, shouted, "All my sources indicate a big win, darling. We're proud of you, Norah!"

"Let's hope, Andy. Thank you! My love to the President." She handed the phone back to Tom, wondering what the chairman's tone would have been if his sources indicated a big defeat.

Tom was saying, "Fine! Fine! She's got him on the run. We're feeling confident. Be in touch when the early votes come in. Good-bye for now." Tom put the receiver back, turned to Brookings, who was leaning against a green file cabinet, and ordered, "You come with us, you martyred celebrity. Norah's going to hit the precincts." He smiled wryly and slapped the press secretary's shoulder. "We'll even let you sit in the front of the bus." Barbara Potter was leaning over a wastebasket, holding a filled ashtray in her hand, picking over the cigarette stubs to make sure they were cool. "Come on, Barbara. You're the true heroine."

She shook her head. "Thank you, no. If that bus goes near Isaiah Smith's church—and they see me—!" She rolled her eyes. "Especially my Aunt Ethel! Anyway, the supreme slob"—she nodded her head toward Mellon —"has promised to clean up this pigsty before tonight, and I guess I'd better help him since he's stopped calling me 'Hey-you'! Besides, I've got to stay in touch with the campus people."

Tom took Norah's elbow. "Okay, Dan, let's go—and bring Lisa. She's good at this."

Brookings hesitated and then, caught up in the excitement, reached for Lisa's hand. The blue eyes looked at him with amusement. Perhaps, she thought, he's finally decided he might as well be hung for a wolf as a sheep.

By the time they'd worked their way back through the headquarters, well-wishers and the curious had crowded the sidewalk. Norah had opted for a bright red silk dress, nipped in the waist by a wide belt. It exaggerated her slimness. She'd always felt red to be her lucky color, and the dress gave her the added pleasure of defying Chisholm's monolithic smear tactics. She most certainly looked like an actress now.

Tom eyed her admiringly as he helped her onto the red, white, and blue bus decorated with "Ashley" signs. Giving her a friendly pat, he whispered, "Win or lose, you have the best-looking ass in all of California, Mrs. Ashley."

By late afternoon, Norah, with Lisa behind her, had managed to shake hands with workers at two aircraft plants, surprised the customers in a major shopping complex, eaten a sandwich at Cantor's Delicatessen, visited a retirement home, and stopped off at most of her campaign headquarters.

Arriving home, they found Mrs. Manley waiting for them, dressed in her best black silk, explaining with a prim smile, "Mrs. Lowman invited McPherson and me to the headquarters for your victory celebration. That is, if you don't mind, madame."

Norah grinned, "Why, Mrs. Manley, how wonderful! Of course I don't mind. I just hope to God it'll be a victory celebration."

The short, plump figure, hands on hips, sniffed: "Damn right it will. Not to worry! We'll give that bloody little bastard what for, tonight!" With a toss of her head, she walked toward the pantry.

Norah's eyes filled. She turned to Tom, who had been taken aback by Mrs. Manley's outburst. "Tom, I'm undone; she really cares!"

She looked suddenly young and frightened to him, unlike the self-possessed, determined woman she'd become in the last months. Her vulnerability aroused him deeply. "Of course she does, dummy. Don't cry!" he whispered gently. He leaned over her as she closed her eyes and kissed her neck, his hands sliding over the small, firm breasts. "I know just what you need—" He lifted her up, and she wrapped her arms tightly around his neck as he carried her to their bedroom, firmly kicking the door shut behind him.

By six forty-five Norah had showered, washed, dried, and set her hair. The early years of tight budgeting with no money to spend on hairdressers still stood her in good stead. She knew exactly what to do. Scrutinizing her reflection from every angle, she could see the toll the campaign had taken. The dark shadows under her eyes and the pallor of her skin betrayed the fatigue and the months spent indoors. With swift expertise, she applied the necessary camouflage and emerged from her dressing room looking radiant and rested. What was it her angry mother had said when she'd found the lipstick and mascara, purchased with carefully saved lunch money, hidden beneath her stockings in the dresser drawer? "Powder n' paint'll make you what you ain't!" God, she certainly hoped so, knowing how brutal and ruthless the camera could be. She'd chosen a simple pink silk dress for the evening, certain it would televise well and add to the illusion she'd created.

Tom was in the library, phone in hand. He gave her an appreciative whistle and said, "It's Peter."

Norah's face lit up with pleasure. A fierce longing for her son came over her when she heard his voice, very male and optimistic, wishing her well.

She hung up and said, "He really believes I'm going to win."

Tom laughed. "We all do. And so do you. Besides, you've already had your first victory of the evening. You didn't ask him if he was eating properly, driving carefully, and getting enough sleep."

"Don't laugh. It wasn't easy! Here I am, about to cross the great divide, and I long for my son like an old peasant crone."

"Well, you certainly don't look like one, darling." Eyebrows raised, he asked, "Do you realize that the next woman I sleep with will be a senatorial nominee?"

"Oh, Tom, will I really win?" Norah grew earnest.

"You really will," he answered emphatically, baffled by her self-doubts. "The question isn't 'if,' it's by how much? Chisholm's finished!"

"But will I win?" she insisted. "Because they want me, not because they don't want him?" She swallowed hard. Mellon's revelations were what had brought Chisholm to his knees; not her overwhelming popularity. Was a negative primary victory enough of a victory to take her to the final one over Richard?

Tom said sharply as he drew her to him, "Cut it out! Now! You're not some insecure ingenue, actress-to-be, fresh off the boat from Philadelphia. You are," he said, enunciating each word slowly, "Norah Jones Ashley, running for the Senate of the United States! That's who you are! What's more," he added impatiently, "you're in the seventh month and the delivery room opens in November. Let's go—it's going to be a long night. Enough of this emotional see-sawing!"

He gripped her hand firmly, and they walked together to the waiting limousine. Norah was about to step into the car, then hesitated. "My God. Manley and McPherson. Where are they? We almost forgot them."

"Crazy Tillie sent a studio limousine for them. Mrs. Manley looked like the Queen Mother, waving graciously to her subjects. McPherson looked embarrassed. By the time we get there, she'll have reorganized the buffet and driven Chasen's people crackers," Tom predicted.

Norah had decided against the usual small dinner with a few intimates, the customary way for candidates to begin the long vigil of an election night. Instead, she hired Chasen's to take over the headquarters and serve supper there. The restaurant protested that the chaos would make proper service impossible. Norah had been adamant. And Karl Auerbach scolded her, saying, "That's too posh for 'the people's choice.' Call McDonald's!"

"You're just afraid *you'll* blow your 'just plain folks' image when your rank-and-file membership see their great plebeian leader being served by red-coated waiters. You old fraud!" Norah chided, determined to have her way.

By the time the Ashleys arrived, large numbers of people were milling about. Some had not left the main headquarters since early that morning.

Mrs. Manley was, as Tom had suspected, rustling her breast feathers and directing the harassed waiters and dinner-jacketed captain. McPherson was behind the bar dispensing drinks, and from the look of him it appeared to Norah he was fortifying himself well for the long night's vigil. The drab headquarters looked festive and unfamiliar. It was transformed by balloons and bunting and the long buffet, its surface laden with shining platters and chafing dishes. A bar was placed at the far end of the room. Media equipment and TV sets replaced the battered worktables. Smoke mingled with the scent of chili; the clinking ice counterpointed the sound of excited voices.

Norah and Tom made the rounds from one end of the crowded room to the other and gradually worked their way back to Karl's office, where Barbara, Mellon, Brookings, Lisa, Evelyn, and the Lowmans were standing silently around a desk littered with half-empty chili bowls and glasses. Tillie put her finger to her lips. Karl held the phone to his ear, his face red with excitement. He loosened his tie and opened his collar and reached for a scratch pad.

"Jesus! Sixty percent?" His voice was incredulous. "You'd better repeat that. It's going to be a rout! Call me the minute you get a reading on the early returns." He threw up his hands in disbelief. "The absentee ballots show Norah leading by sixty percent!"

Tom questioned, "Leading? Are you sure? That's hard to believe!"

Norah couldn't speak. She had resigned herself to taking the smaller share of their support. The absentee ballots, traditionally the first to be counted, invariably went to the conservative candidate. The early returns augured a landslide.

Lisa looked puzzled. "But what about the votes that were cast today? Isn't that what counts?"

Walt Lowman explained patiently, "If Norah gets the absentee votes—they're cast by the affluent, who're more likely to travel than the average working man—you've got yourself a winner the first time around, Lisa."

She hugged Walt and smiled at Brookings, triumphantly. "I told you."

By nine o'clock scattered precinct returns began drifting in. Norah was gaining strength in areas which, earlier on, had been considered Chisholm territory. By ten o'clock CBS, NBC, and ABC projected Norah as the victor by a two-to-one margin. Well-wishers crowded the headquarters, standing three deep at the bar. Chasen's waiters gave up all pretense of clearing away the soiled dishes and simply refilled the buffet platters. They could barely maneuver themselves through the press of bodies.

Microphones in hand, reporters pushed toward Norah, demanding a victory statement. To the thousands watching, she appeared calm and poised; only the flush of color on her cheeks betrayed the inner excitement. "With due deference to the computers," she began, "although there's good reason for optimism, I think any statement on my part concerning the election outcome is premature. We still have a lot of places and people to hear from, including Dr. Chisholm." She was determined to hang in until Chisholm withdrew. She would savor his defeat to the finish line.

Tom made his way toward her through the crowded room. The TV cameras suddenly returned to the Biltmore.

Chisholm, drawn face frozen in a nervous smile, his wife beside him, her lips pressed to hold back tears, raised his hands to quiet the shouts of

"No! No!" "We want Chisholm." "Orange County hasn't come in yet!" The room was body to body full with his supporters now. Some were dabbing eyes, others held their arms aloft, making the victory sign.

The orchestra fanfared for silence. He faced the cameras and said, "My friends, Mrs. Chisholm joins me in gratitude to all of you who have kept faith with me and our cause during this difficult campaign. The things for which we have fought together, the Christian values we treasure, and the America we love have been strengthened by our crusade. The bitter vilification, the attacks upon my honor will have been worth the enduring if our party and our nation have been served. The voters have spoken. Mrs. Ashley is the nominee of our party. We must pray for her and hope she will be worthy of the people's trust."

Karl Auerbach put both hands to his mouth and brought forth a huge raspberry.

Pandemonium broke loose. The screens on the TV set showed Tom embracing Norah, surrounded by the chaos of the undiluted joy of victory.

This may be my finest hour, Norah thought; there's still November. She wondered if the enemy was watching. There was no time for her to brood; a wave of people surged toward her.

*   *   *

Senator Richard Hardwick was watching the television screen in the presidential suite of the Mark Hopkins Hotel. Soon he would descend to the banquet room to accept his party's uncontested nomination and the cheers of the faithful. It was as if he could feel Norah's eyes looking into his. He muttered to the image on the screen, "No way!"

Marianne stood beside him. "That's some charismatic lady—!" she said admiringly, her voice turning worried. "She's going to give you—!"

His face reddened. Before she could finish the sentence, he snapped, "The hell she is! When I'm finished with her—!" He switched off the television set, Norah's image fading from the screen.

"Where's Bailey? We're late," he grumbled.

"He went back to the Casa this afternoon. He suggested we could manage without him," she said, her tone noncommittal. "Rather—*I* suggested he leave, since he showed symptoms of acute boredom."

"That's the first good news of the day," he said as they left the suite.

Later that evening, during an interview, Hardwick was questioned as to whether or not he'd heard Norah's victory statement.

"No, I have not."

Was he aware that she challenged him to debate?

No, he was not.

Would he accept the challenge?

He was swift to reply, the handsome face breaking into a smile. "That's the standard underdog ploy. All contenders give it a try!" His expression turned serious. "I'd be happy to debate the President. That's who's running *against* me instead of running the country. That's whose pawn and spokesman—or should I say, spokeswoman—she is," he said contemptuously.

A *Times* reporter asked, "Do you think Mrs. Ashley will make an issue of your involvement in the Chisholm scandal?"

"I have already explained that I have no such involvement!" he insisted irritably. Then, assuming a dismayed expression, he said, "I don't intend to dignify the smear tactics of the President's henchman, nor defend myself against trumped-up charges. I'll wage my campaign on my record as a senator against my opponent's . . . as a thespian!"

* * *

John Mellon, sitting with Dan and Lisa, a champagne glass in his hand and a bowl of chili on his lap, looked at the screen in disbelief. "The son of a bitch. It was deliberate! It's what Smathers did when he ran against Claude Pepper in Florida, haranguing the backwoods crackers with 'I hate to say this, but the senator's daughter is a thespian.' " I don't give a shit what it takes to beat him, he vowed to himself. I'll find it. I'm going back to Washington, but I'll have his scalp first.

* * *

Bailey Redfern looked up at the screen above the crowded Thayerville bar. Lonny McFarland leaned toward him, pressing against his thigh. "Now what'd he say that for?" he asked. "She don't look like no dyke."

"Because he's scared shitless," Bailey said with satisfaction.

Lonny gulped his drink. Didn't Bailey really want the senator, his wife's pappy, to win? He knew he sure as hell didn't like his father-in-law, so maybe it'd be all right to tell him about the joker who asked him all those dumb questions. He'd felt kind of funny about that. 'Course, he'd had a lot to drink and a hundred bucks was a hundred bucks. Still— No, he'd better shut up about it. There were too many ears around. Maybe later.

* * *

In Sacramento the governor of California studied the election returns and made note of the landslide proportions of the Ashley victory. He decided he'd better call to congratulate Norah and offer her his full support. He signaled the operator.

* * *

In Indio, California, Concha Romo had watched the election night broadcasts at the home of her sister, where she stayed when she needed to retreat from the Casa, its tensions and its memories. She was unsettled by the Ashley woman's authority and beauty, her magnetism and the size of her victory. Somehow, she'd stupidly envisioned her as a nonentity. But that this actress could cost Senator Richard his chance for the presidency —shatter the Colonel's dream—*Dios!* In a shocked voice, she spoke to her nephew, who stood at the other end of the beamed room, "Can she win, Manuel?"

He nodded the affirmative and came toward her. Seating himself alongside her, he took her hand in his. The dark, deep-set, troubled eyes, so much like her own, looked into hers. "Aunt Concha," he said, wrestling with himself, knowing he was delivering a blow to her heart, "I must help her do it."

CHAPTER
Twelve

Giving her stallion his head, Marianne Hardwick Redfern leaned forward, pressed her thighs tight against his chestnut flanks, and galloped across the west field at Casa Thayer toward the stream.

Her hair blew free in the wind. She felt at one with the racing horse beneath her. And free! She was grateful her father had released her after the Veterans' Convention. The strain of being the gracious daughter had been more exhausting than a week of cross-country road running. Breakfasts, luncheons, teas, receptions, and dinners, always at her father's side, smiling, mumbling politeness. She had dozed on the plane trips in between the cities and towns they visited, had fallen exhausted into bed in strange hotels. For several weeks, she'd stuck it out faithfully, as she'd promised her father she would.

"I really am beholden, Marianne; you've gone beyond the line of filial duty," he'd said. She certainly had. She'd endured all the silliness the occasions demanded. She knew she was nothing more than a female symbol for the widowed candidate.

She'd stood alongside her father and that frozen-smiled couple, the former governor of Colorado, himself an unsuccessful candidate for the presidency, and his wife. They must have shaken a thousand hands. The governor was the faded boy-beautiful, darling of the flag wavers. Fine wrinkles crisscrossed over the aged face, belying the full head of dyed brown hair. His wife was overdressed as usual in obsolete elegance, the skirt a touch long, concealing the unshapely legs—her one visible flaw! Madame Perfection.

The governor's own chance for the presidency had passed, but the strength of his support was too heavy to be ignored. His hold on a still-devoted following within the party gave him the balance of power in the National Convention. He had enough clout left to withhold the presidential nomination from Hardwick if he chose to do so.

But now Marianne had a temporary reprieve. She felt herself come alive with the rhythmic movement of the great stallion.

She planned to ride him to the shallow end of the stream and then walk to the rocks. By the time she got back to the Casa, Bailey probably would have returned from wherever it was he'd been. Not that it mattered. Nothing mattered about Bailey. Their marriage was a farce, and she knew she should end it. But for now she was content if he would just leave her alone and keep his distance. She wasn't ready to cope with a divorce. She shut him out of her thoughts and remembered Manuel. The big rocks had been their secret childhood place. Later, when they were older, it was here he'd kissed her. She smiled as the shallow end of the stream came into view, surrounded by great fronds and tall gum trees, dappled with sunlight. No, he hadn't kissed her. She'd been the aggressor; he'd pushed her away. Sighing, she recalled how stricken she had been by his rejection, asking, "Don't you love me, Manuel?" He hadn't bothered to answer her. He had taken her face in both his hands, found her lips, kissed her with bruising fierceness.

Then he had released her and stated quietly, "Marianne, I'll never again come here with you. In the fall I'm going to Harvard, and then to law school. After that, I'll do all the things for my people Chavez couldn't do. Forget about me and marry a beautiful, blond WASP, just like your father. Do you understand?"

She hadn't understood and she still didn't. She had flung her arms around his waist in anguish, her head pressed tightly against his chest, feeling the beat of his heart, sobbing, "I want you, Manuel; I want you, only *you*!"

He stroked her hair gently, saying, "I'm something the Thayers can't have. Everything else you can buy with money and power—a senator for your mother, my Aunt Concha for the Colonel, the state of California, even the country, but not me!''

He was cruel and hateful and sick with pride. And she was sick with loving him and hating him and wanting him, not that he cared a damn. He kept his word, and she had done what he told her to do.

At the time she married Bailey, Manuel was organizing field hands, defending immigrants, and getting himself elected chairman of the Society of Public Interest Attorneys. Concha, who had pridefully brought her news of him during his college years, the scholarships and grants and *cum laude*s, had not spoken of him to Marianne in recent years. And when his name was mentioned, she would promptly change the subject. Perhaps she saw his activism as betrayal. Her loyalty to the Thayers made his defection from them an affront to her as well. He was not to be discussed at the Casa.

Marianne brought King to a halt, dismounted easily, and tethered him to a nearby tree stump. She walked along the edge of the brook until she reached the rocks and scrambled onto the lichen-covered, large one, its flat top shaped by time into a natural seat. Settling herself, she dug into her shirt pocket for a cigarette; inhaling the smoke, she scanned the winding stream toward the little waterfall. Suddenly she stiffened.

Two naked forms were entwined on the distant bank. One body was supine, resting on the lap of the other. The seated figure was curved forward, head covering the other's face, stroking the inner thigh of the raised, long bronzed leg. As if sensing a presence, he looked up. It was Bailey, locked in an embrace with Lonny McFarland, the young ranch foreman. She gasped with the shock of the recognition.

Scrambling down the rocks, her heart beating wildly, not glancing back to see if they knew she'd observed them, she just ran. Fighting a sickening wave of nausea, the taste in her mouth bitter, she mounted King, frantically kicked him into a gallop, and rode back to the house. Flinging the reins to an astonished stable boy, Marianne bolted into the great entrance hall of the Casa, screaming, "Concha! Concha!"

Theresa, the little housemaid, and Luis, the manservant, came rushing toward her. "Señora, Señora Marianne, *qué es?*"

"Where's Concha, *dónde está?*"

Concha's heels clicked rapidly across the tiled floors. Her eyes were large with shock, horrified by Marianne's appearance, the disheveled hair, the deathly pale face.

She rushed forward and put her arms around the hysterical young woman, holding her tightly.

"What happened? I had no idea you were home. I thought you were with Senator Richard!"

Marianne couldn't speak. She held on to Concha and trembled, her breath coming in small gasps.

Concha led her to the library, silently signaling a frightened Theresa and Luis to go away.

"What is it, *mi niña*? What has happened? I will fix you something to drink." The troubled dark eyes probed hers with concern.

Marianne sank into the deep leather armchair that had been the Colonel's. She pulled at her hair and rocked back and forth, her breath coming in gasps.

Suddenly, she burst, "Oh, my God, the bastard! The goddamn dirty bastard! How could he?"

Concha must have known. Nothing escaped her vigilance and scrutiny. Surely she'd read the smoke signals, heard the sick drumbeat.

"You knew about Bailey, didn't you, Concha? Didn't you?" she said accusingly.

The high-cheekboned face remained impassive. "Knew what?"

"That he's a goddamn homosexual," Marianne shrieked.

Concha placed the whiskey on the table. Knew? Of course she knew. There were no secrets from her at the Casa. She, Concha, was its eyes and ears, the repository of all its secrets. She'd hoped and prayed Marianne need never find out the truth about Bailey, that somehow his sick obsession would go away—disappear. Wasn't it enough that the poor child had never known her mother's or father's love. Only the Colonel and she herself had given Marianne any warmth or affection. And now this—the hurt, the shame!

She'd failed Marianne. She could no longer protect her. She'd locked away the knowledge of Bailey and that creature in the same chamber of her mind where she kept her most terrible secret burdens. Stupidly. Her other burdens were in her control. She would keep the Colonel's confidence and his trust. But that Bailey; he was no secret in her control, he was blatantly evil. Sighing, Concha pulled up a straight-backed chair for herself and placed it next to Marianne. She reached for the young woman's hands and held them in hers.

"Marianne, stop this screaming and tell me exactly what happened."

Marianne closed her eyes; the words came in a whispered rush. "I came back early this morning. Father didn't need me any longer. It was dreadfully boring and tiring. The day was so beautiful. Bailey wasn't home and I didn't see you or the others—I'd been cooped up in that horrible Veterans' Convention. I decided to saddle up King and ride to the stream." She paused and said bitterly, Concha's eyes never leaving her face, "I saw Bailey making love along the bank with that—that dirty—that Lonny."

Concha's eyes closed.

"*Dios,* my poor child," she whispered.

Marianne leaned forward and repeated the question: "How long have you known? I want you to tell me the truth, Concha!"

Rising to her feet and smoothing the black silk skirt, Concha's words came slowly. "I have had knowledge for a long time that Bailey has very" —she hesitated for a moment—"peculiar tastes. I believed he would have at least the sense to be discreet. It is well the Colonel is dead. It would destroy him—a ranch hand!"

Marianne burst into high-pitched laughter. "Jesus! My husband is fucking a man in my sight, on my land, and *you,* you are shocked because his lover's a ranch hand! That's really too much—!"

Before she could finish, the library door burst open. Bailey, in faded denims and checked shirt, open to the waist, exposing the lithe, brown, long-muscled torso, roared at Marianne.

"When the hell did you get back?" Without waiting for the answer, eyes narrowing, he turned to Concha. "You goddamn bitch, *you* sent her to spy on me!" Walking close to the horrified, silent woman, his finger pointing, he snarled, "You've always hated me, haven't you?" His voice grew louder, "Haven't you? You wanted Marianne to marry that snotnosed, dumb Mex nephew of yours. Or is he your son?"

Throwing his head back, he said with a sneer, "Senator and Mrs. Richard Hardwick take pleasure in announcing the betrothal of their daughter, Marianne, to her Uncle Manuel Whatsis—"

Marianne jumped up, reached for the untouched glass of whiskey, and silently threw the contents in Bailey's face. Turning, she ran from the room and raced up the wide, circular staircase. Bailey followed swiftly, grabbed her wrist just as she reached the door to their room, and flung her on the large canopied bed.

Marianne lay, immobilized, her breath coming in gasps. Bailey searched her face for a sign of tenderness. "Marianne, for Christ's sake, don't look at me like that! Lonny's the only one who ever loved me . . . really loved me. Do you understand that, do you? Lonny thinks I'm *somebody!* Can't you accept me? You're my wife! That's all I ask," he pleaded. He shook his head and grimaced to hold back the tears of self-pity filling his eyes.

"Even my own mother couldn't bear the sight of me. She hated me. I reminded her of my father. Christ, the only thing I can remember about her is her standing at the door saying, 'Goodnight, be a good boy and obey dear Nanny.'" He closed his eyes for a moment. "I can still smell her perfume and hear the rustle of silk." His voice grew bitter. "Dear Nanny could hardly wait to hear the front door close before she'd find a reason to beat the hell out of me. That's how *she* got her jollies.

"Marianne," he whispered, looking into the agate eyes large with horror. "Let's try—I'll give him up. Let's start from the beginning—"

Begin again? Oh, God, from the beginning of what—to where? She loathed the sight of him, this sniveling, pleading half-man. The same hand that pinned her to the bed had stroked McFarland's body. She gathered the saliva in her mouth and spat in his face.

Abruptly his self-pity and pleading turned to rage. He made no effort to wipe away the spittle. Instead, he reached for her shirt and ripped it open, baring her breasts. When she tried to rise, he threw her back on the bed.

The cold cunt! He'd tried begging and she spit in his face. Give up Lonny for this—? Who the hell did she think she was? No better than a whore, a goddamn whore. She'd married him to be married. The *bitch,* the frigid bitch!

Terror froze her as his face twisted with hatred. Closing her eyes, she lay limp, too terrified to fight. He tore off her riding breeches, hands groping, and entered her body with a violent thrust, exploding in a shuddering spasm.

Marianne shrieked. He slapped his hand over her mouth to muffle her cry and lay limp across her body, still clutching her wrist. At last, rolling over on his back, he released her. His mood was triumphant.

"I'm a universal man. I like cock and cunt. They both feel good."
Running his fingers across her body, he whispered, "You're built just like
your dear mama—although she used hers with more enthusiasm, I'm
told."

She pulled herself up to the edge of the bed, her back to Bailey, and
hissed, "Get out!"

He reached for her hair and pulled her head back, raising himself to
his knees, buttocks resting on his heels, and said, calmly, "No way,
princess, no way. I know too much, much too much. You can't throw
me out!"

Releasing her with a thrust away from himself, he reached for the
cigarette box on the night table.

She stared at him with silent loathing.

He drew the tobacco smoke deep into his lungs and looked at her
through hooded lids.

"Marianne Thayer Hardwick Redfern. My darling, devoted, and naive
little wife. Your distinguished daddy wouldn't like you to be nasty to his
son-in-law." His look was malevolent. "Because of what I know—he
wouldn't like having me tell all."

Marianne remained silent. Her husband's satyr face had become handsome again as his sense of power had returned.

"Chisholm and the nigger preacher. That's just for starters. Don't you
think I know all about those high-class partners of his who visit him here
at the Casa?"

Without answering, Marianne staggered to the bathroom and turned on
the shower. She lathered and rinsed herself in the steaming water until all
sign of him was gone.

What was he implying about her father? What partners? She knew
better than to believe anything he said. It was all a part of the blackmailing
little bastard's nastiness. Why would her father need any partners in any
deals? Weren't they rich enough? She felt a gnawing doubt. No, her father
wasn't, was he? She herself was the heir to the Thayer fortune. She
resolved to ask him herself if there was any truth to Bailey's implications,
but for now there was only one thing that mattered—getting Bailey out
of her sight.

Drying herself, she wrapped her head in a towel and returned to the
bedroom, tying her robe.

Bailey was still lying on his back, the long, tanned body immobile, watching her through half-closed eyes.

She observed the graceful, muscular body, the elegance of the long-fingered hand holding the cigarette. He was beautiful and disgusting and frightening. She longed to kill him.

In a hoarse whisper, she said, "Concha will move your things to the guest quarters, and *you* will get Lonny, lover boy, off this place in *one* hour. I will deposit some money in your account from time to time. And, you will stay the hell away from me!"

He sat up, drawing his knees to his chest, the voice mocking. "My goodness, gracious, the senator's daughter is giving orders and is ever so morally indignant! Listen, baby, you're hardly in a position to be so high and mighty, considering that it's worth your while to keep me quiet." Shrugging his shoulders, he queried, "What the hell do you care whom or what I fuck as long as I service you, or are you still pining for wetback prick?"

She was beyond hysteria now. Her words poured out in an enraged torrent. "I don't give a shit, Bailey, what you say or do. But just remember, this is my land, my home, and you will not do any fucking—or raping—on my property if you want the bank account to stay open. You will not start spreading lies about my father. And you'd better pray he wins, you dirty, twisted son of a bitch. Now I repeat," she shouted, her voice climbing to a crescendo, "get out!"

With studied ease, Bailey slid off the bed, picked his clothes up off the floor, and blew her a kiss. "Anything you say, princess."

CHAPTER

Thirteen

Norah swam the length of the pool without stopping, turned, shoved herself off the tile with all her strength, and cut back to the shallow end. She savored the unrestrained physical release after the long months of travel, tension, and smoke-filled rooms. Coming up for breath, she approached the steps. A long-legged figure was running toward her. It was Peter. Good God, could he still be growing? She climbed out of the water to embrace him. He leaned over, hugged her, and planted a scratchy kiss on the wet cheek.

"Why aren't you and Dad recovering in some luxurious tropic place?"

"Recovering from victory isn't a problem, it's a joy! So we chose to remain in *this* luxurious tropic place." She reached for a towel. "Oh, Peter, how lovely you're home," she said, smiling at him. He was a duplicate of his father. The resemblance had been visible from earliest childhood on. Now it was striking. Tom's were presumptuous genes. Only the eyes were hers. At least she'd marked him with those.

Settling herself on the chaise, she motioned for him to sit.

"Who are all those plainclothes-looking characters loitering around here?" he questioned, scowling.

Norah's face clouded. "Just that, bodyguards! Your father, Walt, and the others are paranoid. They've developed some sort of assassination fixation." Noticing his concerned expression, she changed the subject. "It's just nonsense! Now tell me about your grades!" Before he could answer, she fussed, "You look awfully thin. Are you eating properly? Do you get enough sleep? Are you *all right?*"

He shook his head in disbelief. "I don't believe it! Nominee for the United States Senate, and you're still doing the crazy momma routine. For your information, I eat like a gorilla and made the dean's list. What do you think of that?" he asked.

"Oh, I love it, I love it!" Norah answered, glowing with pride. "Does your father know?"

"No, I haven't talked to him yet. Where is he?"

"You might call him. He's at work." Norah shook her head. "Poor dear. No vacation for him. He's neglected the office; he's got lots of catching up to do." She paused and sighed. "The primary's been tough, Peter, much more so than we expected."

The youth leaned forward, looked at her with intense green eyes so like her own.

"They really socked it to you, didn't they, Mom?"

Norah grimaced.

"How's Dad taking it? I mean your being in orbit. Is his male ego out of joint?"

Norah chuckled. "Are you mad? Your father's male ego is as firmly attached as his nose. He and the President see me as some sort of idiot woman whom they have to keep in line as they shoot me out to fight the dragons. My dear Peter," she said, eyebrow raised, "I suspect I'm cast as a bit player in some major scheme I don't know about."

"Some bit player," he mused. "But you look great. I really thought you'd be wiped out."

"You have no idea how beneficial winning is for your health," she said, laughing. "As a reward, your father and the brain trust have granted me two weeks to swim, to get fat, muck around the garden, and restore my nervous system, which by the way is in great order. I think *they're* more wiped out than I am. I'm really great at winning! What's your summer program, darling?" she asked.

He looked at her with astonishment. "I'm going to work in your campaign. What else? I've rapped about it a lot with my poli-sci professor, Sam Feuerstein, who, by the way, is very much in your corner."

"Why in the world would your Dr. Feuerstein be interested in my campaign? Boston's a long way from California."

"Well, number one," he said and smiled, "I think he's got a thing for you. He's some kind of ladies' man and a film buff. He's up on all your old movies, Mom. Secondly, he's followed your political life pretty closely and likes what you stand for. Mostly, I think he's big on the President and his programs and can't stand Hardwick. Feuerstein sees him as a threat to the administration and the President's reelection. He's convinced if Hardwick ever gets his foot in the door of the White House, he'd kick the country so far back he'd make McKinley look progressive, and hand it over to the oil lobby, big business, and the military."

"Okay, Machiavelli, what do you and the professor have in mind?" Peter obviously wanted to do some theorizing with her.

"Now don't get smart, Mom!" he snapped, catching her tone. "I'm not kidding. We've really been into this. You don't have enough youth in your campaign. True, 'Plumbers West' made hot copy for a small minute when they exposed the Chisholm-Hardwick duplicity, but they're really invisible, now. The *old* bunch has the high visibility—Lowman, Auerbach, Brookings, Mellon, Dad, you—it's establishment, establishment—labor establishment and White House establishment."

Norah bristled. "Thanks a lot! I don't think I chalked up a two-to-one majority across the state exclusively from the *establishment* vote. There must be something we're doing that's right."

"Cool it, Mom. You won two-to-one against a nobody with his hand in the till. You can't out-establishment Hardwick. Feuerstein thinks you should know about two protégés of his, a Chicano public interest lawyer, Manuel Vasquez, and a sharp woman, Sylvia Gannon, who helped him with the PR on a couple of campaigns in Massachusetts. They're both in California now. He'll contact them for you if you'd like."

Norah studied her son and thought, Politics, theater, movies, there was no difference. Everybody is a director, writer, producer, manager, or agent. They all wanted a piece of some action. Well, at least it would involve Peter in the production, and she loved having him near her. "Let's use them," she said.

"When do you want me to have Feuerstein call them? After your two weeks' hiatus or whatever you call it?"

Rising from her chair, Norah slipped her feet into her sandals and put her arm through his. "I'm hiatused out, Peter—yesterday, tomorrow, as soon as—now!" She shook her head. "You've graduated from son to political advisor."

He leaned down and kissed the top of her head and whispered, "Thank God!"

Norah looked up at him, straight-faced, and said, "*She'll* be pleased you're grateful."

* * *

Sylvia Gannon lived in Los Angeles with her lawyer husband and four children. Since her home was in the Hancock Park area, Norah suggested Perino's, which was close by, for lunch and invited Tillie to join them.

Tillie and Norah pushed open the heavy doors leading into the hushed pink calm of the famous restaurant. The solicitous maître d' greeted Norah warmly. "Ah, Mrs. Ashley, your guest is here, and I've taken the liberty of seating her at your table."

"Good sign. I like people who are prompt!" Tillie, who seldom was, commented.

They followed the captain into the main dining room. A slim, tanned woman with short brown hair rose from the corner booth to greet them. Norah's first impression was that she was very young, but when they drew closer, she observed a weather-beaten, birdlike quality about her, inconsistent with the slim, youthful outline.

For a time they went through the usual small social noises, sizing each other up before addressing themselves to the menus. As they talked, Sylvia stared at Norah relentlessly. Norah was accustomed to that; people who'd seen her films had a way of "searching for warts."

Sylvia's expression was almost one of disappointment when she blurted out, "You really *do* look like you photograph. Sam Feuerstein was right." She smiled archly. "I think the professor's in love with you."

"At a certain point in time," Norah said laughingly, "as they say, with the help of Tillie's husband, his studio, and my own irresistible charms, of course, which may be difficult for one as young as you to discern— everybody was in love with me. Let's hope the voters will be in November," she added ruefully.

"I'm sure they will, and we must try to emulate Mr. Lowman's success," Sylvia said archly.

Norah thought, I dislike this woman and I don't even know her. I shouldn't indulge in prejudgment, but damn it, she makes me uneasy. Birdlike? Bird of prey perhaps? She glanced at Tillie, who was engaged in animated conversation with Sylvia and appeared to be quite charmed by her. Norah decided to cut through the small talk. "Peter tells me Dr. Feuerstein believes you would be an invaluable asset to my campaign."

Sylvia smiled broadly, her eyes crinkling at the corners. "He's my political guru," she explained. "Before I settled into domesticity, I worked with him on the Massachusetts senatorial and gubernatorial races."

Tillie, whose only route was the direct one, inquired, "What do you think is *your* greatest political asset?" She rested her elbow on the table, chin in hand, the elegant head turned toward the younger woman.

The answer came thoughtfully, the face serious now. "I suppose I don't threaten anyone."

Norah was puzzled. It seemed a negative attribute. "I wish you'd explain that."

Sylvia became animated, the slim, browned hands, nails clipped short, fingers unringed, gesticulating. "You see, Dr. Feuerstein drilled his favorite rule into me, 'Never get involved in any intracampaign factions.' It's a waste of time and hampers mobility. I know," she said raising her eyebrows, "that I look like the girl next door, and I find that helpful. But I'm tougher than you think."

Oh no, you're not, Norah thought. God, she's going to wrinkle her nose!

"I keep my sights on the goal I have in mind," she continued, "and I hang in there by the teeth, doing my own thing, making as few waves as possible."

"What would you consider your goal if you were to join my campaign, Sylvia?"

"Beating Hardwick, of course!"

Norah laughed. "I have that in mind, too, but what do you think *you* should or could do toward accomplishing it?"

"For one thing, I'd like to gather momentum for you on the campuses." She was quick to add, "I know about those statistics that show students don't vote, but there's got to be strong anti-Hardwick sentiment in academia. He's a Reaganish type in their minds, and rallying campus support correctly could give your campaign a sense of crusade." She grinned. "It makes very good press as well."

Norah had to agree. There was an aura of vitality about this woman, and admittedly, she had a point. Her early misgivings were somewhat dispelled.

Sylvia continued, "You tend to underestimate the value of the Hollywood charisma factor. Since you're a star yourself, you might be taking it for granted. But out there where the voters live, it's political gold. I'd like to get a nice group of stars out hustling for you."

Norah thought, She's a creative doer all right, and that simple little outfit is pure Paris. I don't trust her.

"How would you put their notable attributes to use?" Tillie questioned.

Laughingly, Sylvia said, "I'm glad you asked that question. Ever since Sam called, I've been brooding about your campaign. Natalie Wood, R. J. Wagner, Charlton Heston, Marlo Thomas—people like that could gather a lot of support in your behalf, especially in the small towns, the middle America places, where you need some help. I know you have Lisa Ryder." She gave Tillie a knowledgeable smile. "Of course she's marvelous, but I'm certain Paragon has quite a few other personalities in its stable who'd be willing to assist. Hardwick would find himself hard put to compete with the galaxy we could put together."

"I've already been labeled a thespian by my distinguished opponent," Norah protested. "A caravan of actors might sharpen the stigma."

"Bullshit," Tillie snorted. "Richard Hardwick will rue that cheap shot. It was such obvious cynicism nobody in California's going to buy it. It denigrates the voters' intelligence. We'll make the son of a bitch choke on it." She waved her hand toward Norah. "At least you'll get the gay vote. They're political as hell since Anita Bryant!"

"Come on, Tillie," Norah snapped. "Don't be so sure. Look what happened to McGovern, and he was up to his hips in show people support."

Sylvia was quick to defend her position. "If you recall," she said in an even voice, "George McGovern did stunningly in the primaries when he barnstormed with all those Hollywood personalities in tow. After all, it was McGovern who defeated McGovern. He polarized himself into a kooky position and lost his credibility. Your credibility has been well established, courtesy of Chisholm and Company."

"I thought I had it pretty well established myself," Norah answered testily, "and that was why Hardwick backed Chisholm and felt it necessary to contribute to such a vicious attack on me."

"Of course I meant that," Sylvia explained quickly, catching Norah's displeasure. "It's just that he *emphasized* it by challenging you the way he did."

"Oh, for God's sake, Norah wasn't exactly the captain of the 'Good Ship Lollipop' either," Tillie said impatiently. "But she beat him. Period."

Norah flinched, remembering the meeting with Mellon, and changed the subject.

Over coffee it was agreed that Sylvia would put her ideas on paper before meeting with the campaign leadership the following week.

On the way home Norah asked Tillie, "What do you think?"

"Grab her!"

"Why?"

"For God's sake, Norah, she's smart as hell, and she'll pump some new blood into our tired old veins. Hardwick's going to be a lot tougher than that pious crook Chisholm was. What's to lose?" she asked. "I'll have Walt put her on at the studio and then loan her to you."

"Is it legal?"

Tillie snorted, "Humph, that's why we hire all those costly brilliant lawyers—to make sure it is."

Norah invited the Gannons and the Lowmans to have dinner with them the following week. Tom had been favorably impressed by Sylvia's written proposals, and Norah was anxious to find out how he and Walt would react on meeting her.

William Gannon had much the same look as his wife—tanned, craggy, impeccably tailored, and visibly Ivy League. He made a point to pay special attention to Tillie while Sylvia deferentially drank in Walt's every word, punctuating her conversation with easy, open laughter.

Peter arrived when they were having their afterdinner coffee. Sylvia Gannon reminisced with him at great length about Sam Feuerstein. The professor was in much of her conversation during the evening. When the time came to discuss the campaign, she grew silent and listened attentively. She interjected her own thinking only after the others had spoken, displaying an incisive intelligence.

William Gannon did not enter the discussion. Norah, in an effort to make him feel comfortable, sat down next to him and asked, "Will your children mind if Sylvia comes into my campaign?"

He stared at her in amazement. "Sylvia has her own life to live, Mrs. Ashley. She isn't just a wife and mother or some dumpy little housewife, any more than you are!" Leaning forward, he looked directly at her and asked, "You're the same kind of women, aren't you? Isn't that, in part, what this campaign is about?"

"*This* campaign is about getting the best person to Washington. It's not an offshoot of the feminist movement. Nor, I might add, is it a vehicle to get me out of the house!" she snapped and walked away. Damn it, he had stung her and scratched a nerve. Hadn't Tom drawn the specter of her growing bored and restless and narcissistic the night they had argued about her entering the race? I don't like these people, she thought, but I can't afford the luxury of hostility to anyone who can help me get elected. That Feuerstein character is right. Sylvia's smart as hell. She knows exactly what she's about.

When the Ashleys were alone together, reviewing the evening, over a nightcap, Norah asked Tom, "What do you think of the Gannons?"

"I don't quite understand him," Tom answered. "He doesn't look to be the sort of fellow who'd ride on his wife's coattails, but"—he paused —"he's very low key, very much background material to her. Perhaps she's bird-dogging clients; I can't fathom it. She's obviously a sharp number, Norah, and could be invaluable to you. I think we ought to take her on. Walt is very agreeable about having Paragon hire her." Then he added with a smile, "And as a major stockholder, I find nothing wrong with that."

Norah frowned and said, "I think she was hustling Walt, and I suspect she was more involved with Feuerstein than she cares to admit."

Tom laughed. "I disagree. She very much cares to admit it! She sounded like the old maid with the one sin, the way she was broadcasting it. She made it very plain that they've been lovers and her husband doesn't give a damn. That's obvious. As for Walt, he has a Ph.D. in handling hustlers, he's been worked on by some of the world's best. For God's sake, Norah" —he gestured impatiently—"we're not going to sit in judgment on Sylvia Gannon's morals, are we? The issue is, will she be an asset to the campaign, or won't she?"

"Damn it, Tom, I'm *not* sitting in moral judgment; if I did, we wouldn't have anyone working in the campaign, including *me*. What I'm trying to say is that I just don't *like* that woman, although everyone else seems quite taken with her. What's more, to be blunt, he's not 'low key,' he's a houseboy. And he sucked up to Tillie because she's Mrs. Walter Lowman. I think he convinced her she turned him on.''

"I don't give a damn about the Gannons' ambitions or sexual problems or what turns them on or whom they turn on. This whole conversation is totally out of character for you!" Tom wailed. "She appears to be a valuable PR person on a political level, which is the only thing that should concern you, Norah. If they're kinky, it's not your business. And, the one thing of which I am absolutely certain is that Tillie and Walt are well equipped to protect themselves."

Norah made a face at him. "You're right! You're right! I know it. It's a visceral reaction, and I'm being bitchy. But I don't trust either one of them."

Before the month was out, Sylvia Gannon was firmly settled in a small office in the executive tower of Paragon Studios, with a direct telephone line to the Ashley headquarters.

*   *   *

Manuel Vasquez, Feuerstein's Chicano protégé, was quite another story. For one thing, it took days to track him down. When they finally reached him, he was at the Farm Workers Office in the heart of the Imperial Valley. He indicated interest in becoming a part of Norah's campaign but was at that moment deeply involved in renegotiating farm labor contracts with the growers. He was courteous but firm. He couldn't leave. Not now.

Norah was determined not to be put off and insisted on flying to Indio to see him. Peter, who was as anxious to meet Vasquez as she was, joined her on the journey.

The plane landed at the small private airport, used for the most part by rich ranchers. They were driven from there to the farm workers headquarters, accompanied by her usual security men. Norah had grown accustomed to her guardians, but it didn't make the thought that she required protection any less appalling to her.

They sped past the vast acreage of cultivated fields laden with summer vegetables. This was the heart of the great California agricultural abundance. Its harvests fed the nation and half the world.

The "office" proved to be an abandoned store, sandwiched between a doubtful-looking café and a dilapidated gas station. Dusty vehicles of unrecognizable vintage were parked in front of it. The street itself had an abandoned air reminiscent of the depression towns in *Grapes of Wrath*. Norah noticed a silver Mercedes driving slowly in front of them. It turned at the end of the block, its sleek elegance out of place on the potholed dusty street.

The activity inside the office was in sharp contrast to the desolate quiet of the steaming town. Spanish-speaking men and women dressed in faded cotton clothing were busily sorting stacks of printed material. The sound of clacking typewriters countered their voices. At the far end of the room women stood behind a long table, their backs to the entrance, serving food to people clustered at the rear door. Small children milled in and out around them.

Bulletin boards covered with scraps of note paper and a large poster portrait of Cesar Chavez decorated the pockmarked plaster walls.

An astonishingly handsome, swarthy young man disengaged himself from the others and walked toward Norah, his face showing concern.

"Ah, Mrs. Ashley, I am so sorry you were obliged to come here in all this heat—but," he said apologetically, gesturing to the activity, "as you can see—"

"I understand," Norah interrupted. "You must be Manuel Vasquez." Then, indicating Peter, she said, "This is my son, Peter, who has all sorts of messages for you from Dr. Feuerstein."

His solemn face lit up with pleasure at the mention of the professor's name.

Whispers of "Señora Ashley" telegraphed excitedly across the room. Norah was recognized at once, and there was a movement of people toward her, hands outstretched in greeting. The security men stepped forward instantly.

"I'm safe *here!*" she said emphatically. "It's all right."

Manuel watched the men hesitate and then move back reluctantly, eyes scanning the room.

"Have there been threats against you, Mrs. Ashley?" he asked with concern.

Norah nodded. "It seems to be a part of political life—"

His face darkened. "I'm not surprised," he said, taking her arm. "But you are quite right about these people. They know all about you and believe you are their friend."

"I am, you know," she said.

He nodded noncommittally. "Come, Mrs. Ashley, I'll introduce you." He took her through the headquarters. "Antonio Garcia, Alberto Riverra, Theresa Pasqual . . ." He called their names one by one until they reached his desk. He pulled up some chairs and motioned for her and Peter to be seated. The dark eyes looked at her suspiciously.

Of course she was in danger, Vasquez thought to himself. How could it be otherwise? She threatened Hardwick's power. Chisholm had merely been Hardwick's puppet. The senator wouldn't be the one to harm her, oh no, not the great Richard Hardwick! That wasn't his style. He would incite and inflame, and then other hands would do his filthy work. He studied Norah with some misgivings. True, she had a good political record. But was she merely taking politically adroit positions in order to win? Or did she have a commitment to his people? She had nothing to lose in wooing the Latinos. *La Raza* represented 18 percent of the vote. No mean number. The growers would never defect from Hardwick to support Norah, even though she was as much an elitest in her own way as that swine was in his. Her backers were simply a different breed of power brokers. None of them gave a damn about anything except winning. Still, if Sam Feuerstein thought highly of her—and hadn't he already made the decision to help her on election night?

"You may find me a burden rather than an asset to your campaign, you know. And I think you should take that into consideration," he said to her finally.

"A burden?" she questioned.

"I am to the left of you and the President on a good many issues, Mrs. Ashley. My support could create problems for you," he warned.

Norah's eyebrows shot up. "I'm to the left of some of my strongest supporters, including Peter's father. Our party hasn't been exactly famous for unanimity of opinion. So where do you think we differ?" she asked.

"Well, for starters. I'm in favor of national health care, or what could be called socialized medicine." He leaned forward and spoke with intensity, the long-fingered hands gesticulating to emphasize his words. "I don't believe in the preservation of inherited wealth and would *really* close the tax loopholes, not just make talk. I think cash subsidies for the poor and doing away with welfare payments altogether is the best way to go. For my part, I think the government should take control of all the natural resources, such as the coal and oil industries. What's more, Reuther was dead right about workers receiving an annual income." He shrugged. "Ironically, so was Nixon."

"Do you think the country can afford it?" Norah asked.

"The worries of the rich," he said bitterly. "It *has* to afford it. There must be radical reforms. If you're committed to the status quo"—he waved his hand to the people milling about them—"why should we support you? The status quo hasn't brought us a decent life."

"How much reform can you expect if Hardwick is reelected? He *is* the status quo!" she shot back.

She's shrewd, he thought. This beautiful, rich woman comes to me and makes the gracious gesture. She is, for whatever her reasons, the only hope for us. The fencing is out of politeness. I have no choice but to support her, and we both know it. By the time Norah was ready to leave, Manuel had agreed to come to Los Angeles and discuss his role in the campaign. He stood at the door with Norah and Peter as they shook hands with the workers. Peter had listened with quiet attention as they spoke. But Norah could sense his excitement. She could hardly blame him. Vasquez had the reformer's passion and an intense charismatic aura about him.

When the last of the workers had said farewell, Manuel, holding Norah's hands, asked warily, "Suppose you could accomplish for my people only one thing, what would it be?"

Norah thought for a moment, surveying the weather-beaten men and women and the scrawny, large-eyed children, all of them centuries older than their chronological ages. They, with their itinerant families, moved from place to place, wherever the crops were ripe for harvest, and worked for pennies. The children never attended the same school, any school, for more than a few months at a time.

"If there were only one thing I could do," she said quietly, "it would be to make certain that each of these children be taught in the same classroom for a full school year, which is exactly what I thought should be done twenty years ago. Unless we educate the children, we won't break the hopeless, self-perpetuating nightmare of poverty."

The dark-haired young lawyer looked at her respectfully and then leaned over her hand and kissed it, "*Vaya con Dios, Señora.* I shall see you very soon."

In the silver Mercedes Norah had observed when she entered Vasquez's headquarters, Marianne Hardwick Redfern sat and watched the candidate's arrival and departure. She felt her insides turn over when she saw Manuel bending over her father's opponent's hand.

No wonder Concha no longer mentions his name, she thought bitterly. Plus everything else, he's mixed up with this Ashley creature. She felt a twinge of jealousy. He'd fawned all over Ashley, the traitorous ingrate. After all the years of generosity and kindness and love her grandfather had given him. What did he know about loyalty? What did he know about family feelings, about love? Hadn't the two of them been reared like siblings? He, the older brother figure, she playing the younger, adoring sister. The memory of Bailey shot through her. The venomous attack on Concha, the implications that were too horrible to contemplate. Bailey had called Manuel her "Uncle Manuel." Could there be any truth in his allegation that the man she had always loved might be her grandfather's son? Her uncle? How sick!

She knew Manuel's mother, Juanita, well. She was Concha's younger sister and had often helped out at the Casa. Manuel looked just like her. But then Juanita and Concha bore a strong familial resemblance. No! It was impossible! She willed the thought out of her head. Anyway, even if it were true, Manuel was still betraying her, and everyone at Casa Thayer who had cared for him. He was in Norah Ashley's camp, working against her father, the Colonel's son-in-law! He had betrayed them because he was a power-driven, spoiled bitter bastard. That's what Manuel was. He was nothing more than a Chicano upstart with a Harvard diploma and a heartful of hate. So why did she long for him so desperately, pursue him, why was she here, making a fool of herself? So he could kick her in the teeth? She was the sick one, asking for it. She knew she should force herself to get away from this dreary misbegotten place instantly and forget him.

Instead, she pulled the Mercedes forward and parked just beyond an ancient eucalyptus tree, its leaves dusty and browned by the heat. Sheltered from sight, she had a clear view of the rear end of the store through the car mirror. She had to see him, touch him, be near him just once more. So what if he rejected her again? Rejection was an old familiar thing. She was the reject of all times. Only Papa Colonel and Concha had ever cared about her. Papa Colonel was dead, and after the horrendous confrontation with Bailey, Concha had withdrawn into a studied remoteness. No more visits over coffee, no motherly questioning. Not that it mattered a damn. The only thing that mattered was that Bailey didn't exist for her anymore as a figurehead husband. It was Manuel she wanted more than anything else in the world. Right now. This minute. She had a house waiting, empty, in the Springs. They could go there. In Manuel's arms she'd be a whole woman. A loving, alive human being. She'd done what he'd told her to do, hadn't she? She'd married a WASP—Bailey. So now she was among the living dead. Manuel had to take her, comfort her, tell her she was right. They belonged together. Nothing else mattered. She pressed her eyes shut to erase the remembrance of Bailey's twisted, leering face, and she felt a chill of fear. Even though she hadn't believed Bailey's implications, she had paid him off to avoid hearing him out.

Her thoughts drifted back to the house waiting in the Springs. She'd made all the arrangements to rent it a week ago. She was determined to have Manuel. And here she sat after weeks of stalking, parked on a hot dusty side street, shaking with doubts and despair, wallowing in self-pity, knowing in her heart he'd probably tell her to go to hell.

Peering into the rearview mirror, she observed men and women cleaning away the debris of dishes and food from the long wooden tables which had been placed in the parking area. A short while later, there was the sound of sputtering motors and the creaking of the dusty vehicles leaving the street.

Finally she saw him. Manuel emerged from the rear entrance of the building, looked out toward the street, and locked the door. He spotted the car and began to move toward it. Face stern, body erect, muscles tensed as if in preparation for an unpleasantness, he approached her. Marianne switched on the motor and backed up the car, drawing to a halt directly in front of him.

Recognizing her, his face registered relief and surprise. Then anger clouded the chiseled features. "What in God's name are *you* doing here, Marianne?" he asked sternly.

She felt her heart sink. I'm a fool, she thought. The only positive emotion he feels is relief that I'm not some Teamsters' goon sent to do him in. Her voice was calm when she answered lightly, "Waiting for you!"

Manuel leaned on the car door and scowled at her. She'd removed the large dark glasses and pulled off the bright scarf, freeing the auburn hair, burnished bronze in the red sunset light. The agate eyes flecked with gold returned his gaze without blinking.

"I had to see you, Manuel." She caught her breath in a sigh and pleaded, "Don't be angry—please! I didn't mean to frighten you. Did you think I was some goon sent to do you harm?"

He shook his head. Of course, he'd observed the parked Mercedes. No, he hadn't thought it contained a goon. Goons don't drive Mercedeses. But it might well have been one of the enraged vineyard owners out to threaten him. Manuel wasn't afraid, but he'd been through enough to be wary; and his wariness had been fueled by the sight of Norah Ashley's bodyguards. There was an ominous quality developing in her campaign. And now Marianne! Here? Why?

He stared at her, suspicious of her presence. Was she Hardwick's emissary? Had she been sent on some kind of mad mission? To spy on him perhaps? Why would his support of Ashley be of any interest to the senator? An unknown Chicano lawyer could hardly be that important a threat to the great Senator Hardwick.

He opened the car door and slid into the passenger seat, breathing in the smell of leather mingled with her perfume. She'd been a memory for so long—a fantasy—that the unexpectedness of her presence startled him. "What do you want? Did your father send you to spy on me?" His voice was deliberately cold, to mask the tumultuous emotions that raged through him at the sight of her.

She stared at him, unable to answer, struck dumb. All the anticipation, the planning, the brooding, the hysteria of her need to see him again had been insanity. He hated her!

"Is this some sort of joke? Does it pleasure the *padrón's* daughter to spy on the peons? A new sport perhaps? Tell me, is that why you're here?!" The dark eyes looked at her with hostility. His sarcasm hurt her as much as the cold greeting.

Flushed with anger, she cried out, "No, my father didn't send me. No one sent me. I came because I wanted desperately to see you, be near you, you arrogant bastard. *Not* to spy on you or anyone else!" She turned away from him and stared straight ahead, unable to face him. Her embarrassment was mingled with anger and frustration and an overwhelming sense of loss.

Manuel instinctively reached for her hand. He turned it over and traced his fingertip across the calluses where the long fingers joined the palm. He wanted her and detested himself for the desire. She was the same parasitic breed that had spawned him, exploited his people for centuries. They were all unable to bear the smallest frustration. Every appetite must be satisfied, everything touched, owned. She was the true Thayer, *padrón* incarnate in a woman's body. They consumed the land, the air, the water, the lives of his people, Concha, himself. "Ah, you earned these by holding reins and tennis rackets," he said mockingly. "But have you ever washed a dish or scrubbed a floor with these fine strong hands? What do you use them for except your own pleasures, Mrs. Redfern? Am I to be your new diversion? Are you that bored?"

Without a word, Marianne lunged at him and hungrily pressed her mouth against his. Her hands groped under his shirt, digging into his flesh. Desire for her flamed through him. In a rush, his own suppressed longing exploded. He had never loved another woman but this one. He had never longed to possess another as he longed to possess Marianne, both for herself and for what she symbolized.

As if she'd read his thoughts, Marianne pulled away from him abruptly and faced him. "Why did you say such hateful things? I've come only because I love you, Manuel! You know that. Come away with me—just for a little while," she pleaded, all pride gone, her eyes brimming.

He took her face in both his hands and kissed her gently, the dark eyes intense with desire. "We have no choice, do we, my Marianne?" His voice was a hoarse whisper.

She pushed him away gently and turned the key in the ignition. She looked up at him, her mouth drawn into a crooked smile, and repeated, "No choice!" She headed the car in the direction of Palm Springs.

CHAPTER
Fourteen

Weeks later Marianne lay on her back, her head resting on Manuel's outstretched arm. She traced his ribcage with her finger, committing him to memory, and she asked absently, "What were you up to in Los Angeles? Were you conspiring to do evil things with the enemy?"

He was resolved not to be drawn into a discussion of the campaign and sensed a danger signal. Although she claimed disinterest in it, he knew her family loyalties were too deeply ingrained for her to be indifferent. His hostility to her father made the subject potentially explosive. God knows, she didn't owe that bastard Hardwick anything. She knew it, too. He'd pawned her off on the Colonel and Concha without a pang. If he didn't need her help now in the campaign, he still wouldn't give a damn about her.

But Manuel hadn't driven half the night from Los Angeles to the Springs, full of demon longings for her, in order to have her spoil their time together with campaign talk. He breathed in the scent of her hair. Christ, she was desirable. He longed for her every minute they were apart. She was in his blood. His passion for her had become insatiable, and he still half hated himself for it. "I just did a bit of or-ganizing," he answered offhandedly, and then, because he couldn't resist, he said, "And you, of course, were being a dutiful daughter to your dear father."

Her head shot up, and she snapped angrily, "I thought we weren't going to talk about it!"

Laughing, he pulled her toward him. "Perverse one. *You* started it!"

Before she could protest, he covered her mouth with his, stroking her back, pressing her close. He rolled her over on top of him, caressing the small muscular buttocks, and then with a brisk slap, he ordered, "No politics in bed."

She looked at him with a troubled expression. "Oh, Manuel, you unhinge me. Let's call a moratorium. You're right. No politics in bed. But tell me, do you really believe the Ashley woman is any better than my father? They're both politicians. It's just some personal craziness with you that makes you think there's any difference between them beyond the meaningless party label." She rolled over abruptly and lay next to him.

Manuel leaned on his elbow and looked down at her. She was so damnably beautiful. He could never have enough of her. He was becoming possessive, too. He didn't probe her about Bailey. He couldn't bear to think of him, much less envision his touching her. But maybe there were others. Did she go from one bed to another? Bitterly, he thought, Here I am desperately trying to block her husband, whatever other lovers she has, her goddamn father and grandfather and everything they represent out of my mind. And she won't let me, true Thayer that she is. She's incapable of relating to any head but her own.

"Okay, Marianne, so they're both politicians," he said, brows drawn together in a scowl. "That's true. But at least Ashley has the ability to feel for the underdog. She has some measure of compassion. Your father has only one purpose: his own. And he'll do anything at any cost to obtain his goal." His voice grew louder. "He's anti everything but his own ambitions. If you think the Chisholm exposé was it, you're wrong. There will be more revelations. That man Mellon and his troops have only begun to scratch the surface, and before they're through, your father's going to be lucky if he stays out of jail."

Marianne sat up and faced him. "You want to see him beaten and humiliated, and you don't care how they do it, do you?" Her eyes filled with angry tears, remembering Bailey's ominous threats and the checks she furtively put into his account so regularly to keep him quiet. Without waiting for Manuel's answer, she said bitterly, "You don't care about anyone. Just abstract humanity, not individual people. Not me. Screw the senator, right? Maybe you want to ruin me too! You can't love." Her voice broke. "I thought once you loved me!" she sobbed.

Manuel took her face in his hands and kissed her gently, tasting the wet salty tears. With great effort, he whispered, "I do love you. I've always loved you, Marianne, always."

Marianne flung her arms around him, pressing her body close to him. There was no further need to speak or to think.

But her decision to campaign for her father remained unaltered. She felt she had to do it for the Colonel's sake. Papa Colonel would have wanted her father reelected. Perhaps she herself desperately wanted to see Norah beaten, out of jealousy. She resented Norah's hold on Manuel. She resented his allegiance to someone else, especially that woman. But she admitted to herself that most of all she couldn't bear the thought of her father's losing, and thus being deprived of his chance to be President.

Bailey's innuendos about Hardwick and his partners troubled her. On one hand she knew Bailey would do or say anything if he thought it gave him leverage against her. On the other hand, since when were politicians a saintly breed? Of course, her father's record was less than lily white; it had to be. What politician was untainted? But what about his opponent's record? Surely that ex-actress was no saint. Wasn't the President throwing the full force of his political machine into California in order to beat her father. Why?

Still, there were residual benefits for her in the campaign. Her participation established a pattern of absence from the Casa. She could be with Manuel without the necessity of a complex charade of alibis, not that she felt an obligation to explain her comings and goings to Bailey.

Palm Springs was anonymous. There was no place else for them to be alone and unobserved. Manuel would never have risked exposing himself or her by meeting her in a more public place.

Concha's remoteness, which would have distressed her deeply under other circumstances, was a relief now. She was the one person in the world with whom Marianne would have difficulty dissembling and whose disapproval she could not have endured.

Marianne lived for her nights with Manuel. She was in love, and he had said he loved her. She had waited her whole life to hear it from him. It was enough. She lived the time away from him in a haze. She had no past, and no future. He was her reality.

* * *

Richard Hardwick spent the summer months making himself highly visible on the floor of the Senate. He led the opposition's attack on the administration and studiously ignored his own forthcoming campaign, which would not go into full gear until fall. He hammered at the President wherever he could. Currently he was agitating on the foreign imports and trade deficit problems, two almost certain no-win situations for the administration. If the President capitulated to the ever-increasing demands for import quotas, particularly in the field of electronic equipment, he might propel the United States into a "high tariff" posture. This would be certain to offend allies abroad and risk their retribution against our own exports. On the other hand, to permit our marketplaces to continue to be glutted with foreign products could cripple American industry. The result could be a chain reaction of unemployment, still unacceptably high, and a business recession. The tightrope-balancing act required sophisticated handling. The President was in no position to take a positive simplistic stand and play to the gallery. Hardwick was—and he knew it. He was not required to resolve the complicated problems as was the man in the White House. He gloatingly mounted the attack against the administration wrapped in prolabor, probusiness, pro-national-interest rhetoric.

While the senator was flourishing in the limelight, his aides were already well into his campaign. His Washington office, by now a well-oiled machine, had hired a famous and ruthless public relations firm in California to spread the senator's message. Hardwick flew coast to coast regularly in his private Lear jet, addressing conventions and civic groups, always playing the statesman, the incumbent senator, ignoring Norah's candidacy.

If he sustained any private anxieties concerning his own vulnerability, he gave no public sign of them. Richard Hardwick never lost sight of the ultimate goal.

Marianne's presence at his side helped deflect any questioning, or discussion concerning the doubtful circumstances of Virginia's death. His daughter evoked sympathy for him, an emotion which Richard felt invaluable to his image. She, a younger version of Virginia, was the symbol of his loss. She proved him the proper widower. He noted with pleasure a new warmth and friendliness in Marianne's manner. Gone was the aloof remoteness, the Thayer grandee fixation, which had been such an in-grained part of Virginia's character. The physical resemblance to her mother hadn't changed, but a new happiness, an inner glow, made her a much more dazzlingly effective prop. He was certain that her radiance could not be attributed to Bailey.

No, Bailey had given up the pretense of showing interest in the Hard-wick campaign. He no longer bothered to accompany Marianne when she joined her father at public functions. Hardwick wondered if Marianne's serene radiance was due to relief at Bailey's absence. Did she have a lover? Perhaps. God knows anything was better than Bailey.

He hoped to God she wasn't involved in some kind of a scandal that could rub off on him. He had no wish to pry into his daughter's private life; his need for her presence was too great to risk offending her. But Richard Hardwick was taken aback when his radiant Marianne began to manifest a political toughness that matched his own. Abruptly one evening she questioned him outright about his involvement with Chisholm and Isaiah Smith. Masking his surprise, he said, "Of course I was involved. Obliquely, that is. In my mind, it's hardly a shocker to attempt to weaken your opposition before he gets to the starting gate, or should we say 'she'? Does that offend you?" he questioned.

"Of course not," she said, laughing. "It substantiates Papa Colonel's theory. If you can't grab the brass ring, *buy* it!" Her face serious now, she asked nervously, "How oblique?"

"Plenty," he reassured her. "Don't worry. There's absolutely no way I can be faulted. I've taken good care of that department. If the Ashley campaign is going to consist of beating that dead horse, it will be even easier for me to win than I originally thought!"

Marianne felt a wave of panic. She believed her father. But whatever else he might be, Bailey was no fool. Bailey had hinted at a scandal more threatening and ominous than the one that was already half exposed. And so had Manuel. What did Bailey know? What was the Ashley camp up to? How could it hurt the senator? The Colonel taught her a great many things, and the use of money was not the least among them. She could keep Bailey silenced by regular deposits to the bank. Still, it bothered her.

If a Bailey could be privy to some sort of damaging information, then the Ashley forces could be too.

"What did Bailey mean about the Beau Soleil business?" she asked her father apprehensively, taking advantage of his candor to her, fearing the answer.

"Christ, Marianne, do you think I'm some kind of an idiot! Bailey's a horse's ass trying to look like a big shot," he snarled. "Beau Soleil was a business deal. Being a senator doesn't deprive me of my right to make as good a deal as the one a private citizen makes."

And that was the end of it. The most important thing to Marianne was that she was her father's daughter and the Colonel's granddaughter and she couldn't bear the thought of her father losing against Mrs. Ashley. She would help him make the fight, and they would win.

*   *   *

Manuel began working seriously in the Ashley campaign toward the end of July. In Los Angeles he exchanged his faded khakis for a well-tailored sport jacket, button-down shirt, and dark tie, remnants of his Harvard days. He foraged for support among his former classmates. Many of them were now junior partners in large, distinguished law firms, whose senior members, for the most part, were committed to the reelection of Richard Hardwick. He zealously began organizing the Chicano community, persuading, cajoling, and pleading Norah's cause. Chicanos had good reason to distrust all "gringos." But Manuel persisted. He patiently campaigned through churches and meeting halls. He set up plans for an Election Day push to get his people to the polls. And he rushed back to the desert to be with Marianne whenever he could spare the time.

Peter Ashley attached himself firmly to Manuel's operation. Not only because Dr. Feuerstein had suggested it might be the best place in the campaign to make himself useful, but because Peter genuinely admired the Chicano activist. Manuel found himself developing an equal fondness for Peter, who served surprisingly well as Norah's surrogate in the Chicano community. With Manuel's help and his high school Spanish Peter memorized and gave several effective speeches in his mother's behalf. At first, he was known as "Señora Ashley's *niño*," then as "*niño*," and finally, the "keed." Sensing Manuel's need for privacy, Peter never questioned his frequent late-night disappearances but would await him in his office early each morning to receive his instructions for the day. When Manuel traveled for the campaign, it was Peter who went with him.

Manuel teased him, "You will be the first gringo Chicano in California, Peter. Your mother'd better watch out or *La Raza* will elect you instead of her."

For Norah, the summer months were primarily low-profile season. The campaign would surface into public visibility after Labor Day. Her activities were twofold. Foremost was fund raising: "digging for gold." She hadn't felt as impoverished waiting on tables at college. It was as if she had a beggar's rice bowl clutched in her outstretched hands, and she loathed it. When she complained to Tom, he was unsympathetic, reminding Norah that she herself had vehemently campaigned for the passage of the election reform laws which made it necessary to grovel for small, individual contributions. The second most pressing chore was to gather as many of Chisholm's supporters into her camp as she could before they jumped over to Hardwick's. Ironically, the first meetings she held after her victory were with the Chisholm aides who had opposed her in the primary. They for the most part were more than anxious to join the winning side; slates were wiped clean.

Tom watched with amusement as she played the hypocrite. Her performance was so convincing it was hard to imagine her capable of holding a grudge. He knew her too well to be deceived. Norah had a street fighter's instinct for self-protection. Old hostilities were buried, and the facade of a united front was established. But the former enemies were not to be completely trusted.

The new recruits were never questioned. If mistakes were made, she moved on to the next step without agonizing or challenging motives. But trust? That was reserved for those who had been with her through the primary. She had developed a stunning quality of leadership. She wrung the best out of her supporters and created a loyalty to her cause which went beyond the call of duty or partisanship. Tom's pride in her was limitless.

They were both stubbornly convinced that Hardwick would go to great lengths to avoid a debate. Since she was the challenger, they knew she must continue to demand the confrontation until his refusal backed him into the coward's position. Norah found herself discussing Hardwick on such a totally impersonal level that she could barely recall him as a man. She believed his ambition was so intense that what he might remember of her as a woman would be irrelevant. She knew she was the roadblock Richard Hardwick must remove at any cost if he were to make it to Pennsylvania Avenue. She had no illusions. The fight would be grim.

CHAPTER
Fifteen

It was time to launch the campaign publicly. Tom Ashley chose the Hollywood Bowl to do it in.

On a warm evening directly after Labor Day William Seavers, the manager of the Bowl, scanned his huge open-air arena, shook his head in dismay, and announced in a pained voice, "It doesn't look promising. We're usually more than half full by this time." The bowl was barely sprinkled with small clusters of people.

Tom checked his watch. "Don't panic, Bill, it's going to be fine. Norah will play to a full house."

Seavers thought Tom Ashley had gone mad. As if dealing with a stubborn child, he said in a calm tone, which camouflaged, he hoped, his incipient hysteria, "Tom, do you see those TV cameras near the stage?"

"Um-hum."

"You are aware, no doubt, that they can be turned in any direction the operator chooses."

"I know."

"Well, then"—Seavers' voice went up several octaves—"I take it you also know that they will spend the major part of the evening scanning thousands of empty seats. Norah's campaign is about to open with a full-blown disaster."

Ignoring him, Tom calmly surveyed the great shell. Its banners flapped briskly in the warm autumn breeze. Musicians tuned their instruments, engineers tested microphones, and the Pacoima Marching Band was receiving last-minute instructions from an harassed-looking teacher. Huge searchlights scanned the skies. Tom took a deep breath. "Seven and one-half minutes more and they'll be here," he told the distracted manager.

Seavers was exasperated. "If you had an ounce of common sense, Tom Ashley, you'd call for an ambulance and have Norah carted off to a hospital before she, the governor, and half the congressional delegation wind up in the greatest political embarrassment of all time! There is *no* way this place will have eighteen thousand bodies here tonight. Don't you understand, for Chrissakes?"

Tom squinted and searched the long road winding in the distance. He faced the agitated manager and said calmly, "Look down to the bottom of the hill, and tell me what you see, Bill."

Seavers squinted, his rimless eyeglasses sparkling in the glare of the searchlights, and gulped. "My God, you actually programmed it."

Tom lit a cigarette, slowly blowing the smoke into the night. "I sure as hell did. That's my line of trade."

As far as the eye could see, bus after bus snaked toward the Hollywood Bowl. They drew closer. Seavers could discern the signs, "Glendale for Ashley," "Sherman Oaks for Ashley," "Glendora loves Norah," and the like. They read like a map of southern California.

"Better get your ushers moving. They have exactly twenty-eight minutes, which should be more than enough time to settle Norah's supporters. Each busload has a map indicating the seating arrangements, so things shouldn't be too difficult. We've seen to that!"

Before the astonished man could answer, Tom was loping downhill toward the Bowl restaurant.

Tom had judged correctly. His engineers functioned as flawlessly as the complex machinery they employed. The concept of busing rather than relying on the vagaries of individual car drivers had been his. But it was Sylvia Gannon who had traveled to every Ashley club and headquarters for the past month to organize the operation. Whatever reservations he'd felt about her had vanished. She was competent as hell. Even Norah's instinctive dislike of Sylvia had been replaced by a healthy respect for her talent and willingness to work through a project down to its minutest detail. Walt Lowman told Tom he was so impressed by Sylvia's efficiency he was considering keeping her on at the studio after the campaign.

Entering the Bowl restaurant, Tom saw his wife and caught his breath. She was radiant in a pale green chiffon dress, one white shoulder bared. They had become so interlocked with each other, he'd forgotten how great a beauty she was. Strange that she was more physically visible to him in this room filled with hundreds of people than when they were alone. She was seated between the governor and Senator Sam Bradshaw. Andrew Watkins at Tillie's left was to deliver a message from the President. Tom caught Norah's eye, made a circle of his forefinger and thumb, and winked. She read the message, smiling with relief. She had argued vehemently that a small, packed theater with standees spilling down the aisles was a more sensible goal for her first rally. The prospect of gathering and delivering eighteen thousand people to a specific place at a specific time terrified her. Tom's self-confidence and faith in his own expertise had run over her objections like a panzer division. He had never known the fear of playing to an empty house. Norah had known it well.

The governor commented, "I take it that little domestic pantomime indicates a full house."

"That's what my Tom promised, and that's what we'll get. He's a man of his word," Norah said proudly.

The governor turned to Tillie, seated at his left. "Didn't you feel nervous about filling this place? It could have been an all-time disaster!"

Tillie looked at him contemptuously. "Just because you're not inclined to take a chance, Governor, is no reason to believe the rest of us are cowards!"

The governor tucked in his shirt front. Goddamn it, he was gaining weight again, he thought. Rankled by Tillie's reference to his studied neutrality during the primary, he said, "Come on now, Tillie, we've been good friends for too many years to start quarreling. After all, my own margin of victory was so narrow, I couldn't afford to lay myself wide open," he cajoled. She was Walt's wife and he wasn't going to risk that support.

Tillie snorted, "Then it'll be the only thing you haven't laid."

The plump hand patted Tillie's cheek. "Be a good girl and stop behaving like a mafiosa. You know I love you, honey. I've forgiven but not forgotten that it was you who sent me to that son-of-a-bitch dentist to have my teeth capped. I remember the pain and think of you."

Tillie laughed. "You won the election, didn't you? Considering that you're capable of killing your mother to win, it's little enough for you to have suffered." She bent toward the plump face and whispered, "Now behave yourself if you ever want to run for office again with or without those beautiful teeth!"

Noticing the governor's angry expression, Norah leaned across the table and asked, "What's wrong?"

Tillie modestly fluttered her eyelids. "I'm just reminding the governor that he'd better get off his duff and give you some real support."

The governor drew back in his chair. "Norah, Tillie's forcing me to prove that fat men are not jolly!"

Sam Bradshaw suddenly opened his eyes and leaned across Norah. "What's that you said, Governor? What's that about fat men's bellies?"

*　*　*

In his ornate suite in the Mark Hopkins Hotel in San Francisco, Richard Hardwick extended his free arm and reached for his wristwatch. Dorothy Johnson lay across his chest. He absentmindedly stroked her back. She felt him move and bit his shoulder with her strong white teeth. "Time up, senator?"

He switched on the night table lamp and rolled her over onto her back. "My opposition goes on in a few minutes. I want to see what she's got to say."

"We wouldn't want to miss that for anything in the world, would we?" she said sarcastically.

He leaned over and kissed the hollow in her throat and reached for his robe. "Business before pleasure," he said as he turned on the television.

Dorothy sat up, pulled her knees to her chest, and wrapped her arms around them as she silently observed Richard. He settled himself in an armchair and took an apple from the ornate basket of fruit placed on the coffee table for his enjoyment by the Hopkins hotel manager.

Christ, they *ought* to be solicitous! Dorothy thought. The Hardwick campaign was sponsoring a thousand-dollar-a-plate black-tie dinner for five hundred big spenders to open Richard's fight for reelection.

Eyes riveted on the screen, Hardwick was totally absorbed by the TV. With his hair disheveled from their lovemaking, he looked extraordinarily young. Their lovemaking had meant no more to him than the apple he was eating. Politicians are basically lousy lovers, Dorothy mused. The only thing that really turns them on is a voting booth. Her television rating had a greater aphrodisiacal effect on him than she did. Power was his passion and he meant to have it. She knew it and accepted the fact that sex meant little to Richard. He made no pretense of feeling any strong passion for her as a person, and she was grateful for the honesty. He wasn't about to have their affair go public either, now that his wife was dead. His role of the bereaved public servant endeared him to women voters. And there were a lot of women voters in California.

Well, she didn't much like it, but she was too good a reporter not to know that his daughter standing by his side was a hell of a lot better for his image than she'd have been. Nobody cared what politicians did privately as long as their indulgences weren't splashed across the front pages of the paper or TV screens and billed to the taxpayers. She gave Richard every advantage she could on her program, and she chipped away at Ashley subtly and relentlessly in front of her viewers. She had every intention of collecting on that effort, if not now, then later—when he took up residence in the White House. She could wait.

Dorothy looked at him carefully. He may be more interested in my power than he is in me, she thought. But if he weren't potentially the next President of the United States, I wouldn't be here now, either. The score's even.

The Hollywood Bowl flashed on the screen, cameras panned the huge amphitheater. A stunning young man wearing denims and faded blue work shirt, his hand held near his heart, was leading the salute to the flag. Thousands of people stood up and in one voice joined him. Richard leaned toward the machine and squinted. "My God, it's Manuel! The son of a bitch," he snarled.

"Who's he?" Dorothy asked.

"He's a dirty, snotnosed bastard who owes everything he's got, including his Harvard diploma, to the Thayers," he said angrily. He hoped Marianne was watching. Maybe it would prove his point to her that the ungrateful bastard was no damn good.

"I wonder what Mrs. Ashley has got that you don't, Senator," she goaded.

He ignored her. Dorothy went to the bathroom, pulled on a negligee of white satin, bound with marabou. She fastened the waist, pulled the belt tight, and arranged the collar to make certain the ample breasts, of which she was inordinately proud, had proper visibility. She brushed her hair in place, sprayed some perfume on herself, nodded to the mirror with satisfaction, and returned to the bedroom, settling herself at Richard's feet.

The crowd was going wild. Norah Ashley was heading toward the podium, a nimbus of green chiffon floating around her. The camera zeroed in. Dorothy had to admit that she looked marvelous and hated her for it.

She looked up at Richard, wondering what he thought. His face was expressionless. She ran her fingernails along his thigh; he flicked her hand away as if it were an unwelcome insect. He was intent on the screen.

Norah smiled at the huge assemblage, her face illuminated with pleasure. "What an opening night," she exclaimed, "for a former thespian."

The applause and cheers were deafening. She was throwing it back at him and they loved it.

After making the customary thank-yous, she waved her hand toward Andrew Watkins. "Mr. Chairman, I am deeply grateful to you for being here with us tonight, and especially grateful for the words of support and encouragement you bring from our President."

Turning her face toward Watkins, the flawless profile facing the camera, she added, "Please remind him that my political undergraduate career began during his first campaign for Congress, and that I fully intend to complete my postgraduate work in the United States Senate under his leadership."

That brought another round of applause and cheering.

Norah placed both her hands on the podium and faced her audience. Dorothy noted the large emerald on the fourth finger of her left hand and envied it. The face on the screen was earnest now, the large eyes direct. "It has been an extraordinary experience for me campaigning against an invisible opposition, and I sincerely hope that Richard Hardwick will surface before November.

"Where is Hardwick hiding?" she asked, meaningfully, lowering her voice. "Or—*what* is Hardwick hiding?

"During my primary contest, my opponent barricaded himself in Washington behind a smokescreen of obstructionism. He berated the President's programs while men funded by a mysterious foundation belonging to him attempted to destroy the very basis of the primary system. They attacked my honor, my validity, my person, and, worst of all, they unleashed a hurricane of dangerous emotions.

"Is Richard Hardwick running for the presidency or for the Senate? Will he receive the vote of Californians without campaigning for it? Are we simply going to hand it to him?" she asked.

The crowd roared back, "No!"

Norah shook her head, echoing the crowd, "No! No, we will not! The people of California will reject him." Her voice strong now, she demanded, "Come out, come out, wherever you are, Richard Hardwick! Explain your positions on the issues that affect our lives in California! The bread-and-butter issues! Come out of hiding and tell us what you will do for us in the next six years. Or are you afraid," she asked accusingly, "to step out from behind the cloak of incumbency and money and power and deceit?"

Richard sat mesmerized. She was a fucking rabble-rouser. She had the crowd in her hands and could play them anyway she wanted to. He listened to her tear his voting record apart and remembered the last time they were together.

It was impossible to conceive that this woman was the girl who'd lain in bed with him that summer evening, the humid New York night caressing their bodies. Drowsy with lovemaking, she had rested in the crook of his arm, her hair a damp mass of ebony ringlets, the perfect miniature body curled into his. He had told her about his visit to Casa Thayer, that the feudal grandeur of it had been unlike anything he'd ever known. She listened quietly while he described the baronial Casa and the Colonel and told her about the Spanish-looking Mrs. Danvers–type housekeeper. Even about Manuel, a little boy then—that bastard! He was careful to mention Virginia in a light way, including her presence in the general atmosphere of the place. Norah made no comment. Instead, she asked him the childhood question.

"What do you want to be when you grow up, Richard?"

Without a second thought, he'd answered, "President, of course."

She had been silent.

"And you?" he questioned.

"As of *this* moment, a great actress."

She sat up on the edge of the bed and looked at him, the huge eyes glistening with tears. "And there's obviously no place in a future President's life for an up-and-coming young actress, or even a great one. You have other plans, I think."

"Come off it. You're in my life now. Do you think I could give you up so easily?"

Instinctively she had grasped the depth of his ambition. He tried to kiss her, but she pushed him away and asked coldly, "Are you planning to make Virginia Thayer your First Lady?"

He was stunned by her prescience. He hadn't even admitted to himself that he had it in mind. But of course it was the logical step to take.

He'd been quick to protest. "That's crazy, Norah." And then he stupidly added, "Even if I did, what difference would it make? Nothing can change things between us."

She'd stared at him in disbelief. "You bastard!"

He tried to kiss her, but she pushed him away.

It was over. From then on she refused to return his calls or to see him. His letters were returned to him, unopened. She ended their affair as abruptly as it had begun.

He was mesmerized as the electrifying voice of the woman on the screen rose, then fell, casting a seductive web.

The crowd was hers. The camera panned the rapt faces across the stage. He recognized John Mellon, leaning forward, caught up in the drama Norah was weaving. The senator was seized with anger. He should have known the President would send the little shitheel out to help her.

Dorothy, sensing his anger, leaned against him. He caught the scent of her perfume. The robe had fallen off her shoulder. He leaned over and put his hand on her breast. The nipple hardened beneath his palm. With his free hand he switched off the television. More in fury than in lust, he pushed her down onto the floor and took her.

*　　*　　*

Richard Hardwick bowed his head in the massive banquet hall of the Mark Hopkins Hotel as the minister thanked God for the sumptuous feast he had placed before Hardwick's five hundred most affluent supporters. He prayed that the man they all honored would have the strength and courage to continue his selfless work for the nation, persevering and promoting decency and morality, the ideals that had made America strong.

Dorothy Johnson, seated at the press table, looked up toward the dais. Richard's eyes were closed, his handsome face earnest in prayer. The widow of the former President was at his right. She wore a high-necked powder blue dress, blond overcoiffed hair topping a thin-lipped face. To his left was the first woman elected national chairperson of her party. She was large-bosomed and motherly looking in her dowdy black lace dress, but her frumpy exterior concealed a ruthless politician. To have her support was not as crucial as to avoid her enmity.

Dorothy, seated with the media people, at some distance from the head table, wondered what Richard was thinking. This campaign kickoff was not going to be half as effective as Norah Ashley's Hollywood Bowl extravaganza had been. She really should have that Ashley woman on her program, but she didn't want to risk her picking up any support. She projected much too well. But she sure as hell was newsworthy. Dorothy made a mental note to get in touch with Dan Brookings, whom she had met in Washington, and ask him to arrange an appearance for Ashley the day *after* the election. If she won, which wasn't likely, it would be a coup, and if she lost, it would make her appearance doubly interesting.

* * *

Marianne wasn't listening to the minister's intonations. She was thinking about Manuel. Her father had carried on about Manuel being at the Ashley rally. He'd watched it on TV. She wasn't surprised. Why not? Manuel *was* working for that woman. He could have made himself less conspicuous. But then she doubted he had any concern about her father's feelings. All she knew was that she longed to be on her way back to the desert to be near him, to touch him.

The "amen" interrupted her fantasies. She looked down at the attentive and quiet, bejeweled crowd. The master of ceremonies began the introductions of the guests at the head table. She heard him say "devoted daughter," and placed one foot in back of the other, readying herself to rise and bow gracefully. She received a large round of applause and as usual heard a voice whisper "image of poor Virginia." It happened every time she appeared with her father.

* * *

Richard Hardwick himself was introduced by the famous actor whose credentials included unsullied patriotism and the all-time-high record in backside pinching. Five hundred well-dressed humans rose and applauded with genteel enthusiasm when Richard Hardwick came to the podium.

Hardwick smiled broadly, raising his hands for them to be seated. His face turned serious, and in a voice touched by sadness, he began, "Friends, how I wish my dear Virginia were here to share this wonderful evening."

* * *

Marianne listened to her father blame the President for high taxes, uncontrolled inflation, continued unemployment, and the welfare mess, accuse him of pandering to big-labor minority bosses and inhibiting the rate of business growth. By the time he called for a balanced budget, a strong military defense, and an end to knuckling under to the Soviets, Marianne felt herself squirming in her seat. It was a mundane performance, nothing like Norah Ashley's dramatic telecast in the open-air amphitheater. And he still wasn't even mentioning Norah's candidacy. She looked out over the ballroom and studied the faces of the men and women in the well-dressed audience. They were listening to her father with polite attentiveness. Why not? He was telling them what *they* wanted to hear. But how many of them were there? Weren't *they* perhaps the true minority? For the first time Marianne felt concern for her father's reelection.

"It's a bleak day for this nation when we hear on the morning news that the dollar is reported to be weak against the Italian lira and the Japanese yen." He brought his fist down on the lectern and leaned forward, glaring angrily. "The yen? The lira? It's worse than sad. It's a disgrace!"

There was a burst of applause.

Dorothy Johnson felt her stomach turn over. She couldn't believe what she was hearing. Not only was he risking the votes of Californians of Japanese and Italian descent, he was making a bore of himself. The only thing that could be said for his performance was that the audience at which he was aiming his hackneyed prose wouldn't vote for Ashley in any case. Incumbent or not, she thought, it wasn't going to be easy for his nibs.

CHAPTER
Sixteen

The plane lifted up out of San Diego. Her political foray there had turned into a nightmare. Not only had she made a fool of herself, Norah thought bitterly, but that so-called brilliant Sylvia Gannon had produced a scheduling fuckup that should warm Hardwick's heart.

Norah unbuckled her seat belt and stretched her cramped muscles. How could she have been so stupid? Why had she listened to Tom when he lectured her on the way down to that hellhole? At least if she'd followed her own instincts, she would have grabbed them on the abortion issue and ERA, over which she had strong personal convictions. Instead, she'd waffled around just like he'd asked her to and then shot her mouth off on the Bakke case, which the courts had decided anyway. Worst of all, she'd been badly misquoted, her words twisted and distorted.

She recalled Tom, his face set sternly, admonishing her: "The President wants the abortion business *out* of this campaign, and he certainly doesn't want the ERA mess surfacing all over the place again! It's a no-win. Most of all, he doesn't want you stirring up problems for him, forcing him to explain *your* positions. You are his direct representative, Norah. Do you understand?" he asked, as if she were some kind of idiot.

"Yes, his stooge," she'd answered contemptuously. "You and the Presi-

dent want me to be vague and noncommittal with the usual 'It's a matter
of conscience,' 'I'm glad you asked that question,' and any other 'Don't
take any wooden nickels' garbage that comes to mind. Right?"

"Precisely," he'd snapped.

So what had it gotten her, doing it his way? The whole goddamn day
was a chain-reaction disaster. The President wasn't running in California.
She was! She'd been a fool to listen to Tom. Now she'd blown it. Her
stomach turned over. One lousy day and her whole momentum was shot.
Down the tube! Wasn't this a duplicate of the Muskie fiasco, when the
black caucus questioned him about the possibility of his choosing a black
for Vice-President and he'd answered, "Too soon!" Nobody in his "off-
the-record" meeting had been offended. They thought he was being
candid and liked him for it. That is, until someone leaked it to the press
and blew up the whole thing into a monumental drama. He never re-
couped! Would she?

Paralyzed with anger, Norah slumped back into her seat. She had been
there and back a thousand times with candidates she'd supported. How
could she forget the absolute number-one rule: Nothing is "off the record" for a political candidate, no secrets, no private statements. It was
basic. And if she'd been fool enough to forget it, then where the hell were
her "knowledgeable" advisors? They permitted her to march into the
booby trap, and she, with all her experience, had behaved like a goddamn
amateur. And where was Sylvia? That bitch! So certain her arrangements
were foolproof she hadn't even bothered to come along. Students were
notorious for staying away from the polls. Now they'd probably rush to
them to vote no on her.

Norah looked over at Tillie, buried in her camel's-hair coat, pretending
to be asleep. Damn her. Norah hated them all—Mellon, Dan, Tom, Tillie,
Lisa—all of them. Especially Sylvia Gannon. She was probably in the
executive dining room at Paragon this very moment, sucking up to celebrities.

Her bones ached, her throat felt like sandpaper. She reached for another lozenge. She was fast becoming a lozenge junkie. What did they care
that she had been put through a ringer? No matter to them that the whole
terrible day had been a killer. First, they were late for that awful lunch at
the Grant Hotel. Of course, the people were restless and hostile. So she'd
had to go from table to table spreading goodwill, and that made things

worse. Instead of arriving at the aircraft factory when the shifts broke, she was so late that she stood there in the ninety-degree heat shaking hands with a few stragglers, feeling like a fool. And that meeting, the interminable, frustrating meeting with the local brass. They proved to be the worst collection of bickering politicos in the entire state, complaining about one another. She didn't give a damn as to who did what to whom. It was what had been done unto her that mattered.

Totally disoriented, trying not to look frazzled, she smiled till her face ached. The endless photographs, the continual, "Look this way, Mrs. Ashley"—"Smile, Mrs. Ashley"—"Just one more, Mrs. Ashley." They'd dragged her from hotel to restaurant to meeting hall until she'd forgotten whether she was having lunch or dinner or where the hell she was.

She'd actually felt a sense of relief when she met with the student minority caucus in the conference room of the university's political science department. The young people gathered around her as she sat on the desk, drinking coffee from a paper cup. The questions that shot from every corner were intelligent and earnest. It was the way politics should be, not the hokey business she'd endured earlier in the day. It all seemed so simple and friendly and stimulating. She liked them and they liked her. The first cooling came when a frizzy-haired, pale, tight-faced young woman who hardly looked like a candidate for unwanted motherhood threw the abortion question at her. Swallowing hard, she did as Tom had asked her to, and said, "Isn't it really a matter of conscience?" Hating herself.

"No, it's not. It's a matter of justice. Poor women are being punished, Mrs. Ashley, or wouldn't you understand that?" the young woman protested bitterly.

A male student impatiently called out, "Oh, Christ, it's for the courts. There *are* other issues, Doris."

"Damn right there are," the young feminist retorted. "What about the ERA? They're going to try to shaft it too, aren't they, Mrs. Ashley?" She looked at her for support and questioned, "Why? Why?"

"Because it apparently scratches some terrible nerve, Doris!" Norah answered, deliberately making use of the young woman's name. "Maybe we should have ironed out the differences between us and the men and women who feel threatened by the feminist movement. We unleashed some deep psychotic fears and brought about an avalanche of lunacy, which the vultures are playing on." Norah shook her head. "It's an absolute madness that there's even a necessity for an ERA. And worse yet that we have to fight for it." Before the young woman could comment, that clean-cut little bastard, looking all over Brooks Brothers, asked her about her position on the Bakke case. What did she think about lowering college entrance requirements for the disadvantaged, the reverse quota system?

Without hesitation, she waded in and blurted out off the top of her head, "I agree with the courts. Otherwise, we'd have an exercise in futility." The words echoed in her mind. The fact that she herself had been a scholarship student probably had something to do with it. Suppose she had been passed over simply because she'd been a majority or a minority. She had an ingrained hostility to the concept of quotas. But it was thoughtless and unnecessary to lay herself wide open like this. The thing had already been decided. Yet when she'd spoken, no fists were shaken, no angry voices raised. Besides which, it was a *private* session. That's what the students had requested. They could speak freely to each other. No holds barred. A candid dialogue!

A young black woman calmly asked, "Why do you think so? Isn't there some justice to compensating for past oppression?"

Smugly, relieved to have skirted the abortion issue, feeling sure of herself, certain she was on the side of the angels and that everything she said had the sincere ring of truth, she explained, "Because the lowering of standards defeats the purpose of higher education for everybody, including those for whom the compromises would be made, the disadvantaged. An inadequately prepared student, lacking the basic tools for learning, is predestined to failure. Bitterness, frustration, and the sense of defeat would be compounded—the very thing we're trying to eliminate. The inequities must be reversed in the early years of education." And she'd meant it.

The discussion continued in a positive way. Why not consider forming a "learning corps," similar to the Peace Corps? A crusade to implement learning skills at the lower school level. Wasn't that where the problems began?

All very cool. Norah, pleased with their enthusiasm, made a mental note to discuss developing the idea with Sylvia. It might be a proper campus project. She had more than that to discuss with her now, all right!

Several of the students volunteered to work in her campaign. Knowing

San Diego to be a political rat's nest, she suggested they work through Evelyn Auerbach's "Bag-Its" and circumvent the local party machinery.

The meeting gave her pleasure. She enjoyed the thoughtful questioning, the give-and-take rapping with the young. If she'd had any sense, she should have been prepared for the entrapment. But her directors and producers, she rationalized, let her become exhausted to the point where her judgment was warped.

She'd left the room surrounded by students. Brookings stood at the door, chatting with the reporters assigned to her campaign, smiling affably.

"No, no, ladies and gentlemen. We promised the caucus that this would be strictly off the record." He took Norah's arm and said to her, "Let's go, it's time to get to the airport."

Suddenly she felt him stiffen, his eyes riveted on Jim Stone of the *Thayer-Herald,* who, notebook in hand, was talking to the "Brooks Brothers" creature.

Her heart stopped. She knew instantly and so did Brookings that she'd been had. He dropped Norah's arm abruptly and sprang toward Stone and the youth, shouting indignantly, "That meeting was 'off the record' at the *students'* request. *Not* Mrs. Ashley's."

"We're not in the meeting *now,* are we, *Mister* Brookings?" the young man said, sneering.

Brookings grabbed the front of his jacket, lifting him off the ground. "You dirty little motherfucker."

Pandemonium broke loose, flashbulbs exploded. People surrounded Brookings, pulling him away.

Jim Stone sidled up to Norah smiling archly. "Would you care to elaborate on your statements that minority students should not receive compensatory treatment and that the opponents of the ERA are psychotics, Mrs. Ashley?" Before she could speak, the students began shouting, "She was off the record." "You've got *no* right." "She didn't say that." "You're twisting what she said."

Brookings, regaining his composure, raised his voice loud above the shouting and stated, "Mrs. Ashley will have plenty to say, and *when* she says it, it will be at an open press conference." Heading Norah toward the exit, his eyes on Stone, he snapped with contempt, "Why don't you just pay Judas Iscariot his thirty pieces and let me get Mrs. Ashley to the airport?"

Norah closed her eyes. She could see the stark headlines and the photographs of Brookings freaking out, quoting his words. Somebody should have stopped her before she went into that room. Protected her! What the hell were they there for, for God's sake?

Why didn't Tillie say something? She nudged the silent figure. "Tillie, *say* something!"

Tillie turned her head toward her, shrugged her shoulders, and said coldly, "You blew it."

"*I* blew it? Where were all those geniuses who're supposed to advise me? It was a goddamn booby trap. Who set it up? Our dear Sylvia?"

At that moment, a smiling, fresh-faced young stewardess with an excess of white teeth, leaned toward her across Tillie and inquired in her permanently cheerful voice, "Would you like some coffee, tea, or perhaps a soft drink, Mrs. Ashley?"

Instead of snarling "hemlock," she smiled and said, "Nothing, thank you." She was in no position to lose even a single vote. Stepping over Tillie, she headed toward the rear of the DC-6, which had been converted into a work area.

There they were: Mellon, Brookings, and Tom—the flawless ones, the masterminds—and Lisa, poor Lisa, looking desolate. No detail was too small for them. They thought of everything, even this dilapidated tub of a DC-6: "Norah's Ark."

Hardwick sashayed up and down the state in his private jet. But not she. Oh no. Tom's company jet was resting comfortably in its hangar collecting dust. She was the "peepul's" candidate, and there would be no posh nonsense for her. Bert Lance had seen to that. Well, she had just lost a large segment of those "peepul," her crucial base, made a monumental ass of herself, and *they* had let her.

She slumped into an armchair and faced Dan Brookings. Bitterly, Norah leveled her rage at him full force. "You're going to be *turr*ific on TV. A smash! Attacking a student!"

Lisa stared at her with dismay and put her hand protectively on his shoulder.

Ignoring the gesture, Dan rested his elbows on the table, covering his face with his hands.

Norah waited, studying the table's surface, strewn with yellow pads, overflowing ashtrays, and coffee cups.

She turned to Tom; his face was expressionless. "Any ideas, my darling, my mentor? Won't the President be pleased? Abortion never got off the ground. Just an eensy-teensy ripple." She sneered. "And the scheduling. What a well-oiled machine I'm blessed with!"

"Stop it, Norah!" Tom ordered. "We're trying to think of some way to turn this mess around."

"Stop what, may I ask?"

"This high-handed little Miss Martyr act. *You* bombed, you know!" He felt sick to his stomach. Hadn't he been the one who laid the dictum on her about abortion? In reality she would have been off and running on that one, which was consistent with her image and character, if it weren't a smoking pistol over the President's head. There was no way to explain it to her, and anyway it wouldn't change things now.

"I bombed?" She could taste her rage. "*You're* supposed to protect *me!* Why didn't you check out the caucus? How could I have been so mis-scheduled? Dragged around to the point of exhaustion?" Her voice grew loud. "That little creep was obviously on Hardwick's payroll. Am *I* expected to check those details, too? I was set up for the kill and *you* let them," she shouted.

Tom looked at her furiously. "Stop it, Norah. You're not new at this. You've been through enough campaigns to know there is *no* such thing as 'off the record' and no new questions and that you don't have to answer every damn thing you're asked. You were so bloody pleased with yourself you couldn't imagine one of those stargazing young darlings giving you the knife. All you had to say on the Bakke case was 'The court's have decided!' And you certainly didn't have to label opponents to the ERA as 'psychos.'"

" 'It's a matter for the courts,' " she mimicked. "That's your answer for everything! Even a Jesuit dropout governor felt free to discuss abortion. He can say, 'Poor women are being unfairly victimized.' But not I! Oh no, the President wouldn't like it. And as far as I'm concerned, the opposition to the ERA *are* a pack of psychos, but I *didn't* say it. They twisted it. Even exhausted, I'm too careful for that, but my staff isn't careful enough to keep me out of a goddamn trap. Maybe Hardwick's right. I'm nothing more than the President's puppet. I can assure you the people aren't going to vote for an idiot puppet." Her voice grew louder and angrier. "If you hadn't Svengalied me for *his* sake, I'd have never gotten myself into left field!"

"You're piss-assed mad at yourself, Norah, so you're flailing around looking for a whipping boy." Tom stood up and put his hands on the back of the chair, his anger whipped up by his own guilt. Even if what she said was true, no one forced her to be a fool. "If any of us had suspected you'd be suckered in like a neophyte, we'd never have let you loose. Christ!" —he sighed—"we can't protect you from your own performance."

He's despicable, she thought. Still, she shouldn't have jumped for the bait. And that booby trap "off the record"—! She knew better. It would have been so simple for her to have gone into the need to bolster lower school education, make a small, proper noise about ERA, and sidestep the whole fiasco. Poor Brookings would look like a fool all over TV and it was her fault. She was flooded with self-pity and remorse and rage. Tears began to well up.

Tom bent over and kissed her mouth. He took out his handkerchief and handed it to her. He couldn't bear the tears. "Don't start crying. Please!" Her anger was easier for him to handle.

"There's no way! Hardwick must be delirious with joy," she wailed.

Dan had leaned back in his chair, looking distressed.

"Oh, Dan, I'm so sorry. What's to do?"

"Dunno," he muttered, giving her no comfort.

Mellon, who had been oblivious to Norah's tirade, looked up from his papers. "Suppose you tell us *exactly* what happened in that classroom, from the beginning. Do you remember?" He put his cigarette down in the overflowing ashtray.

"Only too well." She took a deep breath, trying to recall the details. She told them all she could remember of the meeting. They listened carefully.

Mellon, brows knitted, asked, "Did you feel the group was essentially friendly?"

"Of course, or why would I have suggested they contact Evelyn's 'Bag-Its'? They acted in good faith—it was that one little bastard—!"

Tillie left her seat and made her way to the table, settling herself into a chair next to John Mellon.

"If they acted in such good faith, wouldn't they feel they themselves had been had as well as our own Miss Wonderful?" she asked.

Norah shot an angry glance at her. Did she have to rub it in? Some friend! *She* hadn't been put to the fire, had she?

Tom nodded. "I hope they do. We may need them to help bail Norah out. What do you have in mind, John?" he asked Mellon.

Mellon scowled. His mind had been elsewhere. "Oh that! Yeah, you're right. Why don't we have a carefully rigged campus straw vote that comes out heavily in favor of Norah. Should defuse the whole tempest." He paused and smiled. "Be sure to have Auerbach analyze it!" He turned his attention back to the material he'd been working on and added without looking up, "Guess *la* Gannon should implement the action for Norah on *all* campuses. Shove it down Hardwick's throat."

"Marvelous," Tillie sniffed. "She did such a great job on this one! You'd better leave academia to someone else."

Norah wasn't really listening. She was worrying over their arrival at the Santa Monica Airport. "What'll I do if the press is waiting when we land, hungry for raw meat—mine!"

Tom raised an eyebrow and sighed. "They'll be there all right. We better have a statement ready."

They cut away the non sequiturs and boiled it down to Norah's saying in as many ways as possible, "I'm telling it like it is." Norah felt comfortable with that. It would be a proper theme for her campaign, no matter how she phrased it.

She was the first to step off the plane, Dan close behind her. Drawing the cool night air into her lungs, she reached for his hand and whispered, "Behave yourself, they're waiting."

The press was gathered inside the gate. As soon as Norah reached them, the questioning began.

"Mrs. Ashley, you were quoted as saying that the opponents of the Equal Rights Amendment were psychos. Is that true?"

"No, it isn't. I said the *issue* brought out psychotic fears!"

"What's the difference?"

"The difference is," Norah said thoughtfully, "that you don't have to be psychotic to have them." Before her interrogator could further belabor the point, she quickly said, "Next."

"Did you state that you believed no concessions should be made for disadvantaged students?" "Why did you call an off-the-record meeting?" "Do you think your statement will cost you votes?" "Have you heard Senator Hardwick's comments?" "Do you approve of Daniel Brookings' performance?"

Norah put up her hands. "Ladies and gentlemen, one at a time, please!" Nodding toward the UPI correspondent, she said, "I feel very strongly about implementing learning skills at the lower level. College entrance standards are not the real issue."

"Why did you choose to discuss this subject off the record?" an attractive young woman asked.

"*I* didn't," she said emphatically. "The students themselves requested a closed session." She smiled at her interrogator. "For some reason, I can't imagine why, they seemed to feel the presence of reporters inhibiting."

A black reporter waved his hand for attention. "Why was Mr. Brookings so belligerent when that student talked to Jim Stone?"

Norah shrugged. "For one thing, he didn't want me quoted out of context, which, after all, is exactly what happened." Then she threw up her hand in mock dismay, rolled her eyes upward, and sighed, "Ah, men!"

They laughed. She felt the tension break. The "actress" had served her well. A man she recognized to be from the Thayer press chain said, "Senator Hardwick is quoted as saying that your remarks are indicative of an arrogant disdain and a hostile attitude toward minority students. Have you any comments on that, Mrs. Ashley?"

Norah raised her eyebrows. She had anticipated that kind of question but was taken aback by the source. Swiftly she took advantage of the opening. "Yes, I do. For one thing I'm delighted to hear that Mr. Hardwick is finally aware that there's an election going on in California and has taken some time out from his race for the presidency even if only to distort my statement. I don't believe honesty indicates prejudice. I'm hopeful that the majority of the people who attended the caucus will support my campaign because they know I will say the same thing to you that I said to them."

Before he could interrupt, she continued, anxious to grab her advantage. "I would remind you that Senator Hardwick has voted against the President's request for additional aid to education and specifically against the bilingual education bill, which is crucial to minority students, not to mention day care centers and other devices necessary to raise the level of learning skills." She looked at the Thayer representative with a benevolent smile and suggested, "Why don't you report to my opponent that I'm anxious to debate him on *all* the issues, *on* the record?"

There were no further questions.

When Norah slid into the limousine with Tom and Tillie, Tillie whistled. "Well, that's more like it. At least you got your licks in." She made a clicking noise. "And about time!"

Tom squeezed Norah's knee. "You redeemed yourself." Then he asked Tillie, "Do you think Walt is at home pacing, or could I interest you ladies in some pasta? I'm starving."

"Walt's working later hours than he did when he was scratching up the ladder. I'd love to have him pacing," Tillie complained. "He loathes Italian food. This could be my big chance." She looked at Norah, "Are you up to it, Norah? It's been a long day."

Norah brightened. "Up to it? I'd adore it. I'm beyond fatigue. Do you think Luigi's has room for us? It's only a few minutes from here. I've earned it, Tom, haven't I? Am I really back on the track?" she asked, longing for reassurance.

Tom winked. "You smoked him out! With a little bit of luck, we may even make lemonade out of your lemon; it'll take some judicious squeezing." He tapped the driver's shoulder. "We'll stop by Luigi's before we go home."

CHAPTER

Seventeen

I t was late and the secretaries had left for the day. Walt checked his watch, hesitated, and then reached for the phone. Why not? Tillie was still in San Diego and probably wouldn't be back for hours. Gannon was in the East on business. And Walt had never taken Sylvia Gannon out for dinner.

They'd never been beyond the suite in the Bel-Air. God, she was good in bed. Not that he had any complaints about Tillie. But there were no surprises left. They knew each other's signals too well. Theirs was a familiar road and they'd traveled it too often. He'd always been careful not to involve himself with anyone in the industry, not to befoul his work nest. But this was hardly that sort of thing. She wasn't really his employee, she belonged to the campaign. The large breasts, incongruous on the boy-slim figure, roused him. But it was more than that. She made him feel as if he were a virtuoso in bed. It wasn't possible she'd learned what she knew from Gannon, that stick. No! Walt thought. She's a natural! Or was he a menopausal old fool? What the hell's the difference? He hadn't felt like this for a long time.

It had come about so easily what with Tillie involved in the campaign and Gannon being away so much. They'd go back to the hotel after dinner. Suppose they were seen in a restaurant? There was nothing extraordinary about that. They could be discussing the senatorial race, couldn't they? It was a perfectly proper thing for him to do. After all, she was working for the Ashley campaign in *his* studio, and he *was* the finance chairman—

"Get me extension 214, please," he said. "Hello, Mrs. Gannon, this is your friendly finance chairman. Would you consider joining a poor lonely executive for dinner?" He felt a surge of pleasure at the sound of her voice. "Good! Now what kind of restaurant would you enjoy? *Italian?*" He gulped. Walt had reached the stage in his life where his digestive tract demanded certain gastronomic limits. Highly spiced foods topped the forbidden list. What the hell! She had said "Italian" so emphatically. He'd take a large shot of liquid antacid before he left and risk it!

"Meet me at my car in ten minutes. Nonsense! Leave it overnight. I'll take you home and have a limousine pick you up tomorrow morning. No problem. Ten minutes!" he commanded.

He felt twenty years younger as he quickly gulped the white chalky liquid kept in permanent supply in the medicine cabinet in the marble bathroom adjoining his office. He brushed his teeth and splashed his face with cologne. She was waiting when he reached the garage. Her sense of promptness pleased him. Oh God, the man-hours he had wasted waiting for Tillie, who had absolutely no respect for anyone's time but her own.

Sylvia was wearing a white silk shirt, open at the throat, emphasizing the tanned skin, and a beige wraparound linen skirt that parted to expose her leg when she entered the car. She looked so cool and unruffled. It was hard to believe she'd put in a ten-hour day in that cubbyhole. He felt a twinge of regret that he couldn't offer her a job at the studio after the campaign. He didn't approve of mixing things up; it would be impossible now.

He looked around the garage as he got into the Rolls. It was deserted. He closed the door, leaned toward her, and kissed her mouth. Her lips were soft and moist. Sylvia wore no lipstick. She tasted fresh and young. He sat back and switched on the ignition. First, they would have dinner.

* * *

Luigi's was situated on Westwood Boulevard, well below the ornate skyscrapers shadowing Wilshire, surrounded by tacky discount houses and small shops; a neon sign and an unimpressive canopy indicated its presence.

The food was good enough, but it was the latter-day speakeasy atmosphere that gave the restaurant its character. The clientele was a well-mixed bag of prosperous, plump, middle-class men accompanied by stiffly coiffed wives, informally dressed celebrities feeling a comfortable "off-duty" anonymity, occasional businessmen wining and dining young secretaries, hopeful that the darkened atmosphere would add an element of romance to their quests.

Pepe, the maître d', recognized Tom the moment he came through the door into the dimly lit bar, which served as an entrance to the dining room. Hundreds of wine bottles of uncertain vintage decorated the spaces between the booths. The walls were adorned with mediocre paintings of village scenes and happy Italian peasants, the men lusty, the women, large-breasted and Madonna-faced.

Pepe threw his arms around Tom's shoulders. "Ah, Tom Ashley! Welcome, my friend. How is the divine Signora Norah?" Sighting her, he whistled, "*Bellissima*! I am overjoyed to have you here!"

He motioned a waiter. "Naturally Pepe has room for the next senator—!" He stopped short, recognizing Tillie, and lowered his voice. "Mrs. Lowman! It's been a long time." Touching the waiter's arm, he said, thoughtfully, with careful emphasis. "The table in the *far right* corner will be perfect, yes? So these good people can eat in peace!" Nodding to the man to lead them, he himself took Tillie's arm and steered her into the dining room.

It was customary to seat celebrities in the central area of the room; some unwritten law inhibited the diners from gawking or asking for autographs, yet their presence was meant to be felt.

Pepe settled them in the semicircular booth, Tillie with her back to the other diners, Tom between them, and Norah facing the room.

The waiter immediately asked for drink orders; Pepe hovered over them with menus for them to study, surrounding them with bustling concern.

"You order for us, Pepe," Tom suggested. "Not too complicated. We've had a hard day."

"Of course, Signor Ashley. A nice little salad perhaps and maybe some cannelloni and a good wine." He turned to Norah and Tillie. "Does that sound agreeable?"

"Very agreeable," Norah said, pleased not to have to make the decision. "Mrs. Lowman and I have perfect faith in your judgment, Pepe. Don't we, Tillie?"

Tillie grimaced. "That's about the only judgment I have faith in after what we've been through."

"Gracias." The smiling maître d' collected their menus.

Norah, eyes adjusting to the dim lighting, observed a distinguished-looking man involved in deep conversation with a young woman sitting in a booth at the opposite end of the room. Standard Luigi's, she thought to herself with amusement. There was always a seduction or two going on in the place. Then the man leaned back in his seat, and she recognized him. It was Walt! She closed her eyes for a moment, hoping she was mistaken. But she wasn't, and the woman with him was Sylvia Gannon.

Tom looked at her with alarm as she drew in her breath, gasped, and turned pale.

"Are you all right?" he questioned concernedly.

She nodded and reached for the water goblet, unable to speak.

Walter Lowman, who had been exposed to the most seductive women in the world, with Sylvia Gannon! Unbelievable! No one but Tillie had ever interested him. His resistance to female blandishments was part of Hollywood folklore. The little bitch. Norah had never liked Sylvia Gannon, and it was ironic that Tillie should have been the one to urge her to take her on.

Tillie stared at her with alarm. "My God, you're ashen, Norah. Are you sick? Tom," she ordered, "let's get her out of this place and to bed. Tell them to cancel the—"

Before she could finish, Walt was at the table with Sylvia Gannon in tow. He leaned over and kissed Tillie, shaking his finger at her. "Aha, I caught you sneaking 'Italian.' Move over and make room for us." He slid into the booth next to her, motioning for Sylvia to sit beside Norah. He called to the astonished maître d', "We'll have our dinner here. Please have the waiter bring our drinks over."

Sylvia, breathless with exaggerated excitement, bombarded them with questions. "How did it go? Did my people deliver enough students? Did you have good media coverage?"

They were obviously going to bull it through, Norah thought. She had no way of knowing that Sylvia had been terrified when she saw them come in.

"We are *only* having dinner, and of course we'll join them," Walt had said firmly. "Just act normally and matter-of-fact. We have nothing to hide."

Well, they didn't, he thought, not here at least, and he wasn't going to slink away. Goddamn it. How did he ever get himself into this? He'd probably blown his prostate to boot. He must have been insane.

Tillie was glacial, her over-well-bred voice level. "Yes, indeed, Sylvia, they delivered, and we had the most extraordinary coverage!"

She's a better actress than I am, Norah thought. I'd kill him and that clean-toothed all-American little slut here and now.

There was no holding Tillie, who continued calmly, "What a surprise to find you here, my darling, knowing your devotion to Italian cooking!"

Before Walt could speak, Sylvia Gannon leaned across the table. "He's such a *darling,*" she exclaimed, anxious to appear unruffled. "Do you know what he did for me?"

"No! Tell me!" Tillie's dark eyes opened wide.

"Well, there I was, beating my brains out organizing Norah's whistle-stop long after everybody else had left the studio, and who should walk by my office on his way out but—?"

Tillie, her voice breathless and in perfect imitation of the young woman, broke in, "Could it have been *darling* Walt himself?"

Sylvia gushed, "He's so gallant, he asked if I'd had my dinner." She broke into a smile, eyes crinkling at the corners. "Of course, I hadn't and I was starving, and so"—she gestured coyly—"here we are. He's so thoughtful." She opened her eyes wide. "We never dreamed you'd be back this early!"

"I'll bet not."

Norah, heart pounding, was speechless. Tom, his head held perfectly still, sat immobilized, except for his eyes, which traveled from face to face, showing no outward sign of distress.

The waiters arrived with their drinks and salads and baskets of hot crisp bread.

Walt sloshed the ice around his glass, pretending to be oblivious to the mounting holocaust, waited for the waiters to leave and asked Norah casually, "How did it go?"

"It was a total disaster. Not the least of which was the scheduling."

Taken by surprise, Walt said, "I don't believe it! What the hell went wrong?"

"You better believe it!" Tom answered and began to tell him what had happened.

By the time they'd been served the cannelloni, at which they picked indifferently, Tom had given Walt a full accounting of the day's fiasco. He reassured the distressed maître d' that the food was delicious, ordered coffee, and explained that their fatigue had cost them their appetites. He wished that had been the reason.

Walt turned to Sylvia. "I thought you had it all wrapped up," he said sharply.

Indignantly, she answered, "I did, but I'm not responsible if Norah gets herself entrapped in a Hardwick setup and mishandles it!"

Norah bit her lip. The little bitch! She was about to answer her when she felt Tom's nudge. He'd had enough.

"Look, it's been a long day, and this is not the time for rehashing. We're worn out." He motioned the waiter for the check. "We'll talk about it tomorrow." In an offhanded manner, he said to Walt, "Oh, by the way, I think Sylvia'd better start to work out of the headquarters, and perhaps we ought to have Barbara Potter take over the campus operation. She's a student herself.

"God knows, we need Sylvia to publicize Norah's minority support. If it hasn't dissolved. Mellon's been uneasy all along about her use of the studio office. He thinks it could be considered a contribution under the new election code. You and Tillie have already contributed your maximum legal amount." He thought to himself, If he doesn't think it now, he sure as hell will be thinking it tomorrow. Tom lit a cigarette.

Tillie looked at him gratefully and shifted her glance to Walt to see how he had reacted to the obvious reproach. Although his face was expressionless, he resented Tom's interference, even though he knew Tom was extricating him from his own mess.

Sylvia, anxious to mask her disappointment, accepted with forced enthusiasm. "I'd just adore it. It's rather lonely in that marble tower." Her expression saddened. "Oh, Norah, I feel just awful about San Diego. Perhaps Barbara could do a better job at it. After all, there are so many minority students these days—"

Turning to Tom, Norah said, "This day has taken its toll. We'll give you a lift home, Sylvia, since we have the driver." Some lonely! She's a self-serving bigot to boot, she thought.

The Lowmans drove home in silence, Tillie engulfed in a rage so great she was unable to articulate it. Walt debated with himself as to what tack to take. Should he ignore the entire episode and act as if nothing out of the ordinary had happened and hope it would blow over? He'd only been caught taking her to dinner! Knowing Tillie, he had little faith in that route and decided the best strategy would be for him to grab the offensive, feign outrage, attack Tillie's bitchiness and Tom's obvious ploy to remove Sylvia bodily from Paragon. Who the hell did they think they were?

Jesus! How could he have known they'd turn up at Luigi's, of all places? He really didn't feel a great passion for Sylvia. Sure, she was bright as hell and a good lay. She'd given his ego a monumental boost, gushing all over him and making him feel like the king of the world. It had been so inconsequential. She was safely married to a man who obviously didn't give a damn what she did and was probably flattered that his wife was attracting studio heads. The whole bloody mess wasn't worth making a federal case about. Walt felt sick at being made to look the fool. And most of all he detested the thought of having to explain himself.

But Tillie never gave him the chance to grasp the initiative. As soon as they walked through the door, she flung down her purse and coat and turned to him. "All right, you dirty old bastard. If you think I'm going to sit still and let you screw around with that slut and humiliate me, you're dead wrong!" Her voice was ominously low. "Do you understand, or would you prefer I spelled it out?"

"Just what the hell are you talking about?"

"Don't give me that crap. You know damn well what I'm talking about."

Walt, outraged, answered in a tone of moral indignation, "I certainly do not! If you think I'm going to put up with some neurotic jealousy seizure on your part, you're dead wrong. I haven't got *anything* to explain. And if you and the Ashleys want to make an issue out of my taking that young woman, who's been working her tail off for Norah, out for a bite of dinner, go right ahead. *I'm* going to bed."

Who the fuck did she think she was? He'd provided Tillie with every luxury known to man. She was the beneficiary of his success, his prestige and power, and she could go to hell as far as he was concerned. He'd been as good as faithful to her all these years, and this was what he got for a *nothing!* He started walking toward the door when Tillie screamed, "You get back here and listen to me." She headed toward him, her face contorted with anger. "There's something we're going to get straight right now. I'm too old to be humiliated by a menopausal fool and that fawning cunt. If you want her, you've got her. You're free to leave any time you like. No one's stopping you, but just remember, Walt Lowman, *I* own half of everything you've got, your stock, your holdings, your bank account, and that tower where you sit and run this town. So suppose you make up your mind right now that your little fling's over." Her voice rose to a shriek. "Over! Do you hear me?"

He looked at her with contempt. "Indeed I do, and so do the servants and the neighbors. If you don't mind, I'll go get my things and sleep in the guest room." He turned his back to her and left.

Tillie sank into the couch and put her face in her hands. She was a fool, a goddamn fool. She had just managed to wipe out the quarter of a century they'd lived together over that two-bit broad. She felt ill. How could she have been so stupid? The whole day had been one lousy thing after another. She could have taken care of Sylvia without saying a word. Gotten her out of the tower and had her shipped to sea. Instead, she'd built a small thing into a federal case.

Listlessly, Tillie washed her face and brushed her teeth, put on a nightgown, and prepared for bed. She pulled back the covers, hesitated, and then resolutely marched down the hall to the guest room. Walt was lying on his back, his hands behind his head. His eyes were closed, and he made no move to acknowledge her presence. She slid in beside him and lay silent, tentatively touching her foot to his. Walt sighed and slowly brought his arm down and reached for her hand.

* * *

In his Washington office Richard Hardwick smashed his fist on the desk in rage. His executive assistant was taken aback. He had anticipated plaudits for manipulating the Ashley woman into the San Diego gambit. She had played into their hands beautifully. Hardwick's unexpected outburst astonished him.

"I don't understand your reaction, Senator, she's been pawning herself off as the friend of the great unwashed, and we showed her to be an elitist."

"It's *obvious* you don't understand," Hardwick roared. "This nonsense will bring on a shriek of 'foul play' from her supporters, and worst of all, we've now publicly acknowledged that she's running—a fact I wanted to studiously avoid. So now Ashley winds up attacking me and calls for the fucking debate again. To add to that, Brookings comes off looking like a macho black buck in her defense, and whatever good we could have gotten from the black vote for calling her an elitist is diluted," he shouted. "Have you read the polls?"

"Yessir, of course, sir!"

"How do you read them?"

The baffled aide wondered what this lunatic was talking about. "Senator, they show you with a formidable lead. Ashley has gained a few points from her primary win exposure but nothing world-shaking."

Richard looked at him with contempt. "Did you, by chance, note the size of the undecided vote?"

The aide, looking knowledgeable, answered, "Oh yes, sir, it's large. Surely you're aware, sir, that the undecided turn out in pretty much the same proportion in the end as the committed votes do."

Richard sighed with disgust. "Unfortunately, we're *not* at the end. Although they may be uncommitted at the moment, it's absolute madness to give that woman anything to create sympathy, much less exposure, for her. For Chrissakes, that *huge bloc* is movable. The public thinks all politicians stink, that voting is just a question of picking lesser evils!" He shouted, "Now suppose you tell those geniuses who planned this idiocy to get their asses over here because I intend to chew them out!"

The harassed young man left hurriedly, relieved at the chance to escape.

Richard looked out the window, blind to the brilliant day. His mind re-created the image of the handsome black man leaping for that silly little bastard's throat and Norah, eyes widened in dismay, then swiftly gaining control, her expression changing to one of earnest concern. She had been dealt a low blow and managed to look marvelous, goddamn it!

The news had flashed her airport press conference directly after showing the fracas. She'd handled it brilliantly. There was no way he could continue to ignore her challenge.

His own idiots had handed the bitch credence by inventing a statement he'd never made. Some crap about "Ashley's arrogant disdain and hostile attitude" toward minority students. Garbage! No one would buy it. And even if it weren't unbelievable, it portrayed him as recognizing the existence of her candidacy. And that was exactly what he hadn't wanted to do. Damn them! He'd better get back to California and shore up the campaign.

CHAPTER
Eighteen

To Marianne's relief, Bailey appeared to be as anxious to avoid contact with her as she was to avoid it with him. On the few occasions when their paths did cross, they had merely nodded to each other.

Concha had seen to it, without making comment, that Bailey's personal belongings were taken to the downstairs guest suite.

The upstairs living quarters were so removed from the guest rooms that she and Bailey hadn't felt the other's presence in the immense house.

McFarland had been replaced by a new foreman. Marianne suspected that Bailey had his lover living nearby, but she saw no reason to pursue her suspicions. She had no interest in how or where or with whom Bailey spent his days or nights, as long as he kept his distance from her.

Whenever she returned to the Casa after a political junket with her father or from a stolen moment in the Springs with Manuel, she would sleep late in the morning and Concha had taken to serving her breakfast on a tray in her bedroom.

The evenings when Marianne dined alone at the Casa, she was served in the library.

On the few occasions her father stayed overnight, he made no comment about Bailey's absence. To her relief no questions were asked.

For Marianne all that mattered now were the moments she and Manuel had together. She had no interest in or intention of coming to grips with the disintegration of her marriage, such as it was.

Her father's campaign provided her with mobility and cover. Best of all, it made it unnecessary for her to explain or justify her frequent absences from the Casa.

Therefore, it came as a shock to Marianne to find Bailey beside her car, holding open the door for her in mock chivalry just as she was preparing to leave for a bit of precious time with Manuel.

"Good morning. How lucky for me to catch a glimpse of my own dear wife. I've missed you, my love. You look radiant, more beautiful than ever."

She slid into the car without a word. Bailey closed the door, pushing his face close to hers.

"Off to help your daddy? Or off for a little love in the afternoon."

She turned the key in the ignition, but her hand was shaking. He knew! How? Had he followed her? Or was he just bluffing, testing?

The handsome face she had come to loathe turned ugly. "I have a message for that Mex of yours, *Mrs.* Redfern," Bailey said menacingly. "Tell him that humping my wife could prove dangerous to his health!"

Marianne pressed her foot on the accelerator full force. The car jerked forward, throwing Bailey off balance. Through the rearview mirror, she could see him pick himself up off the driveway and slowly dust the sleeves of his jacket. He stared after her, undiluted hatred distorting his face.

The encounter ruined the drive from the Casa to Palm Springs. The sense of escape, the anticipation of seeing Manuel, of making love to him again, should have made the trip joyous and swift. But it was spoiled by the sight of Bailey, her own anxiety, and his ominous threat. Damn him!

She arrived at their desert hideaway in a foul mood. She turned the key in the lock and kicked open the brightly painted door, as the desert wind whipped her body and Bailey's hateful face floated before her. She slammed the door shut quickly, threw her coat on the chair in the hallway, and carried the bulging grocery bags into the miniature kitchen. She shrugged as she put the salad greens in the colander. Surely she was overreacting. Bailey wouldn't risk his neck any more than he'd risk losing the money she regularly placed in his bank account, she reassured herself.

She put steaks in the refrigerator and a bottle of red wine on the kitchen table. Marianne loved preparing their meals, playing house. Other than as a place to visit over a cup of coffee with Concha, the kitchen had never before been of any interest to her.

The cottage was her *petit Trianon.* Oh God, Marie Antoinette, she'd gotten hers. Poor thing. The analogy enveloped her in a mood of sadness. She sat down on the brightly painted bentwood chair and lit a cigarette.

How could she have fantasized that they would be insulated here from the outside world? How could they have pretended Bailey didn't exist for them? They were locked in the present. They had no future, nor could they dream of one. Even if she were free of Bailey—then what? Would Manuel marry her, spend his life with her? Love her?

She sighed. He loved her; she knew that. But he hated what he thought she represented. She knew that too. It was a powerful bigotry on his part. She was no more responsible for being a Thayer than he was for being a Vasquez. That is, if he was. She couldn't erase Bailey's dark hints about the Colonel and Concha from the back of her mind. Suppose they shared the same blood? Someday they'd have to talk about it. Throw it out into the open.

She shook herself. Bailey had spooked her, the bastard. She must get busy, move, forget the doubts. She put out her cigarette. Manuel loved seeing her in a long skirt and shirt, hair loose, awaiting him. She went into the bedroom and changed her clothes, opened windows, plumped pillows. By forcing herself into activity she felt her spirits rising. The sun lowered abruptly behind the mountains, the shadows lengthened. Now the street became active with sounds of cars heading into carports, children's voices, the early evening noises. Men coming home. Hers, too. For once in her life Marianne felt herself at one with the rest of the world.

She checked the grandfather clock in the entrance hall. It was after six, he'd be "home" in a little while. She had read in the newspapers that the following morning Manuel would head a delegation of farm workers to meet the train the Ashley campaign was running across the state. She herself would be flying to the wine country with her father to attend a festival the vintners were giving in his honor. She and Manuel had so little time together. But tonight would be their own.

Forgetting her earlier misgivings, she set the little table in the kitchen with plates and cutlery and began the preparation of their dinner.

By seven o'clock the street had grown quiet, dusk had fallen. She turned on the lamps and listened for the sound of Manuel's car. He was late.

By eight o'clock Marianne began worrying. She eyed the telephone. Whom could she call? The silence increased her sense of isolation. Hesitantly, she dialed information for the Farm Workers Office telephone number. No, she must not. He might resent it. She'd be embarrassed asking for him. She could always hang up, couldn't she? She drew in her breath and dialed the number—three, four, five rings. She tried again. There was still no answer.

Could he have forgotten? Her heart sank. They had made the arrangements ten days ago. Surely, if his plans were changed, he could have gotten a message to her, somehow!

Marianne went to the kitchen and poured herself a glass of wine. The house had grown chilly. She lit the gas jet in the fireplace. The imitation logs gave the illusion of warmth as she settled herself in a brightly patterned armchair and waited.

Marianne heard the screeching of brakes and a thud, and the slamming of doors. She realized she must have fallen asleep. Rousing herself, she ran to the door. Her eye caught the face of the clock as she hurried past it. It was after midnight. The bone-chilling cold of the desert wind cut her as she went outside. Moonlight caught the rear end of a blue van speeding into the night. She ran across the lawn to where he lay, motionless, blood pouring down his battered face. His eyes were closed.

She flung herself across his body. The last thing she remembered was the sound of her own voice, a piercing animal-like shriek that shattered the perfect stillness of the night.

*　　*　　*

"I did it for *you,* Bailey! I didn't mean to break his goddamn head open; the son of a bitch fell back into the fucking toolbox!" He shuddered and tightened his grip on Bailey's knees, resting his head on the lean thighs, pleading, "Don't make me go away, Bailey! I only wanted to sock it to that bitch on account of you." Raising his head slowly, Lonny said, "I hate that rotten cunt."

Bailey's hand reached for the back of his head. He loved the feel of the crisp, curly hair growing at the nape of the muscular neck. Looking into the troubled, tear-filled eyes, he said gently, "Jesus, Lonny, I didn't mean for it to turn out like this. You were only supposed to follow him so I'd be able to shaft Marianne and get some more bread for *us*. I've got to get you out of here *fast* for your own good." Bailey's fingers moved rhythmically, stroking the strong back under the denim shirt. "You know that, don't you?"

Lonny raised his head silently and nodded.

Bailey lifted the dark head, holding the tear-stained face in both his hands.

"There ain't nobody ever gonna love you like I do, Bailey."

Bailey was sure of it. He bent over, tasting the salty tears as their lips met hungrily.

CHAPTER

Nineteen

⌇⌇⌇

The governor of California, looking like a riverboat gambler in his white linen suit, stood alongside Norah on the observation platform of the "Ashley Special." Others in the party had left to recover in the air-conditioned lounge car. He waved to the crowd with exaggerated vigor, smiling broadly, revealing the perfect white teeth. The train slowly began to pull out of the depot to begin its whistle-stop pilgrimage into the sunbaked flatlands, the heart of agrarian California.

Norah was engulfed in nostalgia. Like everybody else in America, she too had succumbed to the pressures of time and forsaken trains for planes. She remembered the golden coach that had carried her away forever from Broad Street Station and north Philadelphia. She remembered particularly the luxury of the dining car. In later, affluent years nothing had ever tasted quite as wonderful as the succulent baked apple, dripping with thick cream, the indulgence she'd permitted herself her first day away from home, en route to New York.

The waving crowd of well-wishers, the brass of the high school band's instruments, golden in the bright sunlight, gradually receded from view. The "oom-pah" sounds of "California, Here We Come" were muted by the chugging and whistling of the Special as it gained a rhythmic momentum.

For Norah it was more than a political foray and an exercise in nostalgia, it was a sentimental journey back into the beginnings of her political life. It was Tom who'd brought her to this valley. Here she'd felt the first stirrings of her political conscience. She reluctantly accepted Tom's thesis that the migrant farm workers were archaic, latter-day dinosaurs. Soon they'd be replaced by machines marching across the fields. Mechanized fingers would pick the grapes, strip the fruit from the stems, and place it in little baskets to be shipped to the marketplace untouched by human hands. But she was equally aware that the battle for unionization was still crucial to the protection of the survivors.

There was no question but that the main thrust of her campaign had to be directed to the complexities of today's world. Tom's demand that she lean hard on the issues of the interdependence of nations and the protection of the individual from the overwhelming power of big government made good sense. Although he took a dim view of emotionalism, she'd seen him turn livid with rage when he got going on the managerial military complex and the reckless destruction of the environment. Despite the huge orders his company filled for government, he never lost sight of the potentially destructive effects generated by its by-products. Somehow this journey brought on a longing for her original passionate commitment. She could easily see why Peter chose to attach himself to Manuel. There was a right and a wrong in his cause. There were none of the vague areas in which she was forced to flounder. She'd promised Lisa she'd reopen the abortion and welfare issues with Tom when the whistle-stop trip was over. And she would keep her word. There were no gray areas for her on these issues. There was only a pang of remorse for the one time she'd compromised on it.

The morning after their return from San Diego Lisa had asked Norah why she had spoken evasively on the two subjects. "Don't you believe in a woman's right to free choice and equal rights?" she asked, her eyes troubled. Norah found it difficult to meet her gaze and fiddled nervously with the emerald ring.

Feeling her years, she'd finally looked up and said apologetically, "Of course I do, Lisa—but—"

"*But*—what?"

"The President and Tom don't want me to make an issue of them, especially abortion. The President must be getting some heavy pressure."

"And *you* agreed not to?" Lisa asked, her expression one of shock. Norah nodded. "Reluctantly."

"You mean you're not going to take strong positions on things *you* believe?" she asked, more in disappointment than anger.

"I don't know what to do."

"Remember what you said on the plane? Why should women vote for you? Why shouldn't they go for Hardwick? At least they know where he's coming from. Remember?" she questioned.

Norah sighed. "I remember all right. And I loathe myself for rolling over and playing dead, for equivocating. Do you trust me, Lisa?" she said to the serious-faced young woman.

"Of course!"

"Then give me time to sit down with Tom and lay it on the line. I promise you after the whistle-stop is over, I'll have my way. There'll be no more bland side steps from me. Okay?"

"Okay!" Lisa was quick to answer, her face lighting up in relief. Her idol hadn't tumbled and smashed, just tilted a bit. Poor dear Lisa, she hadn't the slightest notion of the compromises she herself would be obliged to make before she became a star, much less a politician. For a moment Norah wistfully remembered her own innocence. No, she didn't want to go back and repeat that journey. But whatever else, she wouldn't fail Lisa or herself, not on these issues. Tom and the President would have to respect her position. She wished Tom were with her instead of in Los Angeles editing her television commercials with Walt. Tom was no film expert—no one knew more about film than Walt—but Tom was convinced he understood political impact better than Walt did and he wasn't about to let any part of the operation take place without his supervision. In his mind it was the most important facet of her campaign. To him the whistle-stop was only a gimmick.

No ballet was choreographed more fastidiously than the timing of a political contest. The whistle-stop satisfied the desire to "see in the flesh" the image projected on the screen. The phenomenon was especially valuable to Norah, who still retained "screen power" in the public's mind.

The current polls indicated a strengthening of her credibility as a political personage and a lessening of her lightweight actress image. Her percentage gain against Hardwick's majority was still small. But the climb appeared steady. The time factor, itself a mystique, was crucial. The pacing of the race took expertise. She would never reach the finish line if she peaked prematurely. The campaign strategy was to force her strength to mount and Hardwick's to diminish at an accelerated rate so that she could overtake him at precisely the right moment. All stops were pulled, each detail planned. Sylvia Gannon had even conceived the idea of using a small gold star to replace the standard campaign button. It was a way of making the actress issue a plus, throwing it at them. No hokey ploy was too small. Norah was the underdog.

The whistle-stop was the curtain raiser for the home stretch. From now until the fateful Tuesday in November she would be marketed to the public from one end of the state to the other. Her managers wanted no backward glances, no reappraisals or hesitancy.

The governor put his arm around her waist, pulling her toward him. The train curved into the endless, flat acres of farmland.

"Stop dreaming and I'll buy you a drink," he said. "That's some broad, your Mrs. Gannon. She wouldn't remove her teeth from my throat until she had me on this train. Hell"—he chuckled, holding the heavy door for her, giving her a gentle pat on her behind as she walked past him—"I wouldn't have missed this for the world."

Norah glanced over her shoulder. "I'll bet you wouldn't. You're an old lecher, Governor, and please—for both our sakes—easy on the drinking! At least until after Fresno."

The car was packed with her supporters, reporters, "Bag-Its," staff, and —to Norah's relief—a large number of students. The San Diego fiasco was still painfully fresh in her mind.

Barbara Potter, wearing the inevitable jeans, was sitting at a table with Mellon, Brookings, and Lisa Ryder. Norah looked anxiously for Manuel, concerned that she hadn't yet seen him. This was his territory. Strange, she thought, he wasn't here. Perhaps he was gathering up his people and would meet them at Fresno. He had a disconcerting way of disappearing, that one.

Gold stars sprinkled jackets and dresses. She must remember to pin one on the governor at the Fresno stop. It might be a useful maneuver to cut him off, should he become swept away with his own oratory. He was famous for his lack of terminal facilities. Once he got started, it was hard to get him away from a microphone.

Norah spotted the Gannons standing at the bar in the rear of the car, engrossed in earnest conversation with Evelyn Auerbach.

Thank God, Karl wore his mantle of labor leadership with indifference. Had they suspected him of being the power center he was, known the influence and money he could wield, they would have zeroed in on him, just as Sylvia had on Walt, and Norah would have had another crisis to contend with. Most people felt a reluctance to use their friends. The Gannons seemed reluctant to choose friends they couldn't use. She wished she didn't need Sylvia, but she did. This was no time to make changes.

God, what a time Evelyn, in her overbred innocence, had given her earlier in the week. Eyes blazing, she'd marched into her office and slammed the door behind her with a crash.

"Have you gone mad, sending Sylvia Gannon to Sacramento?" she hissed.

"What do you mean?"

"The governor will try to screw her, and from what I hear, Sylvia will probably let him."

"So?"

"Scandal," Evelyn said. "And we don't need it."

Norah was annoyed. It was probably a geriatric symptom, but the older she got, the more she resented criticism.

Making an attempt at conciliation, she said, "For God's sake, Evelyn, we've been good friends for years. Trust me, sit down, and stop glaring."

"I prefer standing," was the hostile reply.

Norah sighed, her patience thinning. "Okay, my friend, then just let me tell you this. Sylvia Gannon is a brilliant political entrepreneur who happens to be in charge of the whistle-stop arrangements. The governor's presence is a crucial part of those arrangements. Sylvia can be relied upon to get that bastard on the train, as well as to take care of herself. Both she and her husband are power addicts; the very scent of it sends their tails wagging. Believe me, William Gannon is delighted to piggyback his career on his wife's conquests."

"You're crazy, Norah." Evelyn's glance was contemptuous.

Leaning across the desk, temper mounting, voice raised, good intentions forgotten, Norah shouted, "Sylvia Gannon would be *thrilled* to be invited to Sacramento, and by the time she's done her thing in the governor's bed, if necessary, her husband will be offered a place in that idiot's administration. What's more, he'll grab it!" She sure as hell wasn't going to betray Walt by telling Evelyn how Sylvia had seduced him. Evelyn would have to trust her, take her word for the Gannons' ambitions.

Making a constrained effort to conceal her impatience, she said, "Come on, Evelyn, calm down. You've been in politics long enough to know that the purpose of a campaign is spelled W-I-N. I *need* the governor's help. So he ducked the primary campaign. You can't minimize the value of his support *now!* He happens to be *the* ranking political figure in the state of California, whether or not he meets your patrician standards of good breeding."

Evelyn bristled. She had made a life's work of proving her liberalism. She straightened herself to her full height and walked to the door. Hand on the knob, she turned her head and looked at Norah with mournful disapproval. "Everybody's a whore. All that matters is the price."

She'd pointedly kept her distance since then. At the sight of the governor, who followed a few yards behind Norah, Evelyn's face took on an expression of stiff disapproval.

Sylvia, of course, broke into a broad smile at the governor's approach. As she offered her cheek for him to kiss, she made certain her full breasts brushed his arm. The governor lingered an extra moment over the proffered cheek, straightened up, offered his hand to her husband, and said, "Ah, there you are! You must be the lucky fella."

Tillie stood watching the scene with a mixture of distaste and relief. The transferal had taken place. Too bad Walt wasn't there to witness it.

William Gannon said, "I'm pleased to meet you, sir. Sylvia's told me so much about you."

Norah flinched. They were about to have a contest in clichés. The governor had a doctorate in political science. Gannon obviously had earned his in the law, and here they stood swamping each other in banalities. She looked at Evelyn as the governor slapped the lawyer on the back and said, "After we get our girl here elected, I'd like us to have a little chat, Bill. I think my administration could use a bright, young lawyer." Fixing his best "cornpone" benevolent look on Sylvia, he winked, "I think this little lady would add a lot of sunshine to Sacramento."

"Why, thank you, sir," Gannon said, solemn with respect.

Evelyn's eyes widened, meeting Norah's glance. Norah shrugged, relieved that the only loss was Evelyn's own innocence, not Evelyn's friendship. Bitterly, she thought, she couldn't afford to lose a friend any more than she could afford to offend the Gannons.

The blaring of the Mariachi Band above the sound of cheering voices thrust Norah back into the present. The train was groaning its way to Fresno. Sylvia Gannon had done her job. The "pro-Ashley" groups were gathered, as planned, at their appointed stations. Their bodies had been delivered en masse.

Sylvia had carefully rooted out a group of disgruntled growers, the owners of smaller vineyards and ranches, whose survival was threatened by the absentee landlords, the Hardwick aficionados. These men were anxious to make their support of Norah visible. The farm workers themselves wore holiday dress; many of the women were in the native costumes of the countries from which they'd come to California. Placards waved in the air, reading, "*Viva* Ashley," "*Viva La Raza,*" as well as "Yugoslavs and Armenians for Ashley." Leaders of various groups were to join them on the train and travel with them as far as Delano.

Lisa Ryder stepped onto the observation platform. She looked undressed, despite her high-necked, demure linen outfit, and she brought appreciative whistles from the cameramen. She's where I began, Norah thought wistfully. All she's doing now is adding a bit of dazzle. And she's becoming hooked on politics. Twenty years from now she, too, might run for office. From sex symbol to senator.

Tillie stood at her side, gold star ready in her hand, and surveyed the crowd. Norah spotted Peter shoving his way through the crowd. He was clearly looking for Manuel, who surely would join the train here in Fresno.

The governor, arms held aloft for attention, stepped forward to the microphone and began, "My friends, Californians, and countrymen." The crowd was then treated to an extensive litany on the virtues of his administration. Finally he remembered he was there to support Norah. At long last, he exhorted, "I need her. The President needs her." He pointed his finger and bellowed, "You need her!" The crowd roared approval. Before he could qualify his endorsement, Tillie elbowed Norah and handed her the pin, commanding in a whisper, "Stick it on Mark Antony *now* before they die of the heat and oratory!"

Norah moved to the microphone, pin in hand, took a firm grip on the white linen lapel, and said, "With this, I do pronounce thee my star supporter, Governor," kissing him for the benefit of the onlookers, the networks, and the national press. She had the old sophist locked into her campaign despite himself. She made a short speech of gratitude and plunged into the business of shaking hands. The crowd surged up the stairs to the platform where she stood with the governor beside her. If only the election could take place here and now. Was she beginning to believe her own publicity? The scent of victory was heady stuff, but it was wise to stay realistic. She'd better watch it. Illusions could be fatal.

Peter returned to the train followed by a group of farm workers anxious to shake hands with Norah and the governor.

The governor was visibly wilting. His jowled face had turned scarlet from the heat. He clutched a handkerchief in his left hand and mopped the gathering beads of perspiration, while he continued to shake the proffered hands. "Let's get the show on the road, Norah," he whined out of the corner of his mouth. "I'm fading fast."

Norah signaled Sylvia and noticed Peter in the crowd milling around again. Christ, he was still searching for Manuel. Damn it! We're ready to leave and he's running around looking for Manuel, who bloody well should have been here by now. Why the hell didn't Tom come along on this crazy trip? It's unbearably hot, the governor's about to have a stroke, and that boy is holding things up. I'm not supposed to be running this circus, Tom is. And he's in a nice air-conditioned studio in Los Angeles when I need him here! She turned to Tillie and said, irritably, "Will you please get that kid of mine back on this train?"

All her earlier pleasure in the warmth of her reception dissipated in the heat of the sun. Just before they pulled away, a small, starched, large-eyed child presented her with a bouquet of flowers, the trumpets of the Mariachi Band blared "Auld Lang Syne," and the train began to move. Sylvia hadn't missed a trick.

The governor whistled, "If I had known this trip was going to be a death trap, I'd have brought along that silly son of a bitch, the lieutenant governor. Least I could do for the state of California." Taking her elbow, he ordered, "Get me a drink!" He looked up from under his brows. "Thought you were putting one over, didn't you, lady, when you stuck that pin on me? You dealt me the proverbial hook, just as I was waxing my most eloquent."

"Come on, Governor, you've earned your drink." Norah put her arm through his, anxious to return to the cool indoors herself.

A drawing room directly beyond the lounge had been set aside for

Norah's exclusive use. She made her way through the car slowly, forcing herself to smile and chat, trying to look composed, making a special point to thank Lisa, who still managed to look cool and beautiful despite the pressure cooker heat. Observing the young woman's excitement, she said, "Perhaps you'll be my successor, Lisa. Politicking is addictive."

Mrs. Manley was waiting for her in the compartment with a fresh beige silk dress, the exact duplicate of the one she was wearing. She had insisted on playing lady's maid, rejecting the offer of Norah's old studio dresser to come out of retirement to help. She had rebuffed the dresser huffily: "I know perfectly well how to take care of Mrs. Ashley." When Norah had shown concern as to *who* would take care of Tom's needs in Mrs. Manley's absence, the crusty housekeeper assured her, "That lazy bastard, McPherson can do very nicely, madame."

"Why, Mrs. Manley, how can you talk about him that way?" Norah chided. Mrs. Manley was really getting out of hand.

"I think that business of yours of 'telling it like it is' is very good, madame, and I've taken it to heart," she answered primly.

Her personality had taken on a whole new character since she had become a camp follower.

Norah slipped on the fresh dress and repaired her face.

Mrs. Manley studied her appreciatively. "Well now, you look like something!"

Norah hugged the plump figure and said, "Mrs. Manley, please tell it like it *ain't* to me!"

*　*　*

The faces at Delano told the whole story. There were no young. The merciless sun burned away youth. Children were born old. Even the adoption of the long-handled hoe, which put less stress on bent and weary backs, had not significantly eased the physical burden of these protein-starved people. Norah felt a strong emotional attachment to the men and women who greeted her. Forgetting the fatigue and heat, Norah took the governor by the hand and walked into the crowd with him, overriding the protests of the security men.

Peter tapped her shoulder excitedly. "Mom, Dad and Mellon just arrived. They're waiting for you in your drawing room."

"It's about time!" she exclaimed with relief. "Tell him to come and join us, darling."

The governor laughed, "I knew Tom'd never leave us alone."

Peter shook his head. "I asked him to, and he said he'd rather wait for you inside."

"That man's no fool," the governor growled.

As soon as the last farewells were made and the usual bouquet presented, Norah rushed to her private drawing room to see her husband. It was strange that he and John hadn't joined the others in the lounge, she thought. She opened the door, took one look at the two men, and her spirits fell. Tom, his face drawn, drew her to him in a perfunctory embrace. Mellon sat smoking, staring out the window. Peter stood silent at the open door. His father motioned for him to enter, saying to Mrs. Manley, who was sweeping up clothes and cosmetic jars, "Just let it be, Mrs. Manley. We'll call you as soon as Mrs. Ashley needs you."

"What's happened? You look terrible!" Norah asked.

He seated himself opposite her, taking her hands in his. "Norah, there's been an accident."

Before he could continue, Peter, the color drained from his face, said flatly, "It's Manuel, isn't it?"

Tom nodded.

"*Tell* me, Tom! Is he hurt? Ill? What's happened?" She should have known something was terribly wrong when Manuel hadn't joined them in Fresno. "Oh God. Is he dead?"

Tom shook his head and said quickly, "He's alive. But he's been seriously injured."

Peter's anguish had cut into Tom. He'd carefully rehearsed how he'd break the news gently to his wife and son. Now, damn it, he'd forgotten how he was going to do it. There was no way to minimize the horror; he couldn't cushion the blow. Norah and Peter were staring at him, waiting. He took a deep breath, trying to keep his voice calm.

"Manuel was found unconscious on the lawn in front of a house belonging to Richard Hardwick's daughter, Marianne Redfern. He's probably in surgery now. Apparently, he took some kind of a fierce beating. There's a blood clot on his brain. If they can get to it and break it down, he may just make it. There's hope, Peter."

Peter's voice was icy. "Who did it? What was Manuel doing *there*?"

Tom shook his head. "We don't know. We just don't know, son. Mrs. Redfern's in a state of shock but has some vague recollection of seeing the rear end of a van speeding away. They found one abandoned twenty miles from the place. It contained bloodstains and fingerprints. The police are checking it out. It was registered in the name of somebody called McFarland."

Norah frowned. The name meant nothing to her.

John Mellon turned away from the window and faced them. "McFarland! Christ! He's the man I talked to in the bar at Thayerville." He scowled, cigarette dangling, the ash growing precariously long. "He sure as hell didn't sound as if he had any love for Hardwick." He shook his head, spraying ashes. "In fact, I had the feeling he was downright hostile to him. This is crazy."

Peter's face flooded with color. "I'll kill the dirty bastard. I'll kill him. I *knew* something terrible happened when Manuel didn't meet us," he shouted.

Tom glared at him. "Shut up and sit down," he ordered. "We don't need any adolescent hysterics."

Norah leaned back against the seat and closed her eyes. Whatever he might have become, Richard couldn't have been a party to an act of raw brute violence. Or could he? And why Manuel? His role in the campaign was not that important, nor particularly visible. Was she somehow to blame? The guilt and doubt were unbearable.

She opened her eyes and looked at her son. He was quiet, slumped forward in his seat, holding his head in his hands. She reached out and touched his face. His angry outburst had chilled her. And the thought of gentle Manuel bruised and battered fighting for his life was too horrifying to grasp. "Where is he?" she asked.

"At the Memorial Hospital outside of Palm Springs."

"I want to go to him, Tom, please get me off this train. He's so private about himself. Does he have any family? Is anyone with him? I can't bear the thought of him suffering alone." Her eyes filled. "Please!"

"Calm down, Norah. We've second-guessed you. The plane is waiting in L.A. We've called the hospital, they're expecting you. As for family, apparently he has a mother and an aunt who're with him now." Tom addressed himself to Peter, his voice stern. "I want you to go with your mother and help her through this. No matter what you feel, I expect you to keep yourself under control and to take care of her. Do you understand?"

"Yes, sir. I understand," Peter answered, meeting his father's gaze.

"Aren't you coming with us?" Norah asked Tom.

He shook his head. "I really have to get back to the studio. Walt and I should have all the film spots pulled together by tomorrow. John will go along and handle the press. I'm sure they'll be hovering. Brookings'll take care of them in L.A. All the arrangements have been made, Norah. The hospital superintendent is expecting you. You'll be driven to the emergency entrance, to avoid the reporters. There's nothing you can or should say to them. Okay?"

He kissed her, putting his fist under her chin. "You all right?"

She nodded. But was she?

CHAPTER
Twenty

The superintendent of Palm Springs Memorial Hospital nervously hurried into the hospital's emergency entrance, bypassing the crowd of reporters standing vigil in front of the hospital. Violence was newsworthy, and violence in a political campaign had enormous possibilities for exploitation. Mellon, hoping for any new leads on the beating that might have cropped up, left Norah inside the entrance so he could join the press.

The anxious superintendent accompanied Norah and Peter in the service elevator up to the surgical floor. The only information he could give Norah was that Manuel had been brought to the hospital in critical condition and was in surgery. He assured her that word would be sent as soon as possible to her and to Manuel's family, with whom she would wait during the operation. He escorted them down the hall to the reception room. The immediate effect of the dreary, sparsely furnished room on Norah was to intensify her gloom.

The room contained several occasional chairs and a long rectangular table of doubtful Swedish origin. The scarred surface of the table was cluttered with glass ashtrays, outdated copies of the *National Geographic*, and a bouquet of wilting flowers. A large bleak desert painting of mauve hills and barren flatlands added to the depressing ambience.

At the sight of the harassed superintendent, two women seated on the dark couch at the far end of the room immediately stood up and hurried toward him. They must be Manuel's mother and aunt, Norah thought. The taller of them was a striking-looking woman. Her graying hair was cut close to her well-shaped head, which exaggerated her unusually large eyes fringed with heavy lashes. Her dark brows were arched and clearly defined. The shorter, softer-looking woman had black hair knotted at the nape of the neck and pulled back from the rounded brow.

The taller woman, ignoring Norah and Peter, asked the superintendent in a hushed voice, "Is there any word?"

"Not as yet, Mrs. Romo, it's too soon!" He introduced Norah and Peter, explaining, "Mrs. Romo is Manuel Vasquez's aunt, and this is his mother, Mrs. Vasquez."

Norah felt the austere figure hesitate, but Manuel's mother quickly offered her hand.

"May we wait with you?" Norah asked. "I cannot understand why anyone would harm Manuel. He's a fine man, Mrs. Vasquez, and we honor him," she said, her face reflecting their own anguish. "Do you know this McFarland? Does he have something to do with the farm labor dispute?" Juanita Vasquez, dark eyes brimming, shook her head. Biting her lips to hold back her own tears, Norah asked hesitantly, "Could it have been something to do with my campaign?"

Concha, her voice firm, said, "Mrs. Ashley, we know very little." She paused. "But we do know the motive for the beating had nothing to do with politics." Searching Norah's face, she said, "You are blaming yourself. That is wrong."

"But, my god, then who—what—?" Norah asked in anguish.

Concha studied her hands, averting Norah's gaze. Her thick lashes shadowed her high cheekbones and veiled her dark eyes. "It was a personal matter."

"What can I do to help?" Norah pleaded.

Concha looked up at her sharply. "Please, Mrs. Ashley—just pray."

Clearly, Norah thought, the woman wanted no further discussion. They lapsed into silence, each one encapsulated in private agony.

Concha thought, She is very beautiful, this Ashley woman. And the boy —I can see he is suffering. They are fearful that it is her campaign against Senator Richard that has brought about this evil act. I will tell you something, God. You too, Blessed Mary. If Manuel lives, if you will let him live, I will tell this woman what I have done. What I did for Senator Richard, knowing it was dishonest. Now I am ashamed. Politics are filthy, what difference who wins? It is all the same. I tried to do as the Colonel wished. Did I not, God? He would have wanted Senator Richard to win. Was that not what the Colonel desired more than anything in the world?

Juanita sat beside her, praying quietly. Poor thing, she'd been horrified when Manuel told them he'd joined with the Ashley forces. In her mind, a betrayal of Senator Richard was a betrayal of the *padrón,* the Colonel, their benefactor. But now as Manuel lay fighting for his life, she found she understood why. It had nothing to do with betrayal. It was an act of independence, and morality. "Let him live, God," she pleaded in silence, "and I will not be a slave to the past any longer. I vow it," she bargained.

The sound of footsteps in the corridor roused them from their private thoughts.

Richard Hardwick stood at the door. A young woman, her face hidden by the scarf tied around her head, rushed past him into the room. "Oh Concha, he can't die!" she sobbed. Concha held her, patted her shoulder, and rocked her gently as if she were a small child. Her dark, questioning eyes sought out those of Richard Hardwick.

Hardwick had seated himself in the chair next to Juanita and taken her hand in his to reassure her. "Conway, the surgeon, is one of the best in the world. I had him flown in from San Francisco. He'll do everything possible to save Manuel, Juanita."

Concha whispered something to Marianne. The young woman pulled away from her and stared at Norah, who had risen from her chair, Peter beside her. Richard looked up, recognized Norah, and froze in disbelief. He got to his feet slowly, the handsome features drawn, the sun-etched lines deep with fatigue.

"Norah Jones!" He came toward her, arms outstretched in greeting. What in God's name was *she* doing here? Then he remembered. Manuel was working for her. A flash of anger ran through him. He checked himself. Poor bastard, he was dying.

Norah remained motionless and unsmiling, as shocked to see him as he was to see her. She made no move to offer her hand. She was taken aback by his presence.

"Norah Jones *Ashley,* Senator!" she corrected. "This is my son, Peter." Her tone was cold and impersonal.

Richard looked at the tall youth, who had taken the cue from his mother and made no gesture of greeting toward him other than a nod of recognition.

He could have been my son, he thought, his chest tightening. No, he's too much like his father. Only the eyes. The eyes are Norah's.

The youth stared at him, equally shocked that he would be at the hospital, speaking familiarly to Manuel's family. There was no doubt in Peter's mind that Manuel had been victimized because of his role in his mother's campaign, no matter what the aunt told them. Hardwick recognized his mother instantly—and called her by name. Jesus, everybody in the world who'd ever seen her movies thought he knew her. Even this bastard. This murderer.

Hardwick felt Peter's unspoken accusation. "Manuel is like a member of our family," he exclaimed, waving his hand in Marianne's direction. "He and my daughter were reared in tandem, as siblings. And I'm as shocked as you are by what has happened to him."

Norah looked at the fine-boned young woman; she had removed her scarf. The cloud of auburn hair fell to her shoulders.

She didn't resemble her father any more than Peter resembled her. For an instant Norah tried to equate the middle-aged man facing her with the golden, sun-bronzed young god of the West who'd caught her eye in that crowded penthouse living room the night they'd first met. He had been so unlike anyone she'd ever met before.

Now a quarter of a century later, here they stood, facing each other in this miserable place, total strangers, opponents, equally bewildered by grim tragedy. She could see nothing of the young Richard in the man standing before her. Even in his distress, she sensed the steel-edged hardness of this well-preserved middle-aged man.

Norah was too deeply involved in her own feelings and the guilty fear that her campaign was responsible for the nightmare of the attack on Manuel to comprehend what Richard Hardwick was trying to tell her. She couldn't untangle her own feelings, much less the complex relationships of Manuel's family and Hardwick and his daughter, who was acting more like a grieving widow-to-be than a fond childhood friend.

"This McFarland, whose truck is evidently involved, used to work at Casa Thayer. He's no longer in our employ, by his own choice. I barely remember the man. You *must* believe me," Hardwick pleaded. "I have no idea why McFarland would want to harm Manuel."

Hardwick appeared desperately anxious to convince Norah of his innocence. Her silence bewildered him. Was it an accusation? "Do you think
I have time for the running of the Casa, the Senate, the campaign, *and* a
murderous assault on a man who was raised with my daughter?" His laugh
was bitter. "Why in God's name would I wish Manuel harm? Don't you
believe me?"

Believe him? Yes, she did. Surely the Richard she vaguely remembered
could not have turned into a murderer. Obviously he was deeply anguished. He stood before her a stranger, comforting his daughter and two
women who were clearly a part of his life. Whatever vague, personalized
fantasies of revenge she'd nurtured dissolved. This middle-aged man was
a senator whose policies she deplored, but who nevertheless shared with
her an agonizing concern for the young man struggling for life in the
nearby operating room. Quietly, she said, "I must believe you, Senator,"
and moved closer to Peter, who stood silent beside her.

The visible depths of Norah's anxiety roused Marianne. The poor
woman imagined her political campaign was in some way responsible for
this horror. But there was only one person responsible—Bailey! Marianne
shuddered, recalling Bailey's leering threat. It was she herself who'd
unleashed the disaster, by loving Manuel, by forcing him to love her.
She'd brought him to this. *She* was the leper! She'd tell them—everything
—about Bailey and McFarland, about Bailey's sick hatred for Manuel. But
before she could speak, there was the sound of voices and hurried footsteps coming down the hall.

A large man in a blood-spattered, sweat-stained surgical smock burst
through the door, his head wrapped in a surgical cap, a gauze face mask
loose at his neck.

"Mrs. Vasquez?" He looked around the room.

Juanita rose and went toward him, hope and fear mingling in her face.
"Will he live, Doctor?" she whispered.

He nodded. "Yes, Mrs. Vasquez, he will live."

"Thank God! Thank God!" Juanita sobbed.

The burly surgeon dug into his pocket for a cigarette and snorted.
"Thank George Conway!" He introduced himself to Hardwick. Then he
saw Norah and asked in astonishment, "Aren't you Mrs. Ashley?" He
couldn't figure out what she was doing here. The man she was running
against, Richard Hardwick, had called him in on the case.

"Yes, Doctor." Observing his surprise, she explained, "Manuel is a dear friend. He's part of my campaign." Offering her hand, she asked hesitantly, fearing the answer, "Will he recover—? I mean, fully?"

His answer only confused her further. Conway exhaled the smoke of the cigarette through his nostrils, the heavy brows drawing together. "If we're lucky, yes. If he hemorrhages again"—he shook his head—"then I don't know." A lopsided grin flickered across the ruddy face. "Now is the time to pray, Mrs. Vasquez," he said. The bushy brows knit into a scowl. "Your son sustained a terrible blow. By the time we got to him, he was decerebrating and his life signs were feeble." He shrugged. "We lucked out. The hematoma was located in the central part of the brain, and we were able to reach it in time. If he doesn't have a setback, there should be no permanent paralysis. Jesus, what a blow he took!" He let out a low whistle. "He's in intensive care now. He must be forced into consciousness. He'll resist waking, most people do after this kind of surgery. We have to fight that. I need someone he can recognize to come with me." Questioningly, he looked at Juanita. "We may have to be a little rough to force him awake. Are you up to it, Mrs. Vasquez?"

Before Juanita could reply, Concha spoke. "Marianne Redfern will go with you, Doctor."

Hardwick explained hastily, "Marianne is my daughter, Doctor. Manuel will recognize her."

"Come," Conway commanded. "You and I are going to bring the patient back to life."

Marianne felt the blood rushing through her veins. Hope had replaced the torpor of fear in her body. Manuel was alive!

Taking her hand, Conway led Marianne swiftly down the dimly lit corridor until they reached a heavy door with the words "Authorized Personnel Only" painted across it. The doctor pushed the button on the adjoining wall and spoke into the small speaker beside it. "Conway here!"

A disembodied woman's voice replied, "Come in, Doctor." There was the sound of electronic clicking as he pushed open the door and held it for Marianne.

They entered a large, brilliantly lit room filled with trays, test tubes, and machinery. Screens flickered with jagged streaks and bouncing lights. Nothing was still. The semicircular periphery held curtained cubicles. The endless activity and bright light came in sharp contrast to the quiet of the dark hallway. Marianne felt removed from time and space. A faceless, starched figure said, "Over here, Doctor." Marianne felt Conway's hand gripping her arm.

The nurse pulled back the curtain. Marianne gasped. Manuel was unrecognizable, a swollen mummy, connected to bottles and machinery by tubes and wires. Conway shouted, "Manuel, wake up! Tell me your name. Say it! Do you hear me?"

The response was an almost inaudible guttural noise. Manuel's eyes remained closed, his breath came in shallow gasps.

Conway leaned close to the supine figure, put his mouth next to the thickly bandaged head, and bellowed, "What's your name?"

Manuel stirred momentarily and relapsed back into his comatose state. The nurse at the other side of the bed looked up at the doctor, her face grim.

"Come here, Marianne." Conway reached out and pulled her beside him. Looking at her searchingly, he asked, "You all right?" She nodded.

Pulling back his right arm and making a fist, he delivered a heavy, thudding blow full force to Manuel's shoulder and boomed, "Marianne's here, Manuel. Do you see her? TALK!"

Marianne winced with the blow. Manuel opened the swollen eyes and saw her. "Who is it, Manuel? Tell me!" Conway yelled.

His mouth moved soundlessly at first, then with great effort he mumbled a barely audible, "Mm-arianne. Marianne."

"Louder!" Conway commanded.

"Marianne!"

CHAPTER

Twenty-one

Richard Hardwick sat in his San Francisco office and stared out at the Bay through the large uncurtained plate glass window, unseeing, blind with rage, waiting for Bailey.

The newspapers strewn across his desk carried headlines screaming, "Violence in California Senate Race," "Ashley Supporter Brutally Beaten," "Alleged Suspect Former Hardwick Employee," "Mysterious Circumstances Surround Political Violence," "Suspect Disappears." He, Richard Hardwick, was being implicated, and he goddamn well wanted to know where the suspect had disappeared to. He'd get the whole truth even if he had to wring Bailey's neck. He'd be damned if that perverted son of a bitch was going to do him in. Bailey sure as hell was going to come clean, and if Hardwick had to hang him along with McFarland, he'd be happy to see them swing in the wind together—at the end of an oiled rope if necessary.

Marianne had finally told him the entire disgusting story about McFarland and Bailey, and how Bailey had threatened her. He'd listened with disbelief as she hysterically poured out the saga of her liaison with Manuel and the house in Palm Springs, reiterating again and again that she was the aggressor. As if it mattered. Manuel wasn't forced to play house with her. But she kept insisting on wallowing in guilt, blaming herself for the disaster. He rubbed his hand across his eyes. He couldn't believe it. He didn't want to.

Christ, what crazy fascination did that servant's phony, self-righteous offspring have for her? He shrugged. She was his child; God knows, he wasn't in any position to sit in judgment of her. But to have this happen in the middle of his campaign . . . ! He was certain of one thing, he could goddamn well sit in judgment on that bastard Bailey. A ranch hand yet! A faggot rapist living off Marianne's money. He had to have been living off her money because he sure as hell never made any of his own! Hardwick's anger erupted again at the thought of it. And Bailey had raped her!

Hardwick hated his son-in-law, hated him with a passion stronger than any he'd ever felt before. His desk phone rang. "Bailey Redfern has arrived for his appointment, and a Mr. Fitzpatrick is calling from overseas," the operator told him.

"I'll take Fitzpatrick, tell Bailey to wait."

Oh God, he'd better get it over with. Fitzpatrick must have heard about the beating and the goddamn van and McFarland's connection with Casa Thayer. He could just see the beefy labor chieftain sitting in the sun boiling with rage in that banana republic he just about owned.

Let that son-of-a-bitch Bailey cool his heels! Christ, what a mess!

No matter how hard the attorney general's office, the press, and assorted reformers had tried, they'd never been able to stick Jimmy with mobster connections. He'd been too shrewd for them, scoffing openly at their unsuccessful attempts to link him to the underworld. James Kevin Fitzpatrick was a secure man, certain in the knowledge that the rank-and-file union membership would need a hell of a lot more than innuendos to push them into challenging his leadership. His people were the highest-paid workers in America, and they weren't about to turn on the man who increased their paychecks and fattened their pension fund every time he renegotiated their contracts. Let him live high on the hog. He produced. But criminality—that could be another story.

He'd dump me in a minute, Hardwick agonized, if he thought being in my camp linked him to a criminal act.

He felt his chest tighten. "Put him on," he told the operator. "Hi, Jimmy. How are things down there?" he said lightly, but his scowl intensified. He paused and listened.

"I'm looking at the headlines right now. What the hell do you think I think? It's a nightmare."

His insides turned over. "Are you out of your mind? My campaign didn't have a damn thing to do with it," he protested. "The fucking press is having a field day."

The voice at the other end of the line grew loud. Hardwick held the phone away from his ear. When the tirade subsided, he said, "Of course I want to win! What the hell has that got to do with it? . . . So he worked at the ranch. He's disappeared. For all I know, he could be in Mexico by now! . . . Did you say he's in Florida? Where in Florida? . . . Are you sure it's the right guy?" His heart dropped. "Oh Christ! The bartender! He blabbed to the bartender in some backwater swamp saloon? That's like taking out an ad! How do you know the bartender won't talk to the press? . . . Sure, I believe you, Jimmy, if you tell me he's your guy!" He listened in disbelief and spluttered, "Oh no!"

The facts didn't matter, he knew that for sure. He was going to be blamed and the shit could really hit the fan if Bailey's connection with McFarland were known. One thing was certain, he'd put his feet in the fire and swear he'd never heard what Jimmy Fitzpatrick had just said. Whatever the hell Fitzpatrick and his boys had in mind, he didn't want to know about it. "For Christ's sake," he shouted. "I don't want to know anything about this, do you hear me? Do you understand? I never talked to you." His voice dropped. "Good-bye, Jimmy." He hung up the phone. God, the goons were afraid it would rub off on them. They were afraid *his* connection with Beau Soleil would hurt *them* because of McFarland. What an irony. *He'd* given them respectability and now they saw him as an albatross. They were going to take care of McFarland in their own way. Hardwick was certain of it. He wanted no part or parcel of that kind of thing. Sick with hate for Bailey, he leaned toward the intercom and spat the words, "Send him in!"

The door opened; Bailey entered the office, half-grinning in studied nonchalance.

Richard spun around, his face congested with fury, breath coming in short gasps. "Shut the door."

"Sure! How are you, Dad? You wanted to see me?"

Hardwick clenched his fists and bellowed, "Don't you 'Dad' me, you son of a bitch. Sit down before I kill you."

Bailey settled himself in the armchair, facing the eighteenth-century table that served as the senator's desk. He slid down in the seat and stretched his legs. He waited in silence, his handsome face impassive.

Richard rose and moved toward him. He trembled with fury and pressed his hands together to keep them still. Standing over the sprawled figure of his son-in-law, who was impeccably dressed in Harris tweed, the brown tie faultlessly arranged in a wide Windsor knot, he snarled, "Okay, you little bastard, suppose you tell me all about that cocksucker McFarland. I want to know whether there's anything on him that can connect him with you and—"

Bailey interrupted him. "McFarland?" he questioned. "Who's McFarland?" the voice arch with feigned innocence. "Oh yeah, the foreman at the Casa! The one who left!" He looked up at his glowering father-in-law and smiled. "What would I know about a ranch hand. After all, I'm not all that palsy-walsy with the help. Ask my wife; she's very intimate with servants and maybe she—"

Hardwick's head exploded with rage. With all the strength in his body he struck Bailey across his face. His hand ached with the force of the impact.

The athlete's reflex was instant. Bailey jumped to his feet and drove his knee into Richard's groin. Hardwick doubled over with the searing pain. Swiftly, before he could recoup, Bailey swung his fist under the older man's jaw and sent him reeling back against the desk.

Stunned, Richard wiped the back of his hand across his mouth; it was covered with blood.

Bailey removed the carefully folded white handkerchief from his breast pocket and handed it to Richard. Resettling himself in the chair, he straightened his tie and said quietly, "Okay, Senator, what is it you wanted to know about some cocksucker? Or would you prefer to talk about the Beau Soleil deal?"

There was no question in Bailey's mind that his expense money would continue to be regularly placed in his account.

CHAPTER
Twenty-two

No movie mogul of latter-day Hollywood enjoyed as lavish a life-style as did Walt Lowman with his wife, Tillie. It was only natural that they should be the ones to entertain for the President when he opened his cross-country swing in behalf of his party's nominees in Los Angeles. California was crucial, Norah's victory was crucial, but above all Richard Hardwick's defeat was crucial to the President's political survival. It was his prime goal. As unacceptable to the professional politicians as his intervention had been in Norah's primary, it was not only acceptable but anxiously welcomed in the finals. Especially since the latest opinion polls showed public approval to be tilting slightly in favor of his administration. Despite the bombast of the opposition's rhetoric, the President was finally beginning to hold his own and then some.

The Lowman household had been in a state of chaos for days. Trucks rode through the gates delivering food, flowers, and furniture. The projection room was stripped bare. Its furnishings, placed in waiting vans parked at the rear end of the estate, were replaced by rented gilt chairs and round tables. The vast area would be transformed into a dining room for the three hundred guests. Tillie's own greenhouses had produced hundreds of red and white cyclamen, and every nursery in town had been raided as well. Electricians, florists, workmen, caterers, secretaries, and finally the Secret Service swarmed the estate. The President and the First Lady would stay in the main house, staff members in the guest quarters. No detail was overlooked by Tillie.

Although she'd been known to complain that she couldn't complete her good-mornings to the staff until dinnertime because of the enormous number of servants required to run the complex household, she was the supreme commander-in-chief of her operation.

The Italianate house had originally been built by an ill-fated oil tycoon from Oklahoma on five of the choicest acres in Beverly Hills. An impressed movie colony promptly dubbed it the Palazzo; the less respectful called it the Post Office. The house boasted the town's only private ballroom, which the tycoon had built for the purpose of launching his three daughters. Before his mission had been accomplished, several dry wells and a Senate investigating committee had made it necessary for him to sell the house to Walt and Tillie. The Lowmans promptly transformed the ballroom into a projection room, its vast dimensions filled with huge, comfortable sofas and deep armchairs. For all its gargantuan proportions, Tillie had managed to endow the house with a sense of lightness and charm. It provided a perfect background for the Lowman collection of impressionist paintings, as fine as any in the world, short of the Hermitage. The tile wall in the atrium off the dining room had been directly commissioned by the Lowmans from Matisse himself. The cutout primary-colored flowers, which decorated the individual tiles, had been reproduced and copied in everything from art books to posters and bed linens.

A two-ton Henry Moore female figure of enormous proportions stood permanent guard outside of the front entrance. It was mounted on a pivoting pedestal which could be turned by the lightest flick of a finger in order to provide the viewer a different angle, according to his whim. Norah still found it so impressive that now, twenty years after she'd first been a guest at the Lowmans', she never entered the house without giving the monumental sculpture a spin.

Tillie's greenhouses produced blooms at her will. Gardeners plucked and pruned the lush trees and foliage and kept the huge flowerbeds in color twelve months of the year. Despite the vagaries of the California climate, velvet green lawns carpeted the grounds as far as the eye could see. The tennis courts, pool, and guest cottage, invisible from the main house, were maintained and manicured in the same flawless fashion.

By deliberate intent, the highly polished, inlaid rosewood dining table with its pale rim of yew seated a maximum of twelve. If studio entertaining needs demanded seating for a larger group, the Lowmans called Chasen's to take over. Walt's idea of a first-class party was six at table, dinner served promptly at seven forty-five, followed by the running of a film in the projection room at eight forty-five.

His preference for small evenings created an additional aura of prestige to evenings at the Palazzo. Invitations to dine with Walt and Tillie were cherished by their friends and dreamed of by the social climbers because they were hard to come by. Hollywood parties were a part of Walt's work life, but he and Tillie found them dull and exhausting. They seldom entertained on a large scale.

The lowering of the bridge across the moat and the throwing open of the gates was a true testament of the Lowmans' devotion to the President and Norah.

Tillie insisted that Norah disinter her famous red velvet dress.

"You're crackers, worrying about my costume, Tillie, with all you have to do," she protested. "Besides which, if it should fit, which isn't too likely, it'll disintegrate on my back from sheer old age. Anyway," she grumbled, "I'm certain it's been given away by now."

"Bullshit! It'll fit, it won't disintegrate, and it's hardly the kind of drag the Salvation Army collects for the worthy poor. I'm doing my red tablecloth number again and"—she hesitated momentarily to conceal her embarrassment—"I'm sentimental about it!"

"Sentimental? *You*, Tillie?" Norah said, laughing. "It's out of character!"

"Well, *superstitious* is probably a better word," she countered quickly. "It worked the last time, didn't it?"

She had a point. After all, she had worn it the night the Lowmans introduced her to Tom. It was a good-luck dress. Tillie in her own brusque way was telling Norah the production was being built around her. But if Norah tried to thank her, Tillie would deny the plan vehemently.

The night was brilliantly clear. Searchlights scanned the sky. Helicopters droned overhead, an airborne reminder of the President's need for constant protection.

Armed guards and Secret Service men, intercom radios plugged into their ears, checked the Ashleys against their guest lists, then allowed their limousine to proceed through the gates. The blockade against crashers was complex and tight. Along the winding driveway leading to the house the trees were bejeweled with hundreds of tiny flickering lights. Cyclamen filled the flowerbeds. The sound of violin music floated through the night. More cyclamen surrounded the brilliantly lit approach to the house and lined the sides of the huge entrance hall. Pot after pot had been placed between the bannister spokes of the circular staircase leading to the upstairs balcony.

Tillie greeted them, arms outstretched, sheathed in a high-necked "little black nothing," slit up the side, revealing her long slim legs, of which she was justifiably proud. A king's-ransom jewel at her throat broke the elegant severity of her costume.

Norah embraced her. Tillie stood back to study her. "You're worthy of the backdrop!" She approved.

Walt, standing at her side, appraised Norah with admiration. "It still fits, Norah, after how many years?" Turning to Tom, he laughed. "I'll bet Tillie made her wear it. And she was right."

Tom leaned down and kissed Tillie. "I like *your* style, General."

"Stop the nonsense and get yourselves next to us at once. This is in *your* honor, you know," Tillie snapped sternly, failing to disguise her pleasure. She was in her element, doing what she did best. Walt ruled the tower, but here she was the empress.

"Where's the President?" Norah asked.

"He and Liz are dressing and will be coming downstairs at eight twenty-two, exactly," Walt replied.

Tillie looked toward the door and shuddered. "Oh God! Here comes Malice-in-Wonderland with that poor boob, Henry Goodrich."

"Shut up and smile, Tillie," Norah admonished. "He's not a 'boob.' He's given the President and me a fortune. I can't afford to alienate anyone, much less big spenders."

Catherine Goodrich sailed toward them, with Henry, her husband, a few paces behind her.

Despite his vast inherited wealth and descent from one of the early California pioneer families, Henry Goodrich was as liberal in his political attitudes as he was with his money. His unprepossessing appearance belied his strength of character. Henry was a staunch supporter of the President's party despite the disapproval of his reactionary

Pasadena relatives. He was among the first openly to declare himself in favor of Norah's candidacy.

Catherine Goodrich née Kelly had had a short-lived career as a film actress. Her one great triumph had been in inveigling Henry to marry her.

Her glimmering black sequin gown was cut low to expose breasts pushed into a billowing cleavage. A priceless necklace of square-cut diamonds encircled her long neck. She pressed her cheek against Tillie's in a phantom kiss and gushed, "It's divine, Tillie, divine!" She raised her finely arched brows and greeted Norah. "Norah, darling, you look heavenly in that red dress! Who else would have the *coraggio* to wear something of that vintage?" She paused, the brows drawing together. "Don't tell me Tillie's doing those same old red velvet cloths again?"

"Don't worry, Catherine, they'll give your gown high visibility," Norah countered. My God, Catherine remembered Norah's dress. She'd known her that long! Time hadn't mellowed Catherine. She was still the Harrion of Holmby Hills. Norah leaned forward to kiss Henry, and moved Catherine firmly along the line to Tom, exclaiming, "Henry, dear, you get younger all the time." It was the absolute truth; his pudgy looks had babyfied with age. He was singularly pink and white as well as a head and a half shorter than his wife. Tillie suggested that astride his pile of gold, Catherine managed to see him as tall and dark and very handsome.

Guests began arriving in a steady stream. No one would dare be late for the President. As soon as they had been greeted by their hosts and the Ashleys, the guests were tactfully ushered into the main living room by discreet butlers, offering them drinks. Tillie's expertise extended beyond the visual; her party strategy was skillfully planned, her staff facile and well trained. There would be no loitering or blocking of passageways. She was an old hand at the techniques of controlling crowds. The Secret Service could take lessons from Tillie.

When the huge, brilliantly lit room was filled, the mingling was inevitable. The congressional delegation fused with Hollywood celebrities, judges with business leaders, university presidents with union chieftains. Small candles placed among the greenery and two sparkling chandeliers added luminosity to the women's jewels and buffed complexions. A large Blue Period painting by Picasso dominated the far wall, and a rounded Maillol figure surrounded by greenery interspersed with small candles and flowers dominated the central part of the room.

The governor made his entrance with Sylvia Gannon, dressed in white chiffon, one tanned shoulder bared, holding on to his arm. William Gannon was a few steps behind them.

Norah, feeling Walt stiffen as they approached, went forward to meet them in order to ease the encounter.

Tillie, for all her bravado, was fiercely protective of her private life. Despite the intimacy of their friendship, she'd never once mentioned the episode at Luigi's to Norah. Norah had no knowledge of what had taken place between the Lowmans that disastrous night. But she could imagine.

In an attempt to lighten the moment, Norah tucked in the governor's shirt front as she greeted him.

He winked and said, "I hope you're being personal."

"Can't the state afford to hire someone to tidy you up, Governor?"

He flashed his large smile and pinched her cheek. "Norah, honey, think what I'd miss."

Tillie greeted him and the Gannons with frosty politeness, moving them along quickly.

Tom nudged Norah and tilted his head toward the door. Dan Brookings and John Mellon were following Lisa Ryder into the room. She was dazzling in a low-cut black velvet gown, the hem bordered in sable. Her hair was piled high on her head.

Norah greeted her with genuine pleasure. She saw her own youth reflected in the young actress. "Lisa, those two will never be the same! How will the President ever get them back to Washington after they've grown accustomed to spending time in your company?"

Norah never heard Lisa's answer. Glancing over Lisa's shoulder, she saw Walt, who'd left his place alongside Tillie to come toward her, accompanied by an elderly man.

Impeccably tailored, ramrod straight, the man looked familiar. Suddenly he was standing before her and took her hands in his. The gray hair shot with streaks of darkness exaggerated the bronze tan of his face, which was webbed with fine lines. The deep-set eyes studied her affectionately.

"You're still my beautiful *cara,*" he said, drawing her to him in a tight embrace.

"It's *you!* Guido!" Her voice rang with pleasure. "How did you—?"

"We thought we'd surprise you," Walt interrupted.

Eyes sparkling with joy, Norah reached for Tom excitedly. "Darling, it's Guido—Guido Di Brazza! Remember, he *discovered* me. My darling guru! Guido—my husband, Tom Ashley."

The men shook hands and Norah called to Tillie, "Oh Tillie, you *knew* he'd be here, and you didn't tell me!"

Tillie kissed Guido's cheek.

"What a wonderful surprise for Norah!" Tom said, trying to look pleased, studying the distinguished face with the high-bridged, triangularly nostriled nose. Very elegant, very European, very thoroughbred. He must have dazzled Norah. A pang of jealousy ran through Tom. Norah looked so young, so delighted, to see her old mentor. The look of the determined woman she'd become had vanished. Before the party Norah had demanded that he promise to sit down with her and the President and have a discussion about the issues she wished to stress in the remainder of her campaign. He'd been forced by her vehemence to agree. Now, two hours later, she was transformed by the sight of Di Brazza into a breathless ingenue. It rankled him.

So Di Brazza discovered her. He had been her earliest mentor. Her lover perhaps? Christ, Di Brazza was an old man now. He cursed himself. What was the matter with him? Why must he punish himself with jealousy this way? Norah was surely all his. It was under his tutelage, by God, that she'd become the woman she was today. The past was none of his business. Putting his arm around Norah's waist possessively, forcing himself to share her pleasure, he vowed silently to himself not to fall into the sickness of jealousy.

A Secret Service agent whispered to Walt, who promptly announced to the guests remaining in the foyer, "Ladies and Gentlemen, the President and the First Lady will be with us shortly. Please join us in the living room, where they will greet you."

The President and his wife, escorted by Walt and Norah, circled the room, greeting the guests one by one. Tillie and Tom lagged behind to give Norah the full benefit of the presidential aura.

Liz, although thickened with age, had developed into a handsome, distinguished-looking woman, her simplicity unaltered. The First Lady had traveled up the political ranks with her husband, and now, at the pinnacle of his career, she still managed to maintain her role as the humanizer with consummate skill. The long apprenticeship had lessened her innate shyness and augmented her quality of gentle grace. Liz lived her political life on the premise that people didn't vote for a man's wife and children but might very well vote against them. Protecting her privacy and her children's with a fierce consistency, she looked forward longingly to the day when she would again be back in the house in Santa Barbara and the gardens she loved to tend.

Tillie and Tom stood near the Maillol at the back of the room and were watching the President's progress among the guests when suddenly Catherine Goodrich swooped toward them, thin-lipped and angry.

"I'm leaving directly after dinner!" she said. Her face was livid with rage. "I can understand *Norah's* sitting at the President's right. After all, we know he's here to promote her. But *Lisa Ryder* to his left? It's just too much! *I* bear the name of one of the first families of California, and when I think of all the money Henry's family has poured into the President's campaign—and Norah's—and you put that little strumpet next to him. Well!"

Tom tried placating her. "Come on, Catherine. Tillie seated herself at another table. The President's entitled to a vicarious thrill."

Tillie, regaining her speech, demanded, "How the hell did you find out where you were sitting?"

"I asked your secretary. I suspected you'd manage to stick me in left field. I know you hate me, Tillie Lowman!"

Henry Goodrich, observing his wife from the distance, worked his way apprehensively across the room to her, inquiring solicitously, "What's the matter, darling?"

Tillie, dark eyes flashing with rage, snapped, "*Darling* has informed me that she's taken umbrage at *my* seating arrangements and is leaving directly after dinner! Would you believe?"

Catherine drew herself to her full height, straightened her shoulders, and looked down at her husband imperiously. "Tillie seated the President between Norah and that little nobody, Lisa Ryder. We'll leave promptly after dinner," she commanded, glaring at him.

Henry drew in his chin, the bald head reddening, looked up at her, and said, with unaccustomed firmness, startling her, "No, *we* won't, Catherine! I suggest that if you intend to leave this house before the President of the United States does, *you* do so this instant!"

Catherine's jaw went slack. Tom gave Henry a furtive congratulatory pat on the back and took Catherine firmly by the arm. "Come along,

Catherine, you haven't said hello to the President and Liz." He steered her into the crowd before she could answer her husband.

Tillie kissed the bald pate. "Jesus, Henry, I don't envy you the ride home. *Darling's* pissed!"

He smiled, expansive with self-pleasure and pride at his new-found courage. "Don't worry about it, Tillie, I never felt better."

As soon as dinner was announced, the President and Norah, followed by Walt and the First Lady, Tom and Tillie, led the guests down the great circular stairs into the transformed projection room. There was a group intake of breath at the sight. Feathery trees, sparkling with hundreds of lights no larger than a fingernail, lined the walls. Red velvet cloths covered the thirty tables; low clusters of the white cyclamen with small votive candles in crystal holders interspersed with greenery decorated the center of each table.

The orchestra played light dinner music at a low volume so as not to interfere with conversation. Butlers stood at attention, ready to assist the guests as they found their places.

Despite their well-cut dinner jackets and black ties, the Secret Service men were easily discernible. Their eyes were constantly directed around the room; they never glanced at their dinner partners. The President's table, out of necessity, was backed against the far wall at a maximum distance from the bay windows, which opened onto the brilliantly lit gardens, where the ever-present terror, an assassin, could be hiding. Despite all the security measures that had been taken, the fear remained, ever-present.

The President held Norah's chair and, before a butler could reach for Lisa Ryder's, he helped her as well. As they settled themselves, Lisa said shyly, "Mr. President, may I tell you something?"

"Of course, my dear." He bent his head toward her.

"When I call my mom in Louisville, Kentucky, tomorrow, which I intend to do, sir, and tell her the President of the United States held my chair, she's going to say, 'Lisa Ryder, God's listening to you and he don't cotton to lyin'.' "

The President threw his head back and laughed.

Tillie, observing him, whispered to Tom, "Screw that Catherine. Our Lisa's got the leader laughing." Her face turned serious. "We never dreamed of the things we'd put up with when we started the campaign, did we?"

"No," he said, remembering the scene at Luigi's with discomfort. "We didn't. And God knows what else we'll be put through before it's over."

Reassuringly, he said to her, "It'll be worth it if we win, Tillie."

She looked at him questioningly. "And if Norah loses, will it have been?" Tillie recalled her own despair the night they returned from San Diego to find Walt and Sylvia Gannon dining à deux.

Before he could answer, the waiters began serving Walt's favorite first course: caviar spooned into small baked potatoes. On the basis of three per plate, at least nine hundred evenly sized new potatoes had been gathered for this course in the evening's dinner. The soup was clear with thinly sliced lemon floating on its surface. The entrée was boeuf en crout, pink and tender enough to cut with a fork, its crisp brown crust stuffed with imported pâté. The cold salad plates held crisp greens. The butlers passed trays of crackers and perfectly aged Brie cheese.

The final tribute to Tillie's managerial prowess was the dessert: three hundred flawlessly puffed-up chocolate soufflés in individual little ramekins.

The three crystal glasses at each place had held white wine for the caviar, red for the meat, and now with dessert, champagne. A curt nod from Tillie quieted the music. Walt rose to his feet, glass in hand. "Ladies and gentlemen, I would like to propose a toast." He faced the President, holding his glass aloft. "To the President of the United States."

Chairs scraped as the guests rose to join him. When they were reseated, the President rose and proposed a toast to Walt and Tillie and Norah's victory.

"For Liz and me, it is more than an elegant and beautiful evening, it's a coming home to the people we love." He nodded his head in Tillie's direction. "To you, dear Tillie, I want to say that of all the palaces Liz and I have visited, none has been more beautiful or flawlessly run than this one. I am going to suggest to Liz, after the perfection of tonight's dinner, that she fire the White House chef and commandeer yours."

Tillie laughed and said, "You'll have to fight for him, Mr. President."

Serious now, the President faced the room. "I am grateful for this opportunity to visit with all of you, so many of whom have supported me across the years, and to tell you how proud I am to be in California on Norah's behalf.

"Andrew Watkins, our National Committee chairman, informs me recent samplings of the California situation indicate that Norah is running so closely to the incumbent, no reliable pollster dares to predict the outcome of this election."

There was a burst of applause.

"I cannot overemphasize the importance of her election. The public is finally beginning to understand the need for a responsive Congress. I'm proud of my administration, but the proudest day of all will be when I greet the new senator from California, Norah Jones Ashley!"

The President sat down and soundly kissed Norah, who rose and surveyed the room. Everyone grew quiet, waiting for her to speak. She felt a rush of pleasure. She had the audience with her. "Mr. President, my dear Liz, Governor and Congressmen and each and every one of you. I had a speech prepared to tell you how indebted I am to you for your staunch support during this long and arduous campaign. I also wanted to thank Walt and Tillie, for whom there can never be sufficient words of gratitude for this night and all their support and treasured friendship. But the Commander-in-Chief of this domain—" she scowled in Tillie's direction —"has informed me that under no condition am I to indulge in speechmaking. Therefore I have an announcement to make. You'll be interested to know that there have been feelers put out to our campaign that indicate that a certain incumbent, who shall be nameless, has acknowledged a realistic apprehension and is interested in what we have demanded from the outset—a debate."

There was another round of applause.

Norah raised her hands for quiet, looking sad and serious. "Now," she said, "I am permitted by our hostess to do one more thing, which is to make the following announcement."

Norah picked up a piece of paper and read, as if from a script, "Ladies and gentlemen, coffee will be served in the living room, to be followed by dancing in the ballroom." With that, she sat down, as applause and laughter filled the room.

The guests went upstairs to drink their coffee and brandy, and so were unaware of the swift removal of the rented furniture that had transformed the projection room into a dining room. Soon the gilt chairs lined the walls of the room, turning it now into a ballroom.

By the time the guests finished their coffee and were led back down to the room, the orchestra was playing dance music and butlers were popping champagne bottles, ready to serve them.

The dancing began as the President led Tillie onto the floor. Tom and Norah followed, grateful, finally, for a moment alone. But their pleasure was short-lived.

They'd no sooner begun to dance when Guido Di Brazza tapped Tom on the shoulder to cut in. As soon as she was in his arms, the music changed to waltz tempo.

"Oh, Guido," she exclaimed with pleasure, "a waltz." He pulled his head away from hers and said, "Of course, *cara,* I arranged it!" His face broke into a wide smile. "You're wearing my earrings!" he noted with surprise.

"I treasure them!" Norah answered, remembering how he'd thrust the small velvet box in her hand as they'd waited for her plane to California to be called. "A remembrance, *tesora mia,*" he'd whispered as he kissed her lightly and abruptly walked away. He'd never looked back. She had boarded the plane, clutching the box, a pang of regret filling her heart. It was the last time she'd seen him until now.

Guido held her close to him and sighed as they moved weightlessly in three-quarter time. "You dance beautifully still, my Norah. Do you remember Paris?"

"Of course I do." How sweet he was, she thought with grateful nostalgia. He'd never been anything but kind and tender to her.

They circled past Tillie and Tom. Tillie smiled at them and whispered to Tom, "Cut it out."

"Cut out what?"

"Cut out being so goddamn jealous! He invented her, you know, even though you think *you* did."

"Tillie, let's go have some of your marvelous Dom Perignon." Tom took her hand and led her to the far side of the room, where a waiter offered them champagne.

They stood together without speaking, watching the dancers. Tillie saw Dan dancing dreamily with Lisa. Oh God, that old mother in Kentucky would die if she could see her baby now, she thought. She barely recognized Barbara Potter dancing by in a slim, simply cut black dress that exaggerated her long, lean body. She had never seen her dressed in anything other than jeans.

Tillie nudged Tom, who seemed to be fixated on Norah and Di Brazza.

He turned to her and said, angrily, "Okay, so I *am* jealous, goddamn it, and I don't know why. Do you think I'm losing my mind?"

She stared at him in disbelief. "Norah's been married to you for over twenty years, and you're jealous of that creaky old man?" She shook her head. "He's been locked away in Florida since before you were married, for God's sake! I haven't the slightest idea what went on with Norah when she was nineteen years old and he discovered her, nor do you! What's more, you shouldn't care!" She paused, looking at him accusingly, her voice stern. "Your own prenuptial track record was pretty good, my friend. In fact, when we introduced you to Norah, you were such a regular in the gossip columns I was afraid for *her*!"

Tom grimaced. "You're right. I know it. I haven't the vaguest idea why I feel this way. I trust Norah implicitly. I know she's mine and God knows I'm hers." He took Tillie's hand and laughed. "I'm nuts to worry about my wife's waltzing with a seventy-year-old. Christ, do you suppose it's campaign fatigue?"

"No, I don't," Tillie said, her expression serious. "It's been a long time since you've had to share her publicly. Maybe this new role of consort is tougher for you to play than you think, Tom. After all, Norah's been the wife of a millionaire industrialist for a long time. Now the millionaire industrialist is the *husband* of a candidate."

But Tom wasn't listening. Face ashen, he stared in the direction of the French doors leading to the terrace overlooking the gardens. Guido was waltzing Norah through them.

CHAPTER
Twenty-three

Guido released his arm from Norah's waist, took her hand in his, and led her to the marble balustrade.

The parklike grounds were brilliantly lit, the air velvet warm. The sounds of music and voices drifted into the night.

Guido held out his cigarette case to Norah. She shook her head. He lit his own and looked at her approvingly.

"Is it possible, *cara,* that you are more beautiful now?" He smiled, studying her face.

"Is it possible *you* refuse to age?" she asked in return, thinking what liars they both were.

"What a gorgeous surprise you are!" she exclaimed. He breathed deeply and sighed.

"It smells like Paris in the spring. Do you remember Paris, Norah?" he asked.

Poor old darling. He wanted to reminisce. Why not? She did too. She had nothing but the warmest memories of him. Guido had wanted her dressed by the legendary Chanel for a play he was producing and had sent her to Paris to be outfitted. Norah suspected he planned the trip as a device to raise her spirits after the end of her affair with Richard Hardwick. He met her at Chanel's atelier and supervised the choice of her wardrobe down to the minutest detail. Guido had driven Coco Chanel to the brink of insanity with his obsessive interest. No swatch, seam, or button escaped his notice. He knew exactly how he wanted her to look, and the results had vindicated his relentless attention to detail. Both her performance in the play and her wardrobe received rave reviews.

Together they had walked hand in hand through the great museums, palaces, churches, flea markets, and the Bois de Boulogne. They browsed at bookstalls on the banks of the Seine and feasted in the well-known and lesser-known restaurants of Paris. Guido taught her to appreciate the joys of *haute cuisine* and fine wines. He coddled her, indulged her, and lifted her out of her own despair. It was he who restored the sense of self-worth and joy so badly battered by her ill-fated affair with Richard. He demanded nothing in return but her pleasure in the moment. When they became lovers, it was she who had taken the initiative in gratitude. Norah never regretted it. She bent Guido to her by her pleasure as well as by her beauty, feeding his obsession and his need to play Pygmalion. What she lacked in passion, she compensated for with warmth and affection. Norah felt genuine pleasure in those memories and in seeing him again.

"Of course I remember, Guido. But tell me why you're here. Are you going to produce a film for Walt? Oh, how I'd love to do a film with you," she sighed.

His face grew serious. "No films, *cara!* I called Walt from Florida and made up a story about having to be in California for some make-believe business and inveigled him into inviting me to the party." He put his hands on the marble balustrade and stared into the garden. Slowly he turned his head toward her. "I'm very anxious to talk to you about this campaign of yours against Richard." Norah stiffened and looked at him with astonishment.

Guido straightened up and faced her. "Is it some kind of vendetta for what happened between the two of you years ago? Surely, that is beneath you, darling." He shrugged. "You have a wonderful life. A rich, handsome husband. I hear your son is a fine boy. Your life is full. What more could you want?"

"What nonsense are you talking about, Guido? I have no vendetta, as you call it, with Richard because of the past. I barely remember it. I'm running against him for political reasons in a political campaign, and personal matters have nothing, absolutely nothing, to do with it. I don't want to talk politics with you, please!" The reunion had taken a chilling turn.

But Guido was not to be diverted. "Then you will be honorable, *cara*, you will not make political use of the unfortunate beating of that poor young man." He frowned. "I can't remember his name."

"Manuel Vasquez." Her pique mounted. "There isn't a shred of evidence," she said, "indicating that Richard had anything to do with the assault, and *I* don't believe he did. There's no sense in pointing a finger at him, is there? When they find the man whose name was on the registration slip of the abandoned truck, or a material witness, then we'll see. So you needn't worry." Norah glared at Guido. "I'm collecting enough hard, political evidence against Richard without making a lot of loose charges. Come now, tell me about yourself." Her tone turned gentle. "How many grandchildren do you have?" That ought to derail him.

"Three. All boys."

Then he raised his dark eyes and looked directly at her. The warm and elegant air of the gentleman was gone. "*Cara*, they won't find that fellow."

"What do you mean, they won't find him?"

"My people do not want this matter explored. They do not want Richard embarrassed."

"Your people? What does that mean? Who are they?" She shuddered. "What do they care about Richard?"

"*My* people, the same people who financed the plays that *I* produced and in which *you* starred"—he paused, letting it sink in—"prefer the man not be found. That means that he *won't* be found. Because even if Richard Hardwick was himself not involved in the beating, the fact that the suspect had been in his employ could indict Richard in the public's mind. It is very much to *my* people's interest that Richard be reelected." His eyes never left her face. He enunciated his words slowly and with emphasis. "They will do whatever is necessary to see to it that he is reelected."

Norah felt her blood run cold. Her mentor's threat frightened her unspeakably. He was no longer her beloved friend; he was a terrifying old man.

"They are also very anxious that you stop demanding to debate with Richard, my darling girl," he continued, studying her expression, making certain his words had penetrated.

Norah's fear suddenly turned to anger. "Don't 'darling girl' me," she snapped. "Are you implying that I'm in some kind of danger from mysterious sinister forces lurking in the background? Invisible people who want Richard reelected? Who want me to lose? Are you threatening me?" she asked, eyes flashing.

"Not with *physical* danger, I assure you. My people only harm one another. It would be quite simple to publicize your early life. Your drunken father. The impoverished background. They could prove you were an ambitious young actress, willing to do anything to escape her poverty. To involve yourself with a married man of dubious reputation— me, and possibly others." He added quickly, "It's not that they have ulterior motives, darling. They simply feel that Richard is a very good senator with much seniority and power, and they do not wish to see all that lost. They will go to any length necessary to insure your defeat."

He shrugged and smiled. "It will not be pleasant to be obliged to explain to your fine husband and wonderful son, much less the voting public, the things that will be said about you." His voice turned cajoling. "Look here, Norah. There's no need to drop out of the campaign. Just make nice little speeches at luncheons and dinners and look pretty on TV. Nothing vicious and *che sarà sarà,*" he said with a sigh. "My wife's father was what you call a Don. Now it is her brother who is head of the family. They have been very good to me, Norah. The family made it possible for me to produce plays and to live comfortably. They have only asked two things of me in all these years."

Norah saw his hands trembling. Guido was himself being threatened. This old bully boy was a frightened old man.

"Blackmailing me is obviously one of them. What's the other?" she asked, wondering what horror was in store for him if she proved intransigent.

He looked at her sadly. "It was that I never come to California."

"Why not?" she asked with surprise.

"Because I had fallen in love with you, Norah. That was something my wife could not bear." He sighed deeply.

Norah's laugh was bitter. "Fascinating, Guido, just fascinating. You are permitted to make love to me in Paris, you may make me a star—because *they* permitted it. Permission for whoring was granted, but not for loving. You were exiled to Florida! Right? But *now* you are allowed to leave your exile to come and threaten me." She leaned toward him. "You never loved me or anyone else. You filthy old bastard! Suppose *you* tell your brother-in-law or the Godfather, whoever sent you here, to go to hell! My people have hard proof of Hardwick's crooked transactions in their hands right now and there'll be more. Do you understand? And before it's over, I'm going to force him to explain his ties with your whole unsavory bunch."

His look turned gentle. He was begging her for compassion. "I am only the messenger. I had hoped you would feel some small sense of gratitude to me, my Norah, for giving you your first *bonne chance.*" His eyebrows shot up. "Perhaps if not for me, you would be married to a nice working man like your father and would have turned into a worn-out drudge like your dear mother."

Norah moved away from him toward the house, but she turned as Guido's voice became ominously low. "I do not think you understand how serious a matter this is," he warned. "It is not some joke to be taken lightly. As for me, I assure you I am deeply pained to be put in this unpleasant position."

"Pained, you?" she said with a sneer. "Your whole life is a painful sham, Guido. At least my 'dear mother' wasn't a slave to a bunch of hoodlums. She was free to live her life, you're not! How long do you think it will take for you to be *persona non grata* in your beloved Palm Beach? If I'm to be exposed, you'll be out there in the bright light, too, stark naked for the world to see! Do you think you and the Don's daughter will still be invited to all those grand parties? The clubhouses will bolt their doors to a member of the Mafia, and that's all you are! The only thing for which I can be faulted is for having been an ignorant young fool. But you—!" She looked at him in disgust. "I owe you nothing but contempt."

"*Cara,* I know you hate me now," he said sadly. "But remember always that I love you."

Norah stepped into the ballroom without answering and without looking back. Before she could grasp what had happened, the governor was heading toward her with open arms to claim a dance. Guido did not follow her.

John Mellon stood at the far end of the ballroom observing the people on the dance floor. He'd barely recognized Barbara when she'd come into the room, as lithe and elegant as an African princess. He hadn't really looked at her before. The wine and music warmed him and he felt aroused for the first time since he'd thrown himself into the war against Richard Hardwick. He'd never slept with a black woman. The thought of it was titillating. He debated whether or not he should ask her for a dance. Make some sort of overture. While he was vacillating, the decision was made for him. A White House aide tapped him on the shoulder.

"The President would like you to join him for a conference upstairs. He'll be going up shortly."

Mellon nodded. A wave of fatigue overwhelmed him. Oh God, here he was, too tired to make it to the dance floor, and now a meeting! At this hour! Shit! Well, at least it would give that pompous bastard Brookings a chance to be alone with Lisa. Or was it the other way around? He suspected she had some sort of yen for Dan and that the press secretary was deliberately keeping his distance, managing never to be alone with her. God knows why, now that the hate mail had diminished!

She was some hunk of woman. Maybe it was the black and white thing. Brookings was nuts. He took himself too seriously, a little miscegenation would do him good! That kind of nonsense went out with *Showboat*!

He found them at the bar with the Auerbachs. "I have to report to the Man," he told them. "Damn it! It looks like he's making his exit now. You take Lisa home, Dan. I'll see you in the morning."

Lisa planted a friendly kiss on his cheek and said sympathetically, "You poor thing." Her pleasure barely disguised, she added, "Now, don't you all work too hard." Unhappily, Mellon left the ballroom and trudged up the spiral staircase, cursing his fate and envying Brookings.

The President's departure signaled the end of the evening. Uniformed attendants and chauffeurs drove the cars to the front door. Guests began to drift away, making their good-nights and thank-yous as maids and butlers brought them their wraps.

It seemed to Walt that Norah looked tired as she hugged them good night. Her eyes misted when she said, "How can I thank you, you dear and wonderful friends?"

Tillie kissed her and snapped, "By winning!" When Tom embraced her, she whispered to him, "Behave!"

The Lowmans stood at the open door waving off the last of their guests. Walt's face clouded and he asked Tillie, "What happened to Guido? I didn't see him leave, did you?"

Tillie shook her head and shrugged. "The last I saw of him he was waltzing Norah out onto the terrace and Tom was turning green. He must have slipped out early."

Walt chuckled. "Do you think the old boy made a pass at Norah?"

"Perhaps." Tillie smiled. "Who knows what any of you old boys would do?"

Walt took her face in his hands and kissed her lips. "Come, we'll say good night to Liz and the President. I know what this old boy is going to do." He looked at her fondly. "Tillie, honey, you're not only the best damn hostess in town, you have the best pair of legs around."

* * *

Wordlessly, the President sloshed the brandy around in his snifter, then glanced up at Mellon, who had been slumped in the chair facing him for the last ten minutes. God, even in dinner clothes, Mellon managed to look rumpled, the President thought. The rounded features didn't disguise the marks of fatigue. According to Tom, Mellon had thrown himself into the campaign like a fanatic. They'd been wrong suspecting that his alliance with Virginia Hardwick might have made him disloyal. Still, removing Mellon from Washington had been a precaution he'd had to take. Christ, would he be spending the rest of his presidency looking in corners, suspecting people? The President cleared his throat.

"Tom tells me that you're responsible for uncovering that bastard Chisholm and that your people are doing one hell of a job, John."

"Thank you, sir. We're working on it."

The President hesitated and studied his brandy. He looked up under his brows. "We've missed you at the White House. I've been wondering if maybe it was time to let someone else take over and get you back to Washington. We need you, John." It was as close as the Commander-in-Chief could come to an apology.

Mellon stared at the President in disbelief. He was asking him back. The sentence was being lifted. This was the moment he'd been waiting for. Perhaps his liaison with Virginia hadn't been discovered. All his apprehension hadn't been necessary. The President had assigned him to the Ashley campaign for positive reasons. Now he wanted him back. But how could he leave now? He was hot on that bastard Hardwick's trail, but all he had were a few loose leads and suspicions. Nothing tangible. Not yet.

Mellon lusted to tie it all together and hang Hardwick with it. It was his baby. How could anybody else know what he was carrying in his head? And, even if they could, Mellon didn't want someone else sharing the kill. Hardwick had become his quarry. Mellon could taste blood. He hadn't loved Virginia. He didn't even know what he felt about her or what love was. But he was sure as hell what he felt about her husband. And the move back to the goddamn White House could wait. Fuck the White House and the President.

Mellon reached for a cigarette and lit it, slowly exhaling the smoke. Then he met the President's gaze.

Finally, he said, "That's very kind of you, sir, but I have some unfinished business in California, and if it's agreeable to you . . . I'll see it through."

CHAPTER

Twenty-four

F inally, she was alone with him. In the darkness Lisa studied Dan's profile. He was the most attractive man she'd ever met. She wondered wistfully what he thought of her. It wasn't that he overtly avoided her. He was always friendly and polite to her and had long since given up teasing her about her southern origins. But he treated her no differently than he did anyone else in the campaign.

If the President hadn't wanted to see Mellon, they wouldn't be alone now. She wasn't going to lose her chance. Not tonight. She'd waited too long.

They drove south along the deserted streets toward the shopping district. The houses grew proportionately smaller the closer they came to Wilshire Boulevard, leaving behind the great mansions with their gates and tended grounds. The sidewalks were empty, and only an occasional car sped past them as they drove through the deserted commercial district. Beverly Hills turned into Pompeii after midnight. No Main Street in Iowa folded up more completely than did Rodeo Drive.

The traffic was sparse on the Santa Monica Freeway, one of the great arteries of the ganglia that linked together the disparate sections of the sprawling megalopolis.

The freeway ended abruptly on the ocean front. They continued along the Pacific Coast Highway past the storm-gutted palisades, taco stands and shacks, and the great mansions of the "gold coast," where Norma Talmadge and Irving Thalberg had lived and the huge house which had first belonged to Louis B. Mayer, then to the Lawfords, sister and brother-in-law of John F. Kennedy. It had served as a vacation hideaway for the martyred young President. It was here that he had first met Marilyn Monroe, the tragic figure whose fate haunted Lisa and every other young actress being catapulted into stardom.

Dan turned left at Webb Way and headed directly toward the ocean. At the Malibu guardhouse the patrolman recognized Lisa and lifted the security gate.

Dan slowed the car to a crawl in deference to the asphalt bumps spaced at regular intervals along the private road. Of all the mysteries in southern California, the aura of glamor attached to the "colony" was the most baffling to Dan. Regardless of the pretentious security gates, uniformed guards, asphalt bumps, and astronomical land values, measured by each foot of ocean frontage, it looked like a slum. The houses smacked against each other on narrow lots. Many looked hopelessly dilapidated, victims of the relentless winds and moist salt air. The threat of fire from the hills and of destruction from murderous high tides was constant. Notoriously liberal on political issues, the residents of the colony nevertheless stubbornly resisted the installation of sewer pipes out of fear of population growth. Malibuites weren't about to share their turf with the "folks." As a result, the toilets were given to flushing backward and the Los Angeles mosquito control board maintained a watchful eye. The pungent odor of the exhausted septic tanks commingled with the smell of barbeques, dead fish, seaweed, and pot endemic to the area.

Dan jammed his foot on the brake, narrowly missing a pack of pedigree dogs gorging themselves on the spilled contents of an overturned garbage can. "Jesus Christ, how can you live in this slum?" he asked in consternation as she pushed open the unlocked gate to the tiny beach house.

Lisa pressed the switch and flooded the living room with light. She looked at him with disdain. "It's the *only* place in town to live. It keeps me sane." She stretched her arms out toward the ocean. "Every morning when I awaken, I blow infinity a kiss and my soul is restored!"

She twirled around, her back toward him. "Do my zipper, fix yourself a drink, and I'll be back in a minute." Looking over her shoulder on her way to the bedroom, she added, "And a fire would be nice."

Dan poured himself a Scotch from the tray on the white wicker table and struck a match to the kindling pushed beneath the logs already stacked in the fireplace.

The small room facing the beach was furnished in white wicker, counterpointed by bright blue cotton upholstery. A Calder print hung above the Delft-tiled mantel. Clay pots of ferns and ivy hung by the window.

Dan looked out over the night-black ocean. The lights on the Palos Verdes Peninsula flickered in the distance. The rhythmic beat of the pounding surf obliterated all other sounds. Hanging his jacket on the back of a chair and loosening his tie, he settled himself in the pillowed bay-window seat, mesmerized. Intellectually, he knew he should leave before she returned. Too full of the evening and her, he made no move.

Wheat-blond hair hanging loose, barefoot, and covered in a long-sleeved, white velvet caftan, Lisa padded toward him, pausing briefly to flick off the light switch and pour herself some brandy. She took a pillow and sat on the floor at his feet. "See, I told you! Isn't it bliss?"

He glanced at her and smiled.

Scrutinizing his face, she rested her arms on his knees and asked, "Will Norah win?" She could feel his leg muscles tighten under her pressure.

"I wouldn't take any bets on it. He *is* the incumbent."

She was silent for a while and then asked, "What will you do when it's over?"

"Go back to Washington, I guess, whichever way it turns out."

She felt him gently pull away from her, and she put her hand to his face.

He nodded and touched her hand. Lisa got to her knees and drew his face to hers. Kissing him gently, she whispered, "I loved dancing with you."

He stroked her hair and murmured, "Lisa, Lisa, Louisville Lisa. There is no way for us to dance together."

He had spoken gently, but to her his rejection was as harsh as if he had slapped her face. She pulled away, the hurt turning to anger.

"Why? Because I'm not good enough for you? You're a snob, a full-blooded snob," she said accusingly. "I know all about you, Daniel Brookings, and how your daddy was a great doctor and all that crap." Catching his look of surprise, she threw her head back and laughed. "I looked you up in *Who's Who.* The one they keep in the office so they can get the big shots' wives' names straight when they send out those 'personal' letters from Norah by the thousands," she said with a sneer. "You're a second-generation Who's Who, aren't you?"

He longed to hold her and stop the tirade. But he said nothing.

She leaned toward him, the blond hair cascading forward, eyes blazing. "For your information, *I'm* first-generation trash! I never knew *my* wonderful daddy. He should be in *Who's Where,* the bastard! He knocked up Mama and split, and she kept me alive slinging hash! I got *my* Rhodes scholarship in a carnival. I'm the girl they sawed in half. If the President makes you ambassador to the UN or Great Britain or some other striped-pants thing, I'd embarrass you, wouldn't I? I don't know anything about anything and you know *everything!* All I know is that I'm sexy enough to make millions of boring average men hang my poster over their beds. I turn *them* on. *They're* crazy about me. But not you!"

He was unable to answer her, to articulate the truth. His silence infuriated her. She jumped to her feet and looked at him accusingly. "It's because I'm white, isn't it," she said. "Maybe what you need is a Barbara Potter!" Her anger dissolved. "She's going to law school. Did you know that? Which are you, Dan? A snob or a reverse racist or both? Tell me," she insisted.

He grimaced and pulled her toward him. Holding her face between his hands, he kissed her hungrily. She threw her body at him, flinging her arms around his neck, her lips and tongue meeting his. Finally, breathless, they drew apart in silence, and with a deft, impatient gesture she pulled open her robe, letting it fall to the ground.

The moonlight streaked across the flawless full-breasted body. Dan gasped, but before he could speak, she reached out and with impatient fingers unbuttoned his shirt, hungrily burying her face into the hollow where the long muscular neck met the collarbone. He stroked her silken back and grasped her rounded buttocks in his hands. He pressed her close to his body, which had grown large with desire. All restraints dissolved in his passionate need of her. In moments he, too, was out of his clothes. The dark, lean figure loomed over her as he flung her on the window seat consuming her with his eyes and hands and tongue, his breath coming in gasps. Instinctively, they knew the subtle nuances of each other's bodies.

As he thrust himself into her body, their passion fused and exploded in the perfect rhythm of longtime lovers.

Lisa lay exhausted and sated in the dark hollow of his arm. She stroked him contentedly with a feathery touch. Neither one of them spoke.

It was he who broke the long silence. "I'll always want you, you know that," he whispered. She pulled his face to hers and kissed him deep and long, not bothering to answer. Drawing away from her, he stood up and slowly began retrieving his clothing.

"Oh no you don't," she commanded with a smile, and reached for him. "You're not leaving now or *ever!*"

His dark eyes filled with sadness. "I must," he said bitterly. "Surely you know that if I don't leave now, I'll never be able to give you up." He pulled on his trousers, tucking in the shirt. "And that, my darling, would be the end of Lisa Ryder, the great movie star."

Incredulous, she was on her feet, facing him. "Are you crazy?" she gasped.

Sadly, he shook his head. "No, I'm not. I'm a realist. You would grow to hate me for thwarting your dream—and that would be unbearable."

"We can't see each other because you're black and I'm white?" Her voice rose with dismay. "Nobody cares about that garbage anymore! For God's sake, even my mother, my old-fashioned southern mother, voted for a black man for mayor! All that hate is—gone—done!" she shouted, too stunned to move.

Dan came to her and embraced her wordlessly, with a lingering, almost abstracted wistfulness. He kissed the top of her head softly. Then he broke away and retrieved his jacket from the back of the chair. "Ask Walt," he said quietly. He walked to the door and closed it gently behind him. What was it Adlai Stevenson had said? Dan asked himself as he stepped into the velvet night, filled with the sound of the ocean. Something about "being too old to cry, too sad to smile." He'd cribbed it from Lincoln. It was all right with him. Who better could speak for his pain?

* * *

After forcing themselves to discuss the party in glowing terms, Tom and Norah lapsed into silence on the drive home.

Tom was trying desperately to heed Tillie's admonitions and restrain himself from questioning Norah about her disappearance with Guido, while Norah was lost in a morass of her own anxieties about the frightening confrontation. She couldn't bring herself to believe it had happened. She leaned her head back against the seat, closed her eyes, and reached for Tom's hand. But no way was she going to be blackmailed by a terrorized old man. Let Guido panic and tremble. She wasn't going to be bluffed into submission. Not she!

But by the time she reached her dressing room, her earlier bravado dissolved, and her anxieties overwhelmed her as she took off the pear-shaped diamond earrings, symbolic of her affair with Guido. The horror of her situation engulfed her. Norah put her head down on her arms, leaned on the marble counter, and sobbed.

She heard Tom knock on the door and call out, "Come to bed. It's late and we have to go to Palm Springs with the President in the morning. Remember?"

She was unable to answer him. Of course she remembered. She had planned to discuss the campaign with the President en route to the Springs. She had had in mind to make clear to him that she was determined to take a strong stance on the issues and stop fudging. And then when the men played golf, she was to visit with Manuel, who was very much on her conscience.

When Norah didn't answer, Tom opened the door to her dressing room. She looked up at him in anguish, tears rolling down her cheeks.

Taken aback, Tom cried out, "Darling—what's the matter? What's happened? Tell me!"

Tell him that at best she'd go through the motions of the campaign? Pull back. No debates. No head-on confrontations. Treat Hardwick with kid gloves and hope to God to pick up her life again. She couldn't bear the thought of exposing herself. As far as she was concerned, she was beaten. Hardwick and Guido had won.

Finally she said to Tom, "I hate the campaign. I simply cannot attack Hardwick the way I should. It's over!"

Tom stared at her in dismay. She looked stricken and deadly earnest. Whatever it was that had brought this on was serious business. She'd taken a body blow of some kind, and he was damn well going to find out about it.

"For Christ's sake, what has happened to you?"

Norah shook her head. "I can't tell you. I can't." The tears welled up again. "Please trust me," she pleaded. "Please!"

"Trust you? Of course I trust you." He looked at her with a puzzled expression. "I simply don't understand you. The campaign is only now going into full gear, and you're pulling back? Don't you want to be elected?"

"No, I don't want to be elected," she said flatly.

Tom pulled a cigarette out of his bathrobe pocket, lit it, and slowly exhaled the smoke.

"Okay, suppose you tell me what this is all about."

She shook her head.

"Goddamn it, Norah, what kind of a charade is this? Are we having one of your prima donna performances—or what?" He was outraged. "We are six weeks away from the election and you suddenly decide you don't *feel* like being a senator. You're finally in the running and have a damn good chance to win, especially if Mellon comes through. Which I believe he will. Do you realize how much blood and money and sweat has gone into this thing?"

He looked at her suspiciously. "Is there something going on I don't know about?" Could it be something that happened when she disappeared with that goddamn ancient hand-kissing bastard, Di Brazza?

Tom moved toward Norah and put his hand under her chin, forcing her to look at him. "Tell me what happened," he ordered. "Tell me about that little tête-à-tête on the terrace."

Norah stared at him, thinking. Tell him? How the hell can I tell him? She shook her head and bit her lip. Goddamn it, she loathed being deceitful. She and Tom had never lied to each other. She wasn't lying exactly, she rationalized. She simply couldn't bring herself to tell him the truth.

"Oh Christ, Tom, let me be. If you like, I'll go through the motions. I simply cannot bring myself to launch a frontal smear attack on Hardwick," she said. Trying to placate him and reassure herself, she said, "I'm moving up in the polls anyway. If Mellon does open up a can of worms, it could backfire—there's always that risk."

She was pleading to be allowed to do what Guido had demanded. "I'll make nice little speeches and let *che sarà sarà*!" She remembered the look on Guido's face when he threatened her, and her heart sank.

Tom sat down on the chaise longue, hunched forward, and rested his elbows on his thighs, his hands clasped together in front of him. He looked up at her searchingly. Norah leaned against the counter for support.

"Bullshit, Norah. I'm not going to leave this room until you tell me the truth. What happened with Di Brazza?"

Feeling cornered, she drew in her breath and, with a sense of relief at finally sharing her misery, told him the story as best she could.

When she'd finished, Tom made no comment. The small vein at his temple pulsated. He stood up slowly and began to pace the room.

"Don't you see, Tom," she pleaded. "There's no way I'm going to expose myself like that. What about Peter? How could I face him? The press will have a field day making me out to be the whore of Babylon. It's a no-win. Don't you understand?"

Tom stopped his pacing and faced her. "Jesus Christ, Norah, didn't you have any sense? How could you have been so stupid? Guido Di Brazza, that phony aristocrat—son-in-law of a Don, yet! How many others were there?" he shot at her. "Who's going to come out of the woodwork to blackmail you next?"

Norah's despair turned to wild rage. She felt betrayed by Tom, too. "You son of a bitch," she screamed. "You pious fraud, wallowing in moral judgment! I was nineteen years old when Guido offered me a chance, the chance to be a star! Do you understand what that means when you're dirt poor, waiting on tables because the paltry scholarship doesn't even cover food money?"

She glared at him. "Guido never, never made any advances to me. He asked for nothing. If you must know—I was the one who made the advances out of gratitude. He gave me love and acceptance, which seems to be a hell of a lot more that I have from you, Tom Ashley, after sharing your life and loving you and bearing your son. So why don't you just take the whole fucking Senate race and the last twenty years and shove it?" She shook her head. "My God, I didn't even know the word *Mafia,* much less what it meant, when I met Guido."

Tom grimaced. His insides turned over. His head felt as if it had exploded. The thought of her in another man's bed was unbearable. Norah being touched and stroked and petted by that paunchy aging—. He closed his eyes. Of course there were others. Who were they? But it was long ago, so long ago, he told himself. What was he doing to himself with this insane jealousy? To her? He should go to her, hold her, reassure her. She needed him now. Instead, as if possessed by a demon, he shouted, "Who else? How many others? Tell me the truth." He moved toward her.

Enraged, she spat out, defiantly, "Richard Hardwick! Are you satisfied now?"

He gasped. "Hardwick? Richard Hardwick?"

"Yes!" she answered coldly. "I didn't want to run against him in the first place because we'd been lovers. That was the real reason!" His look of horror fueled her outrage. "Goddamn you, you civilized brilliant captain of industry. You forced me into the confessional. And now you're indulging yourself in a holier-than-thou neurotic jealousy binge. I never assumed *you* were a virgin when I married you. And I never pretended to be the holy Mary, for God's sake. What difference did it make? I haven't looked at another man in twenty years. And considering monogamy is an unnatural state to begin with, it's no minor achievement!"

"I see," he answered bitterly. "You find monogamy a burden, do you? I've managed to live in that 'unnatural state,' as you call it, and I haven't found it to be a burden." Unable to stop himself, he went on, "Perhaps your other lovers were better at satisfying you than I am."

Norah looked at him with disgust. "As soon as this nightmare is over, you can pack your things and go find a vestal virgin. Then you won't have to indulge yourself in this self-immolation."

He tried to move toward her but couldn't; the anger was still too great, holding him back.

He longed to say, Forgive me for being consumed with jealousy, but I can't help it. I'm ill with it. It's in my bones. The words wouldn't come. They stared at one another helplessly.

Finally, Norah screamed, "*You* wanted me to run. You applied all the pressure you could to force me to do it. Because *your* President needed me. I should have told you about Richard up front. Now I'm glad I didn't!" she said defiantly. "When I need you to help me, you're so goddamn jealous, so terrified my problems will rub off on the President, you don't give a shit about me! Jesus Christ," she screamed in frustration, "I didn't know about Guido's nefarious ties, and it's as much to Richard's advantage as mine not to rake over the past. But he won't have the choice, Guido's masters will." The pent-up tears finally streamed down her face.

"I can't, I can't go through with it. And I can't bear what you're doing to the both of us. I want to die," she sobbed.

He took her in his arms and held her tightly. He hadn't been totally honest with her either. She'd hit a nerve. He *had* put the President's interest first. He had never revealed the depth of the President's own desperation to her. He had expected her to accept whatever they demanded of her without question, and now he'd nearly destroyed her because of his inability to reciprocate. He vowed to himself he'd make it up to her. He'd back her to the hilt. He'd make up for his madness.

With great effort, he whispered, "Forgive me, Norah. I love you." He held her tear-stained face in both his hands and asked, "Do you love me?"

She nodded, unable to speak.

"Okay, then," he said, wiping her tears with his handkerchief. "You can't quit now. There's too much riding on this election. You either hang in or you hand Hardwick a passport to the presidency. And I won't let you submit to blackmail. We'll fight this. We'll win."

CHAPTER
Twenty-five

Lisa Ryder checked her wristwatch and entered the executive building at Paragon Studios. It was ten fifty. Walter Lowman was notoriously prompt. She would reach his office precisely at eleven o'clock. The guard recognized her instantly and smiled. She was the newest star in the studio firmament. Walt had agreed to see her without asking why when she had called him at home early that morning. No doubt, he was girding himself for a session involving the usual star complaints about money, directors, costars, or God knows what. Contrary to the heads of other studios, he made his accessibility a point of pride. He never refused to take a telephone call or a request for an appointment.

She rode the private elevator to the fourteenth floor and walked down the long corridor, not bothering to glance at the huge avant-garde paintings hung along the walls. She turned the corner and headed toward the alcove, where two secretaries sat stationed in front of the open door leading to Walt's office. The neatly dressed middle-aged women nodded politely and let her pass. She was expected.

Walt rose from his desk to kiss her and closed the door. "Good morning, Lisa." Walt smiled as he settled her opposite his desk. "You were the most beautiful girl at the party, and the President fell madly in love with you."

He studied her carefully as he talked and noted her eyes fixed on the stark Franz Kline, black-and-white painting behind his desk, rather than on him. She wasn't listening to a word he was saying. She was lost in some sort of distress of her own, and she was not about to be diverted by small talk. What a way to start the day, Walt thought. But he might as well get on with it. He sighed. "Well, my dear, what's the problem?"

Lisa sat forward in the chair, her body tensed, her eyes focused directly on his. "Walt, I want you to tell me truthfully if you have any interest in my personal life."

Christ! What kind of trouble had she gotten into? "Do you mean do 'I' or does the studio?"

"Both."

"Of course!"

"Why?" She hadn't taken her eyes off his face.

"Because Tillie and I have grown very fond of you and happen to think you're a marvelous young woman." In a soft, soothing voice he went on. "The studio cares because it's about to invest a great deal of its capital in a film in which you are to be the star. What dreadful caper do you have in mind, darling? Are you planning to rob a bank? Bomb a building?" he joked, thinking what a lot of bullshit it always took. "Perhaps have an affair with Fidel Castro?"

The blue eyes widened. "No, Walt, I'm having one with Daniel Brookings."

He flinched. "Why are you telling *me,* Lisa?"

"Because Dan insists it can cost me my career, and when I told him he was crazy, he suggested I ask you. So I'm asking. He's crazy, isn't he?" she asked, her voice pleading for agreement.

Walt averted his eyes. He stood up and walked around the desk to Lisa and grasped her hand in silence, leading her to the plate-glass window that reached across the entire wall. Paragon's make-believe world lay in full view before them. Tourists jammed the brightly colored tramcars riding past blocks of one-dimensional city facades. A few moments of travel could take them from New York to Rome, across the Red Sea, and into primitive jungles. Long rows of enclosed stages built like airplane hangars surrounded the amusement center. Streams of people moved in every direction.

"He's not crazy, Lisa. Five thousand people down there depend on this studio for their living and thousands more own our stock. If you become involved with a black man, the film in which you star will bomb in Georgia, the Carolinas, Mississippi, and Texas, not to mention Rhodesia and possibly even Massachusetts. If that happened, the studio could stand to lose a great deal of money it had a right to expect."

Lisa drew back from the window; Walter turned and faced her. "Things are better than they were. At least we could use you in minor films where the investment is small enough to justify the risk." He paused. "The plans we've made for your career would no longer be the same, Lisa." He shook his head. "Dan is not crazy." He swallowed hard and said, "I'm sorry, darling."

Walt stood silent, hating what he was doing. Still she couldn't have it both ways. Nobody could. He knew that better than anyone. Giving up Sylvia had been easy compared to some of the other choices he'd been forced to make. The friends whom he had refused a needed favor. The enemies he'd been obliged to deal with, the bargaining, the compromising. He hadn't gotten to be the head of Paragon Studios without doing things he loathed, without giving up things he longed for.

Lisa was staring at him in horror. "You're a goddamn hypocrite, Walter Lowman! All the liberal stuff you spout is as phony as that street front down there. Everything Norah's mouthing and you and Tillie and the President are supposed to stand for is just crap!" She was shaking with rage, determined to deliver one last blow. "At least the South doesn't pretend," she concluded bitterly.

Walt's stomach heaved. "That's not fair, Lisa," he protested. "I've spent my life trying to change things, just as the President and Norah and Tom and Tillie have. But this is a business, my business, and I'm in it to make money. That's what I'm paid to do. I'm no more a free agent than all those people down there—than you! Dan Brookings is brilliant, first class, and ten times better educated than I am. If you love him and he loves you, Lisa, I'm for it, and I think you're both lucky. But you, Lisa, you're the one who has to make a choice. Do you or don't you want to be a great star? If you choose Dan, he stops being a brilliant press secretary and becomes 'that actress's nigger' for the rest of his life!" He looked at her, stern-faced. "You'd be warmly welcomed as Dan's wife or lover in liberal and creative circles. But don't kid yourself. You'll be the outsider in his world too!"

She sank into the chair and covered her face with her hands. "You bastard."

"It's not me, Lisa, it's reality."

Walt was silent again, still hating himself. Although he'd developed a great deal of cement in his knees across the years, it didn't make things easier. He had no judgments to make about Lisa's personal life. The only judgment he was obliged to make was how what she did would affect the studio, the stock, his job as chairman of the board. No amount of affection he felt for her could change that.

Why the hell didn't somebody walk into his office with good news, a pleasant surprise? His fate was to bite bullets day after day.

Finally, she looked up at him and placed her hands on the arms of the chair. "You mean I have to choose between Dan or being a star and a hypocrite!"

His face was grim as he nodded his head affirmatively. And he never doubted that she'd choose stardom.

At the same time Lisa was confronting Walter Lowman in his marble tower, Norah was streaking toward the desert across the cloudless September sky on Air Force One with the presidential party.

The plane reached cruising level and the President leaned back in his chair facing Norah, Tom, and Andrew Watkins. His mood was jovial. He'd thoroughly enjoyed the Lowman party and was looking forward to a few days of golf. But when Norah, her face pale and eyes filled with despair, hesitantly began to tell him of her encounter with Guido, his heart sank. The President's holiday mood vanished as he listened to her disclosures. His face grew stern. He made no comment while she spoke, trying to conceal the horror he felt.

"Under no circumstances," Norah concluded emphatically, "will there be any head-on confrontations. No debate! No big exposé. No direct attack. If by some fluke, I win—fine! If not—" She shrugged.

The President leaned forward in his seat. His tone was avuncular, but his eyes were as cold as steel.

"Are you telling me that the threat of public exposure over some youthful misadventure is sufficient reason to hand Richard Hardwick a free ride, my dear?" he questioned.

Norah looked at him in disbelief. Didn't he know what it cost her emotionally to disclose the seamy story to him? To have told Tom? To face up to what the press and what Hardwick's campaign could do to her?

"What you so gallantly call 'some youthful misadventure' will be blown up into a full-scale scandal. I'll be dragged through the mud for the whole world to see—including my son. I don't intend for that to happen, Mr. President."

Tom looked from one to the other, wishing Norah had let him handle the President. But she had been adamant that the President had a right to know the truth from her. Tom felt his wife's anguish, but he also knew of the President's desperate need to keep chipping away at Hardwick. He knew that she would not be let off lightly no matter how eloquently she pleaded her case.

Andrew Watkins sighed deeply and shook his head.

The President glared at Norah. "In other words, you have in mind to quit. To walk out on me! If Hardwick is returned to the Senate, that would be tragic enough—but unscathed! That's unthinkable! I tell you"—his voice rose—"there'll be no possible way for his party to deny him the nomination to oppose me under those circumstances."

The President's mind flashed back two decades. He could still hear Colonel Thayer saying, "These are the terms, Professor." They had seemed so farfetched and absurd to him then. He hadn't believed he'd make it to the Congress, much less to the White House. He had accepted the conditions with relief. He was convinced the Colonel was saving him from ruin, and the conditions were so simple. Besides, he had no choice. The memory of the ghastly tragedy still pained and plagued him. The Colonel was gone, but the evidence of the promise he'd extracted from him existed somewhere. Of that, the President was certain. That old bastard, the Colonel, hadn't been the type to make vain threats, and he sure as hell planned for the future.

The President was grimly determined to keep Norah in there fighting. There'd be no backing away, no matter what she had to stomach. She was the only weapon he had against Hardwick's ambitions. She was competent, well beloved, and, best of all, highly visible—more so than Hardwick was, despite his incumbency. And there was no way the President could bring himself to explain his need of her, reveal the terrible story of his own stained past. It was enough that Tom, Andy, and Liz knew. Oh God, what it had cost him to tell his wife! The President was certain Tom would back him up when it came to the crunch, but first he himself must shake Norah's intransigence! What the hell, he rationalized, no one would remember that little a smear story for five minutes after the campaign was finished. Norah was overreacting.

"I would remind you," he said to her, "that it was you, my dear Norah, who insisted that Brookings stay on for your sake, despite my better judgment and everyone else's, including his own, and he did, out of a sense of obligation to you, even though it cost him a great deal of agony. Now *you* tell me that you have no obligation to me."

"But he wasn't being asked to have his personal life laid open, to be accused of adultery, consorting with mobsters, and God knows what," she argued.

"Bullshit," the President snapped, his color mounting. "Dan was being called an Uncle Tom by his own people and much worse than that by that crowd of bloodthirsty racists. It was as tough for him as it would be for you to be called a—"

"A whore!" Norah interrupted, her voice growing shrill. "A gangster's whore!" But he'd made his point and put her on the defensive. He was asking no more of her than she had asked of Dan.

The President went on, ignoring her protest. "It's not just my neck, or even your neck, lovely as it is, that's at stake here. It's foreign policy and domestic policy and everything else we've worked for all these years. Hardwick is dangerous because he represents the worst kind of elitism and has absolutely no sense of the future. He's a goddamned dinosaur. Privileges for the privileged! Is that what you want in the White House?" he snarled. "Because if you chicken out, that's what you'll get."

Norah's frustration and rage exploded. Bitterly, she shouted, "You want me to attack and be attacked, to take the heat for you. But you don't want me to stand up and holler about the things *I* care about. It's your own political fate that interests you. You don't give a damn about me. They're right when they say I'm nothing but a stooge for you. So now I'm to be put to the stake because you're terrified of Richard Hardwick. For what? For the honor of being your puppet?"

Tom reached for her hand. He was deeply distressed by her outburst. Couldn't she see the President was desperate and begging for her help as best he could. "That's not fair, Norah," he chided. "The President has only asked you to soft-pedal your positions on a few of the issues that differed from those of his administration. No one is asking you to be a robot."

Norah pulled her hand away from his, angrily. "What about abortion, Mr. President?" she asked, eyes blazing.

Andy could no longer contain himself. "Jesus Christ, do we have to go into that again?"

"Damn right, we do! Why should anybody bother to vote for a woman who hasn't even got the guts to stand up on *that* one! I'm being asked to have my reputation destroyed to save an administration that waffles on abortion! I happen to feel passionately about it. And so do a hell of a lot of other women, Mr. Chairman." Norah spat the title at him.

The President glared at Andy and shook his head. He was making things worse.

He gritted his teeth. What could he do? Rip off her epaulets? Make her a civilian? Dump her? That's what Norah wanted, but he couldn't possibly let her off the hook. He had to keep her in the ring slugging at Hardwick whatever the price she extracted from him, even if it meant taking risks with his own skeletons.

"Norah, I'm begging you as a friend and as your President to stay in the race and fight. I want you to attack Hardwick, to debate him, to go after him all the way." He swallowed hard, and his voice was low as he said to her, "And if you must, go ahead and speak out on any issue you like—including abortion."

Norah shook her head. "I can't go through with it. I just can't."

"I see," he said bitterly, "your vanity won't allow your image to be disturbed. I'm willing to make any concessions you want to make, even though it could embarrass me and my administration. That's all right with you. But you, Norah, you can't bring yourself to face a bad review, can you?"

Norah felt as if her head would explode. The President was begging her to make the fight on any terms she wanted, and yet she couldn't bring herself to agree to do what he asked. She'd had her mind firmly made up when she got on the plane, and now she was riddled with doubts. Was she being downright cowardly, vain, as he'd accused her? She was sick with her own vacillation and his angry pleading. The pressure was unbearable. He didn't care what she did or what she'd have to endure for his sake, as long as she crippled Hardwick. Yet his own need for her help was so visible, she couldn't ignore it.

"You're pressing me," she anguished. "I can't take any more of this.

I can't make up my mind. I don't want to. Let me think it over. Give me a few days time."

The President nodded, leaned forward, and kissed her cheek. "You think it over, darling." He had a sense of relief. At least she was off the dime. The first step had been accomplished.

By the time they reached the romanesque pink marble villa situated on thirty acres along the outskirts of Palm Springs, the President's mood was restored to its usual affability.

His joyful anticipation of a few days of uninterrupted golf put an end to all political discussion. The subject of Norah's campaign was dropped.

Looking decades younger than his seventy years, the former Secretary of State welcomed them with warmth and old-fashioned courtesy. He had served his country with great distinction under the administrations of three Presidents. His diplomatic skills and brilliance were legendary, as was his wealth.

The multimillionaire heir to one of the world's largest oil fortunes, he had built his desert showplace for the amusement of his young fifth wife. The scandalous divorce brought on by their romance had cost him all hopes of gaining the presidency, for which he had been eminently equipped. To his disappointment, his wife found the south of France more to her taste than the isolated desert retreat. And as he grew older, he preferred the company of the high-ranking political guests and heads of state who made regular pilgrimages to visit him to that of the raggle-taggle international set with which his wife surrounded herself. She'd given him two sons, which none of his other wives had done. He doted on the boys. He was too old now to make any drastic changes in his life. The arrangement had finally grown to suit him. He accepted the role of gracious host and elder statesman with relish.

The compound boasted seven secluded guest cottages, a meticulously tended private golf course, an Olympics-sized swimming pool, four tennis courts, and a Chinese chef.

His estate was so situated as to be invisible from the highway. The grounds and buildings were enclosed by thousands of feet of tall metal fencing, making the golf course and the guest cottages easily protectable. All in all, the estate met the requirements necessary to satisfy the President's golf mania as well as the complex demands of the Secret Service.

CHAPTER

Twenty-six

While the men played golf, a limousine and driver took Norah to Chino to visit Manuel. Speeding past the barren terrain, spotted with oases of date farms and orange groves, she found herself dwelling on the brutal act of violence that had nearly cost Manuel his life. Although the involvement of his former ranch hand implicated Hardwick, she couldn't bring herself to believe that the man she'd seen comforting Manuel's family could have been a party to the bloody act. Perhaps she didn't want to.

Whatever their tangled relationships, the scene she'd witnessed at the hospital between them and Richard and his daughter made it impossible for Norah to accept the circumstantial evidence as anything more than that. But Tom and Mellon were convinced they had sufficient grounds for a broadside attack. Their arguments were strengthened by the latest opinion polls. With the election only six weeks away, Hardwick's lead over her had narrowed considerably. The combination of his wife's questionable death and the Chisholm affair, compounded by Manuel's brutal beating and the disappearance of the suspect, germinated doubts about the incumbent's integrity. They were anxious to publicize the limited data Mellon had gathered about Hardwick's real-estate holdings under the umbrella of the Elwick Corporation. It would add further doubts about his clouded

explanations of the much-publicized support in the primary of her opponent, Chisholm, by the family foundation.

Norah's campaign managers wanted Hardwick put on the defensive.
That in itself might have forced him to blurt out the details, but Norah
had adamantly refused to risk what she considered a potential smear attack
without solid evidence in hand. Too often she had seen that sort of thing
backfire. She herself had been the one to insist that they press for a debate
instead. Norah had been convinced it was the better way to smoke him
out. Now she wished to God she'd allowed them to use whatever little
material they'd gathered and not been so adamant. Perhaps then an attack
on her personal life would have appeared to be a desperate act of retaliation. But now with Guido's threat hanging over her, the very thought of
a debate with Hardwick sickened her.

The limousine pulled up to the entrance of a white stucco, one-story
house on the outskirts of Chino. Manuel stood at the doorway as the car
drew to a halt. He walked toward her, smiling broadly, his gait somewhat
awkward.

Dr. Conway had warned them that it would be months before Manuel's
balance would be totally restored to normal. Norah had been prepared
for that, but something about his appearance seemed disturbingly unfamiliar. She laughed with relief when she realized it was his closely cropped
hair that made him look foreign to her.

Manuel's mother and aunt joined them for lunch in the sun-splashed
patio, filled with bright red geraniums and exotic succulents. He was eager
to discuss the campaign with her, demanding to be filled in on every detail
and recent development. Manuel was obviously still deeply committed to
her cause. Norah watched him anxiously for signs that his head injury
might have caused permanent damage. But to her relief, other than an
occasional hesitancy, a groping for a lost word, he appeared normal and
well.

"There is hope now where there was none," he said with a look of
triumph on his face. "Perhaps what I have been through will be the
turning point. If the senseless violence has hurt Hardwick's credibility, his
defeat will make it worthwhile."

Norah's heart turned over. Would it seem so worthwhile to him when
her relationship with Guido was disclosed? she wondered.

Did Manuel really believe Richard Hardwick had himself been involved in the beating? Even obliquely? How could he? In an attempt to probe the strange relationship, she said, "I don't understand. Here you are, devoted to my cause, and yet while I was waiting in the hospital with your mother and aunt, Hardwick and his daughter were there with us, as anguished and concerned as we were. He told me then that you and Mrs. Redfern were reared as siblings. How then—?"

Before she could finish the sentence, Manuel was on his feet. "My dear Mrs. Ashley," he said, taking her hand and pointedly ignoring her question, "you are so kind to have come to see me, but it is time for me to take my siesta. Conway's orders. I promise you I'll be in Los Angeles for your election. Tell Peter"—he smiled—"I'll see him then." And he dismissed her.

His mother rose to follow him and said anxiously, "The doctor is very strict about rest."

After they left, Norah looked questioningly at Manuel's Aunt Concha across the table, hoping she would volunteer an explanation of the tangled, mysterious relationships and his obvious reluctance to discuss them.

"Mrs. Ashley, may I speak to you about a matter which sits heavily on my conscience before you leave?" Concha asked. The dark eyes, so much like Manuel's, looked at Norah searchingly.

"Why, of course," Norah said hopefully.

"You have knowledge of the Elwick Foundation," Concha stated and paused.

Surprised, Norah nodded, waiting for her to continue.

Concha rested her arms on the table. Her narrow, long-fingered hands were locked together as she leaned toward Norah, her voice low and the look in her dark eyes intense. "I am a trustee as well as the treasurer of the foundation. Do you remember your primary battle, Mrs. Ashley?"

Norah nodded but remained silent, not wishing to interrupt her.

"If you investigate carefully, you will find that the checks made out to the Reverend Isaiah Smith bear my signature."

Norah was horrified. Did this woman know what she had done? Made a political contribution under the false pretense of charity? Incredible. How had she gotten involved?

"Why did you do that?" Norah asked, astonished.

"Because Senator Richard asked me to."

"*He* asked you to?"

Concha nodded. Without pausing to answer Norah, she continued, "You see, I came to the Casa as a young girl, Mrs. Ashley. I had nothing and was nothing. The Colonel and his wife were kind and good to me. When Mrs. Thayer died, I helped rear Virginia, Marianne's mother." Her eyes clouded. "Poor Virginia! And then the Colonel asked me to take care of Marianne because she loved living at the Casa and so disliked being in Washington." Her face lit up. "The Colonel made my sister's life possible"—she sighed—"and Manuel's too. Without him, they would still be starving in a village in Mexico. He was a good man, Mrs. Ashley. A noble man! And Senator Richard was like a son to him. For the Colonel's sake I could refuse him nothing!"

"But how can Manuel be so deeply involved in my campaign if the Thayer family have been his benefactors?" Norah asked, more confused than ever.

Concha's eyes flashed. "Because he is a man, Mrs. Ashley. They are single-minded creatures, not divided into a thousand pieces the way women are. Manuel has concern about the problems of his own people, my people, *La Raza*—*that* is his great passion. In his mind, the Thayers are symbols of the exploiters, *conquistadores,* the *padrones.* He has separated himself from his personal feelings. Women cannot do this so easily."

Norah could feel the woman's agony. Now Concha herself was betraying the family she loved in disclosing Richard's deceit to Norah—the enemy.

"Then why, Mrs. Romo, are you giving me this evidence which could harm the Senator?" Norah asked, truly puzzled.

Concha looked at her with anguish. "I must because I made a promise to God when Manuel lay close to death. When we sat there praying for him, I promised God I would confess what I had done if only he would let him live. He is alive!"

"But Mrs. Romo, do you know that you yourself could be accused of being involved in a criminal act if I use the information you have given me proving that Senator Hardwick lied?"

The dark eyes misted. Concha bit her lip to hold back the tears and nodded.

How could Richard have used this loyal woman in such a shameful way? Norah thought angrily. She had reared his child, his wife. Yet he had jeopardized her for his own sake. Had he grown so arrogant that he thought himself to be above the law? Above human decency? Incredible.

Norah asked, "Would you consider signing a statement repeating what you've told me if I send my aide to see you?"

Without hesitation, Concha answered, "Of course! I promised God."

* * *

Two days later, John Mellon returned to Los Angeles in a state of high excitement with Concha Romo's affidavit in his briefcase.

Norah, torn between the fear of her own exposure and admiration for the other woman's courage, had finally agreed with Tom that even with the risk to herself she had an obligation to use the material. Her anger against Richard Hardwick had hardened. She knew now that he was totally unscrupulous and the knowledge intensified her fears of reprisal. There was no longer any way to dissemble. Her inner circle must be told the truth about Guido's threats.

Tom reluctantly agreed with her and called a meeting in Norah's office. Mellon could hardly wait for them to settle themselves around the desk. Shouting, "We've had a breakthrough!" he read Concha's statement out loud, without stopping for breath.

Karl Auerbach whistled through his teeth. "We've got him by the short hair. This has to be saved for the debate, sprung on him from left field."

Norah shook her head. "No, not in a debate. There will be no debate!"

The room fell silent.

Tom interjected quickly, "There've been some other new developments that need to be discussed. Norah has been seriously threatened with a smear attack. I'm convinced they mean it! We have to see to it that the Romo statement can be discreetly leaked to some sympathetic commentators or newsmen, and not attributed directly to Norah. There are serious risks involved. Norah's willing to take those, but not to debate."

Frowning, Tillie asked, "What kind of smear? What's left to do? They've already called her everything in the book, for God's sake!"

Before he could answer for her, Norah faced Tillie and said in a low voice, "I was involved with a member of the Mafia and they know it."

"The Mafia! That's crazy!"

Norah shook her head. "No, Tillie, unfortunately it's the truth. Guido Di Brazza was the son-in-law of a Mafia leader. His brother-in-law is the

Don now." She turned to Walt, her face pale and ravaged. "Did you know?"

Walt shook his head in disbelief. "Hell, no! He was always the epitome of social respectability. And his wife—" His laugh was bitter. "The most pretentious, social-climbing pain in the ass queen of Palm Beach society! Come on, Norah, you were a babe in the woods. *I* bought your contract from him, for God's sake. If I didn't know, how could you? So let them try to make something of it! It's nonsense," he snorted.

John Mellon, his excitement dissolved into concern, shook his head. "I'm not so sure it's nonsense. The new material we've been working on suggests that Hardwick's hidden partners in the real estate he owns outside of San Diego are part of a Mafia syndicate. How the hell can Norah blast him on that or anything else when she's got this Di Brazza character to explain? She was so damned reluctant to use the material before it was documented," he said reproachfully, reaching for a cigarette. "Whatever we leak now looks like some desperate last-minute attempt to smear him because she's been linked to some unsavory characters herself. They can leak, too, you know. At least if you call for a debate, Norah, you have a chance to go after him hot and heavy. And this"—he waved Concha's confession—"can shake his credibility. But the real issue is the Beau Soleil business. Your best bet is to attack and let it all hang out. But a leak here and a rumor there?" He shook his head. "You might as well give up."

"I can't debate him, John. I just can't," Norah protested, tears welling up. "I even loathe sticking my neck out on the Romo thing, but she was so brave to give it to me. I feel—"

Brookings, who'd been listening quietly, stood up and walked over to Norah. He glared at her with contempt, remembering the demands she'd made on him.

"If you back down now, *you're* going to be the black baby at the Baptist picnic. You've *got* to demand a debate. Now!" His voice rose to a shout. "Christ! They're going to leak this stuff anyway. They'd be crazy not to. You've been moving up in the polls. Why should Hardwick take any chances? Did that old fraud Di Brazza tell you if you played possum, they'd sit on it?" he snorted. "Don't be naive! Even if you get beat, you can still ruin his chance for the nomination by bringing all this stuff out in the open. You *owe* the President that! Isn't that what you told me?"

"She certainly does," Karl Auerbach said emphatically, his face drawn into a scowl. Labor couldn't afford to have her pull out. Bad enough to have Hardwick returned to the Senate, but to send him back a hero? Maybe if Hardwick were kept busy enough on Norah's case, he'd lay off the President. At least there was a chance that the administration could be salvaged.

Ignoring Karl, Norah returned Dan's look, her face grim. "Marvelous! But what about me? If I'm going to lose, why should I go out there and be made a fool of on national television? I'm to be publicly humiliated so that Hardwick won't pose a threat to the President two years from now. Won't my disgrace rub off on him?"

Sylvia Gannon spoke up. "This isn't going to sit well with middle America, especially the women."

She's got a nerve, Tillie thought, little Miss Power-fucker herself.

"But you could do a Checkers number," Sylvia added, her expression thoughtful. "Throw yourself at the mercy of the voters, plead for under-standing—youthful ignorance and all that."

"They'll throw up," Tillie snarled. Nothing Sylvia suggested could meet her approval.

Mellon disagreed. "It's the only way to go, whether they throw up or not! And Norah's going to get it whether she plays dead or not, so she might as well stick it to him before she hits the mat." He couldn't bear the thought of Hardwick's having a free ride. After all the months of digging and prying and searching, Norah's reluctance to use the material he had so painstakingly put together was unthinkable. And now they had the unexpected windfall of the Romo statement, which would shaft the bastard's credibility. How could they waste it? The memory of Virginia Hardwick stabbed him.

"She's got to call for a debate, Tom," he insisted. Maybe Tom could do something with her. "Norah or Brookings has got to announce that we've uncovered some damaging new evidence concerning the Senator's business machinations and that she's not going to try him in the press with leaks and innuendos. No sir, she's going to let him speak for himself eyeball to eyeball. The son of a bitch probably won't sit still for a direct confrontation. We'll more than likely have to settle for one of those question-and-answer things with a panel doing the interrogating, but at least we can stack it a little."

Tom glanced questioningly at Norah. She was studying the faces of the others as they sat waiting for an answer. Evelyn seemed close to tears. Barbara and Lisa, eyes downcast, appeared to be studying the floor, unable to return her gaze. Only Dan looked at her directly, his jaw set, his eyes locked into hers. Norah had no choice and she knew it.

"Okay, Dan, call a press conference and demand a debate. Do whatever you want," she said and reached for Tom's hand.

CHAPTER
Twenty-seven

Swinging his feet up on his desk and tilting back his chair, Richard Hardwick faced the conservatively dressed, distinguished-looking gray-haired man sitting opposite him. Edward Littlejohn, president of the Thayerville National Bank and chairman of the senator's reelection committee, was worried. He'd seen the latest polls and didn't much like what he'd seen. Norah appeared to be making steady inroads into Richard Hardwick's lead.

"Screw the polls, Ed." Hardwick pointed to the stack of newspapers piled in front of him and said with satisfaction, "Last night's dinner proves how much *they* know. *All* the papers, not just the Thayer press, called it 'an overflow crowd.'"

Littlejohn stared at him in disbelief. Was it possible he wasn't aware of the "table game"? It was a classic political ploy. An announcement made early in the day stated that there would be five hundred supporters in attendance, although more tickets than the publicized number had already been sold. The banquet room was deliberately set up for considerably fewer people than those expected. A large empty space was reserved toward the rear of the room on the pretext of making the dinner service more efficient. When the guests began to file in and the tables appeared to be filling, the prearranged signal had been given and several dozen extra tables were promptly brought into the room and set up rapidly and visibly in the space presumably required for serving convenience, giving the press the impression of an unexpected overflow.

Had the senator become a victim of his own publicity? Incredulous, Littlejohn told him, "Richard, it was *planned* to look that way. There wasn't an overflow crowd. They weren't beating down the doors. What's worse, we had to do some pretty heavy arm twisting in so-called 'Hardwick territory' to get those bodies out," he told him. "I know I'm a banker and not a politician, but the polls are telling us something, believe me! Maybe you ought to accept the challenge to debate, my friend. Actress or not, with your experience in the Senate, you should be able to maul her. They've sent a lot of feelers out and I haven't slammed the door shut— We could have one of those press conference things with a panel asking the—"

Swinging his feet to the floor and sitting up straight, Hardwick broke in before he could finish the sentence, and snapped, "Forget it. She's not going to do any more challenging, Ed." He smiled knowingly.

Surprised, Littlejohn questioned, "Then why the hell is her nigger calling a press conference this afternoon? It makes me goddamn nervous, Richard." He picked at a hangnail. "What do they know about the Beau Soleil deal? Do they know about the bank's involvement? It could rub off on me, hurt the bank, if it gets out that we were involved. Especially now, after all that Lance stuff." He shook his head. "Between the Chisholm business and the Elwick Fund and then that bastard who beat up Concha's nephew floating around loose—I just don't—"

Hardwick repeated impatiently, "Forget it, Ed. Stop being an old woman. I don't care what Brookings or that *summa cum laude* bastard Mellon have in mind, calling a press conference. My opponent isn't buying a debate, and she sure as hell isn't going to let them dump all over me. I promise you—she's not going to talk about any real-estate deals." He leaned forward and lowered his voice. "She knows that I know what she doesn't want the public or her husband or anyone else to know. The message was delivered to her personally. If there's one thing the folks out there are not going to go for, it's a has-been actress with a murky past. As for that foreman of mine"—his face darkened and he lowered his voice to a whisper—"that's under control." He was quick to add, "Of course,

I don't know anything about it." He shuddered at the recollection of Jimmy's phone call. "And you don't either, Ed!" he ordered. "And stop worrying! Mrs. Ashley won't be yapping about a debate every time she hits a microphone." Unconsciously, his eyes traveled to Virginia's portrait on the far wall. It was as if she were there in the room staring at him disdainfully. Cool and patrician. The memory of that same haughty visage stained with blood flashed across his vision.

He thought about John Mellon and hated him. If Mellon dared to push Norah into any funny business, he wouldn't hesitate to let her have it. He'd enlighten the voters about her liaison with Guido and what he represented. Her affair with himself, if he had to. He could afford to take the risk. In spite of women's lib there was still a double standard out there. It wouldn't hurt his image. He'd be considered macho. Womanizing never harmed the Kennedys, did it?

But Norah would be made to look the slut. Ed was simply unhinged by the political arena. Bankers didn't have the kind of guts it took to play the game. The Ashley people would be too smart to risk it even if she had told them about Guido, which he didn't think likely.

Later in the day, when he watched Brookings's press conference, he began to think differently. They must have gone ahead and done their thing without knowing what cards he held in his hands. It wasn't likely that Norah had told them about Di Brazza. If she had, they would be off their heads to risk her being exposed publicly. No, Brookings must have called the press conference without consulting Norah. She would never have permitted it. But Concha! That hit him in the solar plexus. Hers was a bald betrayal of trust. It had not been an inadvertent slip. She was too discreet for that. It was deliberate! Had the latter-day Savonarola, her nephew, gotten to her? Still, that was no excuse. She'd signed a sworn statement, hadn't she? She was as guilty as Manuel was. The Colonel must be spinning in his crypt. She was quoted as having flatly refuted his claim that he'd no knowledge of the Elwick Fund's contribution to Smith. Making him out to be a liar. She had been as much a party to it as he was. No one stood over her with a gun and forced her to sign the check. Manuel had gotten to her! Used the beating to turn her against him. Hardwick watched and listened in horror as Brookings, waving Concha's affidavit in front of the camera, his face impassive, his voice matter-of-fact, went on to reveal the findings made by Mellon's investigators, ticking them off like a shopping list. He spoke of the Elwick Foundation's ownership of a large block of stock in a Bahamas-based holding company, saying, "The foundation is known to be involved with Mafia money and suspect union pension funds."

Brookings further charged that the senator had obtained a zoning variance allowing these same interests to build the lush Beau Soleil resort development on property that was to have been reserved for public parklands. He went on to accuse Hardwick of blatant misuse of the powers of his office to procure tax-shelter benefits for large corporations which were heavily involved in financing his campaign for reelection and the national movement to promote his future bid for the presidency.

Hardwick jumped up, clicked off the television, and poured himself a large tumbler of vodka from the bar next to the bookshelves. He'd seen enough. He didn't need to listen to the question-and-answer crap. He knew how those vultures would pitch it. His phone rang insistently, but he ignored it, rattling the ice cubes around his glass. Gulping down the drink, he returned to his desk and barked into the intercom, "Hold my calls! Say I'm out! Gone for the day." He slumped in his chair and his mind wandered into a reverie.

Even now, he could evoke the image of his mother's face glowing with pride and himself, a small boy, standing ramrod straight, as he looked directly at the President, the way she'd told him to. The then Commander-in-Chief was telling him that the nation would be forever indebted to his father for his bravery and sacrifice in battle.

The lantern-jawed, pince-nezed President had leaned down and placed his father's Congressional Medal of Honor around his neck and shaken his hand as if he were a grown man.

The only memory he held of his hero father was the photograph of him standing alongside the plane in which he died. It was placed in the center of the mantelpiece in the living room of the one-story bungalow. Alongside it was the one of his mother, dressed as a bride, looking very young and strangely unfamiliar.

After the White House ceremony, she'd held him close and whispered, "When you're grown up, my darling, *you'll* pin the medals."

He believed her prophecy then, as he did now. He never once doubted his ultimate destiny. Even with death at her side, she'd clung to the dream. Emaciated and drawn, in that dreary, darkened hospital room, she held his hand, a shadowy smile flickering across her face, her voice barely audible, and said it again! "You *will* pin the medals." At least she'd lived long enough to see him sworn into the Senate. The bittersweet memories brought unexpected tears to his eyes. Goddamn that bitch Norah! He'd have her scalp before she or anybody else cost him the presidency. Nobody! Nobody was going to deprive him of Mama's dream. He was at the point of no return. He'd win at any price.

* * *

Norah's supporters were wild with joy. Hardwick had not refuted the charges. Instead he'd responded to them obliquely, saying, "This poor desperate woman is scribbling dirty words across the handwriting on the wall in an attempt to salvage her faltering campaign."

By his not denying the accusations head-on, he was giving them credence. Not only did Richard Hardwick agree to the long-sought-after debate, he vehemently demanded it. His request was made in a tone of moral outrage. He had no choice. He was sliding down in the polls.

Norah's headquarters were filled with confidence and high spirits. Victory was in sight. Hardwick had been put on the defensive, cornered at long last. The light at the end of the tunnel gleamed bright. But that optimism wasn't shared by Norah or those closest to her. They suspected Hardwick would save the Di Brazza story for his counterattack, during the televised encounter. He'd want full coverage. He would use it as the springboard to destroy her credibility and her image.

Whatever losses she sustained from the attack would inevitably be fatal to her campaign. As the underdog, she desperately needed to gain support in the final weeks, not lose it. Hardwick, on the other hand, was in a strong enough position to absorb some losses. She knew that the last-minute thrust to victory she'd hoped for was blunted.

Norah went about her duties mechanically, disinterested in the campaign details, masking the fatigue that mounted as her hopes diminished. She was resigned to the prospect of the dreaded confrontation and defeat.

CHAPTER

Twenty-eight

He'd never be able to figure it out—Bailey forcing him to split like that. Lonny's face was drawn into a scowl as he looked into the mirror. Christ, even *that* was cracked, distorting his features. The whole thing was nuts. And all that cops-and-robbers stuff. What the hell had he done that was so terrible? He hadn't wanted to hurt the Mexican real bad. Just teach the "lettuce picker" a lesson. Rough him up. He was screwing Bailey's two-timing bitch wife, wasn't he? He had it coming. Big deal! The slob botched up his own goddamn head on the toolbox. So what? Bailey was chickenshit scared for no damn reason at all. Crazy! Him having to take the plane to Miami done up like a drag queen! He grimaced at his reflection. The wig had been hot as hell, and those rags Bailey'd swiped from Marianne's closet were too tight. They'd smelled like her, too. It was something else kissing Bailey good-bye at the airport, like he was a broad. And Jesus, having to sit for hours in the ladies' can in the Miami bus depot! He couldn't make it out of there until the place was empty and there were no dames left squatting and peeing. He'd done just like Bailey told him to and mailed all the junk back to him. He could have dropped it in a trash can just as easy. But Bailey made everything complicated. It started out like a crazy joke. Some joke. Now he was holed up in this godforsaken place, ready to climb the walls.

Christ, he hated this backwater cesspool. It was the armpit of the world. And he missed Bailey so it hurt. Bailey'd promised he'd come get him and take him to the Bahamas or someplace as soon as the fucking election was over. It better be soon. He couldn't stand it much longer.

The room was stinking hot, and there was one lousy movie theater in the whole town running stuff from 1902. They called this a hotel? Lonny McFarland looked around the room in disgust. The dingy wallpaper was peeling, and the dampness penetrated everything, including the lumpy bed, which stank. There was no *air,* just wet. His hair was damn near nigger-kinky, and his color had faded to a pee yellow. The bunkhouse at the Casa was a palace compared with this dump. He pulled on his boots and tucked in the khaki shirt. It clung damply to his back before he had it buttoned. What good were the goddamn money orders Bailey sent him if there wasn't anything to spend it on? Hell, he'd go to that toilet they called a bar and have a drink and b.s. with whatever was there.

Lonny walked listlessly down the scorching street. It was all but deserted. A few blacks maybe and some women in faded cotton shifts. He felt someone walking in back of him and didn't bother to turn around. A fat man in a crinkled white cotton suit, his face half hidden by a panama hat, fell into step with him.

"Hi, cowboy, how'd you like to do some sightseeing?"

Before he could answer, he felt the shock of cold metal against his ribs. "This way, sonny!"

He opened his mouth to scream. The fat man jabbed him sharply. "Shut up, or I'll give it to you right here."

A dark-colored sedan pulled up alongside the curb, and the door swung open. The man quickly pushed Lonny in the backseat, jumped in after him, and slammed the door shut. He pressed the gun hard into the foreman's ribs and the car hurtled forward.

"Lemme outta here!" Lonny yelled and reached for the door. The gun handle came down full force on his hand. He felt his bones crack as he dropped down onto the floor, shrieking with pain and terror. No one spoke. He had no way of knowing how long he lay there clutching his mangled hand or where they were taking him. The car drew to a screeching halt. The fat man kicked him, grabbed his shirt collar, and heaved him out of the car as if he were a sack of pototoes. He fell on his knees. The ground was spongy and oozed through his bleeding fingers.

"Up, buster—we've landed!" The fat man broke into a high-pitched whinnying laugh.

Lonny clumsily pulled himself to his feet, pressing the bleeding pulp of his damaged hand to his chest. The fat man pushed the panama hat back on his head, exposing his red, porcine face, glistening with sweat. The thick lips were drawn into a sneer. The gun still pointed at the terrorized McFarland.

Lonny didn't know where he was. Huge trees, dripping with beards of gray-green moss, hung ominously overhead, like a dark curtain. The air steamed thick with heat and the stench of rotting vegetation.

"You're free, sonny boy. Start running." The fat man chuckled mirthlessly and waved the gun at him. "Run, you bastard!"

"Help me!" Lonny screamed at the driver of the parked car. But the man never turned his head. The frozen profile stared straight ahead, deaf to his cries.

"Don't kill me! I ain't done nothin'! Nothin'!" he sobbed, tears streaming down his face. He moved toward his tormentor, arms outstretched in supplication.

The fat man waved the pistol. "Run!"

Slowly, Lonny backed away and with all the strength left in him turned and broke into a run. But the soggy earth gave way beneath his feet. He felt himself sinking. A huge, exposed root, shaped like a giant prehistoric claw, lay in his path as if reaching out to grab him. He stumbled over it and fell face down. A shot rang out and a bullet whistled through the silent swamp. His wailing cry of "Bailey!" was drowned out by the sound of the car racing down the dirt road.

The swampland was reclaimed by its primeval quiet, the stillness broken only by the humming drone of a million insects.

CHAPTER
Twenty-nine

After days of haggling, the negotiations for the debate were finally completed. It would take place on a Friday, eleven days before the election. In the hope that Hardwick's attack on Norah would have the appearance of a last-minute smear, Mellon tried desperately to have it scheduled as close to Election Day as possible.

Hardwick's forces, on the other hand, wanted it further away. The Friday date was the best he could do. The format agreed upon called for a panel of four interrogators, each principal choosing two of them. The moderator was to be a person approved by both sides. Neither candidate dealt personally with the negotiations. The bargaining was left to their representatives.

Richard Hardwick wanted nothing left to chance. Outraged by what he considered Concha's perfidy, he nevertheless saw its predebate disclosure as an opportunity to prepare himself to handle it adroitly. Along with his aides, he pored over every minute detail of the negotiations. There was no question in his mind that either Norah or one of the panelists inimicable to him would lean heavily on the business of his contribution to Chisholm's primary campaign against her. His game plan was to restate that his bereavement had caused him to be negligent, exploiting the sympathy vote which was still a plus factor in his favor. As for Concha, he planned to take good care of her. He'd paint her as a hysterical woman, her judgment warped because of her personal problems. It would be his word against that of an addled housekeeper. His offensive strategy would be to hammer away at the actress-puppet label already glued firmly on Norah, weakening her validity as a bona fide candidate, while he continued attacking the President.

Despite the protests of his staff, he was determined to withhold the exposure of Norah's relationship with Guido and his Mafia ties until the actual face-to-face encounter. Under no circumstances would he permit the hoped-for negative impact on the electorate to be diluted by time. He wanted the full drama of the shock factor and with maximum exposure. Richard Hardwick was sufficiently knowledgeable politically to know he risked being accused of a last-minute smear, but he felt safe in taking the gamble and relished the prospect of Norah's discomfort. It would be worth the risk as long as the smear took.

Norah, on the other hand, evidenced little interest in the arrangements. When Tom made an attempt to discuss them with her, she'd look at him vacantly and change the subject. The only request she made was for a detailed résumé of Brookings' charges and the material Mellon had collected. Then, she locked herself up with John Mellon in his cubbyhole for briefing sessions until she was certain she knew the script by heart. Hardwick would get his, she'd see to that.

As if by tacit agreement, Tom and Norah handled each other with exaggerated care. They were fearful of tearing open the wounds they had inflicted on each other during their quarrel over Norah's disclosures of her past. Whatever bitterness they carried within themselves was patched over by a distant politeness. Each bore his misery in silence. The prospect of the debate loomed over them like an ominous cloud. For Norah, the horror of exposure was compounded by the fear that the sight of Hardwick face to face with her would exacerbate Tom's obsessive jealousy.

His outburst had been inconsistent with the worldly, disciplined, poised man she'd thought him to be. He had become foreign to her. Tom, for his part, was firmly resolved to keep his demons in control. Riddled with guilt, he was loath to rehash the unpleasant scene. He tried not to think about Norah's past nor his own irrational reaction to its disclosure. They played the unspoken game with scrupulous care. Each was wary of unleashing the depth of his private despair, each hoped against hope that their lives would fall into place as soon as the campaign was over. Laughter had always been the device to end their quarrels. The joke was their white flag. Neither one could bring himself to find the humor now.

The fateful Friday arrived with unexpected swiftness. Tom left the house that morning with an air of manufactured heartiness. His manner was conspicuously unsolicitous and matter-of-fact. It didn't fool Norah. She knew he was riddled with anxieties as great as her own.

She resolved to handle the stress of the debate exactly as if she were dealing with a dreaded dental appointment. She concentrated on the knowledge that she would be obliged to endure discomfort for a limited period. One hour was a manageable time frame for misery. There was some solace in the thought that here, at least, she would be able to give as good as she got, which was not true at the dentist's. It crossed her mind that there was, in both cases, a somewhat macabre analogy to marching into the gas chamber voluntarily, rather than being dragged in. She was going to walk into the broadcasting studio on her own two feet and lay her head on the block.

Capless for the first time in months, she plunged into the pool, secure in the knowledge that Bernie, the hairdresser, would make certain she met her fate well coiffed. For once she didn't trust herself to piece herself together. She was grateful Tillie had been adamant about having him come to the house.

Norah was at the far end of the pool when McPherson, phone in one hand, her white terrycloth robe in the other, called her out of the water, his voice filled with excitement. "Mrs. Ashley, it's the White House calling!"

She wrapped herself in the robe, pushing back her dripping hair, as the butler plugged the instrument into the jack on the brick wall. McPherson handed her the telephone as ceremoniously as if it were a crown jewel. Even after the long years of service in the Ashley household, a call from the White House was still an awesome event to him.

She settled herself in a chair, hand over the mouthpiece. "Thank you, McPherson. Will you be good enough to hang up?" She watched him disappear in the direction of the house, waited until she heard the click, and drew in her breath. "Hello, Norah Ashley here."

A voice answered, "Please hold for the President, Mrs. Ashley."

Her heart sank. More than likely, the President had a postdebate statement ready to give the press, describing her in glowing terms, ignoring
the charges. A eulogy! Why should he care? Hardwick would no longer
threaten him. She'd take care of that, even if it was about to kill her.

The familiar voice came through, firm and cheerful. "Hi, darling!
Ready to do battle?"

"I'm overreadied, sir. Mellon's briefed me day after day on all of
Hardwick's machinations. I think I could get a Ph.D. on his case," she told
him, trying to sound confident.

"That's good. I want you to go in there and aim straight for the jugular.
Tough it through, honey!"

Oh God, it was going to be a locker-room pep talk: "one for the
Gipper." She played his game, answering, "Thank you, sir. I'll give it my
very best."

"I know you will, Norah. Liz joins me in wishing you good luck."

I'll need it, she thought.

"We'll be watching you." He hesitated a moment, his voice becoming
gentle. "And, Norah, my dear, I want you to know we both honor you
for your courage. I know what you're going through for my sake. I'll
always be grateful.

He just wanted to shore her up, to make sure she'd go through with
it. All of them, including Tom, were using her as a sacrificial lamb for the
sake of that great American sacred cow, the presidency. If she won, fine,
if not, at least she'd have helped to save the administration and weaken
the opposition. What did any of them have to lose? It was all she could
do to thank the President for his call and ask to be remembered to Liz.
Slowly replacing the phone, overwhelmed with self-pity and anger, Norah
rested her elbows on the table, covered her face with her hands, and
sobbed.

It was Tillie who found her weeping. "What's going on?" she asked
exasperatedly.

Norah looked up at the elegant figure facing her, arms akimbo.

"I cannot go through with this fiasco, Tillie," she wailed. "It's all a crock
of shit!"

"Oh, for God's sake!" Tillie looked at her with dismay. "You're a
mess," she snapped. "Hilda, the masseuse, is here to beat the hell out of
you! *Norah,* stop this sniveling self-indulgence this *minute!*"

"Go to hell, and take that goddamn Ilse Koch with you!" she cried, wiping her arm across her nose. "I'm beat now and don't need help."

"Look here"—the dark eyes fixed on her, the pale skin pink with agitation—"you're a gutsy dame, and I, for one, don't feel the least bit sorry for you. You're going to give that bastard Hardwick a bad time, and I just happen to believe the folks out there are going to stand up for you. And I don't give a damn for what all the geniuses, including your husband and mine, think. Quit this lugubrious nonsense at once and let's do something about you! You're not the only victim, you know," she said bitterly. "But we're all going to survive."

Norah stood up and glared. After all, whatever Tillie had gone through had been in private and not splattered in headlines for the world to see. And Peter? What about Peter? Tillie didn't have a son. How could *she* understand what it was like to know your son was going to hear all about his mother's affair with a Mafioso lover? Maybe more! Her scarlet *A* would be in full view for the whole world to see.

Tears came rushing back. "And my son's going to see me branded a whore or worse. What about that?" she added despairingly.

Tillie rolled her eyes and made a face. "I don't believe it! This isn't the nineteenth century, you know," she put her hands on her hips and said disdainfully. "*Your* darling baby boy, Peter, and his friends all have had sleep-in girl friends, for God's sake. What we did furtively, they do right out front. Strange as it seems, this generation thinks fucking is normal. Peter doesn't give a hoot about *your* sex life. He's nineteen years old, and the only sex life he cares about is his own. Stop the craziness, Norah! Peter's going to be interested in what you lay on Hardwick, not whom you laid a million years ago. You better believe it! But if you chicken out and face the wall, he'll never forgive you!" she said, glaring.

"All right! All right, terrible Tillie," Norah said resignedly. "Let's go and get it over with. It's hard to believe that you of all people are the last of the romantics. You're wrong, you know. The only thing that so-called 'folks' are going to stand up for is to aim the rocks at me."

The two women headed toward the house, where Hilda was awaiting them, her massage table ready in Norah's dressing room.

Hilda was a small, birdlike creature, but her tiny frame concealed the strength of a bull. She pounded Norah with a steady ferocity and in total silence. Knotted nerve ends were attacked relentlessly, tense muscles were kneaded, and Norah was left in a relaxed state of limber exhaustion. The ministrations were completed by a rapid rhythmic pounding that sent the blood coursing through Norah's body with a bolero beat.

By the time she stepped out of the shower, Bernie the hairdresser had arrived, his hipless form encased in tight trousers and open shirt, a primitive gold amulet hanging around his neck. He kissed her cheek, ran his hands through her hair, and began his work with a straight razor, wielding it like a rapier, talking all the time. He'd been Norah's hairdresser at the studio. She was accustomed to his verbosity. He was a nonstop talker. An occasional nod to indicate she was listening kept him happy. He's probably one of those who don't even bother to vote, she thought. Not that it mattered.

Before the hairdresser had finished his work, the head of Paragon's makeup department was opening his leather case and placing vials and brushes and pots of cream on Norah's dressing table. Norah watched her own transformation with wonder, remembering wistfully that the same magic had taken place in reverse when she was an actress. She had been made up to show the ravages of age by the same hands that were now removing them. Hollows, shadows, and lines the last harrowing months had imprinted on her face were being skillfully eliminated.

By four o'clock in the afternoon, Tillie left, satisfied with the results. Norah was dressed in a pale, gray-blue silk dress, hair glistening in a soft nimbus, framing her face, provided by courtesy of Paragon Studios.

Tom looked at her appreciatively. "Where, may I ask, is the haglike creature I left behind this morning?"

"She was beaten, painted, and abused by Ms. Lowman and her cohorts."

Tom took her hands in his and looked into her eyes. "Are you ready?"

Norah nodded silently and then flung herself at him, holding him as tightly as she could. She needed him, his physical being, for the first time in weeks. He leaned down and kissed her long and hard, his heart turning over.

They were interrupted by McPherson's discreet coughing. "Excuse me, madame, the car is waiting."

"Thank you, we'll be right out." Tom offered her his arm.

"I shall refuse the blindfold," she said. She'd found the joke even though it was a bitter one.

*　*　*

By the time Norah and Tom reached the broadcasting station, a huge crowd was assembled in front of the entrance. Her supporters had gathered en masse, as had Hardwick's omnipresent placard carriers. Photographers and reporters pushed toward her as the security men wedged a path for her and Tom. There were shouts of "Give 'em hell, Norah" and a steady chanting of "We want Ashley."

John Mellon, the Lowmans, Evelyn Auerbach, Sylvia Gannon, and Lisa Ryder were waiting for them alongside the reception desk. Norah felt a momentary twinge of pain at the sight of Lisa. She hadn't been near the headquarters in the last week. And Norah had guiltily felt a sense of relief that she wasn't there to challenge her integrity. Now, poor thing, she'd be in for the kill, forced to watch her heroine go down the tube in disgrace.

The inside of the studio appeared deserted. The hushed, tomblike quiet was a sharp contrast to the carnival atmosphere of the street. A blond uniformed receptionist greeted the Ashleys with relief. "We were worried you might be late. Ah, here's our assistant manager now."

A harassed-looking young man rushed toward Norah, nervously checking his watch, introduced himself, and offered his hand. "I'm Gary Krawford, with a *K*. Please follow me, the others are waiting."

Norah spotted Brookings in the distance, standing in front of an open door at the far end of the hall, talking to several men who looked unfamiliar to her. They must belong to Hardwick. He was probably waiting inside the studio. She wondered how and when he would deliver the silver bullet.

Tillie, unnaturally cheerful, gushed, "You look smashing." Sylvia firmly pressed her hand and Walt leaned over and kissed her silently. Lisa stood large-eyed and worried. Norah felt a need to reassure her and said, briskly, "Stop worrying, Lisa. It's going to be all right. I promise you!" Krawford herded them down the long hallway past heavy closed studio doors until they approached Stage 70, where Brookings was waiting, grim-faced.

Hardwick had selected Dorothy Johnson and Jim Stone of the *Thayer-Herald* as his interrogators. Norah's choices were Walter Thorpe and George Bolling, both of whom were known to be sympathetic to her cause, or at least hostile to Hardwick's, within the framework of their confirmed professional distrust of all politicians. William Heit, whose erudite nightly television editorials were famous for their dispassionate, nonpartisan content, was the uncontested choice of both parties to serve as moderator.

Suddenly, Norah needed the bathroom. "Mr. Krawford, where is the ladies' room?" she asked.

He looked distressed. "Please, Mrs. Ashley, don't be long. It's right over there."

"I won't be long," she reassured him.

"It's just that time is running short," he complained. Women and their goddamned bladders! Even this goddess!

Norah pushed open the door and found herself face to face with a familiar-looking woman, who, small brush in hand, was carefully spitting into her mascara case. Oh God, it was that what's-her-name, Dorothy Johnson with the TV show, one of Hardwick's choices.

She vaguely recalled some sort of gossip she'd heard about the woman. Wasn't she supposed to be Hardwick's mistress? Was that it? Hardwick was often seen on her show and she had been obliquely supportive of him and hostile to Norah. Norah's instincts told her Hardwick wouldn't lower himself to wield the knife during the spectacle. It would be beneath his dignity. How much better to have a woman smear a woman! she thought angrily. Ms. Johnson would be the one to wield it. Now she was freshening up for the kill. They probably planned it in bed, Norah thought bitterly.

There was an awkward moment of recognition. Norah forced a polite smile. "It does work better than tap water," she said lightly, wishing the woman an instant attack of conjunctivitis.

Dorothy Johnson looked up. She said, "Why Mrs. Ashley, how lovely you look!" her voice cloying with mock surprise. "I didn't expect to see *you* here."

"I don't think it would be seemly for me to raise my hand to be excused during the inquisition, Miss Johnson," Norah fired back, heading toward the lavatory.

"Mrs. Ashley, I do want you to know that whatever happens today, there's nothing personal involved. I really am a great fan of yours. I'm absolutely *thrilled* you're going to be on my program the Wednesday morning after the election!" Dorothy Johnson gushed.

Norah stopped short. What was this woman talking about? Bewildered, she asked, "I beg your pardon?"

Dorothy looked at her with astonishment. Was she welching? She couldn't believe it. Was it possible she didn't know? "Didn't they tell you, Mrs. Ashley? Dan Brookings promised me you'd appear. He said you'd be delighted and that Mr. Ashley thought it was a great idea."

Norah was shaken with anger. They'd done it again! Arranging for her to appear on this slut's goddamn program without even bothering to inquire whether *she* wanted to, or even to inform her about it. An appearance on a hostile talk show was really what she would need on the day *after* the election. Well, she'd be damned if she'd give this bitch the satisfaction of knowing that she herself was ignorant of the bloody arrangements.

"Of—of course, Miss Johnson! I quite forgot—things have been so hectic." She forced a smile.

Dorothy's face brightened; her words came in a rapid staccato. "It's all so dramatic and exciting. Your being the President's choice and all that, the *whole world* will be watching the debate." She lowered her voice into a little-girl whisper. "And then to have you on my program the morning after the election! I'm thrilled! You're such a glamorous figure, Mrs. Ashley, and you've had such an *interesting* life."

Norah winced.

"My viewers will be undone seeing you on the show, even if you lose. It will be an absolute coup!" she rattled on.

Unsmiling, Norah looked directly at her and said, "I intend to win, Miss Johnson, and I hope that will make my appearance *just* as thrilling for them." She headed toward the lavatory.

Dorothy Johnson scooped her mascara and lipstick off the sink and threw them into her purse. She gave herself a quick final appraisal in the mirror, smiled with satisfaction, and called out gaily, "Of course, if you win, it will be an even greater coup! See you onstage, Mrs. Ashley," and left.

Norah emerged from the ladies' room wild with rage. Coup her! The

hall was deserted but for Tom and Gary Krawford. Krawford was anxiously checking his watch. His face lit up with relief at the sight of her.
"Come along, Norah," Tom said impatiently. "Mr. Krawford's about to
come unglued."

"He's not the only one," she glared. "Did you volunteer me for that
cunt Johnson's program Wednesday morning, *after* the election? Did
you?" Her voice went up.

Krawford's eyes grew large. He was shocked at the unexpected outburst. Would he ever get this madwoman onstage? Tom frowned and
looked at Norah in dismay. "What are you talking about?"

"I'm talking about your volunteering me for an appearance on
'Good Day, U.S.A.'" she shouted, oblivious to Krawford's horrified
expression.

Tom threw up his hands and grimaced. "Oh Christ, I forgot to tell you
about it with this damn debate and all. I'm sorry, darling," he apologized.
"It slipped my mind." There hadn't been too much communication between them these last weeks. "What the hell, darling, you can b.s. your
way through it. It doesn't matter that much. Brookings and I felt that if
you refused to appear, it would have looked as if you were afraid you were
going to lose the election. What's the difference?"

"I'll tell you what difference!" By now she was screaming. "It's my head
that's going to be bashed in. I'm the one who's going to have to eat shit.
And the day after *yet*! Not you, not Brookings! ME! I'm 'it,' and both of
you have one helluva nerve speaking for me!"

Krawford was speechless. Tom moved in front of her and put his hands
on her shoulders. "We'll talk about it later. For God's sake, calm yourself." He leaned down to kiss her. She turned her face away abruptly and
they silently followed Krawford across the hall. Despite her anger, she
pressed his hand for reassurance.

Tom was stricken with remorse. How could he have been so stupid? He
should have remembered to tell her. She had developed an absolute
fixation about being manipulated. Well, it wasn't any wonder, she was
under terrible strain. He wished to God he'd told the President to look
elsewhere when he first called him about her running. It was too late now
to brood about that. The ship had sailed!

As they approached Stage 70, he said firmly, trying not to betray his
own anxieties, "Just don't let the bastards get to you and you'll do fine.

Remember, Hardwick's going to get his. Bollings and Thorpe are as well briefed on him as you are, my darling."

Norah bit her lip, nodded, and released his hand. Tom stood still and watched her walk away from him through the open door to meet Dan Brookings. She hesitated, turned, blew him a kiss, and stepped toward the brilliantly lit stage set.

The set was designed to look like a conference room. But in reality it was a mechanized jungle of wires, cameras, lights, cranes, and overhead microphones. The activity was chaotic. Norah spotted Richard Hardwick, a sheaf of papers clutched in his hand, consulting earnestly with an aide at the foot of the stage. Her heart sank. A young man with a large Hardwick button on his jacket bumped into her, pushing past them. He mumbled, "Sorry," looked up, and gulped, recognizing Norah. She gasped in a flash of recognition—it was the bastard who'd betrayed her in San Diego. He'd come to gloat, no doubt. Brookings, too, recognized the youth as he came through the doorway. "Why you little—" Brookings was about to lunge for him when Tom rushed forward and caught the press secretary's arm, hissing, "Not now—for God's sake!"

Tom felt sick. It was like a recurrent nightmare. One explosion after another. The youth hurried away, heading to the dimly lit area below the stage where folding chairs had been set up to seat the few who would watch the confrontation in the studio. Gary Krawford, nervously checking his watch, said impatiently, "Please, Mrs. Ashley, time's running out!"

The executive grasped Norah's elbow and assisted her up onto the stage. She looked for Tom, but the strong lights blurred her vision. All she could discern was the outline of figures settling themselves into the chairs.

Hardwick and the journalists were already seated in their places at the long, synthetic walnut table. Name signs identified each participant. A carafe of water, pencils, pad, and ashtray were neatly arranged at each place. Chairs scraped as the men rose at her arrival. The set, contrasting with the chaos at the front of the stage, was tidy and antiseptic. Three walls, paneled in the same synthetic walnut as the conference table, and several treelike artificial plants provided the backdrop. It was a business-like atmosphere, subdued and orderly, belying the inner turmoil of the contestants.

Only Dorothy Johnson remained seated. She acknowledged Norah's presence with a nod and a forced smile. Norah noted with satisfaction that the woman's makeup was exaggerated by the merciless lights, hardening her look.

Heit greeted Norah warmly. "You understand the ground rules of course, Mrs. Ashley," he began. "We'll flip for position." He motioned toward the chairs alongside his. Richard jumped up and held Norah's for her, establishing his chivalry. She nodded politely, without looking up. He might as well have been a waiter. Like a catechism, she repeated to herself, "The purpose of the whole nightmare is not personal. I am playing out the game not to save myself but to destroy Richard's credibility and ruin him. I never slept with him. I never knew him. He's my enemy."

Heit tossed the coin, covering it with his hand. "Ladies first?" he asked, looking at Hardwick, who nodded assent.

Norah made her choice. "Heads!"

Heit lifted his hand from the coin. "Heads it is!"

"Mr. Hardwick may go first," she said, deliberately ignoring his title. She was momentarily buoyed by the small victory. At least she would deprive him of the opportunity to smear her in the last unanswerable minute. The final word would be hers.

Hardwick took the loss gracefully. Why not? he thought. He was confident of his ability to discredit her thoroughly before the end of the program.

The cameras were readied. Norah looked up at the young man aloft on the boom, who was positioning his equipment toward her. He smiled almost imperceptibly, making a quick thumbs-up gesture. She fluttered her eye in a hasty wink.

Tom felt Tillie reach for his hand and pat it reassuringly. His mouth had gone dry when he had seen Hardwick hold Norah's chair for her. He observed Norah's wink and wondered if she had meant it for him. Tillie's jaw was set. She was watching Sylvia Gannon engage in whispered conversation with John Mellon. Walt was relieved that the governor hadn't turned up. At least he'd be spared the vision of Sylvia rubbing those tits, which he remembered so well, all over the old lecher.

Richard straightened his tie and looked at Norah across the table. How calm and poised she appeared, he thought. Was she really aware of what his attack would be? His people had assured him that she'd been thoroughly warned. Obviously Norah was a better actress than he'd suspected when they were lovers. He'd have to be careful. She was too beautiful for him to risk attacking her himself. He sure as hell didn't want to stir up any protective fantasies in the public psyche.

It was best for the sake of his image that Dorothy would be the one to attack Norah. Gallantry was still expected from men of distinction, especially senators, but not from women. Richard Hardwick was a firm believer in stereotypes. If the prospect of Norah's humiliation gave him any pause, it was quickly neutralized by the charges she'd made against him. She had it coming. He was convinced that what she was doing was out of her need for personal revenge. In a strange way, it pleased him that she might feel something for him, albeit hate. After all, wasn't that the other side of the passionate coin?

Dorothy observed Richard studying Norah intently and wondered what was going on in his head. Was he feeling outrage or admiration? He was hard to read. Whatever his feelings were now, they didn't matter. Dorothy Johnson would take good care of "Miss Beauty." Nothing was going to stand in the way of her plans for the future. And the plans for her own future included Richard Hardwick in the White House. It was the *numero uno* top priority on her list. This ambitious, rich actress bitch wasn't going to derail her boy in California. She, Dorothy Johnson, was going to destroy Norah Ashley here and now.

The goddamn lights felt like ovens. Dorothy's makeup was about to melt. Well, it was nothing compared to the heat Mrs. Ashley would feel when she finished working her over. No way would Ashley have been fool enough to tell that handsome rich tycoon husband of hers about her carryings-on with Di Brazza. And if she'd been stupid enough to "tell all," he was too shrewd to allow her to hang herself on national television. Obviously Norah didn't believe she'd be attacked on a personal level. She'd find out differently soon enough.

Lights blinked. The director signaled. William Heit cleared his throat and looked into the camera. "Ladies and gentlemen, the campaign for the Senate seat from California has become a focus of national interest. Knowledgeable political observers see Mrs. Ashley's campaign to unseat incumbent Senator Hardwick, minority leader and leading spokesman for the opponents of the administration, as a test of the President's strength. The senator is considered to be the front-runner for his party's nomination to challenge the President two years from now.

"We bring you this broadcast as a public service in the sincere hope that it will clarify the salient issues and answer the charges and countercharges that have obscured them, thus enabling you, the voters, to make an intelligent choice on Election Day."

The moderator proceeded to introduce the panel, unstrapped his watch, and laid it on the table.

The cameras turned first on Richard Hardwick. He ran his tongue quickly across his lips. Hardwick was more nervous than he wanted to admit. But he'd been in the Senate too long and faced cameras too often not to be skilled at concealing his emotions. His face took on an expression of studied sincerity. Looking calm and serious, he reminded the audience of the many years he'd served them in the Senate and hopefully earned their trust. "I have worked diligently to protect your interests," he said firmly, "both here and abroad. I have fought with all my strength to hold back the tide of reckless internationalism and the irresponsible economic profligacy advocated by this administration. My record speaks for itself; it is based on a respect for business as well as labor." He paused and his voice rose. "And above all, the American way of life." Hardwick went on to list his accomplishments, the bills he'd initiated, those he'd supported. He looked into the camera with a shocked expression, his voice resonant with moral indignation, and asked, "Is it possible that the President of the United States is so insecure as to entrust the defense of his administration to a former actress playing a cheap script? Does he think she can impugn my integrity and silence my opposition to his inept performance? This shameful Hollywood spectacular has been produced, directed, and orchestrated by *him,* in order to impugn me and traduce you."

Tom observed Norah's eyes flash with anger and flinched.

Hardwick leaned forward, the handsome face indignant, his tone serious. "What I find to be the most reprehensible aspect of this outrage is that the President of the United States, who is sworn to uphold the Constitution, is deliberately subverting it. The separation of power between the legislative and executive branches of the government is the cornerstone of this great democracy. He is attempting to create a Senate which is no more than an extension of *his* White House. The President is using the California election for his own purposes, to pack that distinguished body of representatives, who are responsible to you, the people, with those whose allegiance would be to him, not to you."

Tillie closed her eyes and dug her nails into Walt's arm, silently praying that Norah would hold her temper. She looked over at Tom. He was grim-faced, eyes glued on Norah. That son-of-a-bitch Hardwick had really managed to kick her right on the battered nerve end.

Listening to Hardwick denigrate her credentials, Norah could feel Tom's presence, as she struggled against her overwhelming urge to spit out an enraged retaliation. She clenched her teeth and recalled Tom's words: "Don't get sucked into a pissing match! Let the viewer make his own judgment! You *must* trust the people!" She wasn't sure she did. She'd try. She sure as hell would try!

Heit was speaking her name, listing her accomplishments, and reciting the many party titles she had held as the cameras swung toward her.

Norah acknowledged the introduction and began by saying, "I am running as the *elected* nominee of my party for the office of United States Senator from California—not as a surrogate for the President, nor as an *ex-* anything, but hopefully as *your* choice to represent *you* in the Senate of the United States." She smiled into the camera.

Tom sighed with relief. She was in control of herself. She was going to be all right!

Tillie's grip on Walt's arm relaxed.

"I was elected," Norah continued, "to run for the office of Senator by citizens who feel as I do that the time has come to rearrange our national priorities. Yesterday's good life may be tomorrow's plague. We must accept the present.

"My opponent is firmly locked into the past. And why not?" she asked. "He is protected by the status quo. 'Rigor mendacious' has set in. Richard Hardwick is the leading spokesman for the vested interests. He wraps obsolete concepts in virtuous clichés. He is among those who in their quest for self-perpetuation are unable to accept change and thus would shortchange the rest of us."

Hardwick watched her through hooded eyes. She hadn't bothered to answer him directly. He had to hand it to her. That was the best technique. How often had he used it himself? Norah's eloquence didn't surprise him. She was an actress and trained to mouth any script they handed her. The real question was how she'd parry Dorothy's charges. That's where it was going to count; none of this kind of high-blown palaver would be worth shit. He listened, detached and calm, as she went on.

"Richard Hardwick's generation dreamed of gas-guzzling, high-powered motor cars. Today's young dream of clean air. Mr. Hardwick sees blighted communities as a bothersome problem. I see them as a tragedy, not to be endured.

"He and his party stand for reworked budgets, shifted tax burdens, and the rearrangement of the same old script. The great difference between us is that my opponent is committed to the perpetuation of his own and his friends' power and influence.

"I am committed to the concept of change. We must be miserly with our natural resources and spendthrift in the development of our human resources. I want to see our human resources—we the people—employed to the fullest. That is how we will once again make our nation preeminent in the world. If that comes about, and pray God it will, it may be that the cure for cancer will be discovered by a scientist who is black and somebody's mother."

Norah thanked the network for the opportunity they were giving her to speak to her "fellow Californians" and sat back in her chair with triumphant satisfaction. She had controlled the urge to explode in anger. She would wait for the axe to fall without going to pieces.

Tom closed his eyes and sighed with relief. Norah had safely reached the first plateau with poise and without a mishap.

William Heit nodded to Jim Stone, who addressed himself to Hardwick. "Senator, you've been quoted as complaining that you have been unfairly attacked in this campaign. Is that true?"

Hardwick, looking offended, jaw set, answered, "Yes, as indeed I have been, Jim." Richard enjoyed calling news media people by their first names, implying an intimacy with them which for the most part he lacked.

"I believe you made the claim, Senator, that you were totally unaware of the donation made to Mrs. Ashley's opponent in the primary campaign by the Elwick Foundation and were not consulted by those in charge of disbursements."

"True!" Hardwick looked pained. "As you know, I was too deeply involved in my own"—he hesitated, giving it time to sink in—"uh, personal tragedy and my duties in the Senate at the time of the primary to pay attention to the foundation's business."

He hoped that by now any cloud over the circumstances of Virginia's death would have dissipated. Losing a wife was surely sufficient reason to be negligent. Anybody could sympathize with that.

Walter Thorpe was quick to interject, "How, then, Senator, do you account for the fact that Mrs. Concha Romo, the housekeeper at your family's estate, claims that, at your request, and with Dr. Chisholm and yourself present, she signed a check to the Reverend Isaiah Smith in her capacity as treasurer of the Elwick Foundation on March twenty-third of this year?"

Norah watched Hardwick's face intently. He frowned and paused a moment. Squirm, you bastard, she thought.

But he was ready for Thorpe. He shook his head sadly and replied in a concerned voice. "I'm truly reluctant to discuss this matter publicly, Walter." Hardwick felt his insides turn over. That Manuel had knifed him came as no great shock. But that Concha would betray him was still beyond belief. No doubt that son-of-a-bitch Manuel, on whom she doted, had pressured her into it. It was too bad Bailey's goddamned cocksucker hadn't finished the job and killed the Chicano bastard. Well, he'd take care of that bitch Concha here and now, but good. Just as he'd planned. Eyes fixed into the camera, his face drawn into a pained expression, Hardwick continued. "This, of course, is an obvious and transparent ploy to drag up the smears of the primary." He was quick to add, "Not on your part, Walter, but on that of those who provided you with this nefarious material. I am reluctant to discuss this nonsense because of my deep devotion to Mrs. Romo, a fine woman, who is, as you know, a valued old family retainer. She has recently undergone a great personal shock. Because of her present condition, I find it extremely painful to criticize her for using her bitterness in this irresponsible fashion. The actions of those who manipulated this poor sick woman are to be deplored."

Norah looked at him in amazement. He had fielded it skillfully, clearly implying that Concha was not in her right mind. But his pancake makeup was beginning to melt, deepening the lines in his face. Beads of perspiration dampened his forehead. Perhaps he did feel fear. Was he fully aware of the depth of her knowledge of his affairs? She hoped so. He returned her gaze, without flinching.

"Are you inferring that Mrs. Romo lied in a sworn statement?" George Bolling asked.

Hardwick shook his head sadly. "What I'm saying, George, is that, unhappily, poor Concha Romo is in a highly agitated state and cannot be held responsible for what she says. I am deeply distressed by the unfortunate incident involving her nephew and wish to reiterate again that neither I nor any people in my campaign were in any way involved in this senseless, deplorable act of violence. After all, Manuel Vasquez was a protégé of my late father-in-law, Colonel Elwood Thayer. And the beneficiary of the Colonel's generosity. But by the same token, I must insist that Mrs. Romo, his aunt, is being badly used and victimized by unscrupulous people who do not hesitate to take advantage of this poor distracted woman in order to defame me."

Dorothy Johnson interrupted before Bolling could continue. "By that, do you mean people connected with the Ashley campaign, Senator?"

He paused and looked thoughtful. "Perhaps the question would be better addressed to Mrs. Ashley?"

Dorothy faced Norah. "Don't you find it strange, Mrs. Ashley, that Mrs. Romo should suddenly attack the senator's integrity when she is known to be a devoted and trusted employee of the Hardwick family? The woman obviously signed the check and now we find her incriminating herself while she accuses the senator of some sort of sinister collusion."

Norah looked at her coldly. "No, I find that completely irrelevant, Miss Johnson. I believe Mrs. Romo's disclosure was an act of conscience. The only question we're asking here is—is she telling the truth, or isn't she?"

"Mrs. Ashley," Jim Stone said, anxious to move the discussion away from Concha, "you have charged in your campaign that Senator Hardwick is involved in some shady business dealings with certain undesirable elements in the labor movement. And now you accuse him of being a liar. Do I understand you correctly?"

"Yes, you do, Mr. Stone," she said evenly.

Dorothy Johnson leaned forward. "It seems inappropriate that you, Mrs. Ashley, should be accusing the senator of improper alliances when you yourself are known to have been deeply and personally involved with a member of the Mafia." Here goes, Norah thought. Her prescience had been on target. Johnson was fronting for Hardwick.

Norah looked across the table at Richard Hardwick with contempt. He smiled almost imperceptibly. He was enjoying her discomfort.

How could he be the same man she'd seen across the crowded cocktail room and gravitated toward all those years ago? The man she'd slept with and adored? He was a craven, corrupt bastard. She loathed him.

William Heit looked shocked. "I think these charges demand an explanation, Miss Johnson."

Dorothy smiled at him. "Of course." She faced Norah. "You began your acting career under the guidance of a certain Guido Di Brazza, didn't you, Mrs. Ashley?"

"I think it's public knowledge, Miss Johnson, that he discovered me when I was a student at Temple University and gave me my first role in the theater."

"It is also well known," Dorothy shot back, "that he is a member of a prominent underworld family."

Norah looked at her with contempt. "I have no idea of *how* well known his connections are or were, Miss Johnson. I only know that he was a gifted, successful producer who had faith in my talent at the time he discovered me."

Dorothy smiled knowledgeably. "I understand that very well, Mrs. Ashley, and I also understand that you were—uh, shall we say—very close to him, personally, although he had a wife and children." She paused, allowing time for her words to sink in. "And that the plays in which you were catapulted into stardom were financed by underworld monies."

"I cannot believe," Norah said, the green eyes large with dismay, "that the people of California will sit in judgment of something that occurred years ago to an unworldly young scholarship student who had never even heard the word *Mafia,* much less understood its meaning. It would not have occurred to me to challenge the integrity of a famous and distinguished producer. Mr. Di Brazza was responsible for some of the theater's finest productions. He developed many young actors and actresses who in turn gave pleasure to millions of playgoers long before he discovered me."

Sylvia Gannon listened carefully as Norah spoke the words she had written for her. She was doing it beautifully, throwing herself on the mercy of the public without sniveling.

William Heit interrupted. "This has very little to do with the issues that concern the voters, Miss Johnson. I believe we should get back on the track here and not indulge in personalized gossip," he reproached.

Dorothy was quick to accept the criticism with a gracious, "Of course, William."

Her mission was accomplished. She could afford to be benign. She was well satisfied with herself for having forced the revelation of Norah's relationship with Di Brazza into the open. As far as Dorothy Johnson was concerned, she'd just sit back now and let the others carry on about détente, budgets, or any other shit that pleased them. Actress! Adultress! The public would be a damn sight more interested in Norah's personal misalliances than in her stand on international alliances. Any doubts they might have harbored over her fitness to serve in the Senate would be strengthened.

George Bolling, however, was not about to let the issue of Hardwick's dealings die. "Senator, there has been considerable discussion about the Beau Soleil partnership. One of your partners is said to be deeply involved with a holding company in the Bahamas. Would you care to elaborate on that?"

"I believe that you're referring to some business people who happen to have financial dealings with the same bank I do." Hardwick was furious. He had as much right as anybody else did to invest his money without this twenty-thousand-dollar-a-year snoop interrogating him as if he were a thief. What the hell was he supposed to do, live on his senatorial salary? No one else did. Did this idiot believe there was a man in the Senate who didn't have clients or outside business interests? He wasn't a rich man because he married rich. Marianne was the heir to the Thayer fortune, not he. But the public didn't know that. They'd never believe this bastard's charges. He was thought to be a multimillionaire.

Bolling persisted. "What people, Senator?"

Hardwick's voice grew harsh. "Business people, Mr. Bolling."

He was not to be put off. "Could they be people involved with certain union pension funds, who, for reasons of their own, would be glad to invest considerable monies in behalf of your candidacy for whatever office you might choose to run? And isn't the president of that bank, Mr. Littlejohn, your campaign chairman?"

"Are you suggesting," he asked, indignantly, "that *I* was in need of financial aid?"

"I am suggesting, Senator, that you managed to have a large chunk of public property rezoned in return for their support and business consideration."

"Mr. Bolling, I find these scurrilous charges beneath the line of decency. Surely it is permissible to make the same sort of investment that any ordinary citizen might make. I invested my own monies in the Beau Soleil development."

Bolling smiled. "Ordinary citizens don't receive the equivalent of a quarter of a million dollars worth of stock for an investment of ten thousand dollars, Senator." Before Hardwick could interrupt, he continued. "Your record shows, Senator, that you took a strong position against the farm workers' union during the grape strike and actively promoted the Teamsters in their negotiations with the growers. That same union proved to be more than generous in financing your share in the development of the Beau Soleil project."

"I believe in the free marketplace, George, and I am convinced the farm workers' strike was detrimental to the best interests both of labor and farmers," he answered.

"As a grower yourself, Senator, didn't you profit heavily from the boycott?" Thorpe asked.

"No one profits from boycotts."

"I believe you sold your own grape crop at a highly profitable price to the army during that time, Senator. Did you not?"

Hardwick looked straight into the camera. "It was my duty to see that our boys were not deprived," he said sanctimoniously, determined to return to attacking Norah. "Mrs. Ashley and the President are more concerned with picking up a few bleeding-heart votes than they are about the welfare of the men in the service. But the people know better. They're not going to deliver the President a yes-man—or should I say 'yes-woman'?—to help him continue his muddleheaded journey to the left. This outrageous attack on my honor is motivated by the President's resentment and fear of my resistance to his programs. He wants a rubber stamp, not a senator. And I don't believe the people of California are going to help implement his extremist positions by sending his stooge to Washington."

The President a leftist? An extremist? Norah couldn't believe what she was hearing. She'd spent months modifying and moderating, for the President's sake, her positions on issues she believed in. Now Hardwick was painting him red! She felt her heart pounding. Stooge? The word itself exploded in her head. Goddamn it. What was she waiting for? She was going to lose anyway, wasn't she?

She felt as if a heavy weight had been lifted. The blood ran hot through her veins. She'd survived Dorothy Johnson's cheap rotten attack. She could survive anything. All the apprehensions, the depression, the torpor of the last weeks dissipated. She was free. Free of fear, free of winning, free of blackmail.

Norah turned to Hardwick and demanded angrily, "How dare you label the President of the United States a leftist or any other 'ist'? And me his *stooge*? I've differed with him on a variety of issues throughout my political career."

"What issues, Mrs. Ashley?" Jim Stone was quick to ask.

Norah glared at the newsman. "I'll be happy to go over them, Mr. Stone. But first, I'd like to remind Mr. Hardwick, in case he's forgotten, that the single largest bloc of minority voters in the state of California is of Mexican–American descent. Eighteen percent, in fact, in case he's forgotten. I've championed their right to decent wages and decent living conditions before, during, and after the emergence of Cesar Chavez. Not out of political cynicism, as Mr. Hardwick infers, nor muddleheaded bleeding-heart sentimentality, but out of moral conviction. Which may be something he's unable to comprehend. But what I'm certain he does comprehend is that the Mexican–American votes are *mine,* not his. There is no way a self-respecting Chicano would cast his vote for the spokesman of the absentee landlords and corporate farmers, the people who would consign the Chicano and his family to a life of self-perpetuating degradation."

Richard Hardwick leaned forward, his mouth open, ready to protest. But Norah's eyes blazed.

"I'm not finished. You've had your say." She faced the camera. "As for my differences with the President—"

"Oh shit, she's off and running," Tillie groaned.

"Shush," Walt whispered anxiously. Tom doubled over and put his head in his hands. His heart sank. All his coaching and admonitions were wasted. There was no holding her. It would be a disaster.

Norah continued, her voice lowered, but defiant. "I have consistently protested the military-managerial stranglehold on the national economy. I openly opposed the development of the neutron bomb. A bomb that's good for buildings and bad for people is beyond the pale of human sanity. I believe the defense budget the President submitted to Congress should be cut back, *not* increased, as my opponent would have it.

"The proposed tax relief measures that would endanger the quality of our lives, our schools, and our government could be accommodated if we cut back our military expenditures by twenty-five percent. We've already stockpiled sufficient nuclear hardware to blow up the world three times over at the cost of billions of taxpayer dollars. Not to mention those we've shot down the drain in Iran and God knows where else. An agonizing reappraisal of the entire defense budget is long overdue. We're fast becoming nuclear junkies at the expense of education, police protection, and even garbage collection. The people are rightfully infuriated by their unconscionable tax burden. The political establishment had better reexamine governmental fiscal madness before they whine about the people's irresponsibility.

"Certainly the welfare program is a chaotic mess, but for every chiseler there are thousands of men, women, and children in desperate need of help. Are we to write them off as untouchables?

"The President believes the welfare program needs overhauling. *I* believe it should be scuttled. The impoverished and the helpless should be provided with an annual minimum income. Ironically, it was Richard Nixon of all people who proposed it. A system that forces parents to divorce or separate or become cheats and liars in order to feed little children is not only unjust, it's downright immoral!"

William Heit pointedly picked up his watch. "In closing," Norah was quick to say, "I would like to discuss the area in which my positions differ the most from the President's—women's rights—"

Dorothy Johnson drew in her breath. Norah was doing herself in beyond anything she could have hoped for. She glanced over at Richard Hardwick. For a moment, she'd been afraid he'd interrupt, but he'd restrained himself. She nodded toward him almost imperceptibly, but he didn't respond. He was staring at Norah, who continued.

"The President has been wonderfully supportive of the Equal Rights Amendment. He has been very strong in support of women's demands for equal pay for equal work. But I go beyond that. There is no equal pay for equal work on a treadmill.

"True, a few gifted and extraordinary women have made it to the top of the power structure. But the pinnacle in every facet of that structure is glutted with mediocre men who by luck, accident, or simply by virtue of being born male were pushed up the ladder with ease. And men and women alike are paying for their mediocrity. Women want an equal opportunity to reach the top.

"But above and beyond all other rights for women, I am committed to the battle for our right to control our own bodies. I firmly believe in legalized government-funded abortions and—"

* * *

The President angrily switched off the television set. "My God Almighty, she's gone berserk!"

"Turn it back on at once," Liz ordered indignantly. "I want to hear what she's saying."

"Well, I *don't!*" he shouted. "She's thrown the election. I must have been out of my mind to press her to run. Why the hell didn't Tom keep her in line—? Bad enough she was mixed up with that Di Brazza character. But this?"

"She has a perfect right to speak her mind after all those things that terrible man said about you both," the First Lady protested indignantly, turning the set back on. "What has she got left to lose? Did you *want* her to be your rubber stamp?

"As for the abortion thing—you should have told her the truth right from the beginning." Liz paused and looked up at him sadly. It still hurt after all these years. "You and Tom should have trusted her instead of using her the way you did, as if she were an idiot. She'd have understood. And I certainly don't think *you're* in any position to discuss *her* liaisons. She was single, wasn't she?"

The President walked out of the room, slamming the door, not answering.

CHAPTER

Thirty

T om rushed Norah out of the studio the moment the broadcast was over. In the back of the limousine, wordlessly holding her hand, he envisioned the President's reaction to Norah's performance. The President would be furiously angry and anxious, Tom thought despairingly. Norah rested back against the seat, eyes closed and silent as the limousine weaved in and out of the heavy downtown traffic on its way back to the headquarters.

Stricken with guilt, Tom stroked his wife's hand. Whatever horrors she'd unleashed with her outburst, they'd know soon enough. Unable to contain himself, he questioned, "Why'd you do it, Norah?"

Surprised by Tom's question, Norah sat upright and looked at him astonished. "Why? Why not? After all the mealymouthed chickening out I've been doing for months, the President got painted 'leftist' and 'extremist.' With me as his *stooge.* The show died on the road, Tom. Who cares about the reviews? It's all postmortem. Over!" She sighed with relief and her tone was lighthearted. "There was nothing left to lose. What joy it was to have had my own say. Let it all hang out!"

Tom didn't respond.

"At least I made Lisa happy," she went on. "Her eyes were filled with pride. I finally stood for something other than banalities. I only regret I didn't have time to go after oil and the Arabs."

Tom felt his blood run cold. "The President's eyes will be filled too," he predicted dryly, "with tears of grief."

"The President!" Norah bridled. "What's he got to grieve about? *He* should be thrilled. He's got enough ammunition, over my dead body, to pulverize Hardwick if Hardwick's fool enough to oppose him now. The President's the big winner! Oh, Tom," she cajoled, "don't look so glum. Whatever happens is after the fact. So I've lost! Eleven days from now I'll make a gracious little concession speech, pick myself up off the ground, and life will go on, darling! Hardwick's won't. He's going to have a hell of a time explaining himself."

Tom felt worse. She was being so goddamn gallant. She was cheering *him.* All her anger at him was forgotten, and yet if it hadn't been for him, she never would have been caught up in this mess. Guilt gnawed at him. He couldn't bear the deceit a moment longer. He turned toward her abruptly, the fine-boned features drawn, his eyes dark and troubled. The words came slowly and with difficulty. "There's something I have to tell you," he began as he leaned forward and pulled shut the glass partition separating them from the driver.

"Years ago, when the President was a young political science professor, about the time he was gearing up to make his first political run for Congress, he got himself into a mess with one of his students." Tom hesitated. Norah's eyes were fixed on his face, her expression perplexed.

"Was he married to Liz then?" she asked, incredulous.

Tom swallowed hard and nodded. "The girl was pregnant, and he paid for her to have an abortion." He covered his eyes with his hands pressing his temples. "She died."

"Oh my God," Norah gasped.

"It seems she was balancing more than one bucket at the time. The question as to who was the father—was rather cloudy." Tom grimaced. "Still the President felt responsible. It was a rough time."

"Did Liz know?"

"Oh yes, she knew, and she behaved like a Trojan. It wasn't easy for her, but she held firm. Ironically—your—" He hesitated, almost blurting out, "former lover's," caught himself, and said quickly, "—your opponent's father-in-law, Colonel Edward Thayer, was the chairman of the board of trustees of the college. The old pirate wasn't about to permit a full-blown scandal to erupt on campus. Not while he was in charge."

Norah was dumbfounded. "You mean Thayer protected the President?"

Tom's eyebrows shot up. "He sure as hell did—but at a price! Hardwick was beginning his own political career at that time! And the Colonel had very ambitious plans for his son-in-law. Thayer was a shrewd old party, you know. His political instincts were sharp. He sensed the young professor's potential and envisioned him as a threat to his ultimate goal for Hardwick—the presidency. Both men were approximately the same age and from the same state. The way the Colonel saw it, which was certainly realistic, only one of them was going to make it to the top. And the one he had in mind was his son-in-law. What's more he wanted to make absolutely certain that the two of them would never be locked into a head-on confrontation. He could have cut the President off at the knees right then and there." Tom paused and thought about it for a moment. "I never quite figured out why he didn't do it. It would have been so simple. But he was a complicated man and preferred the oblique route— and, of course, he didn't want a scandal. That was a part of it. So he offered the President a deal."

"A deal? What kind of a deal?"

"The Colonel extracted a promise from the President that he would never put himself in a direct political confrontation against Hardwick. In return for accepting the Colonel's terms, the girl's vulture parents would be bought off and all evidence of the scandal buried. Closed book!"

Norah looked at Tom with disbelief. "All these years later? Who remembers? How could such a thing be proved?"

Tom cocked his head and sighed. "The Colonel made it clear that even after his death, the agreement would stand. He told the President that a person in whom he had implicit trust would have access to the evidence and wouldn't hesitate to use it against him if he reneged on his word."

"Who?"

Tom shrugged. "Who knows? We investigated everybody who was close to the old bastard and, believe me, they were few and far between. He kept his own counsel and was surrounded primarily by servants and employees. That kind of man would hardly have been the type to confide in people on his payroll. Hardwick himself seemed the logical one." Tom shook his head. "You can be sure he'd have used it long since if he had any knowledge of that kind of a time bomb on the President. That left us Virginia. She was enough of a bitch and sufficiently hostile to Hardwick to withhold it until the last possible minute. Christ, we even checked out her lovers. There wasn't one in the packet who indicated to anyone that he might have a blackmail on the President. A lot of them were outside the political spectrum anyway. We even thought Mellon might have a clue as to who held the deathbed mandate."

"John Mellon! How would John have the slightest—?"

Tom interrupted. "He and Virginia Hardwick were lovers. We thought she might have confided—"

Norah burst into laughter. John Mellon, dusty, rumpled, distracted John, had cuckolded Richard Hardwick. Her laughter died. It was all coming together. She drew in her breath and glared at Tom. "And so he was shipped to California. Exiled from the White House. Not because of *my* campaign. Or should we call it the President's campaign?" she said bitterly. "My campaign was just a diversionary tactic to get rid of Richard Hardwick before this mysterious somebody or other popped open the box and dragged out the dirty linen! You and the President didn't give a damn whether *I* won or lost!"

Norah was stunned by what she felt to be Tom's part in her betrayal. Her voice lowered to a hoarse whisper. "I was the patsy. You didn't give a shit about me. All that business about how it was time for me to use my fabulous talents, move out into the world again, was pure crap! You deceived me. You lied to me, Tom!" She went on in angry staccato. "You could have told me the truth. It didn't take too much to get me to picture myself on the floor of the Senate. It would be my latter-day Paragon Studios," she mocked. "Me, the new star, a sexy Margaret Chase Smith with a new gaga fantasy to act out in my golden years. I'd have probably gone for it, even if you'd told me the truth. But you couldn't do that, could you, Tom? Your allegiance to that noble two-timing professor made it impossible. Your old college playmate had your confidence, but your wife didn't!"

Tom paled. He was sick with self-loathing. "I was wrong, Norah. I should have told you. But it would have meant breaking my word to the President. I just couldn't bring myself to do it," he agonized.

"So why tell me now? Why burden me with that bastard's problems.

I don't *care* what happens to him. Let Hardwick beat him! He's no better than Hardwick. I can't believe the Colonel ever went through with all that rigamarole. It's a lot of nonsense. The President's guilt made him swallow the hocus-pocus. And *I* was hung by the thumbs for having an affair that hurt no one." She glared at him. But she felt a surge of pity for Tom. He'd been entrapped by his own performance. Well, the show was over. Norah was emotionally drained. She was beyond rage. She leaned toward him and said gently, "Forgive yourself, Tom! The President has to live with his nightmare, we don't! Poor Liz!" she sighed. If Liz could forgive the President, surely she could forgive Tom. The fight was out of her, and she reached for his hand. The car slowed down.

As they entered headquarters, Norah was totally unprepared for her reception. Instead of being received with disappointment and reproach, she was met with a hero's welcome.

"You were great!" "You really socked it to him." "He's finished." They clustered around her. Lisa Ryder hugged her and said wistfully, "I wish I had your courage. Oh, Norah, you were wonderful. I'm so *proud* of you."

Tom promptly disappeared into Mellon's cubbyhole. Taken aback by her reception, Norah gradually worked her way to Karl Auerbach's office and closed the door behind her. Auerbach barely acknowledged her presence. He was listening intently to the telephone he held in his hand.

Finally, he said, "Okay. Okay, George, just hang in there. That's all you can do." Replacing the instrument in its holder, he reached for the dead cigar and relit it silently.

"Say something, Karl," she demanded.

He looked up at her, unsmiling. "What's to say?"

"Whatever it is, for God's sake, say it," she snapped.

He leaned back in his chair, pursed his lips, let out a stream of pungent smoke, and said, "You blew it!"

"Then why is everybody out there"—Norah waved her hand toward the door—"acting as if I'm some kind of hero? Are they all crazy—or is there some remote possibility that I did the right thing?"

"They're nuts!" he barked. "Those people are so hysterically involved with you and this stinking campaign they've got no judgment at all. If you committed sodomy in the Grand Hall of the Dorothy Chandler Pavilion, they'd stand up and applaud, screaming, 'Bravo!' Christ, Norah, the Di

Brazza stuff they laid on you was *nothing* compared with what you did to yourself." He shook his head. "You muddied Hardwick but good. When he gets back to Washington, he'll be hard put to get out from under. At least we'll have him taken care of and put away before the next presidential election. That's what the President had in mind from the beginning, isn't it?" He looked up at her and worked on the cigar. "But that isn't going to help you. Whatever chance you had, babe, and it was little enough, is down the tube." He sighed. "Anyway, if it's any comfort, you looked great."

"Thanks a lot, Karl," she said bitterly. "Do you mean to say that *no* one out there among those 'people' I'm supposed to trust might just possibly decide to vote for me because I didn't talk a lot of bullshit? What about the women?" she asked plaintively. "Won't the women like me better for being outspoken?"

Karl looked at her with amusement. "The *women*? Honey, when that lady at the checkstand in Reseda walks into the voting booth, she's going to remember that you're rich and beautiful and an actress, and that maybe you've had more fun in and out of bed than she has now. You've given her an extra excuse to sock it to you because you've taken some far-out positions that aren't so kosher—and she can zap you with a clear conscience. As for those fancy League of Women Voters types, they'll really vote thumbs down on you. Every one of those broads feels in her heart she's better equipped to be senator than you."

"You hate women," she said accusingly. "They've *always* supported me."

He looked at her from under the heavy brows. "Come on, Norah, you know better than that. I liberated Evelyn, for God's sake!" Karl took a deep breath. Those nuts out there had given her false hopes. His voice was gentle. "Sweetie, I've been taking pulses where the *voters* are. My men are solid because they hate Hardwick. We've educated them well. His flip-flop labor record's enough to keep them in line. I hope!" he added. "That bastard didn't exactly paint you a fallen woman himself, but he leaned hard on Little Miss Actress, and then you did your thing. Add to it the Di Brazza crap that Johnson woman threw out. Oh boy!" He puffed on the cigar stub and scowled.

"But Karl, just suppose my people aren't stark raving mad. Isn't there *any* hope for a week from Tuesday? Some small light blinking at the end of the tunnel—a chance perhaps? What about the students? Barbara's been working on the campuses like crazy. They'll like what I had to say. Won't they?" she pleaded.

"Oh, hell!" Karl snorted. "They never bother to vote. I'm not saying there's going to be a mass defection, female or otherwise," he said sympathetically. "If you'd been ahead by a large margin, losing a vote or two per precinct wouldn't matter. But Norah, you've been the underdog all along. Hardwick's the incumbent! You have to pick *up* votes, not *lose* them, just in order to squeak through!" He looked at her fondly. "And that's the truth, sweetie!"

She looked as if he'd struck her, the momentary flash of hope—gone.

The sound of loud voices coming from the corridor broke their silence. Karl went to the door to see what was going on.

Dan Brookings was locked in an embrace with Manuel Vasquez. They were pounding each other's shoulders, Dan shouting, "You dumb Mex, who let you out?" Barbara Potter and Lisa along with a crowd of campaign workers were excitedly waiting to greet him, all of them shouting at once.

Manuel sighted Norah, disengaged himself from Brookings, and came toward her.

"What are you doing back here, Manuel?" she asked concernedly. "Did Conway say it was all right?" At God knows what risk to himself, he'd come to Los Angeles to join the sinking ship. Because of his aunt? Because of her? Norah couldn't bear it.

"Hardwick's a liar and a crook, Mrs. Ashley, and I've come to do what I can."

Norah snapped impatiently, "For heaven's sake, call me Norah, and I don't think you should be here." She couldn't carry any more guilt. "I won't have you doing yourself harm. Haven't you endured enough?"

Unsmiling, he answered, "I will be the judge of that—Norah. Now I want to sit down with Karl and Dan here, and the others, and see what you've got going for you in East Los Angeles." His authoritarian tone inhibited her from protesting further. He turned to Karl. "I want to see all the precinct lists for East Los Angeles. I intend to get every last human being with a Spanish surname to the polls to vote for Norah."

Karl shook his head in disbelief. The poor bastard must have suffered permanent brain damage. Didn't he remember that along with the students, *La Raza* had the lousiest voting record in the state, despite all the noise they made during a campaign? What the hell, he might as well indulge him in his fantasy. One more nut for Norah! Next would come the men with the cold wet restraining sheets to take the entire campaign staff to the looney farm.

* * *

Richard Hardwick threw his head back against the upholstered seat of the limousine, loosened his tie, and closed his eyes.

Dorothy Johnson bent over him, running her tongue across his lips. "You were fantastic, Senator. They're never going to vote for her."

Richard remained silent. She resettled herself and put her hand on the inside of his thigh. "At the risk of begging the question, didn't I shaft her but good with the Di Brazza bit? Not to mention what she did to herself."

There was no response.

"Darling." Her voice rose with exasperation. He could have shown *some* gratitude. "You won! It was beautiful. Ashley will never make it! You're going to be reelected. I'm sure of it! She took every wrong position."

He opened his eyes. "*You* don't understand, Dorothy. I've lost the presidency."

"For God's sake, that's years away; nobody's going to remember all this campaign shit. People forget!"

He sat upright and looked at her coldly. "Right now, this minute, there's a smart-assed eager-beaver young lawyer no one ever heard of, a staffer on some minor congressional committee, who can barely wait to get in touch with that bastard Mellon and start researching my case. I'll be defending myself for the rest of my life. If I'd have known what was going to happen I'd never have—!"

He tapped the driver's shoulder. "We'll leave Miss Johnson off at the Hilton first. I'm bushed," he said to her. "I'll call you tomorrow. Okay?"

She bit her lip. "Okay."

After all she'd done for him, he was dismissing her like some two-bit hooker.

They rode in silence. When the limousine reached the hotel, she said, "I'm tired, too." She stepped over Richard's outstretched legs. "Call me when you have the time, Senator," she said coldly.

"Sure, sure, darling, thanks for everything." He watched her enter the hotel. She didn't look back.

He let himself into his suite. He needed a drink and the bathroom. Dorothy was obviously pissed off. Christ, her sexual appetite was insatiable. Too bad! There was no way he could get it up. Ashley had taken care of that. She knew exactly what she was doing. He had been an idiot to underestimate her. The Di Brazza business hadn't come as a surprise to her. She'd known all along he'd use it. She'd subjected herself to exposure in order to kick his dream of the presidency in the balls, with Mellon and the White House, no doubt, urging her on. It was nothing but spite, from start to finish; she had never forgiven him, the bitch. She didn't give a damn about getting herself elected. She wanted him destroyed.

Marianne was sitting in the chair facing the television set. She looked up, making no effort to move.

"Hi, darling!" He pulled off his jacket and flung it on the couch. "Fix me a good stiff Scotch on the rocks. I'll be right out."

She had the drink ready for him when he returned, handed it to him, and asked, "Did you hear the news?"

"No." He settled himself in a stuffed chair and took a gulp of the whisky. "What did they say about the debate?"

Marianne remained standing. "That isn't what I mean. I mean the news about McFarland."

"McFarland? Who the hell—? Oh God, *that* little bastard. Bailey's lover! Has he turned up?" His voice was anxious.

Marianne fixed her agate eyes on him. "Not exactly. His body turned up. He's been murdered, execution style, and dumped in some swamp in Florida."

He whistled. "Well, what do you know?"

"That's a good question, Father. What do *you* know?"

He looked at her with dismay. "For God's sake, Marianne, you don't think I—?

Icy voiced, she replied, "Do you mean, do I think you ordered him done away with?"

He stared at her, shocked by her tone, as she continued. "No, I don't, but it's not beyond belief that some of your fine partners considered him an embarrassment to you and handled it in their own singular fashion. They might easily have thought it best to dispose of a sticky problem. Mightn't they?" Her eyes were as cold as Virginia's.

Angrily, he shouted, "How the hell should I know?" Suppose they did? So what? He wasn't responsible for what other people did. Hadn't he vehemently protested when Jimmy first suggested doing away with McFarland when he called from that goddamned banana republic of his, screaming bloody murder over Manuel's beating? It was Jimmy who pointed out that he might be held responsible, because the son of a bitch had been on the Casa payroll. He never told anybody to beat anybody or kill anybody. He didn't have blood on his hands. At least his partners wanted him to win, which was more than he could say for his own daughter. If she hadn't been humping that holier-than-thou pain in the ass, Concha's nephew, none of this would have happened. It was Bailey's lover boy who'd started the whole bloody chain of events. *Her* husband's houseboy! After what he'd been through with that Ashley bitch, he wasn't going to sit still and have Marianne give him this shit. The whole thing was sickening. He shuddered. There was no way anybody was going to lay it on him! No way.

His insides turned over as Marianne calmly continued, "They announced that Bailey's flying to Florida to identify the body." That was all he really needed. Richard sank down into the couch and stirred the ice cubes in his drink with his finger. Trying to gain control over himself, he said quietly, "Sit down, Marianne, and listen to me." He patted the couch.

Marianne walked over and sat down next to him, primly crossing her ankles and folding her hands in her lap, like a well-behaved schoolgirl, waiting for him to speak.

Richard Hardwick put down his drink and turned to face her. "I swear to God, I had nothing—absolutely nothing to do with the Manuel business. You know that, don't you?"

She nodded. "And I certainly didn't have anything to do with shooting McFarland either, Marianne. Believe me!"

She stared at him in disbelief. Was he asking her for absolution?

"Your wonderful husband was the one who was involved with that McFarland creature, not I," he continued. "And if he wants to go down there and throw himself across the bier, that's *his* problem, not mine. Whatever else I may be, Marianne, I'm not a hypocrite. I have too much respect for your intelligence to pretend that I give a damn whether McFarland's dead or alive, or whether he was drawn and quartered or killed execution style. At least whoever did it saves us the embarrassment of having to endure the spectacle of Bailey's peculiarities being aired in public. That's been a real possibility all along, you know. Not to mention public discussion of your shenanigans with *your* lover. In fact, my dear, the entire unfortunate mess had the makings of a full-blown scandal, which is not what I need at this particular moment. I want to get one thing straight with you, Marianne. I made a business investment in a real-estate deal, which was a perfectly proper thing for me to do. I was under the assumption that my partners were legitimately investing union retirement funds in the transaction. Whether or not they had their money in the Bahamas or under their mattresses was none of my business. I don't know what the hell the chairman of the board of any company in which I buy stock is up to. I don't think anybody else does either, and I don't know what denotes clean money or dirty money. For my part, if you took all the top business management people and threw them in the slammer and took all the crooks out and had them head the corporate structure of this country, nothing much would change in the world of commerce. If there was a Mafia connection, so what? They've got as much right to invest capital as anyone else.

"I also believe I am entitled to some small loyalty from you." He sipped his drink. "Let's not go on about this unpleasant matter any longer. It serves no useful purpose." He looked at her sternly. "Do you understand?"

"Oh yes, I understand."

"Good, then there's no need to discuss it further. What did you think of the debate?" he asked, changing the subject.

"You'll be reelected!" she stated flatly.

"But lose the presidency?" he asked, hoping she'd refute him.

Marianne got to her feet and stood in front of him. "Yes! And it's just as well. You're an evil thing riddled with ambition, so involved in your own case that you don't care whom you betray. You have no loyalty, love, gratitude. No anything. Only greed. You made Concha, my Concha, look like a crazy fool and a liar," she cried out.

Dear God, must he listen to this hysterical outburst? What the hell difference did Concha make? She'd been bloody well rewarded for her services and then had the gall to betray him. And Marianne was carrying on as if Concha were the victim.

"Concha?" he muttered. "Do you think I'm going to let her get away with this crazy nonsense because her goddamn nephew got hurt?"

He stood up and faced Marianne. "Now let's get this straight. Concha is a rich woman because your grandfather made her rich. God knows why! Although I've got my suspicions. Manuel went to Harvard with money Concha gave him, which she received from *this* family. *Your* family! For those people to betray me, not to mention your grandfather, whose one dream was to see me in the White House—that's *really* evil! To think that I trusted her! And for you to side with a pack of disloyal servants against *me* is downright disgraceful. If it weren't for us, they'd be out there in the fields where they belong, stoop-picking lettuce. As for that bastard who was fucking your husband and beat up your lover, he may have cost *me* the presidency!"

Marianne stared at him in horror, her face hardening. "I don't believe it. You think the only thing in the world that matters is what you want. You don't care if you have to kill, lie, cheat, or destroy to get it, do you?" Her eyes became slits, her voice a frozen whisper. "I'm not going to be like my mother, a middle-aged sick animal, disconnected from everything but my own craziness. I'm going back to the Casa and pick up the pieces and try"—her voice rose—"try to figure out how to be a human being and *do* something, not just live off the rest of the world."

How dare she wallow in self-righteousness like this? What the hell was she complaining about? She had used money, her body, other bodies, any way she pleased. What about Bailey? She'd used him when she wanted a husband and then spit him out like an orange pip. Hardwick picked up his glass and downed the remaining contents in a gulp. He'd give her something to chew on.

"Why don't you try to figure out whether your lover's your uncle while you're going through this marvelous soul searching?" he shot at her, sneering. "Is incest part of your rehabilitation program? Have you asked that sainted Concha who Manuel's mother really is? His father?"

Marianne turned pale and held onto the chair for support. He observed her with satisfaction. She had no answer. He lowered his voice, enjoying her distress. "And how, may I ask, will you handle the problem of your bereft husband, since you've gotten so fucking noble?" he asked sarcastically.

Marianne walked across the room, put her hand on the door handle, and turned around to face him. "I'm going to give Bailey a chance."

Hardwick threw his head back and broke into laughter. "Oh my God, you're going to welcome that homosexual creep back into your nuptial bed. And throw out your dear uncle?"

Marianne pulled herself up straight and looked at him with cold hatred. "For your information, for what it's worth, I'm going to do the only thing I can think of doing, being your daughter and part Thayer. I'm going to give Bailey enough money to start a new life for himself. Money is all we know about. I believe he really loved McFarland and now, because of us, his lover's dead. Just like my mother, whom you never loved, is dead. It's the least I can do."

She closed the door behind her and went into the room to pack her things.

Richard slumped into the chair and reached for the phone. "Operator, please see if you can get me a Miss Dorothy Johnson at the Beverly Hilton."

CHAPTER
Thirty-one

Election Day: Palm Springs. Dawn lightened the desert sky, transforming the mountains that framed the horizon into two-dimensional cardboard cut-outs. Marianne slept, hugging the pillow, childlike, auburn tendrils framing her face. As Manuel awakened, he was filled again with wonder at the sight of her. She had a quality of innocence in repose. It was hard for him to believe that Hardwick was her father. He lay back and closed his eyes. God, what a nightmare it had been. His mother had broken into hysterics after watching Hardwick attack Concha on television. Turning on Concha with a wild rage, gentle, quiet Mama had cried out, "It is your fault, Concha, you have brought all this evil down upon us. You, the Colonel's whore! What has it given us? Manuel beaten half to death and you publicly proclaimed a partner in their infamy—and a lunatic to boot. And my finely educated son is off whoring with the granddaughter of that swine. He'd be better off in the fields!"

He had put his arms around the small, outraged figure in an attempt to quiet her. "Mama, you must not do this."

She had promptly burst into tears, clinging to him, frightened by her own anger.

Concha had remained silent, waiting for the sobs to quiet. Then she had taken Mama by the hand to the couch, facing the tiled fireplace. "Listen to me, Juanita." Her voice had been low and deliberate without anger. "You are saying things you don't mean. You have forgotten where you came from. You have forgotten when your *padrón* had his way with you that it was the Colonel who made it possible for me to bring you out of Mexico to have your baby here. If not for the Colonel, Manuel would be just another unwanted bastard child scratching his way to no place." Her face had clouded. "It is very difficult for me to discuss these things." She had drawn in a deep breath and said, "I loved the Colonel with all my heart." She paused. "And he loved me. It was enough for both of us. If that makes me a whore"—she shrugged—"then I'm a whore who loved and was loved. But I will remind you that the man I loved gave you and your son refuge."

She'd turned to Manuel, the dark eyes piercing into his. "You could not forgive Colonel Thayer for being a *padrón.*" A half smile crossed her face. "I am not as educated as you, my privileged nephew, and my social consciousness is not so highly developed. I do not see people as *padrones* or field hands. I see them as good or evil. His daughter, Virginia, was a bitter disappointment to him. There was a sickness of soul about her. He was overjoyed when she married Senator Richard and gladly made him his son, hoping against hope that Virginia would be happy at last. And when Marianne wished to live at the Casa with him, he said to me, 'My daughter, Virginia, will never forgive her own mother for dying. She is a tormented soul unfit to be a mother herself. You must make Marianne yours, Concha. Help her to be whole. The little one needs you.' "

Her tone grew reproachful as she turned to Mama. "And when I told the Colonel that you, my little sister, Juanita, were with child against your will and needed me, he was quick to say, 'Go to her and bring her here so the child will be born free.' He was a good human being. And you think *I* do not know what was said, that *he* didn't know the gossip? But nevertheless, he enjoyed Manuel and cherished him, just as if he'd really been his own. He was his father in the way I was Marianne's mother. If you must weep, Juanita, weep for Marianne. She loves your son and she loves me, and she will never forgive her own father for what he did to me today. On that I will put my hand in the fire. She will forgive him for anything else, but not this, because whatever else she is, she is capable of love, just like her grandfather was."

She turned her face to Manuel. "She is not responsible for her father, Manuel, remember that." Her eyes bored into his. "Any more than you are for yours."

Awake now, he checked his watch on the night table, leaned over to Marianne, and kissed her bare shoulder. She stirred and hugged the pillow closer.

"We must get up, Marianne," he whispered, tracing her cheek with his finger.

She pulled the flowered sheet over her head.

He put his head close to hers and said, quietly, "It's Election Day, Miss Hardwick, and I must get to Los Angeles as soon as I have cast my vote against Senator Hardwick."

She rolled over abruptly, pulled his face to hers, and kissed him, running her hands through the thick, dark hair, grown back now.

"My poor Manuel. He will probably win, you know."

They had been too hungry for each other to discuss anything last night, much less politics. They had fallen into sleep, exhausted with spent passion, fulfilled.

"I know." He pulled away from her and swung himself upright. She shuddered at the sight of the angry red scar slashing from the nape of his neck across the olive-skinned shoulder.

As if sensing her distress, he reached for the camel's-hair robe she'd given him during his convalescence, when he was too frail to protest.

But before he could put it on, she sat up, fully awake now, and pulled him down again beside her, unable to let him go. Marianne was filled with an overwhelming sadness. She didn't know why, but she felt this was an end for them. The campaigns were over. Things would change, their worlds might separate. Although she'd tried to bring herself to question Concha and him countless times before about his parentage, she had never been able to do it. Something always inhibited her. Perhaps her fear of what the answer would be.

The memory of Bailey taunting Concha, her father's words striking out at her, the whispers across the years, and her own suspicions converged on her. She could no longer bear to leave the monstrous thing that stood between them unmentioned. Filled with a sense of urgency, she must ask him now. This morning! Before he left her, she must speak out. She clung to him and then pulled away, her face raised to his. "I must know who we are. What it is that hardened you against Papa Colonel and me!" Her voice lowered to a whisper. "Was he your father, Manuel? Is what they say true? Tell me! Tell me the truth."

The memory of Concha's outburst still fresh, he took her face in his hands and brought his lips to hers. "*No,* my darling, I'm *not* your uncle. The Colonel was not my father!" He looked at her with concern. "Have you worried over that, Marianne? Did you think we were incestuous lovers?" he asked in disbelief.

"I didn't know *what* we were. Why else would you have held me off all these years? Hated us all these years?" she cried out. "Why, then, why wouldn't you have me?"

Manuel stood up, put on the robe, and began to pace the room. He no longer knew why. Concha had shaken the very core of his being, challenged the bitterness that was the thrust of his life in a way that even loving Marianne hadn't done. He came to a halt at the foot of the bed and sat down and faced her. "I'm a bastard, Marianne, a misbegotten bastard in the true sense. Conceived against my mother's will, fathered by a landowner who bedded her to assuage a moment's appetite. Concha smuggled her out of Mexico, and I was born at the Casa. I equated your grandfather's patronage with the noblesse oblige of his caste. I saw him as an extension of the *padrón* who fathered me. I had to prove myself to be *somebody,* not just a pickaninny on the plantation. And so I fought to free myself from the domination of the Thayers. I could not bear to be swallowed up and tamed like Concha and Mama. Now I no longer know how I feel. Am I not myself the *padrón* for the farmworkers? I love you and cannot accept it. It is a betrayal of all my instincts. I cannot bear the thought of Bailey having touched you, and yet, if I had not been so arrogant—" He shrugged and paused. "The only thing of which I am absolutely certain is that I was right in opposing your father's reelection as best I could!"

Before she could speak, he said, "Up with you. I'll start the coffee. You must be standing beside him when he claims his victory. With the grace of God and anything I can do, it'll be his last one."

"I don't intend to be standing at his side when he claims whatever he claims," Marianne stated, her voice even.

He looked at her searchingly. "Because of Concha?"

She sat upright, facing him, the small perfect breasts exposed, and shook her head. "No, not because of Concha, because of *me!* I'll wait for you here. If not here, at the Casa. But I'll be waiting—forever if need be."

* * *

Election Day: Bel Air. Norah lay sprawled across Tom's body and gently nibbled his rib cage. Rolling over, she sighed, "Oh God, it's Tuesday, and I wish we *were* in Belgium." She sat up, stretched, and said ruefully, "I will get tonight what I got this morning—only it won't be as pleasurable."

Tom pulled her to him and kissed her long and hard. Then with a slap on the small, firm buttocks, he commanded, "Up!"

Norah pulled away from him. "I don't want to leave this bed! I can't bear the thought of tonight—and then tomorrow!" She felt a surge of angry despair and sat up abruptly, their lovemaking forgotten. Didn't prisoners, about to be executed, have great sexual urges? "It's all your fault that I have to stay in that god-awful hotel tonight and eat shit on that bitch's program in the morning," she complained, scowling at him. "And you're going to leave me to go through it alone."

Tom lay back on the pillow, his hands clasped in back of his head, the long, lean frame stretched out, and closed his eyes, pretending not to hear her, hoping she'd make it through the day without disintegrating.

Oh God, she vowed. I swear I won't lose control again and start whining. It was rotten for Tom, too. What with the headlines screaming "Candidate Charged with Mafia Connection," "Charges Fly in California Race," "President's Choice Takes Leftist Position on Major Issues," and all the quotes repeated again and again in the news broadcasts. Not that Hardwick had gotten away unscathed. Some of the headlines read "Ashley Accuses Hardwick of Shady Business Deals." But the most devastating thing she'd been forced to endure was the oversolicitousness of her supporters, their defensiveness and sympathy, once that euphoria wore off. They made her feel the hypocrite. After all, she walked into the meat cleaver knowing full well what Hardwick had in mind. What she hadn't anticipated was her own explosion. Tom had maintained enormous self-restraint in never once berating her for her reckless performance.

Still, she agonized, it was so unfair! She'd have to face being cannibalized by Johnson the morning after—! She kissed her husband's eyelids. Tom reached for her hand and opened his eyes.

"Norah, listen to me now." His face was grave, his eyes met hers. "Let's not go into this final inning as if it were a Greek tragedy. It's not the end of our world. Twenty-four hours from now the whole thing will be over and done. That's what you said to me," he reminded her. He turned her hand over and kissed the palm. "You did accomplish the major mission, you know."

Norah bit her lip. Some consolation! "I know, I know," she repeated impatiently. "But I *hate* losing."

"I hate it, too," he said quietly.

"Tell me the truth, Tom, or I won't get up," she threatened. "Do you *really* believe that the dossier on the President exists?"

"Uh-huh."

"Well, I don't," Norah said emphatically. "If it were still floating around someplace, surely they'd have laid it on the President by now, especially after I carried on about abortion." Norah reached for her robe and swung her feet over the side of the bed.

"That wasn't the deal the old bastard made with him," Tom answered. "With what's come out about Hardwick now, it may never turn up. I hope to God his appetite for the presidency has dulled. But as long as the President lives, he'll have to worry about it."

Norah belted her robe and snorted. "It's all bullshit. The old boy was just trying to intimidate him." She fixed the emerald eyes on him. "Have you talked to the President?"

Tom nodded.

"And how does his nibs feel?" she asked bitterly. "Happy that Hardwick's been muddied?"

"No, just terrible, Norah. Whether you believe it or not, he really wanted you to win!"

Norah looked at him and snorted. "I'll bet." She padded barefoot to the French doors, pulled back the yellow curtains dyed to blend with the small jewel of a Toulouse-Lautrec fan painting. It had been their wedding gift from Walt and Tillie. Norah sighed. The day was brilliant. She suddenly remembered the old cliché. "Happy is the bride the sun shines upon." Well, she wasn't a bride, and as far as she was concerned, good weather was bad news for a candidate who would best be served by a low voter turnout.

She'd hackled at having had to make the usual "get out the vote" statement demanded of all candidates. The hypocrisy of it! They'd stream to the polls to vote no on her. That's what they'd do. The widespread wish to vote no on something or someone was the impetus for a record turnout. Prop. 13 was the proof of it. People had streamed to the polls en masse to vote no on government.

Norah called out to Tom, "You get *yourself* up, and prepare for this preordained fun day!"

She looked out over the garden. November? It couldn't be. White stock and marguerites were in full bloom, the pansy beds bulged with velvet color, the lawn was a shimmering green. Tom was right. Suppose she did lose? Defeat would keep her world intact, and it *was* a lovely world! There were worse fates, and even if she had made mistakes, she knew she'd run the best damn race she could! At least she'd spoken her mind, for what it was worth. And Richard Hardwick was neutralized. She'd seen to that.

Reaching for the house phone, she said, "Good morning, Mrs. Manley, may I have some coffee? When you get a minute, could you pack me for the hotel so McPherson can take the luggage over early.

She was in the midst of applying her makeup, debating over the rouge pot, reluctantly opting for it, when there was a discreet knock at the door.

"Come in, Mrs. Manley."

"Yes, madame." The voice seemed especially high-pitched. Her jaw went slack. It was Peter, carrying her tray. He was wearing a gray flannel suit, blue shirt, and a sedate, wine-colored tie.

She hadn't seen him properly dressed since he had been six years old, when he rebelled in no uncertain terms against wearing his Merry-Mite Eton-jacketed suit. The resemblance to his father, as he stood before her, was close to being eerie. He'd come home only to see her whipped. Her heart sank.

Peter put down the tray and enfolded her in a rib-cracking hug. "Aren't you glad to see me? Dad and I thought you'd like it."

"Of course, my darling. What a wonderful surprise!" She put his face between her hands and pulled him to her. "You look absolutely beautiful. I can die in peace."

He straightened himself and scowled. "Mu-ther!"

Norah broke into laughter. "I thought I'd be obliged to live forever because you wouldn't have anything decent to wear to my funeral."

"Cut it out, Mom," he said, his young face serious, his gaze searching. "How does it look for today?"

Norah's eyebrows lifted. She hesitated. "The odds are against me—" She let it sink in and added, "Whatever happens, it's out of our control now."

He leaned over and kissed her cheek. "Come on, finish with your makeup and we'll go vote." He smiled. "The family that votes together and all that jazz." His face grew serious. "I watched the debate."

She looked at him questioningly. "Well?"

"You carried Harvard. They're big on abortion. You know, enlightened self-interest."

She waited a moment. Thank God, he wasn't going to mention Guido. "It's too bad Harvard won't be voting."

Peter was quick to change the subject. "I'm going to meet Manuel at the headquarters. He called me at school and asked if I'd go to East Los Angeles with him and hustle." He shook his head. "I'll be glad to see that turkey."

Norah grimaced. "What's a 'turkey' these days? It doesn't seem to have anything to do with Thanksgiving."

"It's current semantics for good, bad, or anyway you want to use it. Like Dad's generation uses 'bastard.' 'You bastard!' is bad. 'You old bastard' is good! Get it?"

Norah looked puzzled. "I guess so. I'll be about ten minutes. Go visit your father. Thanks for the coffee, darling. Where's Mrs. Manley?"

He rolled his eyes. "Wait till you see *that* turkey!"

Norah asked with concern, "Is something the matter?"

He stood in the doorway. "You'll see! Surprise!" And he was gone.

Norah's eyes filled. He was being so bloody gallant. It was all she could do to contain her shock when she saw the cook. Mrs. Manley had transformed herself with a heavy hand. False eyelashes fluttered her eyes with their unaccustomed weight, bright triangles of rouge highlighted the plump cheeks; her lips were curved into a carmine bow, giving her face the air of an aging Minnie Mouse.

"Why Mrs. Manley, you're all done up to go voting," she ventured, not knowing what else to say.

Straightening the plump shoulders, she replied, "Of course, madame. The driveway's swarming with photographers and press. Just wait till you step out the door." She admonished, "I don't want you to be ashamed of the staff." The bright red lips became a thin line. "I told that bloody slob McPherson to get ready and look decent. He's perfectly capable of forgetting to vote." She sniffed, "Men!"

Bringing Norah's luggage out of the closet, she carefully folded the clothes Norah had laid out on the chaise longue.

"Jimmy the Greek says it's seven to five against you, madam."

Norah mumbled an "I know" as she slipped her dress over her head, Kleenex gripped between her lips. She didn't need Jimmy the Greek to tell *her*.

"Well, if I may say so, Mrs. Ashley—" There was little doubt in Norah's mind that she would. Hands on hips, eyelashes flapping, Mrs. Manley hissed, "Up his!"

* * *

Election Day: San Francisco. Richard Hardwick groped his way into the bathroom, grimaced at his reflection in the mirror, and reached for the aspirin.

"Jesus. My head." He turned on the shower. He must have been out of his mind last night drinking alone like that. He shuddered and thought of Virginia. Had her ghost entered his body? Hadn't he held her in contempt for using alcohol as a crutch. And now here he stood staring at himself, sick with a hangover from doing the same damn thing. Marianne really could have brought herself to go to the polling booth with him. That wasn't expecting too much of her. Concha stabs him and Marianne winds up walking out on him. Christ! He let the hot water rush over him. The vote would be decided in Los Angeles. That's where the bodies were. As soon as he pulled himself together, he'd fly back to that hellhole.

The senator began to feel better and turned the cold water on full blast. Shivering, he reached for the towel and rubbed his body briskly. The blood began coursing through his veins. His color returned. The prospect of savoring Norah's admission of defeat lifted his spirits. Mellon would, no doubt, write an eloquent statement, which she, in turn, would deliver brilliantly, employing all her dramatic expertise. But, by God, he was going to eat that bitch alive at the polls and maybe still manage to come out from under by the time the presidential election came around. Others had done it. Hadn't he always been a winner? Maybe—just maybe—he thought of his mother for a moment and began dressing.

CHAPTER

Thirty-two

The Ashleys returned home from casting their votes and found Tillie ensconced on the couch, studying the linear Frank Stella painting over their mantelpiece. "I still think it's antiseptic and sterile." She was a rigid devotee of the impressionists and deplored Norah's interest in contemporary art.

She kissed Peter and stood back, studying him with admiration. "There's been some kind of costume upheaval in this household. You look gorgeous! And I thought I'd faint when I saw Mrs. Manley done all over in head to toe Bozo."

Norah nodded and exclaimed, "You should have seen her ham it up at the polling place. She gave the victory sign for the benefit of the photographers, posing like crazy. McPherson came close to having a stroke."

"At least she didn't do a Claudette Colbert and lift her skirt for a little cheesecake. For a moment I thought she just might," Tom commented. Turning to Norah, he said, "Meet you at the hotel around five, darling. I'll give our son a lift on my way to the office. I've got to get myself in order for tomorrow's meeting in New York."

"The office! Oh Tom!" Norah looked chagrined. "Aren't you coming to the headquarters with me?"

"Of course not. It'll be Pompeii. The only thing going on today is the telephone business. You know that, Norah. It's tread-water time, my darling; to all intents and purposes, our work is *over*! Now it's the voters' turn to do *their* thing. Why don't you ladies have an expensive lunch someplace and make the day go swiftly?" he asked as he kissed them both.

Oh God, Norah thought, everyone's pumping sunshine up my ass.

"That's exactly what I have in mind," Tillie answered with forced cheerfulness, as Tom and Peter headed for the door. "I'm taking you and Evelyn to lunch at the Bistro, Norah. There is *nothing* going on at those headquarters that requires your presence. Karl's got the phone bank working like crazy. He's into his George C. Scott General Patton act."

There was no use protesting, Norah thought, wishing she could lie down and face the wall and weep.

Evelyn Auerbach was waiting at the restaurant when they arrived. The parking attendants assured Norah that they had cast their votes for her. She produced her "camera face smile" for the omnipresent *Women's Wear Daily* photographer who snapped them walking toward the entrance. She wondered if he slept there.

An effusive captain settled them in the corner table, the numero-uno spot in the pecking order of the status-conscious eating place. It was early in the day. Their entrance created no particular stir; only a few customers were sprinkled around the room.

"You can't imagine how ghostly the headquarters are. I'm glad we're here," Evelyn stated as she slid over to make room for Norah. "Karl's office is in the back, so his pandemonium is invisible. The only action in front is on the switchboard. They're crazy with calls asking for somebody to get to a particular place, or God knows what. Those long tables where we licked and spit and addressed for months are totally deserted. It's like the beach in Hawaii before the tidal wave," she said wistfully.

As if by tacit agreement, they made no mention of the voting. It would be evening before the early returns trickled in and they would begin to get the feel of the election. Norah was certain that despite their unspoken fears, the image of millions of strangers deciding her fate in thousands of booths up and down the state hung over the three of them more vividly than the sight of the familiar room decorated in old Vienna kitsch.

The captain finished taking their orders, and the restaurant began to fill. Catherine Goodrich, tailored by Adolfo and bejeweled by her husband Henry, swooped toward them.

"Oh, Christ!" Tillie groaned. "Here comes Madame Badrich herself."

"Norah, *darling,* what are you doing here?"

"Obviously she's eating lunch!" Tillie snapped.

Pointedly ignoring Tillie, Catherine went on. "Norah darling, I want you to meet my dear friend, Baron Rudi von Wattenburg." She presented the ruddy-faced, overly erect man who stood behind her. "This is our next senator from California, Mrs. Ashley," she gushed. "That is, of course, *if* she wins."

The baron creaked into a low bow over Norah's hand and looked up at her, admiringly. "*Enchanté,* madame. Such a beautiful lady cannot lose!"

Norah wondered how much he would cost poor Henry.

Catherine went on, "My dear, that debate was just fascinating. You were marvelous!" Her face took on a conspiratorial look. "Tell me," she asked, voice lowering, "was dear old Guido fun?"

Norah eyed her coldly. "I can't remember."

"Humph, I'll bet you want to forget, don't you, darling?"

"My dear Catherine, Tom and I've been married so long, I believe I fell out of my crib right into his bed." Turning to the embarrassed escort, Norah said, "I hope you have a good lunch."

Catherine received the dismissal message and fluttered with a girlish giggle. "Don't forget to vote, ladies. Come along, Rudi, darling."

"Let's hope *she* forgets," Tillie commented.

Evelyn sat silent during the encounter, her patrician face unsmiling. Taking her glass in her hand, she said, quietly, "Fuck her."

Norah gasped. "Evelyn! My campaign's ruined you!"

Evelyn sipped her wine. "Not at all. I think it's liberated me. I'll bet that so-called baron's family ate Jews for lunch, and now God's paying him back. If Henry's lucky, someday she's going to disappear into the sunset with a ski instructor." She lifted her glass to Norah.

After lunch, at Norah's insistence, they made a stop at the headquarters en route to the hotel. Evelyn's description was accurate. Other than a few people managing the switchboard, the huge central room was deserted and desolate, the ambience strangely still. It seemed to Norah that even the campaign posters carrying her photographs were falling away from the walls, curling at their Scotch-taped corners.

Karl, in his office at the rear of the building, was too busy with the phone bank operation to pretend politeness, and he waved them off without a word.

The three women arrived at the Wellington West by five o'clock. Newest of the large commercial hotels, it was a classic example of the victory of money over taste. The central location and plethora of huge, garish public rooms made it an ideal place for the party to hold the Election Night celebration or wake, whichever the fates might bring.

The bilious pink Grand Ballroom boasted six giant crystal chandeliers and an abundance of white plaster statues placed in lighted niches. The statues clutched their crotches modestly and held aloft a variety of neoclassical urns. The gargantuan dimensions of the space provided adequate room for the mass of humanity and media equipment that would converge here later in the evening. No one was likely to notice the hideous decor; the election board set up at the end of the ballroom would absorb all their attention.

The Wellington boasted six so-called presidential suites, decorated in what Tillie termed "Contemporary Bordello."

The most elaborate of these was assigned to Norah in deference to her position at the top of the ticket. Later in the evening she would be expected to join the lesser candidates and the faithful in the main ballroom.

By the time Norah arrived, her campaign was in the throes of establishing itself in the garish quarters. Telephone company personnel were frantically installing direct lines to her various headquarters, extra television sets were being rolled in; the incipient chaos and activity lifted Norah's spirits.

But she was struck by the oppressiveness of the decor. A chandelier of amber glass and iron, hung on simulated antique chain, which looped across the ceiling, dominated the room. Nubby pumpkin orange fabric covered the furniture, and chocolate brown carpeting ran from wall to wall. Its deep pile, intended to promote a sense of luxury, gave Norah a sense of sinking instead.

Brookings and Mellon had commandeered the two smaller bedrooms, allotting the master bedroom to Norah. Mrs. Manley had carefully hung her clothing in a little closet and neatly arranged her toiletries on the dressing table. The king-sized bed was covered with a velvet spread dyed the inevitable pumpkin shade. A smaller version of the living room chandelier hung above it.

Tom was knotting his tie when she walked in. He kissed her and waved toward the dressing table. "Your home away from home. Just what a movie star should have." Observing her dismay, he added, "Wait till you see the bathroom!"

Norah gasped at the sight of the elliptical plastic cast synthetic marble bathtub, complete with golden fixtures and tinted mirrors overhead. "You wouldn't leave me here *alone*?" she wailed.

Tom shrugged. "You just don't appreciate class, my dear." He put on his jacket and checked his watch. "Peter should be here soon. My last report was that he's doing fine and consuming enchiladas like crazy in East Los Angeles. The company plane will drop off Manuel in Palm Springs and then take Peter to Boston tonight. I'll take the red-eye."

"Oh, Tom," Norah blurted out, despite all her resolutions, "why did you bring him back to go through this? It's so grim, really."

"Because," he answered firmly, "he has to, Norah. It'd be a hell of a lot harder for him back there in Boston alone. At least he'll be with people who love you and him. Cut it out, Norah! If you start bemoaning your fate again, everybody else'll collapse."

Norah sighed deeply. Tom was fully prepared for her debacle. Peter was being brave, and so were her troops. She felt a ballooning urge to scream. Instead she said, "He'll be exhausted, Tom. Couldn't he go back tomorrow?"

"Nonsense, he won't break. He has to be in class tomorrow morning."

They were interrupted by a discreet knock on the door. It was Sylvia Gannon. "I've ordered dinner sent up at seven o'clock, if that's all right?"

"How do we know what the head count will be? It has the look out there of incipient chaos."

Tom excused himself. "I leave these housekeeping matters to you, ladies."

"Have you *any* reports, Tom?" Norah could no longer restrain herself. The pretense of acting as if nothing were going on was increasingly unbearable.

"It's too early, my dear, you know that," he chided. "Now just distract yourself and work out dinner with Sylvia."

"I told them to set up a buffet and keep it coming, just in case, Norah," Sylvia said. "Your Mrs. Manley has arrived and offered to supervise; she volunteered McPherson for bartender."

"She'll supervise, all right," Norah assured her. "That should divert us until the polls close. Hopefully by then I'll be allowed to act as if there's an election going on. This charade is ridiculous!"

Sylvia, recognizing her irritability, asked solicitously, "Is there anything I can get you, tea, or coffee, perhaps?"

Dear God, she was offering her a cup of hot something or other—whatever one offers the ailing. "A nice cup a 'ot tea!" She damn well wasn't ailing; she was in a state of potential hysteria and had every right to be.

"Thank you, no, Sylvia. I *really* am fine," she reiterated in an attempt to convince herself. Did they all have to be so goddamn matter-of-fact cheerful?

Sylvia stood in the doorway and smiled coyly. "The governor will be joining us for dinner."

By eight o'clock, as the polls were closing, Norah had toasted the governor, made an impromptu, sentimental speech about her staff, her friends, her husband, and her son, who tried not to show his embarrassment. She, in turn, had been toasted by the governor, her staff, her friends, her husband, and finally her son. *She* tried not to show how moved she was when Peter raised his glass to her and said, "To my mother—the senator, perhaps—but always my mother, which makes me the luckiest."

He, of course, was the only one who managed to consume his dinner. Norah and the others, unable to eat, pushed the food around their plates, despite Mrs. Manley's admonitions about "keeping up your strength."

The TV sets remained conspicuously silent during dinner. As soon as it was over, Brookings and Mellon excused themselves, got up from the table, and headed toward the back bedrooms, where the direct telephone lines had been installed. Tom and Manuel followed them silently. Walt drifted to the far end of the room and turned on the television set. To Norah's annoyance, Sylvia joined him while her husband went to the bar with the governor. At least that was one problem her defeat would resolve. She would no longer be obliged to be polite to the Gannons. More than likely, she thought bitterly, they would eliminate themselves as a problem to her. They weren't about to be bothered with a loser.

She noticed that Lisa had been especially quiet during dinner and had made no effort to play the game of forced cheerfulness in which the others were engaged. Lisa looked downright desolate, and Norah's heart ached for her. She was suffering Norah's loss as if it were her own. Or was she nursing some private grief? If Walt's plans for her career came into fruition, she would have to inure herself against the anguish of defeat and failure. They were certain companions along the route of the upward climb. She resolved to keep in touch with the young actress.

Norah settled herself in an armchair facing the TV screen, next to the couch where Lisa had seated herself alongside Tillie. Tillie, serious-faced and tight-lipped, tried not to glance in Walt's direction, but she brightened when Sylvia moved away from him, toward the bar, where her husband and the governor were drinking brandy.

While the waiters cleared away the dinner debris, Mrs. Manley brought them coffee. Norah accepted gratefully; it was about all she could manage to swallow.

The governor gulped down his brandy and came over to Norah; he leaned down and kissed her cheek and said with forced heartiness, "Well, well, my dear, I must go and spread cheer among the other hopefuls." He wagged his finger at her. "I'll be back at ten o'clock sharp to escort you to the ballroom to collect the kudos from your ardent supporters."

Seeing Peter, who looked at a loss for something to do, he barked, "You come with me, son, and I'll give you an on-the-spot, crash course in political science like they don't know from at Harvard." He grimaced. "No point your hanging around here getting ulcers. Not a goddamn thing's going to happen for at least another hour, just acid dripping slowly."

Tillie looked at him fondly. He really meant to hang in until the bitter end. She hadn't expected it of him. "You know, you're not all bad after all, you old bastard," she said affectionately. "I may even get to like you again."

But Sylvia was quick to defend him. "Really, Tillie! The governor's a warm, outgoing person," she protested indignantly. "And he *is* the governor!"

Tillie's face hardened. "Ah yes, of course, just a cute little cuddles at heart." She paused and suggested, "Why don't you take Sylvia with you, Governor? She'll just love watching you perform."

His face broke into a wide smile. "That's a great idea," he said and put out his hand toward Sylvia. "Come along, young lady, I'm sure my about-to-be legal consultant won't mind." He nodded toward Gannon and took her arm. "I'll teach you a thing or two about flesh pressing."

Tillie's eyebrows shot up. "I'll bet," she muttered.

Walt felt his face turn red. Why couldn't she just lay off? It was over, wasn't it? He turned and left the room without a word.

Grim-faced, Norah leaned toward Tillie and whispered angrily, "Cut it out!" An explosion between the Lowmans was all she needed. Obviously the wounds were still dripping blood.

Deliberately, she addressed her attention to the television screen. It reflected the hotel lobby below them. The crowd was thickening, people appeared to be milling around aimlessly. Many supporters wore straw hats and buttons bearing her name. The carnival atmosphere was building. The TV coverage changed abruptly to the Century Plaza, which had been commandeered for the night by Hardwick's party. The scene was identical. Was he, she wondered, riddled with doubts and anxieties, watching and waiting in a suite like hers? Probably not. Why should he be anxious? He could indulge himself in satisfaction, anticipating her defeat and his victory. He might never achieve the victory that really mattered, the presidency, but he'd have tonight.

The eye of the camera switched abruptly to Norah's nearly deserted headquarters. There was no sign of Karl. He and his people were probably on their way to the hotel, now that the polls were closed. Focusing on the switchboard, the camera moved in on Barbara Potter, who was wearing a headphone and frantically pushing and pulling plugs and wires. Seated beside her, shouting into his mouthpiece, was one of Mellon's young lawyers. They appeared to be the only survivors. It looked deserted, too depressing to bear. "Oh God," Tillie groaned, "they're still getting out the nonexistent student vote." Restless now, not bothering to comment, Norah got up and went to the far bedroom. Manuel, serious-faced, pencil in hand, sat next to Walt, who was on the phone. Tom standing alongside him motioned for her to sit down.

"The registrar of voters has begun tallying the absentee ballots," he said. She felt a sickening wave of despair. Why did *they* always have to be first? This time, unlike the primary, there was no question but that the absentee vote would reflect the usual conservatism. She didn't need to ask how it was coming in; their faces reflected the bad news.

She shook her head and went into the adjoining bedroom. Evelyn was sitting on the bed, watching the TV screen. Brookings and Mellon were locked into the telephones, and William Gannon was scribbling numbers on a yellow legal pad. They looked dour and made no effort to speak to her. But Norah could hear the unspoken message loud and clear. Campaign workers placed in crucial precincts had begun calling into the suite, reporting the earliest scattered returns, a hundred here, fifty there, only bits and scraps, but enough for an experienced politician to evaluate.

By the time Karl and the remains of his crew joined them, some significant conclusions could be drawn. It came as no surprise that she was doing poorly with the absentee voters. Her percentage was no lower than had been predicted. Ruefully, she thought, they hadn't witnessed the debate. But the scattered early returns from polling places in the lower middle blue-collar districts, where she was thought to be strongest, indicated her margin to be less than they had expected. The seesawing numbers were far too close to spell defeat—but! Karl looked grim. These were his people, and he'd wrung every last vote he could out of them, cajoling, threatening, haranguing, and playing on their party loyalties. Still, even a few defectors in each precinct were more than Norah could afford.

By nine thirty, Norah's suite began to fill with people and ABC announced the vote was too close to call. At the same time, CBS computers projected her defeat and Hardwick's reelection by a margin of 2 percent. There were cries of "They're crazy," "It's too early," "It's too close!"

At ten o'clock sharp, the governor pushed his way through the crowded room to pick Norah up and escort her to the ballroom.

"Do I have to?" she asked plaintively. Tom nodded silently. Lisa jumped up and volunteered, "I'll come with you, Norah." Brookings's heart turned over as Lisa put her arm through Norah's. Tom and Peter fell in behind them with the governor. They walked down the hall to the service elevator, which would carry them directly to the ballroom.

The moment Norah entered, the orchestra broke into "California, Here I Come," and the room, bursting with wall-to-wall people, broke into whistles and cheers, chanting, "We want Norah! We want Norah!" If the news was depressing, they were not about to accept it. They reassured her with their applause and cheers and cries of encouragement. She knew that tradition demanded she in turn reassure and encourage them.

They were locked together in this cavernous room, oblivious to the realities that were becoming painfully clear to those monitoring the returns in the upstairs suite.

The governor raised his hands and bellowed, "Ladies and gentlemen, the next senator from California." The crowd responded with wild cheering and whistling.

Norah came to the lectern accompanied by Tom, Peter, and Lisa. The flashbulbs exploded. Gradually the crowd grew quiet waiting for her to speak.

"There is good news and bad news," Norah began. "The good news is that the CBS computer will be refuted later this evening." There was a burst of applause and cheering. "The bad news is that it may take the better part of the evening to do it, and we're going to have a very long night together." She leaned forward and flashed her best movie star smile and lied, "I shall return here later this evening to celebrate *our* victory together. But whatever happens"—her face grew serious—"I will cherish your friendship and devoted support as long as I live." Norah's supporters answered her with their cheers and whistles and applause. The rhythmic chanting of "We Want Norah" once again filled the room.

By the time she returned to her quarters, Norah had been hugged, kissed, squeezed, and touched by hundreds of her supporters. She dared not anticipate their disappointment later that night when she delivered the concession speech, which she had firmly committed to memory. She thought she'd prepared herself for defeat, yet what she felt now, as it loomed toward her, was an unexpected agony of disappointment and despair.

She herself was exhausted by this exercise in self-destruction. What's more, the price the others had paid was horrendous. Walt and Tillie's marriage was shaken. Poor Lisa looked as if she were bordering on a deep depression. A man had been found mysteriously shot to death in the Florida swamps and Manuel was damn near murdered because of her. Even her own marriage had been rocked by shock waves; Tom had deceived her, and she'd had to play true confessions to him, a role she detested.

Norah's head throbbed. The suite had grown crowded and airless. Why had she ever developed a passion for politics? The whole arena was a stinking cesspool!

Where the hell was Tom? Norah looked around the room. He was nowhere to be seen. He was going to leave her alone in this place tonight yet, and worse, leave her to face the morning's television appearance alone. She never should have agreed to go on that bloody program. It was madness to have permitted the Johnson creature to euchre her into it; the nasty bitch would gloat over her political corpse for the whole world to see. On national television! She should have had the guts to tell her to go to hell in the washroom.

Norah spotted Karl standing at the bar, looking disheveled, talking with Walt and Dan. Poor old bear of a man. He'd wrung the last vote out of his people right down to the finish line. The German in him demanded maximum efficiency even with the ship sinking. A lot of good it had done. She went over to him; he reached out and hugged her, saying, "No matter what, we got out the vote."

"Better they should have stayed at home," Dan grumbled.

Poor Dan, Norah thought, he's got to go back to Washington a loser and take a lot of gaff from the White House Press Corps.

"It's going to be awful here without you, Dan," Norah smiled. "Walt, why don't you put him in a film with Lisa." She joked trying to lighten the heavy moment. "Then he won't have to go back to Washington."

Walt shot her a glance of dismay. Lisa's eyes filled and Brookings swallowed hard. Oh God! Norah thought, something's going on there. She'd been so involved in her own misery she hadn't even noticed. Dan and Lisa! She should have sensed it. How could she have been so insensitive?

Walt was quick to jump into the awkward silence and asked offhandedly. "How's about a drink, Norah? You, Lisa?" He knew he sure as hell needed one.

Norah shook her head.

"No thanks!" Lisa told him and began to move away. She glanced back at Dan, their eyes met for an instant. He felt for the telegram stuffed in his coat pocket, turned away from her, and poured himself a large glass of Scotch. The short unsigned message Lisa had sent him read, "I'll be the other loser on the first Tuesday in November. I'll always remember." So would he. Walt filled a glass for himself and clinked it mutely against Dan's. There was nothing he could think to say to him. Nor for that matter could Norah. She leaned toward the press secretary and kissed his cheek, her heart aching. One more campaign casualty. No, two more. Dan and Lisa.

* * *

Six miles away, on the top floor of the Century Plaza, Richard Hardwick returned to his suite after a foray into the Grand Ballroom. The wild cheers of his supporters rang in his ears, their enthusiasm increased by the optimistic projections. His staff were engaged in precisely the same activity as Norah's, taking the telephone calls that came in from their people stationed in the various precincts.

Dorothy Johnson awaited him with a drink ready. "Did the crowd roar approval for the winner?" she asked.

He nodded, grinning.

"I do like winners, and I have a special little victory treat in mind for you later tonight, Senator." She looked at him seductively.

They were interrupted by his grim-faced administrative assistant. "Senator, you'd better come take a look at these figures. There's something screwy going on in Imperial and Orange counties and Santa Cruz."

* * *

By eleven o'clock the Ashley suite was body to body; even Barbara Potter had finally wrenched herself away from the headquarters. She was squatted on the floor, glued to the television set, oblivious to the people stepping over and around her.

Norah found Tom, and they wandered from room to room, attempting to cheer her followers, preparing them for the inevitable. Mrs. Manley, pale and drawn, had lost one strip of her false eyelashes. Her rouge had long since worn off. She stood quietly, pouring endless cups of coffee.

Walt looked exhausted. Even the indestructible Tillie seemed rooted to the couch, spent and immobilized.

Suddenly Manuel pushed through the front door of the suite and shouted, "Turn to Channel Two, quick!"

An embarrassed commentator was saying, "We wish to retract our earlier prediction in today's contest for the Senate seat from California. Our computers did not properly take into account the variation in the voting patterns in Orange and Imperial counties. The senator's lead over Mrs. Ashley appears to be somewhat less than expected, and the extraordinarily high voter turnout in East Los Angeles and outlying Mexican American areas alters our original prognostications. Too, there seems to be a much higher than predicted campus turnout. At this moment, the election is too close for us to call."

"They're doing it!" Peter screamed. "They're voting! Mom's going to win!"

Manuel, afraid of his own optimism, said firmly, "It's too soon, Peter. Cool it! How do you read it, Karl?" he called out to the labor leader.

"I dunno! Who's got the East Los Angeles figures?"

John Mellon stood in the doorway and waved a yellow sheet of paper high above the heads of the crowd and shouted, "The turnout is ten percent above the norm."

Karl let out a low whistle. "That might just do it." He turned to Tom. "It could be enough to neutralize the blue-collar defection. Maybe you'd better start reprogramming the candidate for victory." Barbara jumped to her feet. "Santa Cruz, Berkeley, Westwood. They did it! They voted!" she screamed.

For a moment there was absolute silence in the room. Then, abruptly, the cheers and shouts began. "I don't believe it," Norah said, shaking her head, "I don't believe it." The possibility of victory was incomprehensible.

Tillie hugged Lisa and felt the young woman's tears, wet against her cheek. She looked over her shoulder and observed Sylvia embracing the governor. Walt was standing at the doorway watching them. He turned away abruptly and came toward her, his eyes piercing hers questioningly. He leaned over and kissed her. "Well, Tillie, old girl, it looks like we all may make it, doesn't it?"

Tillie nodded, wondering if things would ever be the same for any of them.

Walt patted Lisa's shoulder. "You'll be a winner too, little one."

Dry-eyed now, she answered, her voice faltering, "It's—it's almost as tough as losing."

"No way!" Walter said. "Not for the likes of us, it isn't."

Barbara pushed her way through the room of screaming, happy Ashley supporters, her eyes blazing, until she found Mellon.

"You didn't believe me, *did* you, you dumb honky? You and Karl didn't think we'd get the kids out, did you? Did you?" she shrieked.

Mellon grabbed her toward him. Without bothering to answer, he enveloped her in his arms. For the first time in his life he'd found a woman he actually *liked*. No, he didn't want to go to bed with her. He was astonished at his own feelings of affection and friendship toward Barbara. It was a new experience. Releasing her from his embrace, he put his hands on the slim shoulders, looked into her eyes, and said, "I'm going to take you back to Washington with me and put you on the White House payroll as my assistant. What do you say to that, Porter, Potter, What's-your-name? You're too good to waste in this crazy place."

Barbara looked at him with amusement as she reached into his breast pocket for a cigarette.

"After I get my law degree in the spring"—Mellon held out a match for her; she inhaled deeply and carefully blew the smoke through pursed lips—"I'll consider your offer, Mr. Legree."

In a corner of the suite, Dan Brookings stared at Manuel, the look on his face incredulous. "The fucking wetbacks did it. I love you, Vasquez," he shouted, hugging him, his personal pain dissolved in the moment of joy.

The governor pushed through the hugging, kissing, screaming bodies, making his way to Norah.

"Let's go, Senator, your constituency is waiting for you in the ballroom."

* * *

Scowling with disbelief, Richard Hardwick snatched the piece of paper from his aide's hand. "What the hell are you talking about? CBS is crazy. Just wait till that vote is counted properly in Orange County." He crumpled the paper and threw it across the room.

The aide shook his head and said flatly, "It's over, sir. They dragged every goddamn Mexican and college vote in the state to the polls to neutralize your lead. What she lost in Bel Air, she picked up in East LA and Westwood and Berkeley. What we had going with the farm belt Anglos, she zapped with Mexican turnout."

Richard returned to the living room, where he was met with murmurs of, "It isn't over," "Wait till we hear from La Jolla." He seated himself next to a grim Dorothy Johnson, who, eyes glued to the screen, was watching Norah's slow progress into the ballroom.

They grew silent with dismay as the screen reflected screaming pandemonium at Norah's headquarters. Straw hats and tally sheets were tossed in the air. Norah's supporters were going mad. The governor and Tom Ashley were body-blocking Norah as the security men slowly cleared a path for her, until she finally reached the podium.

Richard Hardwick's rage made his head throb, he could feel his chest tighten. That bitch! She'd plotted his defeat. She'd done it to him out of pure spite. And there she was raising her arms for quiet while the goddamn rabble went berserk.

Well, she'd have a good long wait before he'd concede. The final vote was still a long way from being counted. And the ball game wasn't over till the last man was out! He sure as hell wasn't going through the hypocrisy of wishing her and that smart-assed husband of hers well. Christ, he was probably lousy in bed, and she was just another one of those frustrated bitches who worked it out by running after power. What she needed was a good screwing. Christ! The students had never voted in sizable numbers before. And that swine Manuel and his goddamn *La Raza* bastards had helped to do him in. He reached for Dorothy Johnson's hand.

"The good news is," Norah was saying on the screen, "that the news is good." Hardwick spotted Manuel standing in the background, looking Ivy League and jubilant. Hatred welled up inside of him. The dirty little bastard. He hoped Marianne was satisfied now. Her lover had brought out every Mexican vote he could to beat her father. And she couldn't even be bothered to stand beside him, her father, through this nightmare. No sir! She was probably waiting for that double-crossing traitor someplace in Palm Springs with Virginia's ghost smiling beside her.

Norah, oozing gratitude, was talking about the victory "being the President's and the people's," or some such rot. The camera focused on her face. God, she was beautiful. He felt as if she were talking directly to him, the green eyes boring into his.

"It's been a long day and we'll wait to hear from former Senator Hardwick!" Norah concluded. "Good night! God bless!"

Former senator! Damn her! There was no doubt in his mind that what she had done to him was motivated by a savage psychotic lust for revenge.

He felt a surge of sexual desire and pressed Dorothy's hand. She withdrew it, yawning, "Richard, darling, I must get some rest; as the lady said, 'It's been a long day.' I have to get up at the crack of dawn to interview the new senator, you know." She stood up and planted a chaste kiss on his cheek. He whispered, "I'll be at your hotel in a little while. Wait up for me."

She looked at him with detachment. "Richard," she murmured, swallowing another yawn. "I really am tired. Good night." She'd place a call to Sam Bradshaw as soon as she got back to her room even if he wasn't a candidate for the presidency. At least Sam was a live senator. Not some lame duck.

*   *   *

Norah rested her head against the hideous marbled plastic tub, trying not to drown in a torrent of anxieties. Where would they live? Who would run the Bel Air house? Would McPherson and Manley consider going with her? Oh God, staff! Might the President consider giving her Mellon or Brookings or both? And Tom, would he really be able to stay in Washington? Tom! She felt a deep sense of panic.

After everybody had finally left, he'd sent Peter and Manuel to wait for him in the car so that he could have a moment alone with his wife. Every available surface in the living room of their suite was covered with dirty glassware and overflowing ashtrays. Tom dug up two clean glasses and poured a drink for her and one for him. Handing her the glass, he raised his own and said, "To you, Senator." His face was solemn.

"Aren't you happy, darling? You look so grim!" she asked, perplexed.

"Of course I'm happy for you!"

"For me?" she cried out. "Not for us? Didn't you want me to win?"

"Don't be silly, Norah," he said, hesitated, and broke into a wry smile. "I guess I overconditioned myself to the inevitability of your defeat and to our going back to things being the way they were. It hasn't quite penetrated yet that you've actually won." He looked up sharply. "My God, I'm going to be sleeping with a senator."

"Oh, Tom." She clung to him. He held her tightly and kissed her mouth, pressing her to him.

He pulled away and looked at her searchingly. "You're your own person at last. No directors or producers. It's what you wanted, isn't it, my darling?"

She felt tears stinging her eyes and pressed her head into his shoulder. "Don't leave, Tom. Stay with me." She felt a pang of loneliness.

He stroked her hair and said quietly, "I have to, Norah. I have to get back to being my own person, too."

He was right, she thought as she lay in the warm soapy water. It *would* be different. He had been both mentor and lover for her. Now he would be friend and lover. The mentor days were over. Whatever agonies the campaign had brought, it was worth it. She swung from panic to joy! She'd won! It would all work out. Somehow, some way. It had to! They loved each other, nothing else mattered. That bastard Hardwick hadn't conceded but—she'd WON!

She *must* get out of this tub. It was almost time for the makeup man and Bernie to arrive. If she didn't get some sleep, even they, with all their expertise, wouldn't be able to do anything with her.

Determined not to further indulge herself in brooding, she reached for her robe and placed a call for six in the morning.

She would force herself to sleep for the few hours left until the telecast. Dear Mrs. Manley had laid out her nightgown on the bed and turned down the ghastly spread. She entered the bedroom, brushing her hair, one hundred strokes a night—craziness. Bernie would unscramble it all in the morning. She put the brush on the dressing table, looked into the mirror, and screamed. Heart pounding, gasping for breath, she spun around.

Richard Hardwick was sprawled in the armchair, drink in hand. He leaned forward, appraising her. The bloodshot eyes mocking. "You said you were waiting for my concession statement, Mrs. Ashley. You said so on television." His voice was exaggeratedly solicitous. "Oh my goodness. I didn't mean to frighten you. I just thought you'd like to receive it in person." He raised his glass in a salute, his hand trembling almost imperceptibly. "Cheers, Senator."

Norah stood frozen, immobilized by the shock of his presence. He looked askew and disordered and was obviously drunk or out of his head or both. She felt a chill of fear. "How'd you get in here?" she whispered.

Sipping the drink, eyes never leaving her face, he said, sarcastically, "Is it possible that you don't know? I'm shocked. Your brilliant staff did such a wonderful study of all my holdings." He shrugged his shoulders. "It's hard to believe those geniuses forgot to tell you that this hotel is owned by the Elwick Foundation. Very sloppy of them," he chuckled mirthlessly. "Anyway, the housekeeper is conveniently corrupt and your security people wouldn't detain a United States senator, now would they? I still am the senator from California, you know."

Norah's voice returned. "Get out at once, Richard Hardwick, now, this minute, or I'll have you thrown out."

He made no effort to leave.

"Would you prefer that I call the desk?"

He got up from the chair, gait unsteady, and crossed the room. Who the hell did she think she was, this two-bit actress ordering him around? "Really, Mrs. Ashley. I expected a gracious welcome. You *said* you were waiting for me to concede, and here I am." He held on to the dressing table, steadied himself, and put down his glass.

Norah backed away, horrified, as he lurched closer to her. She could smell the liquor on his breath and see the stubble on his unshaven face.

Her hair was damp, just the way it had been that last morning in New York. Was it a quarter of a century? A lifetime away. The goddamn bitch. He reached out for her, pulling her to him, tearing at the robe, groping for her breasts. She'd asked for it, hadn't she?

She struggled silently. Finally pushing him away, with all her strength, Norah ran toward the telephone alongside the bed.

Hardwick reached out and caught her arm. "You stupid cunt. Even the press, who loathe me and love you, wouldn't believe you. Much less the hotel operator," he snarled and slumped into the dressing table chair, reached for his drink, and gulped it.

Dear God in heaven, he was insane, stark raving mad. She had to get away from him, somehow. Slowly, Norah backed herself toward the doorway. She must keep talking, divert him, and then make a run for it. "Look here, Richard, I quite understand. You have had a terrible shock and you're obviously upset." She edged along the wall slowly, speaking in as calm a voice as she could muster, her eyes never leaving his face. "It would be terribly embarrassing for you to be found here like this. Rich—"

Before she could complete his name, he cried out, "Sit down and shut up, Norah, for Christ's sake. I'm not going to rape you. I remember when you couldn't get enough of me."

She placed herself at the edge of the armchair and waited. He was obviously off the deep end and paranoid to boot. She shuddered. Was it possible that she'd loved this sick animal? That he had been a United States senator? Presidential material!

He glowered at her from under the half-closed eyelids. "This is what you wanted, isn't it? The dream come true? Ever since I married Virginia." His voice grew loud. "You've been waiting all these years to see me beaten, finished, haven't you, Norah?" He got up and staggered to the door.

She shook her head, unable to speak.

He stood in the doorway, awaiting her answer. "Tell me the truth, Norah." He was close to pleading. "You did this for revenge, didn't you?"

God in heaven, was that what he wanted for comfort in his madness? All she had to do was say yes. She stared at him. This ashen disheveled psychopath had dreamed of the presidency. She would lie to him; she must —the truth would be a cruelty. She drew in her breath, prepared to speak the words he wanted to hear. But anger overwhelmed her. She couldn't mouth the lie. The moment in the hospital when she had stood with her son and he with his daughter had obviated the past. "You're wrong, Richard, it wasn't like that at all. You're no more than a symbol for me, a political symbol. It was your *political* presence I wanted removed from the arena. That's why I ran against you."

She paused and looked at him, her eyes piercing his. Trembling with fury, she said in a strangled voice, "I swear it."

He stared at her with disbelief. Then with a deliberate effort, he straightened himself and looked down at her contemptuously. "I'll spend the next two years of my life going the length and breadth of this country. I'll attend any meeting to which I'm invited—anything, no matter how small—church socials, rallies in a phone booth if necessary, to mount my campaign against that bastard. Mrs. Ashley," he spat, "you tell your President for me, the fight's only begun." He turned away from her and lurched into the living room.

The moment she heard the door close with a crash, Norah rushed across the room to reach for the telephone. But she didn't lift the receiver. Her hand lay there. Whom would she call? What would she say? Who would believe her? And what good would it do now? Hardwick wouldn't be mounting a campaign ever again. Hardwick would retreat. Casa Thayer would be Richard Hardwick's San Clemente, his Elba.

Norah flung herself on the bed, drained and exhausted. She fell into the oblivion of sleep.

* * *

In the house on the outskirts of Chino, Concha Romo looked into a darkened bedroom and listened to the sound of her sister Juanita's quiet rhythmic breathing. Satisfied she was asleep, she turned away and hurried noiselessly down the darkened hall to the living room. She peered out of the large bay window into the moonlit patio and pulled the heavy drapes shut.

Concha moved nervously to the fireplace. Her heart pounded in her ears. She reached her arms high over her head and ran her fingers across the uppermost tiles above the mantelpiece. She leaned forward. She could feel it move beneath her touch. One ceramic tile gave way to her touch as she gently pressed its corner. Concha held her breath, terrified she might drop the tile, clutching it with both her hands. Carefully, she placed it on the small table alongside the wing-backed chair facing the fireplace.

She raised herself up on her toes and reached into the black hollow, hands trembling. The cold metal touched her fingertips, sending a shiver through her body. But before she could get a firm hold on it, it slipped away.

Panicked, she bent down and reached for the footstool, pulling it to her. She climbed up on it and looked searchingly into the dark aperture. An outline was dimly visible. Concha took a deep breath and put her finger into the opening, edging it forward until it touched metal again. She took hold firmly with both hands, and extracted a metal box from the hollow.

Carefully lowering the box, she placed it alongside the tile on the table. A chill went through her body as she knelt down on the hearth. Composing herself, she unbuttoned the collar of her robe, slipped a gold chain over her head, and grasped the key hanging at the end of it.

Placing the key in the rusted lock, she turned it back and forth until finally the lid sprang open. Concha stared at the contents, hesitated, and then removed them and spread them out on the floor.

It was all there—the canceled check, the death certificate, the terrible letter from the poor girl's wretched mother. With deliberate care Concha ripped the papers into small pieces, brushed them into a heap with both her hands, and gently placed them in the fireplace.

She felt an overwhelming wave of sadness and her eyes filled.

A saga was ending, and with it a part of her own life. This key, this box, and its contents were symbols of the Colonel's absolute trust in her.

Shaking herself into the present, she reached for a match, struck it across the hearth and held it to the scraps of paper. She rested back on her heels and watched the fire take hold. A gray spiral of smoke snaked upward, lifting with it the burden of her knowledge.

Senator Richard would not be running against the President. Not now. She thought pityingly of the dead girl as she reached for the poker and spread the gray dust of the ashes, making certain no evidence of the box's contents was left. Evidence to a cruelly wasted life. Death alone gave it importance. It had been no more than the wisp of smoke. Concha crossed herself. At least the President would never know where or when the poor creature might rise from the grave to point the skeletal accuser's finger at him. That was his punishment.

But she, Concha, had kept her commitment to the Colonel. It was over now. He would understand.

* * *

Dan Brookings and John Mellon arrived promptly at Norah's suite in the Wellington West in order to escort her to the broadcasting station.

They hurriedly whisked her through a side entrance to a waiting limousine. As usual, a bodyguard sat next to the chauffeur. Norah wondered when her need for protection would come to an end. She made a mental note to discuss the matter with Tom as soon as possible. By God, she'd won the election! Surely the crazies would soon be looking for a new target. Fatigue forgotten, Norah stepped briskly into the limousine.

To her astonishment, Tillie was sitting in the corner of the backseat and called out gaily, "Trick or treat?"

"Tillie Lowman, you witch! What are you doing here at this ungodly hour?"

Tillie leaned across the seat to embrace her. Mellon and Brookings settled themselves on the jump seats.

"You didn't think I'd let those two"—she gestured toward the men— "have all the fun, did you? After all the nasties we've been through together." Tillie's face lit up. "I can barely wait to see that lovable Miss Johnson's tongue turn brown."

But Norah wasn't fooled. She knew that for all her bravado and brusque manner, Tillie was a sentimentalist and, above all else, a caring friend. She wasn't about to let Norah go it alone—just in case.

Deeply touched by Tillie's unexpected presence, Norah said fondly, "You're something else, Tillie!" She turned to the men. "How am I ever going to be able to tell all of you how grateful I am?"

"Oh, shut up, Norah," Tillie snapped with embarrassment, and, quickly changing the subject, she asked, "Doesn't Norah look marvelous?" The finely arched brows lifted. "It can't be entirely due to Bernie and the makeup department."

"Not bad," Brookings noted approvingly and then questioned Norah, "Did you get *any* sleep?"

She shook her head. "Not very much. Bernie beat at my door at five thirty this morning." She hesitated for a moment, tempted to tell them about Richard Hardwick's bizarre visitation. What for? Instead she commented lightly, "Winning's good for the skin."

Mellon lit a cigarette and looked up at her thoughtfully. His satisfaction in her victory was doubled by his joy in having trounced Hardwick.

"Winning's good for a lot more than that, lady," he said, emphatically.

As the limousine pulled up to the entrance to the broadcasting station, Norah spotted the assistant manager, Gary Krawford, with a worried look on his face, pushing his way through the crowd of onlookers, newsmen, and photographers who were awaiting her arrival.

Breathless, Krawford reached for the car door. Norah had a pang of guilt and greeted him effusively, hoping to compensate for the hard time she'd given him a week and a half before.

"Good morning, Mr. Krawford! How kind of you to meet us!" she gushed, holding out her hand to him as soon as Brookings and Mellon had stepped out of the car.

The moment her feet touched the pavement, flashbulbs exploded, microphones were shoved toward her, and Norah was greeted by shouts of, "Yea, Ashley!" "Congratulations, Norah!" Questions were shot at her. "How does it feel?" "Have you talked to the President?" "Do you think Senator Hardwick will resign early so you can have some seniority?"

Brookings and Mellon and the bodyguard kept on clearing her path and working her toward the door.

Gary Krawford pleaded at the top of his voice, "Please, no questions now! She's late!" and rushed them into the studio with relief.

"Please hurry, Mrs. Ashley," he admonished. "Miss Johnson was afraid you might have forgotten, or overslept—what with winning and all. She was worried sick and had me up the wall," he complained, heading them toward the studio at the end of the hall.

Tillie made little clicking noises in mock sympathy. "That's not all that's making her sick," she noted gleefully.

Suddenly, Norah stopped short. "Oh, no, not again," the assistant manager agonized. He'd been through that with her the last time.

"I won't be long—really!" Norah reassured him. "Dan, you and John go ahead and placate Johnson," she suggested and headed into the lavatory.

"The lady's just a little nervous," Tillie explained, with amusement. Poor dear! It really was a *déjà vu.*

"*She's* nervous!" he wailed, pacing up and down the hall. He checked his watch. "We've got about a minute and—" Before he could finish his sentence, Norah emerged.

"Okay, let's go, Mr. Krawford," she smiled, moving briskly alongside him and Tillie. When they reached the brightly lit studio, Norah looked up and saw the number 70 over the door. It was the same place in which she had debated Hardwick. She paled and caught her breath. The unpleasant memory shook her confidence.

Dorothy Johnson, flanked by Mellon and Brookings, headed toward them, her face flooded with relief at the sight of Norah. She broke into a forced smile.

Tillie gave Norah a gentle pat on her behind. She knew exactly what was going on in Norah's head and whispered, "Same set, but a much better script, Senator. Enjoy!"

"Come along, she'll be fine," Tillie said to Brookings and Mellon. The three of them headed toward the darkened area below the brilliantly lit set. The large studio audience was already settled and waiting for the show to begin, despite the early hour. Recognizing Norah, they broke into enthusiastic applause.

"Congratulations, Senator," Dorothy Johnson gushed. She took Norah by the hand and led her up onto the stage as the applause grew louder.

The unhappy memory of her disastrous encounter with Hardwick dimmed as Norah greeted the director and announcer. The camera crane moved toward her. Norah looked up and saw the same young man who'd given her the thumbs-up sign before the debate beaming at her. He held his clasped hands over his head in a victory gesture. Norah blew him a kiss.

The announcer held out his hands for silence. Norah settled herself in an armchair opposite Dorothy Johnson. This time the set was arranged to give the appearance of a living room. The comfortable armchairs were separated by a low coffee table with a bouquet of flowers on it. A curtained bay window served as a backdrop. The severe office decor used for the debate had vanished.

The lights blinked, the announcer looked at the teleprompter, and said, "It is with real pleasure that we bring 'Have a Good Day, U.S.A.' to you this morning from the great state of California. An enormous political upset has just taken place here. Our own Dorothy Johnson is fortunate indeed to have as her guest, the former Academy Award–winning actress, Norah Jones Ashley, now Senator Norah Jones Ashley, the first woman in the history of the state to be so honored by her fellow Californians."

There was no need for the studio employee to hold up the "applause" sign. It exploded spontaneously. Tillie felt unexpected tears of joy fill her eyes as she stood up and cheered and applauded along with John, Dan, and the rest of the studio audience.

Finally, the ovation for Norah subsided. Dorothy Johnson welcomed her effusively. "We are *thrilled* to be in California and to have the honor of presenting the first television interview with the brilliant, beautiful, and gifted new senator from this wonderful state, and to share this exciting moment with you. Welcome to 'Have a Good Day, U.S.A.' Mrs.—uh-uh" —she caught herself and giggled coyly—"Senator Ashley."

Norah smiled modestly. "I'm thrilled to be with you and all these wonderful people." She gestured toward the audience, savoring the moment, her pleasure enhanced by the knowledge of what Johnson's original purpose had been for inviting her to appear on the program.

Dorothy Johnson addressed herself to Norah. "Tell us"—she hesitated imperceptibly, finding it difficult to address Norah by her new title—"Senator. To what do you attribute your stunning upset victory over Senator Hardwick?"

Norah looked thoughtful, but the green eyes flashed mischievously. "Upset? I didn't find it upsetting at all. I loved it!"

There was a burst of laughter and scattered applause from the audience.

Dorothy Johnson was quick to back down. "I mean, he was the incumbent, and—ah—I—ah—believe he was thought to be ahead in the polls."

"My dear Miss Johnson, there's only one poll that counts, you know. That's the one taken on the first Tuesday after the first Monday in November."

Norah opened her eyes wide and looked into the camera, smiling broadly. "I think my victory can be attributed to the simple fact that more Californians voted for me than voted for my opponent. And I wish to thank each and every one of you."

A roar of applause filled the studio. It sounded more wonderful to Norah than any accolade she had ever received as an actress.

Her mind flashed to Tom. She hoped he was watching.